Gui

The Dark School

By

Michelle MillerAllen

Published in 2014 by Green Phoenix Productions

Dedication

*for the late Rick Allen
and all the Poets and Bards,
those true guardians of the Mysteries*

Foreword

We are so glad that Michelle MillerAllen joined us at our Indie Authors meeting in Glasgow in 2013. Michelle shared her enthusiasm and passion for writing with us and in return we encouraged and supported her journey to self-publish her books in Scotland. Sadly her untimely passing meant that she didn't see her book published. It is with a heavy heart but great pride that we took up the reins to ensure this book would cross the finishing line and be available to the world. We hope that you are pleased with our work Michelle and that those reading it connect with your wonderful spirit through your words.

Kim and Sinclair Macleod, Indie Authors Scotland.

We Miller children, early on, tried to avoid the nine-to-five. Michelle wrote, Laurence became a musician, and I painted and drew. Through the years we encouraged each other, and contributed to one another's work. I recall many a long talk over "matters of the art" with our big sister. Her energy as a creative spirit, and as a contributor to her community, will not cease to be an influence on my habits with her passing, please, Lord.

Lyle Miller

I met Michelle in 2006 soon after she came to live in Scotland. We were introduced as sharing the same passion for the local environment. Michelle and I soon became what she termed as the 'accidental activists' as we dedicated our efforts to improving the local green spaces. Our physical efforts were widely recognised but it was through Michelle's writing skills and the creation of our local newsletter New Leaf News that the work of our groups reached heights we never thought possible. Michelle was entirely responsible for the level of success we achieved as 'Accidental Activists'. Along the way, to me personally, she became my rock, my strength and my mentor in all my environmental works. Above all...my dear and special friend.

Her passion will live on as we continue to deliver on our aspirations to actions. She remain with us in spirit. I miss her in person. x

Christine Bell

Michelle inspired people she met and empowered them to believe in themselves. Michelle's craft was writing and her creativity reaches out and grasps the readers attention in a similar manner. Michelle's energy and belief in the possibility of change and growth were catalytic and it is an honour to have been part of her world.

Jennifer Lim

Author's Notes

Credits, Thanks and About the Spelling

I am grateful and indebted to the following people who generously guided me through the various worlds I needed to visit, in the process of writing this book:

Baltimore & Poets: Janet Maher, David Beaudoin, the Artmobile artists

Computer & "guy stuff": Laurence Miller

Connoisseur info: Lyle Miller

Durango: Chris Lujan, Rob Pivonka, justmeonlyme, wildthing, Rick Baker

Forensics & Crypts: Debra Komar, M.D., A.J. Ferrara, Esq.

General information: mysterybooks.about.com, Rogula Wolf, Gerry and Laura Carthy

Green Man: Simon Todd , Tony O'Callahan, Rick Allen, the folks at Cu Mor,

Green Man: The Archetype of Our Oneness With the Earth, William Anderson & Clive Hicks (HarperCollins, 1990)

Inspiration: The Green Man

The Ireland Experience: Dear County Roscommon friends, Lady Gregory and the sidhe

<u>*Kilns, Masks & Artists: Jill Kiefer, Linda Vozar-Sweet, Brad-*</u>

ford Hansen-Smith, Jude Catallo

Kivas & Anasazi: John Kantner, Ph.D

Living through drafts & feedback: Highway 4 Writers (Linda Vozar-Sweet,

Elizabeth McBride, Judith Isaacs & Erica Kane)

PI info: Michael Chaippellie, TACTICS Private Investigator

Toxicology: Scott Emerson, M.D.

Scottish Publication Advisors: Glasgow Indie Authors Group

I am grateful to Rick Allen, the author of the poem "The Green Man"(c) 1999, for letting Liam Fagan borrow it. And for the loan of his two incredible libraries (one on shelves, one in his head) on mythology, Gaelic and bards, and for the guided tour of Ireland's old stones. For her dedication, invaluable editing, and spirited support of this project, I am most grateful to my agent, Jill Grosjean.

As I am an American author publishing this novel from Scotland, where I now live, it should be pointed out that this book was written during my life in America, hence the Americanisms in both the language and spelling. Although in my daily life in Scotland I have adjusted and spell "center" now as "centre" and "traveling" as "travelling", I have intentionally left my American spellings in this book "uncorrected".

Finally, my process draws in part from insightful dialogue with others. I especially am grateful to Simon Todd, Tony O'Callahan, John Kantner and Chris Lujan for their intellectual and creative generosity.

In loving memory

"The departure from a human body does not end a person's life. As long as one is remembered and loved by those left behind, that person remains alive, in spirit. If one has been gifted and left behind a legacy of creative works this is even more true."

Michelle wrote those words in memory of her husband Rick, who lost his battle against cancer back in 2002. All her friends believe they apply equally to her beautiful spirit.

"But cease your weeping now
Women of the soft, wet eyes,
Till Art O'Leary drink
Ere he go to the dark school--
Not to learn music or song,
But to prop up the earth and the stone."

Eibhlin Dubh Ni Chonaill
c. 1743-1780
(Trans. Frank O'Connor)

"Bird and wing together
Go down, one feather."

Edna St. Vincent Millay, "To a Young Poet"

Chapter 1 - The Wild West

September 1, 1993

Fiona Kelly had been left in an immensely quiet room, filled with more sunlight than she was accustomed to feeling on her skin indoors. The hot light was unexpected, in contrast with the early autumn chill outside. To reach this room she had been led on a long walk through a cool, shadowy corridor of salmon-colored, Mexican tile flooring and thick adobe walls. The wide hallway was dimly lit by old brass sconces and saint-illuminating votives. The small candles rested in *niches*, every six feet, which housed ancient, paint-blistered carvings of Our Lady of Guadalupe, St. Francis of Assisi, *Santo Niño de Atoche*. Those were the *santos* familiar to Fiona from the Southwestern photography books resting on the coffee table back in her Baltimore apartment. The others she didn't recognize. Their upward-cast eyes and outspread hands were unsettling. What terrifying tortures had they endured - or chosen - for their beliefs? What visions?

Before her was a low antique table, inlaid with sky-blue tile. On top of the tile work rested a large cordovan velvet book, hinged and trimmed in brass. The luxurious volume, with deckle-edged pages the color of faded ivory piano keys, begged to be opened. In Fiona's Baltimore basement apartment, books were placed on the coffee table with the assumption that they would be read by visitors. So, on that early autumn day, the young poet leaned forward from the edge of the long, white, leather sofa, reached out her green-gloved fingers, and opened the pages.

The book was half filled with a sepia-colored script. The letters were large, loopy and exuberant. The author obviously felt at ease imposing himself - or herself - into the space between the binding. Fiona closed the book, then opened it again at random and began to read:

It is a place of dehydration here. While we sleep, the soles of our feet crack. We inspect them for blood in the morning, hopeful, as we inspect the arroyos for water.

There is no blood, no water. We wake, dry, with our tongues stuck to the insides of our mouths, our eyelids not entirely closed.

We keep bottled water by the bed, drops for eyes, lotion for skin. I wake, worrying about the lack of water. I creep out of bed and stare out of the window into the moonlight, the brown pine needles that should be green. Longing. For fog, for a walk in the woods. But not this woods. A woods I've never seen, thick with a watery green carpet that squashes between my toes, caresses my skin and curls my hair. Not just a woods - a forest, like in the fairy tales, filled with damping down sounds - not rustlings, too moist for rustlings. Soft thumps, plops, leaves pushed against the ground, which slowly lift and separate after the weight has moved on, making a sound like...

Hearing a faint noise down the hall, Fiona swiftly closed the journal, and moved her fingers, instead, over the cluster of antique cut-glass doorknobs randomly displayed across the surface of the table. Mrs. Fagan - she had said that her name was Talulla, but that Fiona should call her Talle, like everyone else - had been gone several minutes, and in the vastness of the old adobe hacienda, and the complexity of its corridors, it seemed to Fiona that the woman would never return. Fiona feared that she could never find her way out of the mansion on her own, and wondered if she was destined to spend the entire two months of her northern New Mexico adventure on this sofa, contemplating the meaning of these doorknobs, and furtively reading - or not reading - the velvet journal.

Fiona knew the woods the writer described. She had been there, had had that exact same impression, *"Not just a woods - a forest, like in the fairy tales..."*

It had been summer a year ago, on her trip to Ireland, in the forest at Cong in County Galway. At her father's insistence, Fiona used the round-trip ticket to Ireland that her mother had purchased but never got to use, having suddenly died only three months before the long-planned trip. At Fiona's insistence, her father had used some of the insurance money to accompany his daughter on the trip. He was less curious about his one-quarter Irish heritage, or his wife's one-half, but he accomplished some incredible fishing with a droll, white-haired Irish priest he befriended at the edge of Lough Mask. Fishing became the only possible salve for her father's grieving.

Fiona had recognized Cong immediately; in her child's imagination, whenever her mother read her the old European fairy tales. All her life she had assumed the fairy tale forests were just that - imaginary, the human storyteller's image of what the perfect forest would be like. Like the author of the velvet journal, here in this hot, white southwestern landscape, Fiona's imagination was easily pulled into the watery green woods where galoshes were recommended. She had only been in New Mexico now for less than five hours, and already she longed for moisture. Like the writer.

Whose writing was this? Talle's? A 50-something who appeared too hopeful for her age, in a burgundy tiered peasant skirt and off-white Mexican blouse, her long greying brown hair wound into an absent-minded knot at the back of her head, wisps of it falling in her face. Fiona's long hair, in contrast, was worn loose and wavy, a crackling red. She carried well the long, body-hugging black velour turtleneck dress, the silver buttons of which were undone from thigh to ankle, revealing black leather boots.

Maybe the velvet volume was an antique, a collector's item? None of the entries were dated. Perhaps it was the writing of the deceased poet - Liam Fagan - assumed dead, anyway. In fact, Fiona had never heard of him before she entered the competition, which bore his name. Her research into the Fagan Residency had revealed little, only an announcement in the Spring 1980 issue of *Bards & Writers* Magazine that the prize would no longer be known as the "Liam Fagan Bardic School for Emerging Poets". The announcement also included a passing reference to a Fagan poet who, after her stay at the hacienda in 1979, had gone missing. There was no explanation as to the name change.

To add to the mystery, Fiona had been unable to locate any published books of Liam Fagan before her trip to New Mexico. Probably a regional poet, only known locally. Could this be a sample of his work? The daily journal from which came his poems? Fiona listened to the hot white room, to the cool, tiled hallway. Not a sound. She leaned forward again, opened the book to where she had left off.

...sucking, water bubbles popping back into the air.

Yet the woods are not enough for my husband. He loses himself in his study, in his words, and is oblivious to the woods. He might as well live in a city slum for all he notices.

I feel squeezed out of my environment. My husband's new computer was delivered this weekend. Tonight the local computer wizard came by to - already - 'upgrade' it. To connect us to something new he calls 'the web' and 'internet'. It seems daily we bring home more and more that needs to be plugged into the electric. Even my writing - since I can't walk in wet woods, I rise from the bed, from the side of my husband, and go to my computer. Dehydrated insomniac. Even this - electrified, dry static, the air crackling.

The silence too much or not enough.

Like the sounds in our bedroom at night. I pretend the dripping shower is some other sound. Irony of ironies, in our desert the shower drips, drips, drips. He is the man of the house, but he can't fix it. Neither can I. We have done everything, four times, and nothing will fix it. I tell him the only way to fix it is to move.

But of course we never will leave this place. We are rooted in as surely as the grape vines that wrap around these adobe walls, our intertwinings and roots so complicatedly knotted and twisted, we can't be removed. Each year we burst open. Annually we are unharvested, here in the desert. Each year we dry up, raisins on the vine. (We are like the masked ones, in that way.) It is a state of mind, the dehydration...

Silence, not hallway sounds, caused Fiona to nervously close the book again. The reference to the computer. These were not some dead writer's musings, unless very recently dead. Someone living, no doubt living here in this mansion. The hacienda - not to mention all the rooms Talle had pointed out with their entrances to the inner courtyard, and all of its out-buildings (which she called *casitas*) - was certainly large enough to hold a mysterious houseguest or twenty.

In the hallway, a throat was cleared. Thank god she had already stopped reading, thought Fiona. Or...had she been seen reading the entry?

Talle emerged from a doorway carrying a silver tray laden with tea things. As the woman set the tray down on the coffee table, Fiona observed that she either avoided glancing at the book or didn't notice it. No, not hers at all. But had she seen Fiona reading it?

"I know this looks like tea time, but it's actually Mexican chocolate," Talle Fagan spoke quickly and breathlessly. "You do like chocolate, I hope? Oh dear, I didn't think to ask you. Some people are allergic - my husband certainly is - and these are a local favorite, *bizcochitos.*"

Talle moved with a former grace, but bumped her knee against the table, grimaced and awkwardly plopped down on the sofa. She poured a thick brown liquid into two old Wedgewood teacups that were the same blue as the Mexican table tiles. Talle tucked the small sugar cookies into the saucers and handed one to Fiona.

"I'm honored, I love chocolate. Thank you," Fiona accepted the proffered cup and saucer. "Are there other guests?"

"No, just you. Why? Were you hoping...?"

"Oh no. I prefer - well, I *assumed* this would be a very remote, quiet, writer's retreat. It's just so huge! I figured you must have other guests."

"No, no other guests - my dear, please take off your coat, you look so hot! We used to have guests, years ago. But rarely anymore. You'll be left pretty much to yourself - that is what you expected, I hope?"

"Of course," Fiona quickly agreed, pulling off her gloves and tucking them into the pocket of her coat, the sleeves out of which she had obediently slipped her arms.

"We don't have formal meal times. In the morning there will be whatever you need in the dining room, whenever you get up. Feel free to use anything you want in the kitchen. We have all kinds of fresh herbs from my greenhouse - the basil is extraordinary this year - and we put out salad and sandwich things for lunch, or if you want to take a picnic. Dinners we usually have something special from the garden."

"It all sounds wonderful but I don't eat breakfast, just coffee. Juice for lunch. Protein shake for supper - I brought my own."

Talle frowned, sipping her chocolate.

"But, of course, I'll be honored to join you for dinner, if that's what you prefer..."

"Oh, it's really our only requirement. Liam doesn't socialize except at dinner time..."

"He's alive?"

Talle laughed, shaking her head.

"Oh yes, very much so."

"I'm sorry, I didn't mean..."

"Oh that's quite all right. All the young poets who come here assume he's dead, while the older ones assume he's a fortunate recluse. He's living out an old poet's dream - to live in luxury and only write. The young poets have different fantasies. They want to starve and have lots of sex in garrets until their thirties, then become 'well published', receive academic tenure and revel in vast, devoted audiences, right?"

Fiona felt as if her whole body was blushing.

"Anyway, the very-much-alive Liam Fagan likes his chess after dinner, before bed. You do play chess?"

"Of course. It was required."

"Oh yes, I forgot. We added that requirement this year, along with the usual one about spending time in Ireland. How long were you there?"

"As I explained in my letter, only a month. And it was my first time. I hope he isn't expecting me to have a wealth of knowledge of Ireland. I don't, just my love for it."

"But the megalithic stones, you researched them, you said you located many on your trip?"

"I'm no scholar, that was just private research, I used very old books from my childhood, county maps my mother collected. I did it the hard way."

"Oh, he'll like that. He likes people who are inquisitive and adventurous...And your heritage, your lovely red hair -you are Irish?"

"A bit. My mother's mother was one-half Irish, O'Conner. My father is a Kelly, but he's only one-quarter Irish. I hope that is enough?"

Talle sighed what sounded like relief.

"Yes, that will do nicely. Of course, Liam was happiest the year Chahil O'Shea won our competition. A real Irish poet, you see, from Galway. Had only been in the states a few months before winning. His brogue was so thick I couldn't understand a word he said. But Liam did - he studies Gaelic, on his own, for the sheer love of it."

"Was Liam raised in Ireland himself?"

"Oh no. I know that sounds strange, considering his fixation. He wanted to go when he was a young man, but he was very poor. A true starving poet. This is all mine, from my inheritance. Now he's not up to traveling."

"Are you yourself Irish?"

"Probably. I'm a bit of a mutt. I think there's a Mac-somebody back in there somewhere, ha! I'm more of a converted Celt, thanks to Liam. Anyway, he will expect to see you in the evenings. He likes to talk to the poets, you see."

"Well, I...I would be honored to meet him."

"Because you admire his work?"

"Well, I..."

Talle chuckled, rose and went to the wall of book shelves opposite the french doors.

"Here, any time you wish to read them. These volumes represent Liam's life and work. Thirty-nine years of poems.

He began these at age eighteen. The only requirement is that they are returned to this room at the end of your stay."

With a practiced flourish, Talle Fagan indicated a collection of black leather volumes, filling the center shelves of a wall of books. She selected three of the books and returned to the sofa.

"You needn't pretend. You were unable to find his work. You see, he doesn't believe in any of the usual means of publishing, the interference of the government and the big corporate houses," Talle bit into a cookie. "Nor the universities - he believes they produce clones of the poet professors who teach there. He has never published in that sense. Although, by sharing his works with those who come to this room to read them, technically that is publishing. But you will never find an ISBN number attached to his name. And no xeroxing is allowed."

Fiona accepted the three volumes. The memory of the words of her major professor, Dr. Giles Bregman, when she told him she'd won the competition, whispered into her ear:

"No one cares about the work of this Liam Fagan, Fiona. Believe me, I've checked around. Fagan has no publication history. The reputation of this 'residency' of his…" Professor Bregman had grown more angry as he continued, flipping a pen back and forth against the knee of his wool slacks, "Well, let's just say it's a dicey situation at best."

"Dicey?"

"It's the Wild West out there. The Druidic reference is obviously a self-indulgent anachronism! And a female poet was abducted, for god's sake!"

"From the Fagans'?"

"It's not clear. Check 'Bards & Writers', there was a big to-do."

Fiona had already checked the magazine. One sentence was hardly a "big to-do", but she played innocent to find out what he might know.

"When was this?" she asked, yanking her skirt down against his usual glances.

"Who knows? The point is, the place has a questionable reputation."

Like yourself, Fiona thought grimly.

"It's a waste of your time to accept this 'award', when you've just started your MFA," he continued, stabbing his pen into his desk blotter. "It's bad enough you took three years off after your B.A. You're already behind most of those in your class. You need to be more discriminating in your choices at this point in your career. For one thing, you'll lose half a semester! For another thing, you don't want things on your CV that smack of...amateurism...self-indulgence...lack of discipline. Especially following your illustrious waitressing career..."

"Some of the great writers have waited tables. It's a literary tradition in itself!" Fiona snapped. She refused to go into

the harsh economics of her lifestyle with this man.

"I'm sure you can justify your choices, Fiona. Meanwhile, as your advisor, I will tell you which competitions are worthy of your talent. It angers me, really, these charlatans, the nouveau riche who think they can buy their way into the long tradition of…"

"What? The 'poetic elite'?" Fiona had snarled.

"I do what I can for you, Fiona, but you are hopeless. You have no respect for your own craft! So go on, go to your damned desert! Don't say I didn't warn you. You're on your own!"

"I'll be honored to read them."

Talle chuckled again.

"At the rate you're going, you'll be so burdened and weighted down with honors by the time you leave us, you'll have to crawl out of here!"

Fiona blushed and laughed uncertainly, fingering the books.

Talle stood, shaking cookie crumbs from her skirt.

"I'll leave you to your own devices now, if you don't mind. This is my own writing time, until dinner. Your rooms are ready for you - see the casitas out that door? It's the second on the left. It's unlocked, just go on in. Feel free to walk the grounds, don't be shy. We'll call you for dinner. So did you have any questions?"

"I…" Fiona paused, wanted to ask about the abducted poet, but couldn't think of a graceful way to bring it up.

She opted for her second question, "...was curious why the prize name was changed from 'Bardic School' fourteen years ago."

"Oh my! Ancient history! What about it?"

"The idea of a Bardic School in the desert..."

"...Exactly. We changed it to fit the times. Well! Good! We'll see you later, then."

Talle reached down and Fiona moved her knees, thinking she was reaching for the tray. Instead, smiling a brittle smile, she plucked the journal from the table, and wrapped her arms around it protectively. Leaving the room, Talle Fagan twirled her skirt and walked buoyantly like a young girl, in black Chinese slippers with dragons embroidered across the toes.

Fiona sat with her mouth hanging open, staring after the woman's departure. She had obviously brought up a taboo subject. And that journal was Talle's? That fluttery, red-cheeked housewife in the garb of a long-dead counter culture had been the one writing about longing for the archetypal, watery forest?

Had the woman spied Fiona reading her journal? And, if so, had she left the book out on purpose? Everything else in the room seemed so precisely placed. Fiona put down her cup of chocolate which, suddenly, felt heavy in her stomach and too sweet on her teeth.

Perhaps it wasn't Talle's journal. Just because she had taken it from the room didn't mean she was its author. She must have seen Fiona reading it so rudely, graciously chose to not mention that, and would safely return the book to its absent-minded owner.

Feeling chastised by Talle's down-home, good breeding, Fiona fought a sudden impulse to pull on her coat, hoist her bags over her shoulders, and head out for the highway. With an immediate ferocity, she missed her dark, cave-like basement apartment, her familiar brick & board shelves of second-hand paperback poets, her cat Lady Gregory, the Baltimore rain, films at the Orpheum, hot waterfront pretzels at Fell's Point.

Why had she entered this stupid competition?

Maybe she would just stay the night, get a meal, get some sleep, and endure the requisite chess game with the un-publishable poet. No doubt his poetry was horrible, clichés and tired rhymes, why else would you "never find an ISBN number" attached to it? She would leave in the morning. What excuse could she use? She could call home for messages, find out someone had died, that would work. A sudden family emergency, have to leave, so sorry, so honored and so sorry.

Feeling she was being observed from some shadowy corner of the hacienda, Fiona kept her face carefully non-expressive as she gathered up her shoulder bag, suitcase and the three poetry books. She walked through the room, across the sheepskin rug onto the brick flooring, past bronze life-size gods and goddesses, old and dark cathedral-sized paintings of saints, impressively large arrangements of dried desert plants. Out into the court-yard, through the dust, through the chattering autumn trees, past a clutter of tumbleweeds crushed against the adobe walls that fortressed the courtyard. Toward an unfamiliar bed and the hope of water.

Chapter 2 - Santos and Icons

iona awoke to find herself standing in the middle of the hacienda hallway, staring at a dancing circle of light cast by a votive in front of a wooden St. Francis with a missing arm. This feature marked the *santo* as a valued antique, instead of a broken religious *art d'objet* to be discarded or repaired. His facial features were no more than splintered indentations.

Sleepwalking. She had heard of it, naturally, but had never experienced it before. How had she gotten this far from her *casita*, across the courtyard and into the main house? And what was that underfoot? She lifted her foot and pulled an oak leaf from under her sock.

Astounding, the powers of the subconscious, that, her first night in this strange place, her feet knew exactly where to carry her. Fiona rubbed her eyes and looked around. The house was dark, other than the votives in the hallway. Did they burn them day and night, eternally? Were the Fagans

29

Catholics, then? Very possible, with the Irish blood. But this place did not remind her of the churches and Catholic bed and breakfasts she had visited last summer. The Spanish influence was so strong here, yet neither of them was Spanish. So who *were* these people?

Contrary to Talle's insistence that Fiona make her appearance as the greatly-anticipated dinner guest and chess partner, Liam had not shown himself. Talle said he was too tired to join them, and would meet Fiona the following evening. Talle then took her supper upstairs with Liam, and left Fiona in the company of a man she introduced as Hawthorne-tall, muscular, suntanned, scowling, with a tattoo on his forearm - of a man with antlers - and long, blond, stringy hair. The two of them were left to hold up one end of a thirty-foot carved Spanish-style table and an uncomfortable conversation. Not exactly a first-night award-winning-poet's dinner.

She was perplexed by the event, and somewhat irritated. She would have just as well mixed up her usual protein shake and gone to bed early. In addition, the presence of the young man confused her, because Talle had told her there were no other house guests. By way of introduction, all Talle said was "Hawthorne has the *casita* next door to yours."

Stilted conversation with Hawthorne revealed that, true to Talle's description, he was not a houseguest, but a permanent resident - the grounds-keeper for the past fourteen years. He ate moodily, no happier to make conversation with Fiona than she was to do so with him. He kept his dark, sullen eyes focused on his plate, shrugged and answered in low monosyllables Fiona's questions about the grounds. He was actually an artist, he informed her stonily, and doing "this yard work" to support his true work. Hawthorne quickly ate a full plate of blue corn enchiladas, chugged a large glass of ice tea, and barely nodded to Fiona as he departed.

The blue corn enchiladas, and Talle's home-grown spearmint tea, were a new discovery for Fiona. Despite herself, the food from Talle's kitchen was enticing. And the altitude made her more hungry than usual. She finished her dinner in the silence of the large dining room, the sounds of her fork and knife clinking loudly against the dark stoneware plate. A small stack of logs burning in a corner fireplace - a *kiva*, Talle called it - filled the room with the sweet, religious scent of *pinon*. Like the *casita* to which she had been assigned, the hacienda was neat and orderly, but a fine mist of dust covered all the furniture and statuary. She glanced upwards - "*vegas*," Talle had called the large wooden beams, and "*latillas*," the layer of tree branches the beams held in place. Oh yes, she had mentioned something about the silt in adobe houses, that dusting was a daily job. Perhaps this dust was one day's worth? Maybe others lived here, housekeepers and such. So it wouldn't be just herself, the Fagans and Hawthorne for the next two months.

That is, if she stayed. Since Liam Fagan had not shown up for dinner tonight, Fiona would be required to stay at least another night. To leave without ever having met him - the namesake of the competition she had won - would be so rude as to never be forgiven. A struggling poet was wise not to burn her bridges, or that's what her advisor, Professor Bregman was always telling her - his way of saying she should have slept with him. Fiona didn't want to start a reputation for herself as an ungrateful award-winner; so at least another night here was going to be necessary.

Her *casita* was the art of understated Southwestern decor and comfort, as good as any she'd seen in her collection of Santa Fe-style coffee table books. Although the same adobe style as the hacienda, it was built more recently. Small but airy, an open space with a living/dining area on the ground floor, a sleeping loft which overlooked the main room, accessed by a rustic wooden ladder. There were the requisite adobe walls and smooth brick floors, the pristine, white, down comforter on the bed. Even the quintessential *kiva* fireplace, hand-formed in the corner.

Fiona's fascination with the Southwest had led to her ownership of a small but significant collection of photographic books on Southwestern and Mexican folk art, and because she religiously attended any exhibits of such that ever traveled within a hundred-mile radius of Baltimore, she was able to identify many of the pieces displayed on the mantel and along the side *bancos* of the *kiva* in the northwest corner of the spacious room. An antique Zuni bowl; wedding vases and pots of all sizes and shapes, from various decades and pueblos; several Mexican *retablos;* a shelf entirely filled with turn-of-the-century beaded moccasins - mostly turquoise, red and yellow; even three Navajo *yei* masks of spirit gods, and an assortment of Apache peyote fans.

One corner of the dining room displayed a life-sized buffalo *kachina* – spirit effigy – complete with buffalo skin, drums, beads and fetishes - looking very primeval. In the opposite corner, near the hallway entrance, stood a very old church angel - possibly German. Fiona twisted in her seat to see what the wall behind her held: a magical-looking, cracked and faded animal skin with a dancing bird man painted on it, in vegetable dyes of yellow and blue. Finally, in the remaining corner, a weathered replica of an ancient Celtic cross, like those of the fifteenth century which she had seen and photographed in Ireland's cemeteries. Not every belief system in the world was represented in this room, but Talle had covered several bases.

Fiona wasn't quite sure of the protocol after dinner. Was she expected to stay and wait for conversation with her hostess? She sat a while, quietly staring out the windows at the growing dusk. Upstairs somewhere she could hear murmuring, footsteps. Then the sound of silverware, crockery, cabinets opening and shutting in the kitchen. Fiona gathered the plates from her dining experience with

Hawthorne and carried them into the kitchen, pushing her way through the swinging door with her shoulder. A wide-hipped, pleasant-faced woman with substantial cheekbones and sleek blue-black hair smiled at her and continued scrubbing pots at the sink. Fiona put the dishes on the counter.

"Did you make the enchiladas?"

The woman - up close, revealed to be a very young woman - smiled expectantly and shrugged.

"Thank you, very good!" Fiona pointed to the dishes and smiled.

"*Si, gracias,*" the woman laughed shyly and continued her work. Fiona tried to look nonchalant and accustomed to all this splendor as she walked back through the kitchen. The large and steamy white room was equipped with an oak chopping block in the center, a rack of copper and cast iron skillets and pots suspended from the *vegas*. Various white, industrial-sized, state-of-the-art appliances, bright red bunches of chilis hung in long clusters at every corner, and festive blue and white floral tile graced the counters.

Fiona pushed her way through the swing doors, reluctantly leaving behind the strong, earthy smell of onions, garlic, chili and coffee, and the young woman whose presence made the young writer feel less lonely. Right now she wanted someone to talk with, someone who didn't care if she had Irish blood, or played chess, someone who wasn't defending his position as a serious artist who pruned hedges for a living, someone who was truly glad she had been asked to come all this way, simply because she was a poet. Yes, a fellow poet, that's what she longed for.

She then remembered Liam Fagan's leather volumes, the three she'd left in her *casita* to begin reading tonight. It would be the wise thing to do, read some of Fagan's work, so she could discuss it intelligently at next night's dinner. That would make her exit much more possible, and much less transparent.

Fiona shivered her way from the hacienda across the courtyard, surprised at how cold a desert night could be. Back inside her private space, she felt better about things. The lamps glowed golden, and the thick, white, mud walls were warm. The brick floor, partly covered by a Navajo rug of simple geometry, was smooth under her socks. There was a small stack of *pinon* logs outside her door for the *kiva* fireplace. Kindling was already set, so she lit it and brought in the logs. She put on her nightgown and a light sweater, wrapped herself in the white down comforter from the loft bed, and settled onto the small sofa to read Fagan's books.

She opened the binding of the first one, her eyebrows knitted. She didn't expect to like Fagan's poems, but she was ready to defend him, knowing she would have to on her return to Baltimore. Professor Bregman would insist on dinner and a full accounting.

Not modern poetry, she mused, after reading the first two. Formal rhyming schemes, hand-written in a Celtic-styled calligraphy. The way to read them was to assume she had opened a very old book, with pages of crumbling parchment. Once that adjustment was made, they were beautiful, passionate poems, the classic themes of love, death, immortality, honor. Pastoral imagery. References to gods and goddesses - Roman, Greek and Celtic. Yet all of it laced with rage at injustice and longing for deep, human connection. The poet laughed at himself, reminding himself that he was not worthy of such lofty themes.

Liam Fagan was a soul perhaps too sensitive for these times, Fiona thought. She chuckled, imagining Bregman receiving these in the mail as a submission to *The Artisan*. He wouldn't know what to do with them; and yet, if she were to place them, printed out and unsigned, next to any of the traditional forms of poetry he taught, he would ask her from what heretofore unknown collection of which famous bard had they been taken? All in greatly masked irritation that he didn't already know the answer.

There was even a Green Man poem:

"...The Green Man laughed and gave them breath
And daring heart and dancing feet
And none would dream to fear their death
For merry part and merry meet..."

Fiona was quite familiar with the mythic figure, having begun her research into the Green Man the semester before her trip to Ireland. She was herself working on a series of poems using the motif.

Despite her fascination with her benefactor's book, Fiona's journey from Baltimore to this desert mountain had finally caught up with her. She fell asleep after the third page.

And awoke to find herself standing in front of the armless St. Francis in the dark hallway.

She rubbed her eyes again and walked down the corridor, leaves crunching underfoot. She turned left at the forked walkway, looking for the main door back to the courtyard. Now the floors were clean - the clutter of leaves back there seemed, unfortunately, to have been something Fiona had brought in with her.

She hadn't seen these *santos* this afternoon, she must have made a wrong turn. In fact, these weren't Catholic, or even Christian, despite the votives burning before each one. In one *niche* rested a bronze female head, framed by rays of the sun and topped with a slice of the moon. And next - was that a stone relief of the Celtic horse goddess, Epona? She had seen that image somewhere in Galway, in a gallery. Further down, a clay rendering of the famed Oliver Shepherd image of Cu Chulainn, which she remembered from the sculpture in the Dublin post office, with the raven goddess of death - the Morrigan - on his shoulder. Fiona had kept a photo postcard of that piece, drawn to the image of the hero who tied himself to a tree so that, as he died, his enemies wouldn't see him fall.

Finally, a wooden-carved Druidic figure of Hern with antlers on his head - of course! Hawthorne's tattoo! - holding a snake in one hand and a torc in the other, and surrounded by animals. Now Fiona recognized the image, one she had come across while researching pagan Green Man icons for a project at the Institute. Visually, the Green Man was usually found in the form of a mask made of leaves - the head of a man, sometimes with vines and leaves erupting from his mouth, eyes and ears. However, there were other forms, and her research had identified Hern as one Green Man derivative.

Fiona thought she must have stumbled into a private area of the house. Great, she thought, only in her sleep could she find her way around the hacienda. Now that she'd woken up, she was in trouble. This place was so huge!

Now that she recognized Hern, her gaze lifted to the wall above him, and she gasped. Spaced between each *niche* hung a series of life-size clay masks in the traditional form of the Green Man. Fiona recognized them as replicas of that same mythical character from her studies. She stepped back to view them better. These were not generic or modern Green Men – over the past year she had noticed that her Christmas gift catalogues were filled with the icon, in sculpture and jewelry, puzzles and posters. As a fledgling scholar on the subject, Fiona always chuckled at the watered-down descriptions of his origin in the catalogues.

"Fertility symbol" and "guardian of the forest" didn't begin to explain the significance of this character.

Fiona's studies had revealed that the Green Man was an icon of irrepressible life - rebirth and renewal - which (or whom) had evolved from prehistory, appearing, disappearing and reappearing in varied cultures over thousands of years. One researcher had found forty some forms of the Green Man in such places as Japan, Brazil, Egypt, Southeast Asia, the Middle East and Central America. It seemed to Fiona that the Green Man's most popular and purest form came from the Celts, the Druids, and that modern-day European and American pagans were rejuvenating him once again. So were the environmentalists; she'd seen bumper stickers and woven patches of his visage. Fiona found it most interesting that, when the Christians tore down the pagan places of worship and began to build churches, they retained one pagan image on those sanctified walls: the Green Man.

As Fiona stared up at the faces, whose features seemed to animate in the dancing shadows of the votive candles, she recalled another theory - that, when pagans were forced to work as slaves to build the Christian churches, they had subversively incorporated the Green Man imagery. Yet, they were obviously allowed to do so; images as old as the first century A.D. could still be found. She had read that even the walls of Rosslyn Chapel in Midlothian, Scotland, built by the Knights Templar, had only one image of Christ, but over four hundred icons of the Green Man.

At first glance, the Green Men on the Fagans' corridor walls seemed to be replicas of ancient forms she'd seen in books. But a closer look revealed that, although they were all obviously rendered by the same artist, and in the classical styles, each of these Green Men was different from the next. Their features were strikingly realistic, and it seemed every conceivable emotion was represented here. Anger, awe, cynicism, lust, anguish, terror. Some of them had eyes carved, some had only dark sockets. Oak leaves and vines protruding from the mouths of some, others were caught in tangles of grape vines, insects, feathers, pinecones, twigs or other natural formations. One mask had a spider on its cheek, surrounded by a halo of copper-spun web; another had cicadas and grasshoppers hidden in layers of leaves. A bejewelled scarab crawled toward the eye of one mask. Fish swam in and out of the eye sockets and mouth of another. As Fiona walked slowly down the hallway, she counted twelve such masks.

Another surprise in a house full of Catholic saints.

Here, the hallway stopped at a dead end, an alcove under a stairwell, which led into one of the many rooms. As Fiona stood, contemplating which way to go, and fearful any movement would waken the Fagans sleeping upstairs, she realized that the room into which she was staring was a formal library, lit up by the full moon through a tall stained glass window. She stepped closer inside the library entryway, crossing an invisible scent threshold of burnt pinon and old books. Wall to wall books, very tall ceilings, the proverbial library ladder.

Rich oriental carpeting, two antique, green glass lamps on a glossy, dark reading table. A window seat with silk saffron and pewter-colored cushions, their colors luminous in the moonlight.

The most obvious adornment in this not-so-Southwestern room was yet another large resin face formed of leaves on the north wall. Fiona had seen the specific face of this Green Man before. She stepped closer to inspect him, trying to recall. The dark, shadowed crevices between its sculpted leaves gave the illusion of many eyes watching. The lips parted as if about to whisper a secret, the true and watchful eyes stared to the right, as if about to give ominous warning or shrewd observation. Fiona remembered now. Whomever the artist, this was a reproduction of the German Green Man of Bamberg, one of the most fierce, beautiful and terrifying she had found in her readings.

Fiona surveyed the room. The long, stained-glass window depicted an intricate knotwork panel from the Book of Kells, no less. The symbols of the four Evangelists - the lion, ox, man and eagle - in muted tones of blood red, purple, mustard and acid green. Fiona held her breath at the dreamlike indulgence of this room. There, on the other wall, an elaborate, gilt-framed reproduction of a William Blake watercolor. She moved closer and, in the blue of the moonlight, made out the rendering of

Blake's words, his drawing of a bearded man playing a large harp, surrounded by women and children in robes:

Youth of delight come hither
And see the opening morn...
How many have fallen there!
They stumble all night over bones of the dead
And feel they know not what but care;
And wish to lead others when they should be led.

Fiona squinted to read the small brass plate mounted on the frame. "The Voice of the Ancient Bard", Plate 54, *Songs of Innocence and Experience.*

In front of the Book of Kells window were placed a small table and two chairs, an oversized chess set on the table. Fiona stepped near the table, recognized a very old, classic Staunton set. The board was inlaid, aged and cracked walnut and ivory. A game was in progress and, judging by the dust on the pieces, it had not been continued for a while. It seemed an evenly matched game; few pieces were left on the board, but as many black as white. This late in the game, both players had replenished their queens and both kings were well fortressed. She wondered, with whom did Liam ordinarily play? Talle? Hawthorne?

She must get out of here and back to her *casita* before she was discovered. Suddenly she was incredibly tired. As she turned to leave, her elbow brushed against the chess-board, knocking over a black knight, which clinked against the board, and a white castle which fell to the carpet. Fiona paused, her heart beating wildly, expecting to hear voices, see lights as the household woke to her intrusion. It seemed half an hour of total silence passed before she dared move again. She stared at the board, trying to remember where the pieces had been. But it was hopeless; it was too dark to discern dust patterns, best to leave them as they had fallen.

As Fiona left the library, the moon-lit, sideways eyes of the Bamberg Green Man seemed to glare at her accusingly, while his mouth twisted into a knowing smile. She shuddered and turned back from where she had come, heading the opposite direction at the fork. Still wrong. *No, wait, there was the courtyard light.*

Fiona opened the glass doors, vaguely recalling they had been wooden ones earlier, and stepped out into the night. No, this wasn't it either, this was a patio, set with a cast iron umbrella table, a bench, a small fountain bubbling. What was that scent? Russian olive? Somewhere a dog barked, another answered further on. The black sky was busy with stars new to her.

Fiona walked out beyond the flagstone patio into damp grass, to see what she could see. Maybe this path led back around to the main courtyard? No. This courtyard was very small, surrounded by a gateless adobe wall. Passing the umbrella table on her return to the flagstones, Fiona caught her breath. There was the cordovan velvet journal, open, illuminated by a glass-held candle nearby, a half-empty glass of wine, a pen. She paused, looking around. No windows, nothing but this walled-in, candle-lit table, darkness, the bright moon and stars beyond. Talle certainly was absent-minded, or had been interrupted in the middle of her writing.

Fiona was suddenly aware that she was wearing nothing but a cotton nightgown, grass-dampened socks and a lightweight sweater. Not enough to be sitting out on a New Mexico autumn mountain night, and certainly not appropriate clothing in which a guest poet should be caught wandering around. Still, the fascinating book, which had been whisked from her sight earlier in the day, was here, open. This was an opportunity she would doubtless never have again.

Again, that strange suspicion, that the woman had left it there intentionally.

Fiona stood near the table, hugging her sweater to her rib cage, pretending to look out into the darkness. She lowered her eyes and surreptitiously began to read, her ears as alert as a wild animal's to the slightest sound:

It is not that there is not enough water; it is that we fear there will be a time when our bodies will have lost the capacity to take it in.

Odd. The book was open to the exact page where Fiona's previous reading had left off.

So I convert the sound of the dripping shower to the sound of a grandfather clock. It is easier for me to sleep, listening to time dripping away, than for me to listen to the loss of water. (Time does pass all too quickly, but that is a lost resource over which I have no control).

44

Fiona moved away from the table, rubbed her arms against the chill night air, and looked through the glass doors into the hacienda hallway. Nothing in there but silence and darkness, the faint light of the nearest votive several feet down the hall. Fiona returned to the table. The wine glass caught her attention. Fingers of the night air passed its scent under her nose, along with the smell of candle wax, some kind of flower along the adobe wall, again the Russian olive. Fiona picked up the wine glass and tasted. A strong red wine. A *good* red wine. She wanted to finish it off. But, in the morning, when Talle returned to retrieve her things, if she found a drained glass where there had been wine... Fiona wiped the rim with her nightgown hem, again staring at the open page. Why was she so compelled to read this journal? Other than a couple of enigmatic references, it seemed nothing shocking was being revealed, no dark secrets, just a woman's personal musings of no particular note. Fiona would have left at that moment, except a phrase caught her eye.

"...*that He is coming near. For I have no doubt that He, too, longs for us. Perhaps searches, even. I keep imagining myself, just walking out into the woods and following wherever that takes me. Without a map. But I would never be able to carry enough water.*

Because I think He's out there, and that if I found Him, the skin on the soles of our feet would heal, our eyelids would finally be able to stay closed at night. There would

45

be that much moisture for us, my husband and I, if I found Him. My husband would be at peace, finally, and then so would I.

Fiona carefully turned the page.

I can't understand or explain how the three thoughts are connected - the overload of the electrical circuits here, the lack of water...and finding Him. The crackling in the air...it either interferes with the reception or warns - like static - that He is coming near.

I often think, as I drift back off to sleep, if I walked far enough out of the desert, into the woods that becomes forest, beyond the crackling and rustling to the plopping and sucking sounds...there He would be, dark and green, waiting in those places, His eyes filled with compassionate understanding of all that has happened here.

In fact, I imagine He is the <u>only</u> one in existence who could see my part in it with compassion, who is large enough to embrace that which cannot, by most, be embraced.

And so, in my loneliness - and in the fear that sometimes comes - it becomes more and more imperative to find Him.

Now I have written myself back to sleep. Back to bed, to the dreams of the forest, the sound of the grandfather clock.

That was enough. God, if someone had seen her doing this. Inexcusable. But who was this "He" with a capital H? Fiona listened carefully. No sounds other than the same dry autumn rustlings, the distant canines excited by the moon.

She turned to leave, yet, unable to resist putting her finger into the wine glass for one last taste, she almost tipped over the long-stem goblet. She barely caught it in time to avoid a shattering fall, but too late to avoid the splash of red across the open page and the clattering on the iron table top as she set it upright.

Fiona stopped all movement, her breath and pulse on hold, certain again that her bumbling noises would waken the household. Cursing under her breath, she started to blot the wine stain with her sleeve, then realized she might smear the sepia script. She turned quickly and crept back into the hacienda. This time terror made her feet sure. She moved swiftly past the twelve Green Men, back down to the fork, turned left, found the one-armed Saint Francis and the clutter of leaves, continued on and made a right turn at the other end of the hall. There it was, the large wooden door leading to the courtyard, standing open as she, apparently, had left it earlier in her sleep. More leaves had blown in and were scattered at the threshold. Fiona clasped her hands over her mouth to muffle her sigh of relief.

As she entered her *casita*, feeling blessed by having had no embarrassing explain-your-nightgown encounters along the way, Fiona suddenly realized she had left the journal open to the last page she had read. Not the page at which Talle had earlier left it open.

At this rate, she might not have to make up an excuse to leave. She might be *asked* to leave.

Chapter 3 - Bluebeard

oo tired to climb the ladder to the loft bedroom, Fiona slept on the sofa. Barely after sunrise, she groaned and turned, pulling the comforter over the top of her head, to block out the faint trace of light pressing through the simple muslin curtains. She felt hung over, as if she had consumed the entire bottle of Talle's wine, not just one furtive sip.

The *casita* was cold, she hadn't remembered to add another log to the fire last night. Not enough sleep - that was really why she felt hung over. Mostly, Fiona realized as she curled into fetal position under the covers, it was her chagrin about her nocturnal mishaps that made her feel unwilling to face the day. How could she possibly dress and walk into the dining room to claim her morning coffee and bowl of fruit, knowing the look of suspicion she would have to endure in Talle's eyes? Perhaps they would all be there - the sweet cook, the reclusive Liam Fagan, the sullen Hawthorne - all lined up in the dining room, arms folded across their chests, glaring at her. She would be banished, her reputation sullied.

Three hours later, Fiona had only showered and pulled on her stay-at-home clothes - jeans and a sweatshirt. Rather than face Talle, she remained huddled by the glowing fireplace, clutching the mug of coffee she made in her own kitchenette. Occasionally, Fiona peeked through the curtains at the courtyard and hacienda; once she saw Hawthorne, headed in for his breakfast. Later, Talle, wearing a sun hat, a straw satchel slung over her shoulder, wrapped in a large shawl, and carrying the velvet journal.

By now her hostess would have seen the leaves in the hall and the wine stain. Fiona took great hope, however, from the fact that, when Talle passed a few yards from her *casita*, she did not glance in Fiona's direction - not angrily, accusingly or with curiosity. Talle seemed very preoccupied, but with a faint Mona Lisa smile on her lips. She kept her eyes focused on her path, stopping only once, to pet one of the several cats which populated the premises, then walked out into the pine forest in her childlike, black dragon slippers, the cat trailing behind.

The woman seemed quite serene, not at all like one whose day had started out with the shocking realization of night intruders in her home. Of course, mused Fiona, the Fagans did not even start from the mind-set of securing their property. The doors were apparently never locked, Fiona had not even been given a key to her *casita*. (She could bolt it from the inside with a cast-iron bar, but, when she left, it remained unlocked.) Either privacy was assumed to be of no importance, or there was some kind of honor system in place which made privacy a given.

But even with Talle out for a walk, Fiona wasn't up to heading toward the dining room to be scrutinized by the others, despite the fact that she was incredibly hungry. The altitude definitely was affecting her metabolism. She was ravenous. The blue corn enchiladas last night had awakened some craving in her. This morning she urgently wanted rich, yellow eggs drenched in thick, orange cheese, sausages that would burst with fat bubbles as she bit down into them, toast soggy with melted butter. Even cream in her coffee, although she had been drinking it black for a year now! Fiona rose from the fireplace angrily, pulled an envelope of protein powder from her suitcase - not having yet unpacked - and mixed it with water at the kitchenette sink. Its maple flavor was distinctly distasteful this morning, but she forced herself to drink it down. It would fill the emptiness for a while.

So what would she do with this day? This would be her only day here, so she best spend it in a fruitful way. She would definitely make those calls today. One to her father and one to the Baltimore Fine Arts Institute. Professor Bregman was leaving for France tomorrow, on sabbatical, and would be gone until after Thanksgiving. Before he left she needed to find out if the work-study job was still available, that small bit of cataloguing which might pull in wages to compensate for the prize money she would, no doubt, not receive since she was leaving. One of the irritating points about this "honor" was that the promised prize money had not yet been placed in her hands. Her round-trip air ticket had been paid for, between Baltimore and Albuquerque, and the award letter had said the prize money would be presented on her arrival. Would she actually have to remind them?

Nothing, yet, had been as Fiona had expected. Even with the unlocked doors, she began to feel more like a prisoner than an honored poet. No great welcome, no guided tour, no word of the public reading she was going to give. All those unpublished volumes in the sun room. And then that uncomfortable dinner with Hawthorne. She hadn't even met her benefactor yet - too tired, indeed! How tired did he think *she* was yesterday, after traveling thousands of miles!

Perhaps they planned to award her the check at her public poetry reading, whenever that would be, if she stayed that long. Or would she have to remind the Fagans about the reading too? And where, exactly would that literary event be held, and to what audience? The nearby village was minuscule, didn't seem to be an oasis of culture. Would she just read in the sun room to the cook, the reluctant Hawthorne, and the smiling Talle - Liam Fagan being too tired to attend? An angry flush of heat ran up her spine at the thought of all this. Perhaps she had been rude, reading Talle's journal and spilling Liam's chess pieces, but no more so than they!

Suddenly she longed to hear her father's voice, to hear his simple descriptions of planting bulbs and his latest fishing expedition, his upcoming cataract surgery, the brake job he just had done on the old Ford truck. His life was so sane, while she felt overwhelmed by her mad poet's life, with all its vagaries; with her inability to get through a single day without translating its events into metaphor; with the never-ending task of alchemizing her emotions into tightly-hewn phrases that would pass muster at the Baltimore Fine Arts Institute, yet satisfy her soul.

Sometimes she would tell him of her struggles, the faltering relationships that never became substantial, the confusion of her dreams to be a great poet. He would listen, quietly, not having much advice to offer in those arenas. He could easier instruct her on how to clean a fish, change a tire, and build a compost heap. Then he would say, "Well, honey, you'll be fine. You've got your mother's stamina." And, shortly after such a phone call, she would receive a box holding some treasure from her mother's belongings, wrapped in white tissue with a short note explaining.

"*These pearls I bought for her during the war.*"

"*This was your mother's favorite set of table linens.*"

"*She saved these baby pictures of you.*"

Fiona felt tears in the back of her eyes at the thought of hearing his voice. That's what was missing today. Grounding, a reminder of her roots, her true identity kept hidden from her world of poets and professors, because it wasn't colorful or exotic enough to help promote her work. She wasn't an immigrant poet from a military state who had been imprisoned for her words, nor a former felon discovered to be a gritty, raw poet by some out-reach writing teacher. She was just Fiona from the bland Midwest, with a basically non-eventful childhood and no explanation for the inexplicable inner demons (Professor Bregman's phrase) which compelled her to write.

She could go into the hacienda right now, ask the cook where the phone was - a good moment to go, with Talle off in the woods.

Or, better still, she could go exploring. The small village, Ojo de Sombras, was about a half mile down the dirt road from the hacienda, where the bus had left her off yesterday. (That was the first insult, that no one was waiting for her at the bus stop, that there were no cabs here. She'd had to ask directions and then walk the half mile with her baggage.) Next to the bus stop bench, Fiona had seen what appeared to be a coffee shop with an herb-&-book store attached, and passed a second-hand store and a combination grocery/hardware store on her way to the hacienda. Somewhere in the village there would be a pay phone.

In fact, she now recalled having seen one on the wooden porch of the grocery/hardware place. She'd almost stopped there yesterday, to call the hacienda for a ride, but a cowboy in dusty denims and a dirty brown western hat was using it. He was engrossed in a long and aggravated discussion, so Fiona had passed on by and opted to walk. After being cramped up in the airplane and bus, the movement and clean air was refreshing. She was suddenly and literally transported from the grey, rainy brick-and-concrete streets of Baltimore, to the edge of a pine forest, a red dirt road, a mansion formed of red mud. She heard birds and saw squirrels, rabbits and quail moving about along her path, instead of street strangers with questionable motives. Some of her constant city guardedness began to evaporate in the dry afternoon sunlight.

Remembering this, Fiona pulled her grey duster over her jeans and sweatshirt and tucked her wallet into her pocket. She put on sunglasses against this unfamiliar white light and tucked her small poetry notebook and pen into the other pocket of her coat. She would go exploring and make her phone calls in the relative, open-air privacy of a high-desert pay phone.

* * *

"Well, I'm not sure why you went there in the first place. I would advise you to stick it out, now that you have."

"But I'm not sure it's the best use I can make of…"

"I don't see that you have a choice. You said your finances were not…"

"What about the work study position? The cataloguing, you said there was a need in the department library..."

"Filled that, the day after you left. There were several students in line, you know that."

"Yes. I see. Well..."

Fiona sighed and leaned against the wall next to the pay phone.

"Make the most of it, Fiona. Write about it! There's ample material there!"

"How would you know?" Fiona asked in a disgruntled tone.

"Raven Shane Cordova's poems."

"Who?"

"In the upcoming issue of *The Artisan*, you know, that poet from Santa Fe."

"I don't know what you're talking about."

"You didn't see that? We accepted six poems from her just last week, all about her stay at the Fagan hacienda. She was last year's award-winner."

"I never saw them."

"Must have arrived that day you were out - weren't you out? Flu or dentist or..."

"Oh, right. Dentist. But-you never told me about these poems!"

"Didn't I? Thought I did. She's been accepted into the program, come January."

"The next *Artisan* doesn't come out until then."

"Are you hinting?"

"Hinting?"

"That I should fax you the galleys now?"

"Why would I want you to do that?"

Fiona poked at some dried leaves on the ground with the toe of her boot. Bregman loved his mind games.

"Perhaps to give your competitive spirit a kick? Her work is very interesting; you'll both be up for the same honors and funding. Granted, her work is a little on the self-absorbed side, as with all of you young female poets..."

"Excuse me!"

"You know I'm right. And don't go off about sexual harassment again. I'm speaking from a position of wisdom as your elder and your mentor and, within that arena, I am allowed to say anything, I repeat, *anything* I damned well please!"

"And you always do."

"I always do. So. What's the fax number out there? Or do they even have such modern advances?"

"I'll have to check."

"Get me a number where Fagan is likely to review what I send before you see it. Cordova isn't exactly flattering to him, which should liven things up for you. And you can test his grit, see if he even acknowledges receiving the fax or even passes it on to you, once he's seen these."

"I'll be sure to do that, Sherlock," Fiona answered dryly. "What do you mean, unflattering?"

"Apparently he's highly unpublishable, for one."

"He doesn't believe in being published."

"Yes, I gathered that. As do most sinners not believe in hell."

"What else does she say?"

"Well, have you had any weird, pagan-esque experiences there yet?"

"Pagan-esque? Like what?"

"Wood sprites, devas, bacchanalian rituals, sex orgies, strange herbs in your evening tea, the usual?"

"Good grief. They're just a sweet old couple. She's an heiress, he's…"

"Yes?"

"Well, I haven't exactly, uh, spoken with him one-on-one yet…"

Fiona was too embarrassed to admit to her mentor just how neglected she was feeling and that she hadn't even seen the man yet.

"…He's working on something very involving," she went on quickly. "We'll be discussing things this evening. And playing a game of chess."

"Ah yes, the chess thing. Be careful with that."

"Careful?"

"I gather Liam Fagan is something of a Bluebeard. Do you find yourself attracted to him?"

"I, uh-oh, for god's sake, now you're being ridiculous."

"Maybe you like them older? Maybe he can do for you what I never could - or what you never let me try."

Fiona was silent. The affair that she and Professor Bregman almost-but-never-quite-had was still a great discomfort to her. He was attractive but she held him at bay, for many reasons. His wife; his position as her major professor in the Master of Fine Arts program at the Baltimore Fine Arts Institute; their mentor/student relationship; her literary career; her sense that he had had many student lovers; her not wanting to be just this semester's idiot.

"That's not entirely true," she finally responded.

From the porch of the hardware store, Fiona watched a trembling, elderly man help his arthritic wife out of an old truck.

"You refer to that time when you were drunk and got angry because I turned you down?"

"I did not! And I *wasn't drunk.*"

The frail couple, climbing the steps of the hardware store porch, glanced at Fiona in alarm. Fiona turned to face the wall for privacy and, clenching her teeth, reduced her volume.

"And *you* didn't exactly turn *me* down."

"Yes, you were, and yes, I did. I wanted you, Fiona, but not that way. Ah, but that's all ancient history, isn't it, my young poetess?"

Fiona hated it when he called her that.

"Professor Bregman, I will find out if there's a fax machine in town somewhere."

"If you don't get back to me within the hour, it'll be too late, I'm heading home, have an early plane to catch."

Fiona ended the strange - yet terribly predictable - conversation and, instead of calling her father right away, relinquished the hardware store pay phone to the two giggling teenage girls who were waiting under a nearby tree. A sign at the *Extranjeros,* a combination bookstore, herb shop and art gallery across the street, indicated a fax machine was on the premises. Fiona crossed the dirt road and entered the lace-curtained door, breathing in the pleasant scents of sage incense and peppermint tea. A bell tinkled somewhere in the back of the tiny space, which was crammed with new and used books, a showcase of locally-made silver jewelry, a display of herb products, a help-yourself counter which held a tea pot on a hot plate, mugs and a basket of herbal teas. The back corner was set up with a handful of easy chairs, benches and a podium. In response to the bell, a tall, thin woman came out from a back room, arms full of used paperbacks, blowing at the mass of kinky, grey hair, which fell over her lively brown eyes.

"Hi! Can I help you find something?"

"Can I have a fax sent here?"

"Yup, fifty cents a page. The number's on the wall there."

Back at the pay phone, Fiona recited the fax number into Professor Bregman's answering machine and hung up. She walked over to the Wild Shadows Cafe next door to the *Extranjeros* and ordered an espresso, pleased to see that at least that token of civilization could be found along the dusty main street of the little village. She sat and stared out at the tumble weeds, yellowed cottonwoods, the ancient adobe and wooden structures that seemed like loaves of bread baked with low-altitude recipes, sunken in the middle and sprawled at the edges. The espresso was good, and cheered her into jotting some descriptive phrases in her notebook. *Write about it*, he'd said.

Perhaps she could ask her father to send a few hundred, she mused, chewing on the end of her pen. That would get her through until January so that she could go back to Baltimore, get an early start on those "incompletes". But she hated to ask, he kept his retired years so simple, no doubt he was conserving funds to make them last. She knew he would send what she requested, no questions asked. Still, it was hard enough - trying to be something so romantic and useless as a poet - without having to admit she couldn't afford her own livelihood. That was the graduate school dilemma; it would lead to a teaching position, but did she really want to teach?

Fiona hadn't the heart for it. She found the aspirations of the younger poets to be so embarrassing and so like her own, still. She sometimes suspected they - and she - were all deluded and spoiled, would never grow to be adults. That she should give it up, get a real estate license or enroll in a business school. Or go back to the farm, grow a subsistence garden, keep a cow and some chickens. Now *there* was a plan! Live with her father in Oklahoma, a simple and hard life, and write when she could. The very modest farmhouse was paid for, she would inherit it, but could she really live there? Could she really be her father's daughter, the neighbors' neighbor, the bake sale ladies' lady? Could she marry a simple, good-hearted man of the soil and settle in? The way her mother – a socialite with artistic leanings – had done? She smiled at the memory of that old photo on the piano at home, her mother in a ballroom gown in her twenties. Next to the one of her mother in her forties, in overalls, feeding the chickens out back.

No, she was cursed to be a poet, to constantly lift the wings of sleeping things, to wake up questioning - before her morning coffee - Who am I? Where am I going? She could see herself, doing chores on the farm, asking the same ridiculous questions she'd always asked, as a child. Why the udder? Why the egg? Only now passing them off as poems.

And what about this other poet, this Raven Shane Cordova? What funny coincidences, that Cordova's poetry had arrived just as Fiona had left to come to the Fagans' hacienda, and that they would end up in grad school together. As editorial assistant on The Artisan Review, the creative writing department's literary magazine, Fiona would ordinarily have been the first to read Raven Shane Cordova's poems, to decide whether to pass them along to Professor Bregman for consideration. Would she have felt reluctant to come to the Fagans' for a residency if she had read those poems? Or would she have wanted to, even more so?

Another thought came. Had Professor Bregman intentionally chosen not to show Cordova's poetry to Fiona before she left for New Mexico? That would be like him, she could see him rubbing his hands together and chuckling, knowing she was going off into some macabre, maybe even dangerous, adventure, and not warning her. Eagerly awaiting her report, her chagrin, her discomfort.

Fiona finished her coffee and rose to go next door to check on her fax. As she stood, she noticed Hawthorne, the young artist/gardener, sitting in a corner of the cafe, slumped in his chair and watching out the window as if lost in thought. No, as if watching for someone. He then sat up slowly, lifted his hand in a lazy salute to someone in the street. Outside the window, she saw the wide-hipped, blue-black-haired cook from last night, coming out of the hardware/grocery store, wrapped in a dark shawl, with a large sack of groceries in her arms. The young woman ducked her head shyly at Hawthorne, through the glass, and began to walk down the dirt road, in the direction of the hacienda.

Hawthorne's greeting was apparently not as idle as it had seemed, for he moved quickly, up from his seat and out the door, jogging across the street to catch up with the young woman. Fiona smirked; he exerted as much energy in pursuing the cook as he had in trying to escape dining with Fiona the night before. Hawthorne put one hand around the woman's waist and took her groceries with the other. They walked closely, their hips bumping against each other. The young woman lifted her face - did she frown or smile? - and he kissed her. She averted her lips from his, shyly, and a dark curtain of hair hid her expression from Fiona's view. It seemed she also tried to move her hips away from his, but he pulled her closer to him. Whether they entered the woods in collusion or ambivalence was not clear from Fiona's vantage point.

She wished she hadn't seen them. She didn't want to know all these things - or have all these questions raised - about interrelationships at the hacienda. She just wanted peace and quiet and simplicity, no human interactions. For the gardener to be just the gardener, the cook just the cook, the wife just the wife.

Or, better still, to leave, to go back home.

Fiona grimaced as she scanned the faxed pages the bookstore woman handed her. Professor Bregman had apparently been expecting her call, her desperate cry for help. He had quite eagerly and quite obviously prepared this package in advance, planning to send it to her. His cover sheet was dated two days back, and read:

"Fiona, dearest - A predecessor, last year's winner of the Fagan award, to be featured in the January issue of The Artisan. She's also been accepted into the graduate program. No doubt you'll have much to discuss at some point. The long black dress for chess with Bluebeard is the ticket. Regards, Your

'Professor'. P.S. Watch yourself. Don't forget, Fagan poets have been known to vanish."

His message sent a red flush up the back of her neck. And the cryptic post script was irritating.

How dare he bring that up, about her dress, and where others might read it! The long black velour dress had been the one she'd worn the night she...how *did* she explain or define that evening in his office, on his sofa? The dress was so much a part, in her memory, of how far they had gone and at what point they had stopped their erotic play. The black velour was her favorite, her signature dress. She had been trying to disassociate it in her mind with Professor Bregman. And now he had ruined it for her.

Events had not gone as Professor Bregman chose to recall them. He had not turned her away. She had left, in the middle. Although she was not emotionally aroused by Professor Bregman that night, her physical arousal was frighteningly intense. She was so warm from the champagne, so ready to let him pull the dress off, to let the cool air of his office touch her skin entirely. The blatant illicitness of the situation was more than tempting. And then what did he say?

"You pretend not to want it, your lady-like demeanor is so maddening! Like these buttons, who are you trying to kid? Wonderfully maddening-and you well know it, you..."

Thankfully, the phone had rung, interrupting whatever he was about to name her, in his growling voice. His wife called at that very moment, as if she knew, across town, that he and the young poet had left the reception, and gone up into his office on some pretext. Fiona rose, pulled herself from his hands, which still tried to tug at her clothes as he lied to his wife. She felt so ashamed of herself, suddenly realizing that it was not true, that she did *not* "want it". Not with him, not from him. She hated his lie about grading papers late, rushed out of his office, out of the building, not caring if anyone saw her, red-faced and disheveled. The silver buttons were undone to her panty line; the imprint of his hand still clutched her velour breast like a sweaty brand. Of course, students saw her fumbling with the buttons as she passed them. Rumors began.

Until this moment, standing in a bookstore in the middle of these foreign New Mexico Mountains, Fiona hadn't realized how uncomfortable and stress-filled the past four semesters had been for her. Always the undercurrent between she and Professor Bregman, between she and his wife at department receptions. Always pushing away the hints from fellow students, the smirks when she got a high grade from him, the grins when she did not. Unable to read aloud her erotic poetry in class, or submit it for publication in *The Artisan*, for fear it would be interpreted - by him, by the students - as being about him.

In fact, that had been the initial reason she had begun her research and series of Green Man poems. A round-about way of reworking her usual erotic material, of taking it to another level, away from the here and now. The history of the pagan Green Man was a subject of no interest to Professor Bregman. It was a place she could go without his academic intrusion. He seemed puzzled at - and wary of - her Green Man poems, and begrudged the interest and approval her fellow students showed in them. Fiona suspected that Bregman, in his late fifties, had reached that crossroads to which some academics came: he was, finally, one generation too far behind his students for true communion. Not so admired, not so in touch, not so relevant to them. And, to him, the students had finally become tedious, petty and hopeless. His tried-and-true routines of seduction no longer worked with the female students, and the admiration of his male students no longer satisfied. Bregman was exhausted, and that was anathema to his subject matter - poetry. The stale food of the soul no longer sustained him.

Suddenly she felt a great sense of relief that she was not back there in Baltimore; that she was here, in an unfamiliar place, unknown to these people. For that sensation alone, it might be worth staying the two months.

"So you know Raven?"

The wavy-haired woman behind the counter asked Fiona, closing the cash register and picking up her cup of tea, seemingly nonchalant. So this woman had read the fax cover sheet. Not so anonymous after all. How fast would word spread in this village? Oh god, not already; snickering behind her back about black dresses and chess games with Bluebeard. She had to repair this, immediately.

"No, actually. My professor just sent her work."

"We have her books. The one she wrote the year before she came here, and the book that just came out in May. We keep books by all the Fagan poets. Including Aisling Devlin's. You're the new poet, Fiona Kelly, right?"

"Yes..."

Fiona blushed.

"Do you have a book out?"

"No, not yet. Uh, where are..."

The woman came around the counter and guided Fiona past a display of packages of dried herbs, to a small shelf in a corner, almost a shrine, displaying a photo of the Fagan hacienda, a photo of Liam Fagan shaking hands with a middle-aged bearded man, and a shelf of books of past award winners. Liam Fagan's face was craggy and interesting, his white hair tied back in a long ponytail.

"Who's this?" Fiona asked, "I mean, with Liam Fagan."

"Chahil O'Shea, he was a real Irish poet, brogue and all. So...back here is where the readings are held. Let us know if you need anything special. I'm Silver, by the way."

"Glad to meet you."

"One poet needed a certain kind of tea. Aisling Devlin came in the day before to rearrange the chairs; she didn't use the podium because she had this sort of harp thing she played. Whatever you need, we'll do it. We're all excited about your reading."

Her reading? The woman named Silver handed Fiona a flier as she spoke. A bad xerox of the photo that Fiona had sent along to the Fagans with her poetry- one her father had taken of her in Ireland, standing next to the entrance stone at Newgrange - announced that she would give a poetry reading and be awarded the Fagan award at the *Extranjeros* on Friday night, September 17th. Two weeks away.

"I am too, thank you. I can't think of anything I'll need. It's just me and my poems."

"You might be surprised, we get a pretty good crowd for the readings. Everyone always wants to see who's the new poet up there. Liam never comes down except for the reading once a year. He's pretty reclusive. Talle, though, she's always in here, she's our best customer. And, of course, we consign her herbs. You want those?"

Fiona looked at the two books Silver had placed in her hands on top of the flier. *Water Rites*, the back cover bearing a photo of Raven Shane Cordova. *The Wounded Watcher*, the back cover photo the exact same as the first, no clues there. Fiona glanced at the publication dates. Two years ago. Then this year. Before and after her residency with the Fagans. Of course she wanted them.

"I'll cut you a deal, ten for the both. I'll throw in Aisling Devlin's chapbook for fifteen, you'll want that, of course."

Silver pulled a stapled sheath of poems from the shelf.

"I'm sorry, I'm not familiar – who is this Aisling Devlin?"

"The disappearing poet, of course. You don't know about her?"

"Oh yes, I heard something about that. I didn't know her name."

"She was the 1979 Fagan poet. Left a few weeks before the end of her residency, drove to Colorado and was never seen again. Police figured she was kidnapped, probably murdered. There was a big investigation, and we all got questioned. For a while it put Ojo de Sombras on the map. Unfortunately."

So Professor Bregman knew about this all along, Fiona thought. And didn't exactly tell her, other than his cryptic comments. Just like him. Fiona handed Silver a ten and a five from her wallet, and took the three books. The woman tucked the bills into the cash register - an old-fashioned one, with mechanical keys and a bell – and sipped her tea.

"That's sad about the poet," Fiona commented, leafing through the books.

"Yeah, she was cool. Sort of chanted her poems with that harp thing. That's her only book. It's signed."

Fiona turned the chapbook over and scrutinized the poet, dressed gypsy-style in India gauze. Her face had that hopeful, sexualized innocence of the '70s. A bandana held her hair back from her forehead, and it cascaded down one shoulder. She sat on a lawn with a small harp across her shoulders, smiling serenely off into the distance. Fiona turned one of Cordova's books over and compared the photos. Two very different generations. Cordova was dressed in black and white, leather and boots, and looked like someone you wouldn't mess with. She, too, looked off into the distance, her gaze anything but serene.

"Those are real different from each other, you know," said Silver.

Fiona looked up at Silver.

"Raven's books. The first one is real adventurous, hopeful. She was that way, at first. Great sense of humor, always in here telling me some crazy thing or other going on up there. Really liked her at first. But by the time she finished at the Fagans', she seemed to have lost her sense of humor. She'd come in here looking real dark around the eyes, you know? I'd try to talk to her, she was almost rude, didn't want to be bothered. She didn't send that second book when it came out, even though I asked her to remember us. I accidentally saw it in Barnes & Noble in Albuquerque, so I ordered it for us. Real dark stuff. Suicidal, I think."

"Suicidal?"

"Yeah, wonder if she's still around?" Silver picked up a box of silk herb-filled sachets and began arranging them in the display case next to a basket of goddess-shaped candles. "She was renting a cabin up the road. Haven't seen her for months. 'Course, she's a real loner, could be there and we'd never know. I think she's been traveling, too."

"This fax is about her recent work. She'll be in our magazine."

"Oh? Which one is that?" Silver pretended not to have read the fax cover sheet.

"*The Artisan Review* - at Baltimore Fine Arts Institute."

"Are you in that, too?"

"Yeah, I have poems in, from time to time."

"Send that to us. We'll put it on the shelf until you get your own book published."

Fiona had to admit she liked the definitive way that sounded. In Silver's matter-of-fact company, where poets were just quirky neighbors with first names, Fiona began to feel like a real poet, in a way she never felt around Professor Bregman.

"So Raven's ok, then? That's good. One Fagan tragedy is enough," Silver closed the display case and picked up a box from behind the counter.

"I assume she's fine. We just received her poems last week. I'll have my department send you some back issues, and the January issue."

"Great. We'll see you at the reading, then," Silver smiled and made her way to a shelf along the back wall.

Fiona smiled back uncertainly and readjusted her armful of fax paper, flier and books. As she opened the door, over the bell tinkling somewhere in back of the store, Silver's voice called out:

"And good luck with your chess game!"

Fiona chose not to respond or even turn around - her blush would say it all. As she approached the edge of the woods, she turned onto a dirt road leading in the general direction of the Fagans', taking the same path through the woods she had seen Hawthorne and the cook take, instead of walking along the main road to the property gate.

The pine woods grew thicker and the path through the trees became convoluted. In ducking and twisting her way through, she lost sight of the hacienda. But she could hear water, so she followed the sound.

Suddenly the grove of pine trees dropped off into a small valley and she heard voices. Within shouting distance was a hot springs pool, and in the steamy water were a man and a woman. Clothes were scattered along the pool's edge - his clothes. The woman, seated on the edge of the pool, was dressed. Then Fiona saw a bag of groceries on the ground and a shawl, and realized she was looking at the entirely naked Hawthorne and the entirely clothed cook.

The young woman was shaking her head and Hawthorne was apparently comforting her, his hand on her hair, then on her breast. He stood up and pulled her into the water, laughing and embracing her. She struggled free, shouted and slapped Hawthorne, then scurried - as best one of her size, fully clothed, could - out of the water. Crying, she stuffed her feet into sandals, pulled her shawl over her shoulders, gathered up the grocery sack, and stumbled off into the woods toward the house. Hawthorne smashed his fists on top of the water and turned an angry face in Fiona's direction. Fiona quickly ducked behind a boulder. Her pulse raced and she waited, trying to calm her breathing. She could hear the sounds of water splashing, the clink of a belt buckle against stone, soft cussing. Booted feet crashed through brush, then silence. Fiona peered around the boulder and saw that the sculptor/gardener had disappeared, leaving a muddy red trail to the Fagans'.

Fiona suddenly heard another sound. Low, male laughter. Something splashed and rippled in the steamy water. A stone was thrown into the pool. Fiona ducked again, then slowly peered from her hiding place to see the source of the aim. There, on a rocky ledge, frighteningly close, at a height parallel to hers, sat another naked man, staring down at the pool and tossing stones into it. Laughing softly. He must have been there all along, must have seen the whole encounter. Had he seen Fiona? The man was lean, the hair on his chest white, his hair long and rippling. He leaned back and closed his eyes, unabashedly spreading his legs - which were muscled and thickly haired, reminding Fiona of images she'd seen of Pan, a half beast below the waist. He seemed to be absorbing the sun's heat. He spread out his arms on the ledge and lay there, completely still, his face lifted to the sun, his eyes softly shut as in sleep.

Fiona was afraid to move, or to even avert her head, in case he would hear her. She felt pinned like a butterfly to a board, throbbing, unable to move her wings. As soon as the metaphor entered her mind, it expanded. The wings became the folded wings wrapped around her sex, throbbing, and opening. In the sunlight, the man, too, was aroused. Nothing else stirred, he lay absolute in his stillness. Even from here Fiona could see the urgency of his condition.

She was afraid to look at his feet, afraid they would be hooves. Her fear grew as she heard herself breathing heavily, then moaning! She cupped her hand over her mouth, but she could not control her noises. She needed something between her legs, hurry, something, something to catch the sensations, to keep her from shouting out. Fiona pushed the armful of books and papers down slowly, between her and the boulder against which she leaned, positioning the spines of Raven Shane Cordova's and Aisling Devlin's poems against her jeans. As she came - with intensity it seemed the denim could not contain, surely her stolen pleasure would fill the entire valley - she saw that the naked man was coming too. The veins in his arms stood out, his back arched, and his chin lifted to the sky, his mouth open, his eyes still closed. Had he made a noise? Had she? Fiona could ask no more questions, as she slumped softly against the ground and lay there, quickly falling into complete unconsciousness.

In her dream, the naked man rose from the forest floor and came to her. He stood over her, and then knelt beside her. He was entirely green, the almost brown-green of these dry woods. This Green Man was not separate from the earth; the vines and leaves that clung to his limbs were attached to the forest floor, trailing off and undulating like green snakes which then wrapped around every tree trunk and branch, every rock and boulder. As he moved, even his little finger, the entire green forest also moved, a ripple of crackling green like the ripple of water after a stone is thrown into it, or the gyrating dance of a new-log fire.

A wreath of leaves was wrapped around this Green Man's skull, originating from the corners of his mouth. More leaves grew, intertwined in his leg and chest hair, vines wrapped like braids in the green hair that flowed down his back and across his shoulders. The smell of him was complex - that of male sweat and the dusty-wet smell of the ground when it rains. His feet were not hooves, but were green, with tendrils growing and wrapping around the toes.

He knelt beside her and spoke these words:

"Rook to f6. Knight to b5. Can you remember that?"

Fiona was unable to speak, staring up at him.

"Can you remember that?"

"Rook to f6, knight to b5," she answered slowly, each syllable an intense labor of the larynx, her throat aching with the effort of speech.

The Green Man smiled, his teeth a pale green as were the whites of his eyes.

Fiona opened her eyes and was alone. The sun was very low in the sky, squirrels and crows darted nearby. Where was she, what had happened?

Then she remembered. The man, the coming. And the dream. The chess notation! She rolled over quietly and peered cautiously around the rock. No one was there in the little valley. The hot springs were still there, needing no human presence to justify the bubbling activity. She was entirely alone, only the animals rustling, creeping and flying about.

Fiona stood and pulled leaves from her hair, brushed dust from her coat, gathered up the badly crumpled fax pages, poetry flier and the books, which she had symbol-ically defiled. She felt dizzy and heavy with hot exhaus-tion. What had come over her? She felt that the whole day, starting with her sleep-walking, had been one, continuous, sensual assault. Too much preoccupation with the presence of others, their sexuality, which imposed on and seemed to awaken her own, against her will.

What was going on? Which Green Man had that been?

She recalled Talle's journal. Was this the man Talle wrote about, longed for?

Wasn't he familiar-looking? Aside from all that Pan business? Hadn't Fiona seen his face somewhere? And then she remembered. The man in the photo at the bookstore. The almighty, reclusive Fagan! So he didn't spend his entire day locked up in some tower room writing poetry. He wandered up and down his property, buck naked, sun-wor-shiping and spying on the help. In retrospect, Fiona real-ized that he had not been green - except in her dream - but brown, nut brown from head to toe. A nudist, that's all he was. Nothing particularly exotic about that, a person had a right on their own private property.

Fiona looked toward the horizon and, from this vantage point, was finally able to see the hacienda. She checked her watch. Still on Baltimore time. She adjusted the hands to read six-thirty. Barely enough time to get back to the *casita*, change out of these jeans (which now felt terribly clammy), take a quick shower, rush over to the dining room.

As Fiona began her brisk walk toward the hacienda, she grimaced. She'd forgotten the earlier ordeals of the day, now she would have to face Talle. Not only with the knowledge of having read the woman's journal and spilled the wine, but having watched her honored poet husband in the raw, spilling his seed to the almighty sky!

Dared she really replace those chess pieces, according to the Green Man's instructions? She told herself it was her subconscious, which did recall the placement of the pieces, and revealed them to her in the dream. She could slip into the chess room, and no one would ever know.

Chapter 4 - Entry

I suppose what has become normal to me is not what the outside world expects or is prepared for.

Like Him, in the woods. How could I explain Him to the outside world? How could I expect anyone to understand that, although I am fulfilled in my life here, and devoted to Liam...yet I long for Him, eagerly look forward to my naps in the woods, because that is where I have the dreams of Him? I truly do find Him there, dark and green, waiting in the place of dreams. How can the outside world understand that?

Interesting...by saying that, I have automatically included Him in my "inside" world. That is how it feels. He is not an outsider to me. He is more than family, He is – my soul. He is inseparable from the woods, the grounds, the wet forest of my dreams. And the woods are inseparable from Him, He is the spirit of the woods – even when I am in the woods and awake, I feel His presence in the junipers, the pines, the soil, the rocks, the water. The manifestation of the woods, in human form. As if His fingerprints are everywhere, as if I place my feet in the prints of His bare feet along the path I walk. And He is inside of me. I don't have to explain anything to Him, He already knows. Knows everything. Everything.

The outside world. Sometimes I wish we had never started the poetry competition, the residency. It keeps our life here under the constant perusal of strangers, vulnerable to them, to their judgments of us. Complicated strangers, artists and poets. And, in the past, the media.

Like that stranger I found on the compu-net bulletin board - he had too many questions about my life, my marriage, my motives, my activities. His questions and attitude angered me, I stopped responding.

But Liam's virtual chess partner did worry me. Sometimes I would log on as a spectator to their game - Liam didn't object. He and his partner didn't "chat" much during their games - only a few comments at the end of each game. But I could tell, after six months, that the player was becoming very curious about Liam. He/she rarely asked overt questions - seemed agreeable to staying in the realm of "no personal information", as Liam requested. They used handles when they played. Liam was always Finn and the player was Naoise. (Liam was delighted at the coincidence of them both choosing what he explained to me were mythical Celtic warrior-hero's names.) But odd things were asked or said, here and there. Seemingly innocent and polite, Naoise always asked what was the weather, and hinted around to determine what time of day or night it was here. Often enough that I began to think he/she was trying to hone in on our geography. Liam thought I was being ridiculous when I suggested that.

Of course there were the to-be-anticipated questions about how had Liam become such a chess master, and when Liam referred to his chess mentor back at university, Naoise hinted around that he would like to study with such a master. Several times Naoise referred to this, even though he/she was obviously every bit as good a player as Liam and needed no mentor. I don't think Liam should have given the name, but he did at one point. And when I chided him about it, he said no harm done, that old professor had died years ago. But, I thought, he had been a well-published man in his field (the history of astronomy) and easily traced to the university at which he was tenured, easily tied to a time and place, to an annual list of students. Granted, to make connections to Liam that way would be no small accomplishment (Naoise wouldn't have had Liam's name, for starters) and one would have to be very determined to pursue it. But the way my mind works, how very much I want to limit and control the nature of the world's access to us - despite the poetry prize - I do worry about such things. Potential poetry prize winners can be checked out, references, mentors, publications and the like. We have at least some sense of context of the poets we bring here to our home. But a disembodied chess partner could be anyone, anywhere, with any kind of motive. We want no uninvited guests.

I was especially concerned when, in one of the last sessions Naoise, after Liam took his queen, said, "Only a master poet would have pulled off such a move. Bravo!" How did he/she know Liam was a poet? Liam was puzzled by that too, said he had never made any allusions, never offered that information in any of their chats. In fact, when Liam asked, "Why did you call me a poet?" Naoise wrote back "I assumed you were a poet, if you are Finn, the bard warrior. I only meant it would take the mind of a poet, one used to devising metaphor to hide/ reveal meaning; to have made the connection you just made, all the while dazzling me with the threat of moves you never intended to make, in order to slip past my awareness and take my queen." Liam was "satisfied", he told me, that the reference to a poet had been a coincidence, an intelligent deduction by someone who obviously knew their Celtic mythology. <u>Flattered</u> was more the truth of it, I thought. Those who come here - through the contest or through the computer - are not visitors who keep their eyes on the surface, no! They are like an army of psychiatric and spiritual sleuths, crawling around, looking into corners and closets, questioning our way of living, our motives!

For example, this Fiona. She has violated my privacy. Now it is most strange, to write that down, knowing she may well read it at some point. But, damn, it IS my JOURNAL, for the love of all! This is SUPPOSED to be the place of my private thoughts, the dark, secret, protected sanctuary in which I am allowed to grapple with my inner self!

But it is not that anymore. It has become something else, and the original function of it has been ruined. This velvet book is no longer a journal of a woman's secrets but...the pretense of a journal of secrets. It has become the surface, tainted and stained with "what I prefer the world to see", which was the very thing I was seeking to overcome and avoid when I started this writing nine months ago.

I so very much felt the need for a private place to say things I cannot say otherwise. Doesn't everyone have such a need?

I have felt safe writing in it and leaving it wherever, to return later. Because, frankly, Liam would never have any interest in what I write. He has no longing to know my secret thoughts; he's only interested in his own! As well it should be, he is the Real Writer in this house, he is allowed every luxury of privacy and megalomania. That is as it should be.

But now that this stranger has opened these pages, it feels no longer safe to leave this book lying about. Apparently the musings of a middle-aged dilettante are of some interest to this Fiona. (Hello, dear, it feels very strange - oh, it ANGERS me! - to be writing about you, knowing you will read it if you can... So I feel I must not say what I really think or feel, especially in regards to you. Now I even feel I've begun to write this book FOR you - a veritable stranger, and one I distinctly do not trust!)

Of course, I could keep this journal upstairs, but I have grown so used to carrying it with me, especially on my walks.

If I can't write off the cuff or on the run, then I will never find time to write at all. The very thought of having to curtail my pattern of activity because of a rude stranger in my house angers me! Who IS she to instantly claim access to my innermost being? For that is exactly what she did. The very first afternoon - that is, only yesterday! It seems longer - when I left her in the sunroom and went to get our chocolates, she sat herself down and opened my journal and began reading in it! The cheek! It was shocking to me, when I returned and saw her doing that. But I covered well, I think - didn't I, Fiona? - didn't let on that I'd seen. And whisked the book away as soon as I could. I gave her the benefit of the doubt at that point.

After all, it has such a lovely cover, is actually the antique cover of a large family bible I found on this property, hand-carved wood covered with velvet, brass screws and ornate hinges from Spain. I had the bible pages removed - they were badly stained and bug-infested - and had the restorer polish up the brass and refurbish the cover with antique velvet, and insert lovely, deckle-edged paper from a special London paper source. The book was laying there on the coffee table. I can see where a visitor would think it was left there to be opened by guests.

But she didn't stop there. Last night she crept about our home in the dark, while we slept, and poked around until she found it again! I know it was she who spilled the wine on the pages.

Of course, she is very lovely to look at. I'm sure Liam will think so when he sees her tonight, with her fair pink freckled skin and crinkling, long red hair and green eyes. The epitome of the Irish looks that he so favors. The looks I have always wished I had. I know I am not his preferred ideal of woman-hood, with my dull brown (now graying) hair, my murky brown eyes. I am too tall for a woman, I think. I have to work at gracefulness and, lately, I tire of having to do so. So I let myself flounce and flop around, less self-conscious than when I was younger, trying to look "svelte" instead of what I was, "lanky". Of course, no one could accuse me of being lanky now! If anyone called me lanky now, I'd kiss their feet!

No, Liam has never spoken words of praise to me for my looks, but I have had other men refer to me as "a hand-some woman". So I have no illusions about the nature of my appearance. I think I have a strong presence, an interesting one. But not "pretty" or "lovely" or "beautiful". And, as for sexual passion between Liam and me...well, even I have limits as to what I will place in here, for others to read. Suffice it to say, I believe, given our time in life and our separate preoc-cupations, that we are both as satisfied as can be expected in that realm.

But he does have his flirtations, his fantasies. He is the poet. I cannot deprive him of the sources of his expression, his imagination. As his wife, it is part of my duty to nurture his talent, and nurturing, at times, means exactly that. To feed. I believe that sensual fulfilment is an important life-sustaining and prolonging motivator. Therefore, I make sure the table is set with delicacies and healthy fare, flavored with the best of herbs from our garden here. I make sure our lives are graced with the young, soulful and beautiful poets. Little do they realize how he feeds on their presence, their wide-eyed introspection. It does them no harm; in fact, does them great good to have an appreciative, gentle voyeur.

So if this Fiona will just behave herself and observe proper respect...then the residency can go very well for her and for Liam. And, therefore, for myself.

The dinner bell has rung. I must go inspect the labors of the cook. Unfortunately, it appears that Hawthorne might frighten off yet another with his amorous advances - I caught her wringing out her clothes from the hot springs. She tried to pretend she had hand-washed them, but she had obviously been crying. I must have a chat with him, he is wearing on my nerves, increasingly. Despite the bond between us.

What is going on, anyway? Everyone around me is acting like wild adolescents, out of control, no respect for boundaries! Despite my careful and cautious selection of each of them to fulfill their part in keeping this place - and the intent of this place - in functioning order.

Sometimes I suspect He is not exactly monogamous to me. That He delights in making Himself known to all of the others here, as well. That He is a Pan, and delights in stirring things up, creating chaos. The well-ordered chaos of nature. Well, if it is true, I might be jealous. But it would be so like Him. Funny, after all these years of his Green Man mask-making, I've never thought to ask Hawthorne, outright, if he's seen Him. If he knows Him. I think I haven't really wanted to know the answer. Or else the answer has been all too obvious.

Chapter 5 - Emerging Poets

iona hung up the phone and sat in the darkness, feeling the warmth of the dinner wine. She mused over the perplexing events of the evening - not daring to try to give much thought to the strange sexual events of the afternoon. Those she would save for later, back in her casita.

Her conversation with her father had been brief. It was late on his end, and he was just about to turn in after a day of gardening and mowing. They didn't have the conversation she envisioned earlier, the one in which she would tell him how much she regretted having come to New Mexico, and how she would probably be going back to Baltimore by the week's end.

Instead, after dinner, she called and babbled to him about the beautiful New Mexico sunset outside the stained glass window of this room. She was quietly pleased when, asking to use the hacienda phone, she was directed toward, and left at the threshold of the chess library. Talle was entirely courteous, even warm, telling Fiona to use this phone because it would afford her the most privacy of all the other phones in the house. It appeared that her hostess didn't suspect her of having left leaves in the hall or spilling wine on her journal after all. While dialing her father's number, Fiona was able to inspect the chessboard in the soft glow of the green library lamps. The dust patterns exactly matched the Green Man's instructions. The white rook to f6, the black knight to b5. She quietly and quickly replaced the pieces, amazed at her good fortune; no one had discovered her accident before she could correct it.

Fiona chatted with her father from a place of wine and relief, describing in great detail the beautiful mansion, her *casita*, the bookstore. Leaving out the disconcerting fax from her professor, the local mythology of the missing poet, the scene at the hot springs, all of her doubts and forebodings. She told him she would be honored at a poetry reading in two weeks and he said, sleepily, "That's great, sugar plum, I know you'll knock 'em dead." She promised to call next week, to keep him posted on her great adventure.

She found it amazing that the Green Man was right about the chess pieces. Or her subconscious was. Perhaps here, away from the city, she was more able to tune in to her intuitive, instinctual self. Fiona felt her emotions had turned around, and she wanted to stay the full two months. She wanted nothing to do with the restrictive, competitive atmosphere of the Baltimore Fine Arts Institute's creative writing department, and did not long for the dark cave of her basement apartment. She would indeed write while here. The first poem was bubbling and brewing, she felt ready to burn the midnight *pinon* logs, to get back to her Green Man poems. She would write about him from the sensuality of these woods and mountains, from the eroticism of her experience and dream this afternoon. Very different than that dry, intellectual place she'd worked from at the Institute. Fiona stared up at the resin replica. There he was, grinning slyly at her again, as he had last night, and today in her dream. She rose and crept over the luxurious rose-colored Persian rug, to get a better look at the Bomberg replica.

"Did you reach your party?"

Fiona gasped, startled, and turned around to see Liam Fagan in the doorway. It was still hard to believe - as it had been through dinner - that this was the same man she had seen spilling his seed in the valley this afternoon. For one thing, in the indoor light of the hacienda, Fagan - in his late fifties - was very pale, not the nudist brown she distinctly witnessed earlier. His hair was the same - long and white, now tied severely at the nape of his neck with a black cord. He had the same face and eyes, but his body - albeit hidden in the loose folds of 1940's-style, wide trousers, a non-descript white shirt, and an over-sized cardigan which looked like an Irish knit to her - seemed thin and ethereal, not muscled as it had been in the raw. His eyes were distant, a pale blue-grey, and his cheekbones were very lean. The effect was of a man staring right through you into another dimension, not really seeing you or connecting. His hands, picking up silverware at the table earlier, were delicate and long-fingered, fascinating to watch, but seeming to barely make contact with objects - as if feathers lightly dusting over the surface. Somehow she knew that his skin, to the touch, would be very cold. Yet, outside on the sunlit rock, it would have been fevered and damp.

"Pardon?"

"Your call, did you have success?"

"Oh, yes. I was calling my father. Thank you for letting me use the phone...this is an exquisite room."

Liam Fagan moved into the room, pausing at the chessboard. He frowned, lightly touching the two replaced pieces. Fiona froze.

"Odd. These had fallen. I needed to check my computer to see where to replace them. But someone has, already."

He looked up at Fiona, expectantly.

"Really?"

He looked back at the pieces, his fingers still hovering over the horse head of the knight, the castle's turrets.

"They are replaced exactly right, now that I see it. Sometimes, you know, you have to visually see a thing to discern its pattern. It's not enough to remember it in your mind's eye. At least, at my age it is so."

"I know what you mean," Fiona breathed quickly. "I was admiring your Green Man," she added, hoping to distract his attention.

"Was it you who replaced the pieces?"

Fiona froze again, stopping in mid-gesture as she faced the Green Man on the wall, her back to Liam Fagan. She made a quick choice and turned to face her benefactor.

"Yes, it was me. I apologize. Last night I was lost and wandered in here. I knocked them over in the dark, by accident. I felt I had disturbed something quite sacred."

"Sacred. Interesting word choice. But you are one of the poets, after all. I'm curious - why did you wait until tonight to replace them?"

Fiona looked down at the exotic floral carpet. Again, she made a choice about how to interact with this strange man of an obviously dual nature.

"I had a dream. The Green Man told me how to replace them. I checked the dust pattern. He was right."

Liam looked up from the chessboard and stared into her eyes. At first, it seemed as if he stared through her, as he had all during dinner. But now they were focused, intently, and an icy heat radiated from them that was probing, shrewd, kindly, alarmed and, to her surprise, erotic.

It was her body that registered that final implication, a heat starting up her lower spine. At the same time, her pulse increased and her breathing shortened. It took Fiona several seconds - which felt like several minutes - to begin to feel able to receive this disturbing gaze without embarrassment or discomfort. However, just as she began to relax into it, with curiosity and pleasure, their gaze was broken - with apparent reluctance on Liam Fagan's part, for he grimaced at the interruption - by Talle's form filling the library doorway.

Fagan's wife had apparently been in the hallway long enough to hear Fiona's confession. She looked from Liam to Fiona and gave a warm, practiced smile - which struck Fiona at that moment as a "professional" smile - and spoke, in muted, cultured tones, as if noting the name of a pattern on an antique porcelain tea cup.

"That's interesting. Apparently you were not the only one to have a mishap in the night. This morning I found someone spilled wine on my book..."

Fiona looked Talle in the eyes, still warmed and aroused by the gaze with Liam that had been interrupted. *"Coitus interruptus"* came to mind, and she smothered the urge to giggle.

"Or was that you, also?"

Fiona made her third choice of the evening.

"No, I only spilled the chess pieces."

"Probably the *sidhe*, dear," Fagan smiled at his wife. "You know how such things happen all the time, here."

Talle smiled at him in return, herself initiating a long gaze. He responded with a cool, detached smile. The woman then rested her gaze on Fiona, considering the young poet. Fiona surprised herself at how easily she sustained the eye contact, how steady and calm she felt doing so. And how, at some level, she realized she didn't care whether or not Talle believed her.

It wasn't that she disliked the woman; it was that, for some reason Fiona did not yet grasp, she had decided to proceed with honesty with Liam and dishonesty with Talle. Her reward for that honesty with Liam had been a look shared between them, like rich and potent sherry. It was a secret, a knot of decadent chocolate slipped into her palm by a stranger, a knot she wanted to take back to her *casita* and examine. She knew that honesty with Talle, at this moment, would dissolve that chocolate, and something precious would be lost, forever.

It struck Fiona that she felt exactly as if Talle had walked in on Liam and Fiona naked across the chessboard. Fiona now finally blushed thoroughly, recalling Professor Bregman's faxed message. She looked at Liam. He was staring straight at her, a small and knowing smile on his lips.

"Well, don't stay up too late, you don't want to get sick again, my sweet," Talle chided her husband softly, nodded at Fiona and left before Fiona could say another word.

"I suppose it's too late to play our first game, Fiona," Liam sighed and drew up a chair to the chessboard. His voice was weary now, he didn't make eye contact. "I must do as she says. I am under orders to not stress myself. Earlier this year I had pneumonia."

"But surely we're not going to play on this board?" Fiona joined him at the table. "Isn't this a game in progress with someone else?"

"Yes, you're quite right. I didn't mean we'd play this board, I have others. We won't play any games at all, tonight. I'll be going right up to bed. The excitement of new company, of my new young poet, caused me to imbibe more than I am used to, I'm afraid... No, I just want to sit here a moment, I like to consider the game, in case..."

Liam stopped and lifted his head, but his eyes remained lowered, scanning the board. He seemed to be fighting tears - suddenly and strangely vulnerable, not at all like a man who could have initiated, nor endured, the heated look of a few moments ago. But definitely like the sensitive poet who had penned the lyrical verse she had read last night in his books.

"Are you ok, sir?"

Fiona felt puzzled at her deference, and even more puzzled at the low, dusky quality of her voice in speaking so to him.

"Yes, I'm fine. It's just that this game began with such energy, a complete match with a mind like my own. And then so suddenly halted."

He truly seemed to have left the erotic realm he had taken her to before Talle had interrupted them. Inwardly, Fiona sighed, and forced herself to also shift gears.

"Halted? Did...did someone die?"

Why had she asked that? How ridiculously melodramatic. But then, she didn't understand from where came most of what she found herself saying to this strange man.

"I don't know. Perhaps. My chess partner simply stopped returning moves. My last move was to castle my king. Nothing has happened since then, and that was months ago. My partner and I played virtual chess for six months. Sometimes I would predict his every move, until the last, then he would turn the tables on me. We took turns winning, we were even to the end. I would win, he would win, I would win, and so on. Almost boringly predictable, once we saw the pattern, yet, of course, never dull."

"Amazing."

"Yes. And our chats - they were brief, of course, the *game* was the thing, but our quips were...so connected."

Liam Fagan paused, smiling softly, looking up over Fiona's shoulder, as if a very welcome friend had materialized there. Then fixed his gaze on her, continuing intently.

"Do you understand what I mean? There's a spark, even between disembodied voices on a screen - or there isn't. You feel it when there is. So we continued...until *this* game, stopped in mid-stride. Our best game. Brilliant. A dance, graceful and sure of itself. Then nothing."

The older poet traced a line in the dust on the board.

"Being evenly matched. That is rare, in any relationship," Fiona stated.

From where all this sudden wisdom? But Fiona did feel calm and older, ordered and wise in Liam's presence. And aroused, still. After all, this was the man who had moved her to a frenzied orgasm in the woods today.

"Yes, rare. Well...and so your Green Man dream is how you found out the placement of the pieces of my chess game?

Very interesting. You are not the first visitor we have had to talk of the Green Man. And Hawthorne, he carves him, sculpts and draws him. He did this replica for me," Liam gestured to the one on the wall.

"Hawthorne? I had no idea!"

"He is a very talented young artist. We give him a lot of room, how you young ones say, 'space', we give him space."

Yet you spy on his sexual adventures, thought Fiona, scrutinizing Liam's expression. There was no trace of duplicity. But then, Liam didn't know she had seen him on the rock.

"Perhaps your Green Man will come to you again and tell you the next move."

Fiona was startled.

"But surely your partner will return and you'll continue it where you left off. Perhaps he or she had to travel, or is just very busy."

"No, I sense he's gone. For good. *You* think on it, what would be the next move? I only want to play with you from your dreams of the Green Man. Is that an agreement between us?"

Fiona frowned, looking at the board. She was not that good a player, indeed, she had felt embarrassed to enter Liam Fagan's competition in the first place - her chess playing was mediocre and her knowledge of Ireland so limited. Yet he seemed easily pleased.

Fiona looked up. There it was again, the hot light in his eyes. He was blatantly looking at her breasts. She had changed for dinner, into a long, hip-hugging grey skirt with boots, a simple white cotton tee. She waited for his eyes to lift and meet hers. Finally, he did look up. Again, as before, his eyes were probing and shrewd. But now no longer alarmed.

Here, then, was the man who prowled in the nude, the voyeur who had laughed at Hawthorne and the cook at the hot springs.

Again, her body responded, remembering the events in the woods. This time the heat was fire, searing up her tailbone. Watching his lips as he watched hers, she answered:

"Yes sir. Only if it comes in a dream."

Liam Fagan nodded and stood, frowning and averting his eyes from hers. The impact was as icy as if he had turned away from her desire in disgust. Suddenly, again, this was not a man who knew anything of eroticism.

A fierce wind was beating outside, against the stained glass window, howling as if to animate the Evangelist beasts depicted in the stain glass panels. Fiona's cheeks were hot, she felt embarrassed, as if she had misinterpreted and driven a permanent wedge into any further communications with this extraordinary man. As if she had soiled a religious experience with nothing less than lust.

Once again, Fagan lightly touched the tops of the pieces Fiona had replaced, and she again had the impression of wings, not fingers, brushing against objects. He pulled the chains on the two green table lamps, dousing the room with darkness. His silhouette passed before the stained glass Book of Kell images of lion, ox, man and eagle. Impossible that he had been the naked man this afternoon. So slight, his movements so troubled, as from early stages of arthritis. This man did not have the stamina of the man on the rocks.

"Liam, do you...walk? I just wondered, your grounds are so beautiful."

"I spend my days in total seclusion. The woods are indeed beautiful, and I see them from my window. Talle has given up trying to get me to take walks with her - she goes out every day. Also, my skin is too pale to handle this intense western sun."

Fagan paused in the doorway, still a silhouette.

"I am sorry, I hope you weren't counting on walks with me or that sort of thing."

"Oh no, I only meant…"

"You, too, should spend your time alone during the day. You have much writing to do."

Fiona nodded and, before she could wish him good night, Fagan was gone. She sat at the chess table a long while, in the dark, waiting for her body to cool down, for the throbbing to stop. She was disconcerted at the realization that, in the last few moments, she had almost orgasmed again in the presence of this man, and he seemed not to know anything about it - yet, somehow, he seemed to have quite purposefully caused her arousal.

And she was disconcerted at his lie about taking walks. She had chosen to be honest with him. Why didn't he reciprocate?

Fiona studied the moonlit outline of the green man on the wall. She didn't like knowing that Hawthorne had created it. She was predisposed against the young man, yet now she was called on to admire his artistry. She thought back to her impressions of him at this evening's dinner. Warmth didn't seem to be one of his character traits, but he obviously felt at ease in the company of his employer/ benefactors, eating, nodding and giving a cool smile as the conversation warranted.

In fact, everyone at dinner was extremely civilized and cheerful, as if their relationships were simple and on the surface. Talle was solicitous of Liam and Hawthorne, pouring their wine and refilling their plates from the sideboard after the cook withdrew. She said flattering things to Fiona about her hair and attire, each time adding "Doesn't she, Liam?" or "Isn't she, Liam?" Liam Fagan was serene and quiet, focused on his food and wine, saying little, watching Fiona without expression. As if he was thinking something over.

The dinner conversation moved easily, with few silences, from talk of a new book by a fellow poet in New Zealand, to a courtyard wall which needed to be re-stuccoed, to polite queries as to Fiona's comfort in her *casita* and the course work she would continue in the spring.

Yet Fiona hadn't been able to entirely relax in their company. There was a subtle undercurrent, as if secret notes were being passed under the table. Momentary exchanges of glances between Liam and Hawthorne, Hawthorne and Talle. Fiona had confined her part in the conversation to simple responses, taking the position of the polite, nonintrusive guest.

It was time to do so again, she thought to herself, left alone in the darkened chess library. She rose and tiptoed down the hall, past the pagan icons and Catholic *santos*, out the door, and across the courtyard toward her *casita*. The courtyard was softly lit by lanterns set into the adobe wall, and garden lights among the cactus along the stone path. A few feet from the door to her *casita*, an old metal chair was propped under a large cottonwood tree. As she walked past it, Fiona saw a large shawl draped across the seat - the one Talle had been wearing when she walked into the woods this morning - and on the shawl lay the velvet journal. Inwardly, Fiona froze, but kept her feet moving, feeling she was being watched, and entered her *casita* without giving any sign that she had seen the book. It seemed too much like a carefully-set trap. Obviously Fiona was not going to fall for it, not after the encounter with Talle in the chess room. But her cheeks burned at the realization that perhaps she was being tested and spied upon. The whole thing irritated her greatly. Especially because she felt seriously tempted to pick up the book and read it again. Now that she had seen Liam Fagan in the woods, and now that she had met the Green Man in her dream, she so much wanted to go back and reread the passages in Talle's journal about the man in the woods.

The irony struck Fiona as she pulled off her clothes, that the man Talle longed for in the watery woods was actually her own husband. Could it be that the woman didn't know of her husband's secret walks, his sensual adventures near the hot springs? Fiona supposed it was possible that Talle might not know this other side of him. One was always hearing about wives not knowing of their husbands' private lives - hidden stock portfolios, secluded mistresses, secret apartments. Or perhaps Talle assumed her husband's sensual persona existed only in his poems. It really was time to give some serious attention to Fagan's poems. The answer to all this, no doubt, lay between the pages of those thin, unpublished, leather volumes.

In what was quickly becoming a nightly ritual, Fiona pulled on her nightgown, lit the fire, and wrapped up in the white comforter. She sat by the fire with Liam Fagan's, Raven Shane Cordova's and Aisling Devlin's books, Professor Bregman's fax, her notebook and pen. She was quite eager to begin reading the words of these poets, which might unravel the day's mysteries.

But she stared into the flames too long. Within moments, her head nodded and she sank down on the sofa, lost in a warm dream of walking across the mesa, feeling the sun on her shoulders, smiling at the wide blue sky. Suddenly the sky split at a crossroads, one half a cheerful, daylight blue, the other an ominous, storm-crackling black. There was a simplistic sense that the choice was for good or evil. Light or dark. Fiona paused, deciding, and then turned on the path into the cold blackness. She found herself approaching a hot springs in the dark, felt the bubbling heat of the water around her ankles and knees, contrasting the iciness of the cold on her bare shoulders. She realized she was naked in the dream and that before her stood the naked Green Man. He reached out and touched her breast, and she felt afraid and guilty for having chosen the dark path, for having left the blue sunlight. As his fingers brushed her nipples - feeling like feathers - a loud banging noise ripped the dream in two and Fiona cried out, threw off the comforter and swung off the sofa to her feet.

Disoriented, she stood there in the shouting silence and dark of her *casita*, staring into the glowing coals of her fire. Her heart was pumping hard and her breathing was short. She saw that nothing in her *casita* could have caused the noise. As she crossed the room to look out the window, she heard the banging again, then the muffled voices of anger - a woman's voice and then a man's - the slamming of a screen door, and the sound of boot heels along the stone path outside. Fiona rushed to the window, crouched below the sill, and pulled the muslin curtain back a few inches, just in time to see a figure marching down the path, not toward the hacienda but toward the large gate in the adobe wall surrounding the courtyard. A male voice called out and, in front of Fiona's *casita*, the lantern light revealed the figure that paused, looking back.

From Fiona's perspective, crouched under the window, she saw a tall, lanky woman in cowboy boots, black denims, a white silk blouse, and a black leather jacket. The woman's hair was tied back in a long, ebony ponytail. Wide cuffs of polished silver flashed in the lantern light at both slim wrists, silver disks at her ears and a silver concha belt at her waist. The woman put her hands on her hips and glared in the direction of the man's voice. The collar of her shirt gaped open and Fiona could see it was unbuttoned to the waist, revealing the dark curve of breasts. It was Fiona's distinct impression that this was a shirt that was intentionally never buttoned up.

The woman hissed something in an angry tongue unknown to Fiona, then turned and stomped away, yanked open the gate, passed through and slammed it shut, not caring that the cast iron cowbell slamming above the gate might rouse the whole compound. It certainly started the barking and howling of a distant radius of wild and domestic canines.

The source of the male voice now showed himself on the stone walkway, which was only a couple feet from the window of Fiona's *casita*. She peered through the opening of the curtain, careful not to breathe, and saw that it was

Hawthorne, enraged, clenching his fists - and nude again. That made twice in less than twenty-four hours that Fiona had witnessed his apparent lack of charm with the ladies. And the third time in less than twenty-four hours - or the fifth, if you counted the two naked Green Man dreams - she had been graced with a vision of naked male loins, like it or not.

Hawthorne stood a while, staring at the gate. Beyond the adobe wall came the sounds of a truck's indignant engine starting up and racing, big tires in reverse, then brakes applied to gravel.

The metallic sounds of a speeding and rattling truck receded, and the young man returned to his cottage.

Fiona heard a couple of angry thumps from Hawthorne's cottage, and then the *casita* and courtyard were quiet. The only thing moving was one of Talle's cats. It stretched its paws on the ground and tugged at the bunch grass, then rolled onto its back and splayed its legs at the moon. Fiona glanced at the chair under the tree. The shawl and the book were gone. Apparently there had been a lot of human activity in the courtyard tonight.

Now she felt wide-awake. She put another log in the *kiva* fireplace and turned on a lamp. This time she didn't trust herself to the comfort of the sofa, but moved the books and writing tools to the table. She put on a kettle of water to make a cup of strong, heavily caffeinated black tea, and sweetened the cup from a jar of local honey, which Talle had considerately provided. She sat at the table, wrapping the comforter around her legs, and began by opening Aisling Devlin's chapbook. Fiona caught her breath and pressed her hands down hard on the open pages as she read the quotation inside the cover:

"Who is He? When, in the woods,
the corner of your eye notes a movement
or you see one tree, alone, moving,
yet the others are still...that is He,
that is your Green Man."

–Chahil O'Shea

That name was familiar - ah, yes. The Irish poet who had been a Fagan winner some time after Devlin's residency. So Devlin had been familiar with O'Shea's work. Fiona smiled to herself: as usual, the ever-repeating circle of poet quoting poet.

Aisling Devlin wrote a lot about the Green Man. Like so many writing in the early seventies, she wrote about her longing to live in nature, and about sex:

...we fed each other
meals of leaves stones
we became those trees
our skin grew brown gnarled
our hair   fingers toes
fragrant green
our limbs lifted to the sun...

Some of the poems were about the time she had spent in Ireland - a semester as an exchange student. (Perhaps she had even met O'Shea?) Her voice was so innocent, so vulnerable, it dismayed Fiona that this young woman, still finding herself as a writer - as a person, even - should have ended up the possible victim of foul play.

Fiona poured a new cup of tea and went on to Cordova's books. She opened *Water Rites*, with the two-year-old copyright, the poems written before Cordova's stay at the Fagans'. She read the title piece, an erotic prose-poem about desert seduction, eros and death.

"She finds a sculptor who has become the thirst of this place."

Could that be Hawthorne? Only if Cordova had known him before she came to the Fagans'. Fiona skimmed through the book. Cordova's work was strikingly similar to her own in one regard: the poet used the reoccurring metaphor of the male lover to reflect and explore her current interior attitude. In *Water Rites* the sculptor was described as having the taste of salt on his skin, *"...his mouth a twist of lime/his soft voice cracks dry"*. Reflections of the inner drought and longing of the poet, projected onto the figure of the lover who couldn't quench her thirst.

These wee desert hours were cold, despite the fireplace. Fiona got up to find a pair of socks in her still-unpacked suitcase. She pulled them on and re-wrapped in the comforter, thinking about Cordova's book. It was divided into two parts; the poems of the first were filled with metaphors and motifs of the desert, references to the Spanish culture, the Native American, a sprinkling of italicized words and phrases in Spanish and various pueblo languages. Obviously the poet lived in New Mexico; a running conceit was her longing for greenness and water, for the opening of the soul through verdant nature.

Fiona flipped to the biographical notes. Yes, Cordova's home was Santa Fe. She had spent most of her childhood there, and had earned her B.A. at St. John's. Now twenty-six, only a year older than Fiona, this already-published poet had taken a couple years off to travel in Ireland, France and Italy. At least if she had waited tables, they were European tables, grimaced Fiona. That should please Professor Bregman. Cordova was firmly plotting her academic time line now, having been accepted to earn her MFA at the Baltimore Fine Arts Institute.

The politically correct publisher noted Cordova's heritage - her biological father an errant Irish priest, her mother Navajo, her adoptive stepfather a third generation Spanish American. Obviously there were not a few genetics-based grants for which Cordova could apply, none of them available to Oklahoma-born, German-Irish Fiona, which Professor Bregman would be quick to point out. Fiona felt the competitive twinge, as he had gleefully predicted.

The second half of the book was about Cordova's time spent in Ireland, the satisfaction of that longing, the saturation of her soul in endless fields of soft, green grass. She wrote of the magical, algae-filled depths of the bog, the restorative powers of the water and woods, and her discovery of the Green Man. Fiona could see that the poet hadn't spent her entire Irish time in the confines of the city, and had apparently visited there more than once. In contrast to contemporary images were the proverbial, peacefully-grazing sheep, in and around stone castle ruins, the wild flowers amidst Celtic-cross-filled graveyards. The classical Romantic references to hazelnut and trout, muse and music, the reverent allusions to Yeats and Shelley.

Somehow Fiona felt these usages came not from the naive passion of a young poet paying homage to her ancient ancestors, but from a calculation that such nuggets tucked in and amongst her otherwise very contemporary verse, would bring an approving lift of the academic eyebrow, if not an outright nod. Nevertheless, the result was pleasing - whimsical yet effective.

The final piece - a prose-poem – *Water Rites II*, was about the poet's return to the desert. Not to the sculptor, but to the desert's Green Man.

". . .opening her blouse to him
on the ground in the moon
his green tongue and teeth
move deep and hard
bring up milk that was never there
urge all her body liquids high

the ground beneath her clothes runs wet
sand grows white with mammary foam."

The poet's union with the desert's Green Man was depicted in ambiguity, again the theme of eros and death:

"After, on the desert that was beach
she lies skeletal, bleached.
She has lain there for centuries;
she is the clacking sound of vertebrae
of the rattler's tail.
The wind whistles between her joints.
'Is this what you wanted?' the Green Man laughs
now in motion.
'Is this why you came?"

Fiona turned the book over to examine Cordova's photograph. Artfully digitized, the background was unmistakably New Mexican, red rocks and crows, while, in the foreground, the striking poet leaned in a mock-masculine pose, her arm draped over the Castlestrange Stone in County Roscommon, familiar to Fiona from her own photo-documented Ireland adventure.

Fiona pursed her lips and lifted her eyebrows, impressed. It had taken some doing to find that stone herself, since the locals didn't appear to know much about the history of the Bronze Age *Tuatha de Dennan* carving, except that it was "the old stone over in Shirley's sheep pasture". This Cordova person was obviously as persistent and undaunted an explorer as she was herself. Fiona and her father had spent half a day, and the purchase of several pints of Guinness for three farmers in the local pub, to find that stone.

Cordova's grin was cocky. This photo was more proof that Silver's concern - that last year's poet might be suicidal - was unfounded: Cordova was the woman Fiona had just seen outside, enraged at Hawthorne and stomping off to her truck in the dead of night!

There she was in her uniform again - black and white, denim and leather, her blouse slit open to her concha belt, silver gripping her wrists and earlobes. No, Raven Shane Cordova was very much alive - and kicking, one of her cowboy boots was raised in a playful half kick at whomever held the camera - and apparently capable of anger in several different languages. In what language had she been cursing Hawthorne? Was that Navajo?

Much too feisty for suicide.

Seriously exhausted, Fiona rose and stretched, put the tea things in the sink and turned out the kitchen light. However, on her way to the sofa, she was compelled to stop at the table again. She pulled Cordova's more recent book toward her, the one entitled *The Wounded Watcher*, a much smaller volume. The copyright was this year. The photo on the back was the same as on the first book. Fiona suddenly recalled having briefly compared the photos at the bookstore, and feeling frustrated that there was no visual clue to the changes in Cordova's writing that the bookstore owner, Silver, and Professor Bregman had described. Even though

Fiona had seen the photos earlier, she hadn't immediately associated the angry cowgirl outside her window with the sultry poet of the book cover. From her conversations with Professor Bregman and the bookstore owner, Fiona had mentally placed the poet as being far away from here and on her way to take her position in Baltimore.

The implication of Cordova's presence in Hawthorne's *casita* suddenly hit Fiona: her predecessor was local and available. Fiona could meet with her, ask some questions and put all this mystery to rest! Then she could get on with the real reason she had come here: to hide and write. She made a mental note to visit the bookstore tomorrow - no, today, the sun was putting a blue glow on the night outside her muslin curtains - and find out how to reach the angry woman in leather and silk. Silver had said Cordova rented a cabin in the village, and had been traveling. Apparently Silver hadn't yet heard that Cordova was back in town.

Fiona took the book with her to the sofa. Just a few more lines, then she would close her eyes. She curled up with the comforter and opened the book. To her surprise, a stanza of a Liam Fagan poem was at the front:

> *"Where he wends and when and why*
> *And who is it for him would weep*
> *He the Lord who cannot die*
> *The wounded watcher in our sleep."*
>
> *The Green Man*
>
> *Liam Fagan*

Fiona didn't want Professor Bregman and the book-store owner to be right - that the poems in this book would be "self-absorbed", dark and different from the ones Cordova had written before her stay at the hacienda. She felt that same fierce affinity that she had experienced with Liam Fagan's poems - wanting them to be good, to prove Professor Bregman wrong.

She stared into the fire, reflecting that last night she had found Fagan's poems a bit archaic, going against her "good modern poetry" training. But she hadn't cared, had let their lyricism pull her into another time, another aesthetic, one much older than the hallowed halls of the Baltimore Institute. She knew, in her heart, that it was long since time to admit this internal war she fought with her professor, instead of keeping her mouth shut due to that other odd loyalty to him. Once and for all, she needed to admit that he was a man who had proved himself to be without morals, an insulting, condescending womanizer, and one who increasingly did not have Fiona's best career interests at heart. Not since she had refused to sleep with him.

To admit such a thing meant to also question whether or not Professor Bregman really believed Fiona was a gifted poet. Did he find her of interest because of her talent, or simply because she was a woman he hoped to bed? If the truth was that he wasn't truly interested in nurturing and supporting her talent, she would be thrown back on her own faith in herself, in her work. A lonely prospect, since she had relied very heavily these past few years on Professor Bregman's opinion of her as a writer.

Of course, now there was also the faith expressed by Liam Fagan's having awarded her this writer's residency, based on her submission of poems. A secondary affirmation of her talent. Or at least, so she hoped. Fagan's true motivations were yet to be clarified.

Fiona shook her head and yawned loudly. Caught between exhaustion and insomnia, she nevertheless gave Cordova's second book a good skimming. Silver was right: these poems were strikingly different from the ones in the first book. Gone were the geographical references to the Southwest and Ireland, the playful classical allusions. Straight to a dark, myopic interior, no light or landscape present. Nothing with which to ground the reader.

"There is nothing to wrap around these days
impale yourself on the sundial style
this edge of burning stone."

The poet was dragging the reader along with her on a disturbing ride, no brakes, no seatbelt, no sympathy.

"Your shadow spins with the sun
marks the hour
but so slow you seem
not to be moving at all."

In one poem, Cordova wrote of a cruel Green Man:
"He lays him down green leaf and vine
He lies naked inside holding secrets

His thorny embrace bleeds her skin
In darkness her terror is born
This green is not love"

From Fiona's Green Man research, she felt this to be an unfair and one-sided representation of the Green Man's persona. Darkness wasn't necessarily a place of evil. Fiona was puzzled. It seemed unlike Cordova, judging from the first book, to turn her head from the ambiguities she wrote about so eloquently there, to now paint such a negative picture.

Another passage in particular struck her, as it used an image she had seen in a Liam Fagan poem, that of the Green Man's nest.

"To his nest/to his lair/the Green Man brought them/To his nest/to his lair/there he entwined them," had been Fagan's line. As if picking up where he left off, Cordova wrote:

"He kept them there
His green web whispered along their spines
the vines wrapped 'round their elbows and knees
He kept them there
In his eyes they could not move
In his eyes they lost their seasons."

What was that about?

As the sun asserted its undeniable, hot, gold presence through her muslin curtains, Fiona realized how exhausted she felt, but she couldn't stop now. She untangled from the comforter and pulled off her socks to cool her feet on the brick floor. She went to the kitchen, boiled fresh water for more black tea. She reached for Professor Bregman's faxed copies of Cordova's recent poems, which would appear in the spring edition of *The Artisan Review*.

Two cups of tea later, she had finished the poems, tucked them into *The Wounded Watcher*, and stood to stretch. Her back ached; she bent to touch her toes, stretching out her spine.

The faxed poems were not as dark as the ones in the second volume; there were references to light finding its way in. But the rage and cynicism was so alarming it seemed it could burn holes through the thermal pages. Why was Cordova so angry? Was this some of the same anger Fiona had heard outside her window, aimed at Hawthorne?

Fiona had a sense that reality was going on without her permission. For some reason, far beyond Hawthorne's initial rudeness to her over enchiladas that first night, Fiona felt an intense, biological aversion to the man. To imagine that a woman as striking and fiery, as talented and lively as this Cordova could have undergone any serious alchemy at the hands of such a hormonally-driven, cold-eyed male, was unthinkable!

But his Green Man sculpture in the chess room was very good, and Liam had spoken highly of his work. Was there something more to the young man than a conversational reticence and a disposition to sexual assault? Even if Fiona didn't want it to be so?

Obviously there was something more. Had Raven known Hawthorne, or his work, before she had come to the Fagan hacienda? Before she had written the first volume of poems with its references to the Green Man?

How did the disappearing poet, Aisling Devlin, fit into all this - with her own Green Man preoccupation? Or, for that matter, Chahil O'Shea?

Fiona wanted so badly to close her eyes against the insistent sunlight burning through the muslin. Her watch read seven a.m. Another hour before breakfast was served, and today she felt she would really need it, especially if she was going to walk back to town and talk to the bookstore owner, try to track down Raven.

Most of all, she wanted badly to crawl into the bed she hadn't yet slept in, pull the comforter over her eyes and create a false sense of darkness. But there were too many questions buzzing in her brain, and too much she wanted to accomplish today. She needed to continue reading Fagan's books. A critical missing part of the picture was, no doubt, imbedded in his lines of poetry. She checked the dates inside the covers of his leather books, which he dated like journals. One was from last summer, just prior to Raven's residency. The second from the fall - during Raven's residency. The third from the following spring, after Raven's departure. Was it coincidental that these were the ones Talle had handed her? The selection appeared random; the books' bindings were all the same - black and thin, no titles along the spines.

But then, nothing that Talle did seemed random to Fiona anymore. She intentionally left her journal lying about for Fiona to read; of this she was now certain. Talle seemed to want Fiona to discover something in the book's contents as well as to trap her into proving she wasn't trustworthy. Although Talle hadn't shown herself to be as colorful as the other local characters - no tendencies toward nudism, noisy outbursts in the night courtyard, erotic encounters in the chess room - the woman seemed to hold even more secrets from, and evoked even more ambivalence in, the young poet than any of the others she'd met in the last two days. And the woman's relationship with her poet husband seemed very complicated. A fierce and supportive loyalty, laced with condescension.

Two questions remained: Who was the man for whom Talle longed, in the journal? And what was all this business of the missing poet?

Chapter 6- Hawthorne

Fiona was finally unpacking. It was something her father had said when she called him from the chess room again, after breakfast. He was on his way to go fishing because it was a grey and rainy morning. He said it was the kind of weather his neighbors complained about, because it stopped them from their planned activities. To him, a rainy day was a good fishing day. The sun might as well be shining, the way he felt about it.

He had told her this by way of responding to her "I'm not sure I should have come here" phone call.

"But last night you sounded so happy to be there."

"I was, last night. But I'd had wine with dinner and… an interesting day. And the sunset was so beautiful."

"So what has changed since last night - other than the wine wearing off?"

"It's not just since last night. These people are strange, their personal lives seem so complicated and I don't want to get involved."

Fiona didn't want to worry him with the missing poet story.

"Oh, I agree, stay out of people's messes. I always do. They start telling me their sad stories and I just say, 'Would love to chat, but I got to go fishing.' You should try it, sugar plum, I hear there's great trout fishing there in New Mexico."

That's when he'd told her about rain days being good fishing days, and it had, oddly, cheered her up. Also, about that moment in their conversation, the effects of four cups of breakfast coffee finally began to kick in. Things began to seem more possible. She'd come back to her *casita* after the otherwise uneventful breakfast - neither Talle nor Hawthorne had shown up. Liam Fagan was, of course, not expected to show himself until evening. Left alone, Fiona had taken leisurely time with a bowl of cantaloupe, a green chili corn muffin and the four cups of coffee.

After talking with her father, the day seemed sane and opened up. No dark secrets, no murders, no enigmatic velvet books lying about. No angry women raging in the courtyard, no naked men with which to contend. She could stay here, she could avoid all the psychodrama, just write and relax and decide what to do with her life on her return to Baltimore.

But, at that thought, the prospect of the upcoming academic competition with Raven Shane Cordova came to mind. No, even that drama could be avoided, she decided, as she hung her suitcase-wrinkled clothes in the hall closet. It would be better if they met here, rather than first meeting in the academic Baltimore setting which would pit them against each other. She would simply set up a comradery with this Cordova poet, here on potent turf - potent for Cordova since it was her terrain, and potent for Fiona since it was the place, which had invited her to be the honored poet. That was today's task; to find out how to contact her predecessor, she mused as she spread out her toiletries in the bathroom cabinet, and set out her jewelry bag on the white-tiled counter. She climbed the rough-hewn ladder up into the loft to spread the comforter on the un-slept-in bed, then sat at the top of the loft ladder, looking down to survey her temporary dwelling.

It really was a beautiful *casita*. The simple decor soothed her. One big delicious room, white-chocolate adobe walls and red brick floors which gleamed like peanut brittle. The *kiva* fireplace was set into the corner opposite the loft, flanked by an L-shaped *banco* on which white, raw silk pillows were lavishly spread. Sky-blue Mexican tiles outlined the *kiva*, a hue echoed in the velveteen blue of cushions, which rested in a heavy oak-framed sofa opposite the *banco*. The Navajo rug thrown down at an angle in the center of the room bore a geometric weave of grey, ochre and rust and a thin border of the same blue as the tiles.

The sleeping loft was placed so that, from the bed, one could look down and see the fireplace, illuminating the big room and dancing shadows all the way up the wall. Here in the loft was a sturdy box-spring mattress on the floor, covered with a feather bed and down pillows, sky-blue flannel sheets and the white down comforter. This was the first time Fiona had actually examined the sleeping loft, having spent her first two nights downstairs by the fire. Again, only one piece of art up here. A sage green, faux-stone relief of a Green Man hung over the bed, obviously one of Hawthorne's. Circling his head were vine leaves and grape clusters. When Fiona lay back on the mattress and looked up, his green eyes, cast downward, met hers. His lips were opened in a mocking grin. The look was clearly lascivious.

Perhaps she would continue to sleep downstairs, she thought. But, no - indications of rain meant good fishing. To translate her father's message, the rich imagery and verdant sex lives of those around her simply indicated that this was fertile ground for poems. Even the myth of the disappearing poet added to the mix. She could - and would - make of all this whatever she wanted, as a writer.

But she must remain detached. After all, the Green Man over the bed was just one artist's clay rendering of an image in his head, traded for room & board. Consider the source and leave it at that.

* * *

In the *casita* next door, Hawthorne stood at the kitchen sink, scrubbing dirt from his fingernails with an old toothbrush and a bar of Lava soap. This was his necessary ritual, to divide the day between the Fagans' grounds work and his sculpture time; he never mixed the dirt and clay under his nails, although they were from the same place. By noon today he had put in his six work hours already, having skipped breakfast to do so. His chores of the last few days had been to rake leaves and then to drive the pickup over to Cat Mesa to chop firewood for the dozen little fire-places - Talle's *kivas* - in the compound. Hawthorne hadn't slept much last night after that fiasco with Raven. Despite his exhaustion, an urgent need to get into his studio this afternoon had driven him to rise earlier than usual, get his chores done, grab a sandwich-to-go from the kitchen, and get back to his apartment by noon.

He refused to call it a "*casita*". Talle's vocabulary was too affected for his taste. The units were separated, barely, about two feet of dirt between each one, and not big enough to call cabins. To him, they were nothing more than glorified apartments, with pretentious Southwestern decor: those awful protrusions called *bancos*, that stupid, inefficient little adobe fireplace. He never could get the flue to open all the way, so there was always smoke, a dingy grey film over the walls. Dust filtered down from the *vegas* and *latillas*, the stucco always needed patching, there were carpenter ants in the kitchen. He'd told Talle about the ants but she pretended not to believe him. The night he moved into the apartment, he piled up all those decorator pillows outside the door for her to take away, and spread his old army blankets and animal skins on one of the *bancos*. On the other one, he assembled his cans of paint and brushes. He threw tarps down over the rugs to protect them from paint and plaster, stacked Talle's local-artist paintings of adobe ruins and the Rio de Sombras in the closet, and taped his in-process sketches on the wall instead. The dining room table became a worktable, covered with layers of plastic and newsprint. The next morning, Talle blinked and swallowed when she saw the transformation. But said nothing. After all, she had hired him on as the resident artist and was therefore obligated to indulge his idiosyncracies.

Talle had shown up at a Santa Fe gallery back in the spring of 1979, the day he was taking down a show of his drawings and masks entitled "Effigies". The show had brought some good reviews in the local arts rags but had resulted in only one sale, a miniature dark-humor sketch of a human skull with a flower in its mouth, wearing O'Keeffe's famous black sombrero. After adding up the costs of framing, supplies, studio overhead, time, sweat, blood and tears, Hawthorne figured he'd made back one-hundredth on that drawing of what it had cost him to put the entire show together. When the gallery owner brought Talle Fagan over to introduce her to Hawthorne, he was pulling nails from the wall, had a couple of them between his teeth, and was in a dark mood.

It turned out that Talle Fagan was the one who had purchased the drawing, and she was curious to know more about the brooding artist. Over coffee next door, he told her the condensed version of his history - admitting that he was from Michigan, but omitting the part about being run out of Kalamazoo at a tender age. In exchange, she made him the offer he couldn't refuse – indefinite room, board, outdoor work, a fair salary and all the time, space and supplies he needed to do his art. On a remote, mountain estate where she resided with her poet husband. Plus the annual commission of one mask at a very generous fee.

Fourteen years later, the kitchen sink bore the stains of paint and solvents. A couple of the Mexican tiles on the counter had cracked when he tossed down scraping tools in the heat of a project. He was always forgetting to put out his towels to be washed, so once a week Talle sent the laundry lady in to creep around and grab them. His beard hairs peppered the bathroom sink and the unclean toilet seat was perennially in the upright position. The houseplant in the kitchen window was long since dead. He ignored the stench of some indiscernible food at the back of the refrigerator when he opened the door to get at the coffee cream and film. He had truly made the *casita* his own, Talle's attempts to civilize him always failed.

Hawthorne shook the water from his fingers and dried them on his jeans. He began to assemble what he'd need for a long session at his sculpture studio across the valley, the one that held the kiln and made him less accessible to the world. He'd set up the first studio here at the compound before discovering the site of the second. He'd always meant to disassemble this one and make it more liveable, but never got around to it. So now he used the *casita* studio mostly for sketches, conceptualizing and sleeping, and the remote site for making the Green Man masks.

He put a thermos of fresh coffee and the sandwich in his backpack. From a coffee can under the sink he pulled three pre-rolled joints - from the Gro-light, basement crop of a village acquaintance – slipped them into a pencil tin wrapped in a towel and stuffed it into the pack.

Although he hoped his day's work would end at the hot springs, the grass was as much for inspiration as relaxation. Hawthorne knew people who were debilitated by their habit, but he used it to push himself, to create a thick wall around his awareness over which he must climb to create - a pleasant barrier between himself and other people, most of whom he considered to be necessary evils incarnate. Increasingly, he used the grass to warp time and space - three joints a day, to keep certain events of the past at bay until, he hoped, one day he would awaken with no memory of them at all. Which would be very fine; as things now stood, the past and the present were horribly intertwined. He'd have left the Fagans' years ago if he truly had a choice.

But Talle had seen to it that he didn't. He was far too obligated, indebted and compromised to leave. His role at the Fagans' had become like an addictive vice – obvious yet secret, ordinary yet unnatural. Less and less did he feel the "art" hours of his day were truly his. Still, he had become quite dependent on the comforts and amenities of his situation on the estate.

Be here now/ time being what it is – is be here now.

Hawthorne walked out of the Fagan compound and into the woods, turning northwest and traveling briskly in the opposite direction of the hot springs toward his secluded sculpture studio, a mile-and-a-half away. As he walked toward the valley that separated the juniper-and-oak Fagan settlement from the ponderosa wild land of their estate, he remembered that line from one of the poets - the one who wrote those quirky little things that looked like haiku but technically weren't. Or so she had explained. Aisling?

At the thought of her name, his inner visual screen went dark.

No, don't think about her, that one, don't think about that name, about what happened that night, how her eyes...

Hawthorne stopped in his tracks, a cold sweat breaking out, despite the heat he'd worked up in his brisk walk. Damn, no matter how good you got at not looking at a thing, your mind tricked you, slipped it back in. Relentless, the mind, the memory. Like a bad dog, always digging in the garden where it shouldn't, pulling up bits of bony secrets you thought you'd buried deep enough.

Hawthorne shook himself like a wet dog - that same bad dog - and continued to walk, carefully steering his mind away - away from that garden. Carefully replacing the bones, the soil, patting it down smooth. He pulled the memory dog by its collar, up to surface, distracted it by giving it a series of inner pictures to scan, mental photographs he'd taken of all of the poets who had modeled for him - all of them, no particular one. At this point he functioned best if he only allowed himself to remember visual moments rather than particular names or faces. An arm lifted, resting on a forehead against the background of a faded floral pillow-case. The light coming through a vine-tangled window, illuminating a naked hip. A phrase giggled out, in a marijuana fog: *Be here now, time being...* A copper bracelet on a wrist gripping the edge of the pool, a dark-haired beauty with her face turned away in the look of pain that was pleasure.

And then the not-so-pleasurable moments. Like last night. What had been with Raven? All these months she was gone, no word, stormed out of here a year ago. Then suddenly there she is in the dead of night, creeping around his apartment. Kicking him and yelling, "Get your filthy hands off me, you creep, and give me my pictures!" when he tries to kiss her. And then some string of cuss words in that odd mix of hers, part Navajo, part Spanish, part who-knows-what. But what did she expect? Comes in wearing that musk and that silk shirt with everything showing. Those tight jeans. He'd known she would come back. Rules of the game. And he'd figured she'd come back to get those photos he took of her in the Green Man nest. No big deal, she could have them, but she'd have to find them first. He wasn't going to make it easy for her, not after what she put him through. If Hawthorne had a heart to break - and, from what women told him, that was doubtful - Raven broke it. Finally, he'd thought, he'd met his match. Someone as hard and cold as himself. Never let her guard down, not once. He liked that. He hated it when women let their guard down. Most of them hadn't any guard at all, were all "out there" with their emotional needs and how you were responsible to meet them.

But something else was going on with Raven. When they first met, she'd been so aggressive sexually. Liked it rough and unexpected. In the woods, by the pool, in his van. Talle caught them a couple times. Not that Talle minded, exactly - she never said anything. If she had minded, he knew he'd have heard about it.

Then something changed with Raven. She stopped wanting it. No, that couldn't have been it. Not as hot as it had been between them. Not after all the secrets they had kept from each other. The way it seemed to him, the more they didn't tell each other, the more they wanted each other. No, it wasn't that she had stopped wanting it.

Hawthorne reached the edge of the woods that over-looked a valley of grazing land, which was only one small part of "the Fagan Empire", as he thought of it. The Fagans owned every variety of terrain these northern New Mexico Mountains could offer. Their thousand acres were situated above Ojo de Sombras to the northwest, and stretched along either bank of the Rio de Sombras, which passed between the village proper and the foothills of the Sierra de Sombras. Their property ended a few miles below the village, spanning the nine-thousand-foot elevation of twenty-foot-tall ponderosa forest, to the five-thousand-foot elevation of red rock mesa, with an expanse of low, squatty, juniper bushes and scrub oak in between. The Fagan Empire included cougar dens, owl roosts, hot springs, water and mineral rights. Anasazi ruins, caves, defunct lumberyards and shutdown pumice mines. Stark mesas where there was no shade, patches of pines where there was no sun. An inactive volcano was even part of their inventory. The Fagans owned land above the village where cross-country skiers trespassed in winter, while, simultaneously; trespassers in t-shirts scorched their necks climbing the Fagan red rocks below the village.

The Fagans rented out this particular valley to local ranchers for their horses and cattle. In the distance was a small herd, but, between here and his studio cabin, there was only an expanse of pale golden-green grass, crackling and dormant underfoot on this cold, autumn day. He could see his studio chimney from here, although most other hikers would not be able to. It was at the bottom of a foothill beyond the valley. He recognized it by the particular configuration of the pines and scrub oak in that area. The barest tip of a chimney showed itself behind a slab of red rock that looked more like a scaly dragon than a piece of mountain. There were no direct roads leading to the cabin studio. That was a big reason he liked it. When he was in there working, there was little chance of disturbance. Aside from the Fagans, he figured Raven was the only one who would venture that far. Crazy bitch. Too crazy to be cautious. Dark of the woods, cougar, bear, rattlesnake or human – none of them scared her.

The sight of the chimney top helped speed up his gait. He was really itching to get back to work on the latest Green Man mask. This one was a winter mask, which he was crafting from his own face, the first of a series devoted to the seasons. Hawthorne's studio truly excited him as no other place could. He would light the stove; he could almost smell the burning *pinon*, in his anticipation. And then he stopped in his tracks. He *did* smell burning *pinon*. And sage, a bit of burnt sage. Very faint, but definite. He frowned, lifted his nostrils and turned, trying to determine the source. Sage again. Had that same camper returned?

Damned tourists, despite all of Talle's Trespassers Will be Prosecuted and her Absolutely No Campfires Beyond This Point signs, they still just hiked on in. Every now and then, he caught a couple of them pitching a tent or tearing down camp, and had to run them off. It had been a couple of years since anyone had camped here - the villagers warned them off, one benefit of a good rumor mill – until that one camper, a couple months ago. Hawthorne had found the remnants of a campfire one morning, a neat circle of stones filled with cold coals and ash. Appropriately put out, dirt and water thrown over, no forest-fire danger. He even located the hole where the camper had buried trash, and the post holes where the tent was pitched, and could tell where the trespasser had laid a sleeping bag. That guy's fire - Hawthorne assumed it was a guy by the trash he left - had sage in it, too. Hawthorne found crumbled bits of the herb near the circle of stones and could smell it in the coals. He'd gone through the garbage the guy had buried, wrapped in a plastic grocery bag. Disposable razor, used-up butane lighter, empty tuna can, breadcrumbs, coffee grounds, and some paper scraps. Hawthorne had unfolded those. A bus schedule showing routes between Albuquerque and Santa Fe. A crossed-off list of camping supplies. Most of the list he'd been able to decipher, even though it was written in a kind of customized shorthand: slp bg, mtchs, H20, rn gr, ch st. That last item, Hawthorne couldn't figure. Cheese sticks? Check...something? The last two bits of paper were a computer-generated map of the Bandelier area and a computer printout showing the addresses and phone numbers of the few shops, restaurants and churches located in Ojo de Sombras. Amazing, Ojo de Sombras was a destination on the information highway, Hawthorne had laughed to himself. Like in the tourist brochures. What a joke. He'd stuffed the garbage back in the sack and re-buried it.

That had been at least eight weeks ago. Not likely the same camper was still around. Probably burning sage didn't mean anything, folks bought those smudge sticks at the bathhouse and the locals used them a lot, too. The smell of burning sage was part of the Southwest adventure, after all. For the moment, Hawthorne dismissed the fading scent and continued his hike to the cabin, resuming his musings about Raven - a preoccupation which had taken up a lot of his mental time, a lot more than he liked to admit, over the past few months. In fact, whenever he wasn't working on the masks, whatever else he was doing, he was thinking about that damned dark-haired poet and how dangerous she felt to his life. She knew too much. No, she *assumed* she knew too much. And then just walked away. That was what made him crazy.

He'd broken his rules with Raven, and one rule was about memory. Once a woman was gone, he didn't allow himself to remember anything much about her. He'd gotten pretty good at this. Names, faces - all vague and discon-nected, mixed up with one another. (Except for those occa-sional bouts with the bad memory dog.) Yet, he kept having these distinct memories about Raven, not like the others, and not dug up by the dog. These memories were fresh, at the surface; he'd never even pretended to bury them.

For instance, he often remembered that last time, in the van, coming back from Farmington. That was when she started to pretend not to want it. To take them to the next level, he thought, or to keep it at the seduction place, for the excitement. Yeah, she was good at keeping things strung between what was obviously consensual and what was taboo.

He'd tried to come in to her cabin, the night after they returned from Farmington. As was their usual plan. Except, after creeping through the woods at two a.m. he had found her door locked. First time ever. Not only that, but his things were in a box on the porch. T-shirt, razor, his notebook, the mud boots he kept by the door for trekking through that swamp she called a back yard. Even a half-used bag of his favorite coffee beans, for Christ sake. She'd been making a point. So he'd left without knocking. Left the stuff sitting there, so maybe she would think he hadn't showed up at all. And without knowing what had happened to change her mind.

A week later - one week before the end of her residency - Raven had left the Fagans' in anger, with no explanation. During that last week, she pulled away completely. Hardly took any of her meals there, spent little time at all in her *casita*.

Yeah, for that last week, Raven had been about as approachable as that Fiona person was from the start. Talk about a block of ice. He didn't even want to try with that one. He was tired of the routine, of Talle's apparent expectation that he should bed every damned poet that came through the place. What was he, some kind of gigolo, with Talle as his pimp? If so, where was the pay off? Talle never exactly came out and said, "Sleep with them" but she always pushed him and the lady poets together. Made her little sly comments, as if he was some kind of court eunuch if he couldn't bed them by the first weekend. Always arranged for him to drive them here and there, put their chairs next to his at dinner, made sure he was invited to those little cigar-and-brandy salons she liked to have sometimes after dinner. She pretended those little chats were Liam's idea, but they were hers, always.

Hell, she'd even asked Hawthorne - in a hopeful tone - if he had ever considered himself to be bisexual - that time Chahil O'Shea won the competition. He set her straight on that, right off. Kept total distance from the Irish bard. Not that O'Shea wasn't pleasant enough, and minded his own business, which was Hawthorne's favorite character trait in anyone. But just to keep away from any of Talle's weird innuendos, Hawthorne had faked a bout with the flu during O'Shea's stay, a flu that just wouldn't go away all that fall.

The only thing he hadn't managed to avoid with O'Shea was making the Green Man mask. Talle insisted. But even that, he kept at a distance. He had shown her how to do the plaster enough times; she finally got fed up waiting for him to do it. Sometime before O'Shea left the hacienda, Talle took the plaster mould herself. Brought it to Hawthorne after the poet left. He had to work hard to salvage the botched job she made of it - she put some useless plastic coating on it. But he finally was able to make a good mask from the mold. Pity O'Shea never saw it; he probably would have been impressed.

Chahil O'Shea had fulfilled best the criteria for the Fagan residency prize. More poets of his caliber might be selected if Talle didn't have this fixation on nubile, young female poets who had spent trust-fund summers in Dublin and had a few lessons from campus chess jocks. Hawthorne had seen the advertisement for the competition, the requirement that the poets send ten poems and a photo. A photo! Since when was a photo of an artist necessary to sell one's art? How did these naive young things show up here with visions of literary success, when they'd had to submit a photo?

By now Hawthorne was through the woods, approaching the dragon-shaped rock, which hid the studio cabin from easy sight. He grimaced as he thought about the poets' photos. Maybe they were necessary after all. He'd always been better able to secure an appointment with a gallery owner or museum curator (heterosexual female or gay male) if his portfolio included a photo. It was such a joke, the extent to which sex and art were intertwined. Yet everyone acted as if there was no connection. Giving in to, or fielding come-ons from curators and art critics had been part of the game since he could remember. At least for him, it was. He knew that he filled some kind of fantasy expectation of many people in the art world. His appearance did. His manner. They liked his aloofness. He used it well.

However, he was very tired of it now. He wanted out. Out of the Fagans. Out of the memories-of-Raven thing.

Even out of the art thing - what little was left of that in his life. He'd stopped sending out portfolios. Pulled his work from the Santa Fe galleries, put it in storage. Stopped subscribing to and reading art magazines, stopped attending openings, stopped networking.

Now he only made Green Man masks. They were all he cared about. The sex part that was the initial draw. The seductions did become a ritual to him - beyond the meaning they held for Talle. But now it was the actual making of the masks - the work he did alone, away from the poets and the women – which compelled him. He kept thinking, *"enough is enough"*, that he was finished with Green Man images. But it seemed there was always one more, subtle nuance to explore - something he could only articulate with his hands. The Green Man changed and evolved as he did, unlike any other image he had ever explored.

Talle's belief was that the Green Man was the earth's masculine energy (she spoke of him as if he were a living man, and, indeed, the Green Man had appeared in that form even in Hawthorne's dreams) and required the annual ritual of the mask-making, the symbolic capture of the expressions of the poets at their most private moments of sexual climax.

"The potent and *feminine* combination of fertility and artistic creativity is *necessary* to feed and sustain the *earth*," she elaborated during one of the rare times she allowed herself to get stoned with Hawthorne. They were talking one afternoon at his studio, while he worked on the details of the latest mask.

"*All* of the earth, of course," she continued, leaning on his work table and holding in the smoke like a pro, then blowing it out like God's storm cloud, over the clay cheekbone the sculptor was forming. "But, specifically, *my* land. The *Fagan* land."

"Huh," Hawthorne grunted, chiseling away at a nostril.

"In case you have ever bothered to *wonder* about it - that's why it *has* to be the *poets* for the masks, not just some village *bar*fly."

"Why?"

Talle rolled her eyes and sighed, sucking on the home-grown, forgetting to pass it back to Hawthorne. He carefully extracted it from her fingers and took his turn, then handed it back, shaking his head at her ability to completely waste half a joint by waving it around, babbling on.

"The *poets* carry a special power *above* the other art forms, " she explained, obviously enjoying the opportunity to expound. "The Green Man, as the *husband* to Mother Earth, requires sacrificial representations of the feminine power. The poet must lend her *essence* in the mask, in her act of potential creation which *mimicks* all creation."

"You mean when she comes."

"Ah, Hawthorne, ever the poet. Yes, when she *comes*. Although," she added, "the feminine poetic power doesn't always have to be embodied in a physical *woman*. Chahil

O'Shea was the most powerful bard we've had here. It was critical, I mean *critical*, to take his mask. Pity you were so worried about being *queer*! Taking his mask was the...the..."

"Talle, let me finish that if you're going to just waste it," Hawthorne complained, rescuing the last of the joint from her waving fingers.

"...it was the most *incredible* experience, it was the pinnacle, supreme, *ultimate...*"

"Tal! You mean, you got off!"

Talle hammered the work table with her fists, hunkered down and glared at Hawthorne.

"Why did I ever, *ever* bring you here? You have not one tiny *inkling* of the sacredness of what we do, *have* you?"

"Watch it, Tal, you almost knocked off the eyebrow there," Hawthorne gently moved her elbow out of the work zone. "I think you've had enough."

Talle rarely imbibed marijuana, but when she did, she had no sense of moderation. Hawthorne shook his head, half smiling, and carved the tail of a lizard darting in the vines of the Green Man's hair. She was more like a naughty child sometimes, an endearing nuisance. But, as long as she let him do his masks and otherwise left him alone, he didn't mind her.

Nevertheless, over the years Talle's ritual became very real to Hawthorne. From the moment a new poet would arrive at the hacienda, Hawthorne would begin to watch her, to catch her mood, her tone, her way. He would browse through his small, but thorough, library on Green Man history, deciding which period, which style would fit her mask. He joined in with Talle in the game of getting the poet to agree to have the plaster face cast done. He made sure to bed the poet in the studio's Green Man nest early on, so that she would be willing to incorporate the blindfolded sex game with the taking of the impression in the other - the true - Green Man nest in the hidden place, the under-ground *kiva* behind the now-boarded-up Bardic Cabin.

The Bardic Cabin was located about half-a-mile from his studio, further into the red rocks and deeper into the woods. Liam Fagan had come upon the concept of Ireland's Bardic Schools while researching his heritage as an Irish - albeit Irish-American - poet. The 16th-17th century Bardic Schools were born of the Druidic tradition, so they greatly intrigued Liam. In the preface to a 1722 London publication he had discovered, *The Clanrickarde Memoirs*, he learned that Clanrickarde had been a Bardic School, open to poets born of distinguished clan poets. The school was set in a rural area, away from distractions, in a building with no windows, where each student, in his cubicle containing a table, couch and chair, was left alone in complete darkness to compose on a given subject. The next evening candles were brought for the poet to write down his composition, which was then examined by the professors. At the end of the studies, the head professor gave each poet an "Attesta-tion of Behavior and Capacity" to carry home to his clan.

Liam was enchanted with the concept. It seemed to him the antidote to today's cloning of university poets. During the first years of the Fagan residency, the poets were required to spend at least one night alone in the Bardic Cabin, to compose in the dark, without pen or paper. At daybreak, breakfast of Irish soda bread, farmer's cheese, apples and coffee, plus paper and pen were waiting for them in a basket outside the cabin door. They would then write down their poems and, before departing, would recite them for Liam Fagan. Eventually Talle had convinced Liam that the Bardic Cabin was too archaic a concept, not a good draw for the residency. Liam did not agree, but very reluctantly let the Bardic Cabin go. The building had been closed up several years ago and any mention of it deleted from the Fagans' brochures.

However, Talle and Hawthorne continued to use the pit structure behind the Bardic Cabin for the mask-making rituals. It was Hawthorne's task, on each full-moon, October midnight, to lead the blindfolded poet to the nest, to then undress her, tie her to the nest with green cords, and make love to her. The sex was invariably raw and powerful; each woman responded keenly to the experience. As she rested in her afterglow, Hawthorne would apply the preparatory oil to protect her skin, then the wet sheets of plastercraft to her face. Before the plaster set, he would bring the poet to another climax with his hands and lips, to capture her coming in the mask. The mask-making ritual was a secret between Hawthorne and Talle, and the poets who took part in it. That was why it worked; they were made a party to the ritual, they were fully informed, ultimately they chose to be involved. They were never forced.

But the focus had recently and gradually changed for Hawthorne. His increasing need for solitude, for time in the studio here alone, that became what obsessed him, what claimed and named him. The only way he could continue his part in the annual Green Man ritual was to find in it something that was just his, only for him, separate from Talle's intentions, separate from the poets' experiences.

Hawthorne wasn't even interested in the ritual this year; he hadn't really taken a good look at this Fiona Kelly. Oh, he'd noticed she was pretty enough, in an abstract sort of way, like he'd notice a woman walking down a street out of the corner of his eye, and maybe turn his head to look, or not. Fiona was cool, full of herself, so back-east-coming-to-New-Mexico with her prejudices and amazement. That look on her face, coming and going from the hacienda, as if she didn't know how she had landed here and wished she could leave. They all had that look, at first. But on Fiona Kelly it seemed to be a permanent expression, about life itself. Behind that kind of reluctance was a complexity he didn't even want to get near. Sex wouldn't be just sex to that one. Not like Raven, who could put bodily functions and physical needs first with the best of them. He'd always felt used after sex with Raven. He liked that feeling.

Hawthorne unlocked the studio door and pushed it open. He inhaled the smells of his true home – paper-wrapped moulding clay, turpentine, oils, *pinon* logs, marijuana, Nag Champa incense, mildew and dried leaves. He lit a couple of kerosene lanterns to illuminate an adobe room that was otherwise dark in broad daylight, the dust-frosted windows covered with new and ancient cobwebs, with layers of interwoven vintage ivy. The floor was cool red dirt, the walls thick mud bricks, splintered with bits of straw.

The cabin predated the Fagans' purchase of the land. Hawthorne had discovered it an old herder's or hunting cabin - on one of his early walks on the acreage. Propping the abandoned, rusted paraphernalia against the outside mud wall and sweeping out the mouse turds, he'd claimed it for his studio. He'd thrown down buckets of water, watched the generations of dust bead up, and then swept out the small, red-mud pearls. The side porch he'd turned into a kiln shed. It was in this cabin studio that he built all of the masks - the ones of clay that he fired in the kiln, the others of casting plaster, which he finished with various stains and hard wax. In these rooms he worked by kerosene lantern and candle, like an artist of another time, completely void of media and modern fixtures, fine honing with dampened clay, the brows, eyes, cheekbones, noses, lips. The furnishings were a wood stove, an old metal sink - under which were several gallon-jugs of water - a large, rough-hewn table. Multiple shelves and drawers filled with jars, jugs, bottles and paper-wrapped hunks of clay. Half-rusted cans filled with brushes, tubes of paint and rags, a cot with one blanket.

The practice Green Man nest - where he sketched the nude poets, and where the initial seductions took place - was set up in one corner, and needed replenishing. All the greenery was now dried and brown. He made that the day's first task, since he would need to get Fiona in here very soon for a sketching session. He tugged at the dried vegetation, broke and crushed it into kindling, and began a fire in the wood stove.

The site of the real nest was completely secreted, in the Bardic Cabin's underground *kiva*. The *kiva* had been another surprise discovery of Hawthorne's, back behind the cabin. It was hidden under an old metal door which had been covered with antique refuse and kindling. Hawthorne suspected, by the shape of the room - and by the fact that there was an Anasazi ruin within the area - that it had once been a Native American structure, and then converted into a cellar. He had found old jars of something fermented and a couple bottles of 1940's blended scotch. It was the formation of a tiny clay fireplace, the remnants of old ash, and the time-worn shapes of vegetable pigment hand-brushed into one wall which convinced him it had once been a sacred space. On the wall was a faded red hand, a brown bear with the remnants of an arrow down its throat pointing at its heart, several images of corn growing, and representations of clouds, rain and lightning. A few pottery shards were scattered in the area.

Talle had sworn him to secrecy when he'd shown her his discovery of the cellar/*kiva*. She didn't want the archaeologists coming around and declaring this some excavation site. She told him her personal reverence – and that of Liam's – for all things pagan and sacred, made her a sufficient steward of this bit of possible history, and that the academics and politicians didn't need to go poking their noses into it. After all, she'd donated so much of what she'd found on this property to the Church and museums and local families. She'd already done her duty. Talle assured Hawthorne that Liam left such matters entirely to her judgment and didn't want to be bothered with them; in fact, would be angered if it was ever brought up in conversation. Thus had Talle and Hawthorne evolved one of their first secrets together, the secret of the existence of the *kiva*. Later that year, they established their second secret: the Green Man mask rituals - something Talle had conceived of only a few weeks before hiring Hawthorne - would now take place in the *kiva*.

Presumably, Liam knew nothing at all of the Green Man mask-making ritual. The boarded-up Bardic Cabin had been closed down in 1980 and plastered with condemned-building warning signs. Talle had said it was too dangerous for people to enter anymore; she herself had twisted an ankle when a rotting floorboard gave way. The reclusive poet assumed that Hawthorne formed the clay masks directly from the sketches he took in the studio nest, and that the nude aspect of the experience was "art for art's sake", simply an aesthetic choice on Hawthorne's part. As a poet, Liam respected that and was more than willing to allow the other artist all the privacy and idiosyncrasies he required to pursue his work. Being the recipient of a similar blessing provided by Talle's inheritance and her generous belief in his own work, Liam could afford to be gracious in this way. The poet's visits to Hawthorne's studio had been rare and brief through the years; seemingly uncomfortable during the sketching sessions he'd attended. He came and left quietly and quickly - the dutiful host simply looking in on his guests, then back to his own work.

Except the sessions with Raven, Hawthorne reflected as he hauled in fresh branches of ponderosa and juniper, stacking and forming them in the nest corner. Liam had stayed and watched some of those. His embarrassment - Liam was not an overtly sexual man, to put it mildly, was much more of an old-school romantic - had been well hidden. Hawthorne suspected that Liam was sweet on Raven. He also suspected that Talle knew, by how carefully she tried to hide how much it bothered her. Talle always attended the nude sketching sessions with the poets. She came bearing boxes of black English tea and shortbread cookies to set up those insufferable tea trays, as if this weren't the Wild West or the twentieth century, as if she wanted to modify the tone of the very erotic situation she had encouraged from the beginning.

Talle hadn't brought tea and cookies to the Raven sessions. She had only come by once. Yes, things had definitely changed during Raven's stay. Raven switched the game on them. She wasn't the first poet to leave before her two months were up, but she was the first to leave in silent anger, in rage – which she was so good at. It had burned them all. Not that they spoke about it amongst themselves. Just that a kind of dusty depression settled over the compound for a couple weeks after she left. Liam became ill with pneumonia, and didn't come downstairs for his meals. Talle was harder than ever to deal with, her moodiness unbearable. No doubt she was livid that the mask ritual was not accomplished, the tradition broken. Hawthorne had seduced Raven in the practice nest - he had even blindfolded her and taken her to the real nest, unbeknownst to Talle. Not as part of the ritual, but as part of the outrageous, uncontrollable lust between Raven and himself. He had never done that with any of the other poets; he never would have dared disturb Talle's sanctuary that way. Nor had he taken photos of the other poets in the nest, but he had taken a roll of Raven that night.

He wondered if he had perhaps insulted or angered the Green Man by using the ritual nest for a purely sexual liaison. *But then, if anyone understands lust, it's the Green Man*, Hawthorne grinned to himself.

The nest was now replenished. He arranged the branches so that they would push upwards into Fiona's bare skin. The great discomfort of sharp pine needles and juniper berries would border on pain. It was an important element, he had discovered through the years of preparing the nests. The women had a need of that, along with the blindfold, the cords, the not knowing, as he sketched, who might be in the room watching their vulnerable nakedness. Each of them had become somewhat of a hedonist while bound in the nest. He found all of this pleasantly amusing. Raven had been the hottest. And the vulnerability had angered her.

He swept the stray bits of greenery into a piece of cardboard and tossed it into the wood stove. Then he poured himself a thermos cap of hot coffee, spread his first meal of the day - the sandwich - near him on the table, and removed the wet cloth from the unfinished clay face. He nibbled and sipped and began working on the forehead. During that period after Raven left, Hawthorne had never known from morning to morning whether he would be greeted with Talle's girlish giggle and her plans for yet another woods picnic, or her sullen glare. Back then, Talle took to going off by herself for several hours at a time, with no word to anyone of where she'd be or whether she'd be home for dinner. For those few weeks, it seemed the house ran itself and Talle - usually so completely present to the point that the hacienda *was* Talle and vice versa - seemed only a guest herself.

Then, as plans began for the next competition, and the fliers were laid out for the printer, the sun came out again and the darkness lifted. Raven had left New Mexico, no one knew if she would ever return. Her cabin in the village stayed empty. Through the grapevine Hawthorne heard that she paid the rent by mail, but was traveling. Eventually, he retrieved his box of things from her porch. They were still there, rained on, cobwebby and dust-coated. As if to say, even though she was gone, her cold shoulder still stood as her final statement.

Hawthorne still didn't know why. Raven had made up her mind about something, about him, and that was that. Just as well she'd ended it, just as well she'd gone away. But he wasn't so sure about the change she had caused at the hacienda. Was that just as well? Or the beginning of everything falling apart? Months after Raven left, Hawthorne grimly prepared a Green Man mask, working from sketches of Raven, without a plaster form. He gave it to Talle, but he still didn't know what she did with it. He never saw it hanging in the hacienda. Probably didn't want it reminding Liam of anything. The mask had been Hawthorne's best yet. Raven had made a very sultry, ominous Green Man.

Hawthorne finished his lunch and lit one of the joints. He began forming the eyeballs on the winter mask taken from his own face. Unrelenting, harsh eyes, ancient and cold.

The Green Man had been pleased with the Raven mask, Hawthorne recalled. He always was pleased - except that one time. No, twice - Aisling's in '79 and O'Shea's in

'86. Hawthorne had had disturbing Green Man visions after finishing those two. In both visions, the Green Man came into his room during the night and stood over the bed, staring at him until he woke up. Then he lifted his leafy arms and threw back his throat in a gut-wrenching howl, crying out "No, no, no!" - a terrifying sound. The leaves of the Green Man's body burst into yellow and blue flames, consuming him until he was a mass of foul-smelling, burnt vegetation on the floor beside the bed. The heat generated was so intense that Hawthorne had the sensation that his own skin was burning, and for days after these vision/dreams, his skin felt sunburned and his eyes stung as if from smoke.

The most alarming aspect of the visions had been the Green Man's eyes, fixed on Hawthorne's through the whole burning, in an expression of absolute pain, rage and accusation. Hawthorne was left, each time, with heaviness in his belly, a visceral feeling of something gone very wrong in the world, something that could not be fixed. He spent days after these visions feeling ill and unable to leave his apartment, do his work or take any pleasure from his art.

But the Green Man vision/dreams after the making of the other twelve masks had been quite different. Within a few nights after the creation of each one, the Green Man had lifted him from his sleep as easily as if he were a child, and wrapped around him from behind, until Hawthorne felt that the creature's pleasantly scratchy arms and legs became his own. He had felt as if green bubbles of energy were rushing through his veins, and then he and the Green Man had danced through the woods - their steps in synchrony. All the leaves rattled and whispered in their wake, and he felt a lightness unlike anything he could ever accomplish in his waking hours. They hardly touched the ground; their rapid dance was never impeded by stones or branches on the path, the way it would be in waking hours. Hawthorne would waken from these vision/dreams feeling incredibly energized, and all of his senses seemed super-charged. Colors were more intense, tastes more keen, textures and sounds excited him.

Because of these visions, Hawthorne believed that Talle was right; the Green Man *did* require the annual mask making. The ritual to capture the faces of the poets in their orgasm, that potent combination of fertility and artistic creativity *did* feed and sustain the land. The masculine form, the

Green Man as caretaker, steward of Mother Earth, husband to nature, did require those representations of the feminine power. Yes, if Hawthorne had a religion, this was it.

* * *

Fiona approached the edge of the woods, walking back from her visit with Silver at the book-&-herb store, thinking this was her moment to try the hot springs. There would be just enough time before dinner for a short dip. Silver had been appalled to hear that, after being here nearly a week, Fiona still hadn't experienced the waters.

"Hon, people travel from other countries, for goddess sake, to get into these hot springs! They finagle invitations from property owners to use private pools! They pay good money just to sit in the baths at the bathhouse. And there you are, living for free within yards of one of the best springs in the valley, and you haven't even used it? Girl!"

Fiona crossed the tree line of the hot springs valley and peered at the distant pool. A thread of smoke lifted from the water, rising above the rolling steam, and she followed it down to the source: a man's head and shoulders rested on the stones, facing the opposite direction. She squinted in the dusk to see who it was.

Hawthorne. *Damn.* She paused. Should she go, anyway?

She could imagine nothing pleasant about getting into the pool with that man, despite her curiosity about last night's episode with Raven in the courtyard. She'd wait for another opportunity to try the waters.

Fiona backtracked and walked briskly through the woods and through the open compound gate. As she passed through the courtyard, she glanced over to admire the chess library's stained glass window that faced into the courtyard. The lamps were lit within, illuminating the jewel-tone, knotwork rainbow of color - the imagery of the lion, ox, man and eagle from the Book of Kells. Fiona frowned at the shadow of misshapen shrubbery that marred the view of the window. A great gardener Hawthorne was not, she thought ruefully. What an awful place to let a shrub grow out of control, destroying that incredible vision.

Then the shrub moved, rising from its hunkered-down position and shifting to the left. Fiona quickly slipped behind the large cottonwood tree and watched the darkened figure, looking into the stained glass window. After several minutes, the figure turned and moved swiftly toward the opposite adobe wall, hoisted itself over the top and disappeared into the woods. The figure was briefly illuminated by one of the night lanterns set in the wall. Long white hair over his shoulders. Liam again. Creeping around and peering into his own library window? Nimbly climbing the wall to escape, with no sign of frailty?

Fiona had to know what he could have seen. She crept close to the house and up to the window. Faint sounds of music and voices – probably Talle and the cook setting the table for dinner in the dining room. Fiona scanned the courtyard behind her; no one seemed to be out here but herself. She crouched and pressed her nose to the glass. All within was hazy - vague shapes and shadows. Then she saw the thin strips of clear glass wound into the knotwork, forming a braid between the vibrantly-colored strips. She pressed one eye against the narrow band of clear glass and closed the other. This provided a quite different view. Although the perspective was limited, from here she could see details - book bindings, the burgundy edge of the oriental rug, a corner of the chess table in front of the window, if she moved to the left, the pieces.

Fiona caught her breath. The pieces, clearly visible from here. The game in progress, easily charted. So this was how the Green Man had been able to tell her from where on the board the pieces had fallen that night!

No sooner had she thought it, than she shook her head in puzzlement. Why had her mind made that incongruous leap? Liam, the Liam she'd seen nude on the rock that afternoon, wasn't the Green Man. And the Green Man wasn't a mortal man. He wasn't even a real man, just a vision she had had. Visions didn't sneak around peering in windows to get information for their prophecies.

Which still left the question: why was Liam Fagan spying on his own chess game, through the window of his own house? And leaping over walls when he moved so slowly through the halls of his home? What was the connection between him and the Green Man? Even that first afternoon, Fiona had felt a sense of connection between the man on the rock and the man in her dream. Somehow they had been linked from the beginning.

What was she thinking? That the aging poet, Liam Fagan, that pale, sickly man with hypnotic eyes, was the god of the forest, the icon of fertility in all times and cultures? That he could appear in visions? And yet, despite his supernatural powers, he had to spy on his own chess game to recall the moves?

Fiona returned to her *casita* and changed for dinner, still a little shaken by the commingling of personas in her mind.

She hoped to be able to discuss these musings with Raven. She assumed the other poet would have experienced these strange goings-on herself, during her residency. Fiona's conversation with Silver this afternoon led her to believe that would be so. According to Silver, at the beginning of Raven's stay at the Fagans', the poet had been quite vocal about the Green Man lurking in the Fagan woods, and about the weird sexual energy of the place. At first, she had found it amusing. Later, Raven had become less talkative, downright moody and unfriendly. She would come into the store only to order copies of the other Fagan poets' books, back issues of esoteric literary magazines, books about the history of the Green Man and "a lot of books on Celtic lore".

Silver had seemed surprised when Fiona mentioned that Raven had made an appearance at the hacienda the night before.

"I thought she was still on the road. Funny she hasn't come by to say hi. But, of course, that one keeps to herself," Silver waved her tattooed fingers and rolled her eyes. "She must have just gotten back, I'll have to call and fuss at her! Here's her phone number."

Fiona took the card and called from the payphone at the hardware store. She found the poet at home. After establishing the connection facts – the Fagan prize, the Baltimore Fine Arts Institute, Professor Bregman – Fiona asked if they might meet for coffee.

"Why?" Raven had asked.

Fiona was thrown by what seemed a rude question but she realized, a valid one.

"Well..."

She started to say something about being just curious, or since they'd be fellow graduate students, or she'd read her books or...and then decided to go with the simple truth. The way she had with Liam.

"Ok. I'd like to ask you some questions about things that go on at the Fagans'. About the Green Man and Liam and Hawthorne and Talle..."

"The Green Man?"

"Yes, you mention him in your work. And he has occurred in my work for some time before I came here."

"And you've seen him?"

"Seen? Uh, yes. Ok, yes, I have 'seen' him."

"Already? Your first week?"

"In a dream, of course."

"Of course. Hmmm."

There was a long moment of silence, then the exhaling of smoke.

"I'm working on something, I don't go out much."

"I realize that, I'm sorry, it's just that I…"

The Wild Shadows Café Sunday morning. Eleven is good. But I can't stay long. Don't take that personally."

When Fiona hung up the pay phone, she felt a sense of calm. She had the feeling it would be a very interesting meeting. Her dad was right; it was turning out to be a good day for fishing.

* * *

Hawthorne rested his head back against the stones at the edge of the hot spring and drew the grass smoke deeply into his lungs. He could relax now; he had accomplished a lot today. The nest was ready for Fiona. He had finished the features on the winter mask and left it wrapped in a damp cloth until tomorrow, when it would go into the kiln. A good supply of logs was stacked under the tarp for the winter's stove.

And, on his way to the pool, he had discovered that the sage-burner with the shopping list did have a new campsite. He had found it not far into the woods on the other side of the grazing meadow as he'd headed toward the hacienda compound. The camper wasn't there at the time, but his tent and camp area were clearly set up, as if he had been there for a few days. A shirt hung to dry in a sheltering tree, a backpack of food was tied higher up in its branches, and a stack of kindling had been gathered. Hawthorne lifted the tent flap and peered in. There, on the sleeping bag, was the most curious item: a miniature, portable chess set; the kind with its pieces magnetized to the board. It appeared that a game was in progress. Either the lone sage-burner had found himself a companion, or was playing some kind of solitary chess game. Hawthorne verified it was the same camper whose garbage he had dug up, by a notebook tucked under the sleeping bag. The same indecipherable, customized shorthand, plus pages of notations of letters and numbers. Same handwriting, same guy all right.

Hawthorne had been tempted to plant himself in the guy's campsite, await his return and make him pack up and get off the property. However, his loyalty to the Fagans and his desire to smoke his third joint in the warm, bubbling water were in conflict. The hedonistic side of his nature won out. He would postpone his role as irate groundskeeper until he'd had a good night's sleep.

Hawthorne took another drag on the hand-rolled, homegrown and dug his toes into the bottom of the pool. The stars were visible now, as cold and distant as disturbing memories, cruel in their inaccessibility. He closed his eyes against the sight of them, letting the strands of thought soften and intertwine like algae strings, gently buffeted by the water's movement, traveling where they would.

Chapter 7 - Raven

September 5, 1993

For the fourth Sunday in a row, Raven Shane Cordova woke up with an old-fashioned tequila hangover. On the floor by the wood stove again, curled up on the bearskin, wrapped in her father's ancient blanket. Lime rinds and salt spilled on the bricks, the tequila bottle empty, the glass on its side.

But a good stack of poems lay on the other side of the bearskin, away from the wood stove. They were stained and crumpled, some having been tossed, retrieved and tossed again several times during the night. Nevertheless, they had survived – had not been inadvertently burned up for kindling, like last weekend. Must have made that choice before the tequila took over, she thought grimly.

Her dog Dingo whined at the door - he'd probably been waiting there, watching her, since sunrise. She slowly roused herself. Her eyes were puffy and gritty dry, and the inside of her mouth tasted like cigarettes floating in a glass of last night's beer.

That was another thing of late - smoking. Something she had done briefly as a teenager, then given up until now; at age twenty-six, she found herself buying those thin brown cigarettes and smoking them when she was alone. When writing or driving. A habit she knew she'd have to give up. Rumor was that her biological father - the errant Irish priest, Daniel Shane, S.J. - had died of lung cancer, and two of her mother's sisters were headed in the same direction. But it was something she had to do, right now. Like the Saturday-night tequila.

Until she left for Baltimore, she told herself. She'd leave the last cigarette in the last pack at the last motel the night before she pulled into Baltimore. Baltimore - a foreign country to her. She would be new and unknown, she would neither drink nor smoke, nor engage in verbal nor physical intercourse with granite-eyed men. And she would find a good karate school and work for that Black Belt she'd quit just shy of.

But that was not until December. Meanwhile, for the next three months, Raven would sin as much as possible, pay homage to the Great God Tequila, send out smoke signals to the universe from her own lungs, and get a new set of tattoos. Show up in Baltimore armed for bear, as they say, and work hard, keep to herself, give no one any clues. Become new, unknown to anyone. Forget all this, which so enraged her now. That was her self-prescribed medication to heal the illness brought on in her by the Green Man. Green Man Flu, she called it.

Raven leaned over and swept up from the floor the stack of new poems she had scrawled in the tequila night. She relished the moment of reading them, hoping they would bring revelations from her interior. They would be like sardonic letters from a tough girlfriend having a wild adventure a world away. The poems would seem foreign and exciting, messages in bottles, cryptic puzzles from down under to surface above, to contemplate over her morning coffee - or "mud" would be a more appropriate name, she needed her caffeine thick and black.

Raven clutched the wrinkled poems and opened the door to let Dingo out. He was a pueblo dog, a caldron of ancient breeds - with some coyote thrown in - the result of which was a cartoon of a dog, spotted, mottled and white, with aesthetically illogical, asymmetrical markings. His legs were askew, he had extra toes, and each ear pointed a different direction. He had one blue eye and one brown, and the most engagingly stupid grin. Dingo sniffed and wagged and danced out into the morning. Raven grunted at his simple-minded happiness, and shuffled to the kitchen. The coffee machine was ready to go, evidence of the severe split in her current personality: she had ground the beans and filled the white paper cone last night, before ever opening the bottle of tequila. Modern day equivalent to a shaman's preparatory rituals. Making sure that, upon return from the chemically-induced journey of the night, a landing strip was prepared, and antidotes assembled. She was mixing her astronaut and medicine man symbols, she knew, but the Green Man Flu jumbled up time and space and place so badly, anachronisms were allowed - in fact, encouraged.

While the coffee brewed, she splashed cold water on her cheeks, then ran warm water over a rag and pressed it against her eyelids. She gulped down a few aspirin with a swig of orange juice from the refrigerator, lit a brown cigarette, and filled all four slots of the toaster with gas-station white bread. While it toasted - extra crisp and dark - she set out a tub of gas-station margarine, a knife and plate and coffee mug, pausing occasionally to tap ashes into the kitchen sink. She spread the poems on the kitchen table, smoothing the wrinkles and scowling at her scratchings. Where was that red pen? She could already see her standard first-draft clichés staring angrily up at her from the pages. There was a good morning's serious editing ahead. Perfect cure for a hangover.

Raven arranged the yellow-lathered toast, cup of black mud, ashtray and pack of browns on the table, and added wood to the wood stove. Look at that, she'd even banked the coals before passing out! Who else did she know who could take such good care of business on a bottle of tequila? Granted, she'd banked the coals at the two-third's mark on the bottle - but, still.

She only had a couple hours to sober herself up through the wonders of caffeine, nicotine, lard toast and the focus required to decipher her night's rant on paper. At eleven she was to meet the Fagans' new poet, the one from the Baltimore Fine Arts Institute. They would be dealing with each other in the department, so a bit of Sunday-morning brain-picking and academic ass sniffing was probably in order.

It had been a while since Raven had indulged. In fact, until about four weeks ago, Raven hadn't even been in the village, had been touring and camping in her truck, in Chaco Canyon and the Mesa Verde National Park area. She cringed at the idea of stepping back into the small social world here. There was no way to avoid it once you showed up at the Wild Shadows, given the fact that her cottage was smack in the middle of town. Everyone would stop at her table, welcome her home, promise to drop by - completely oblivious to the alarm in her eyes at the prospect of visitors. This afternoon she'd better drag out that old sign and touch up the weathered paint, the one that she'd hung last summer on the gate to her property: *"If the gate is closed, please go away, I'm working. If it's open, enter at your own risk."*

Not that it did much good, people showed up if they wanted to, climbed the damn gate, ignored Dingo - since everyone knew he was hopelessly friendly. The weed-induced, hanging-out lifestyle hadn't changed much in Ojo de Sombras. Not that anyone in her circle smoked much pot anymore - at least, not in each other's company. It had become too risky, these days the local cops didn't look the other way if you grew it in your garden, the way they did in the '60s. But people did what they could to earn enough to get by, grew their own veggies and hung out. A very lazy, sleepy place, the center of the village. Those on the periphery were more industrious, running small trading posts, motels, cafes, shamanistic retreat centers, nail salons and auto repair shops. But dead center, it was the eye of a hurricane. Ominously still and infertile. The perfect place to plant yourself and write poetry. That was about all it was good for.

At least, that was how Raven saw it. Others saw it differently, saw more and more tourists passing through every year; saw ways to make a living off of that. Bed-and-breakfasts had opened up, the bar had added a dining room, and there was a new gas station up the highway. The local librarian was writing grants for more books, and the village had slotted tourist tax funds to put in a new modular marshal's office. No convenience stores, malls movie theaters, casinos, thank you very much. This place still had a night sky ordinance - no neon and everything closed up by ten p.m. Except, of course, the bar stayed open until two on Saturday nights when the cowboy band played. And when locally famous characters died, their western hats were nailed to the wall over the bar, next to the bottles and antlers and skins.

Five cups of mud later, the stack of edited poems was neatly assembled next to the computer, held down square by a chunk of river rock. She would begin to enter them in the computer tonight. The toast crumbs and coffee stains had been wiped away, the empty tequila bottle added to the corner recycle stack, the house in order. Raven tied her hair into a ponytail, stuffed her feet into her boots, yanked on her jacket, tucked a couple of dog biscuits in her pocket, and headed out the door to the café.

Like most cottages in Ojo de Sombras, the door was left unlocked in her absence. It didn't matter that Dingo was useless as a guard dog. Loud but useless. Raven had nothing worth stealing - except the computer, but it was an older model, second-hand from the university computer lab, covered with geek dust and irreverent Bill Gates stickers, pretty grunged up. There was no pretense of a personal life or keeping secrets around here. If anyone wanted to sneak in and read her poems while she ate her red chili burrito and played academic nicey-nice with a "fellow writer" (oh please, could she get out of this, was it really too late?), fine. She really didn't care what anyone found out or thought they knew.

Except that one, Hawthorne. At the thought of him, Raven slammed the cottage door behind her to express a rush of red-hot rage. She threw a few jabs into the air at a phantom, whirled and kicked an invisible opponent. Definitely needed to get back into karate. She tossed the biscuits to Dingo, who wagged appreciatively. Wrapping a pair of sunglasses over her eyes, she stuffed her hands in her jeans pockets as she walked the two blocks. Had to get in to Hawthorne's studio, get those photos. She'd had a good look in his *casita* the other night and couldn't find them there. He'd caught her at it and they'd had a strange confrontation. He actually thought she'd come back for "more" as he called it. At that late hour, she had thought he would be over in his studio, so had let herself in to the never-locked *casita* after midnight. Suddenly he had been on her, from behind, grabbing inside her shirt with one hand, the other at her jeans. What did he think, that she'd go for him again, after all this time? As if nothing had ever happened? He'd grabbed her hair, yanked her head back and rubbed his unshaven cheek against her neck.

"I knew you'd miss it," he'd said.

What stupid, deluded, desperate women had led him to believe he was so desirable? Men like that always found women like that, and they ruined it all for the rest of us, Raven thought, kicking stones as she walked. Someone should have put him in his place years - decades - ago, and none of this would have happened. To think that she had found him attractive at one point! For about a month. Curse that month.

Got some damned good poems out of it, though, and a new following of mostly women readers. She got letters all the time now, pretty amazing for a poet. Letters from total strangers in Texas, Oregon and Massachusetts. *"I thought I was the only one running into men like that..."*, *"Your poetry gives me such courage to go on, I don't feel so alone now..."* *"If I'd found your poems sooner, it would have saved me a lot of heartache."* Etc. Apparently there were quite a few of Hawthorne's breed out there.

So the other night she'd kicked him, elbowed him, cussed him out all the way to the hacienda courtyard gate and drove off. Left him standing there naked in the moon-light, shaken up pretty bad. He'd had a constant hard-on in her presence last year. Flattering at first, then it became a real drag. Not just that he truly did his thinking from below the belt - that was never a threat, she could deal with that, work around it, ignore it, enjoy it. But that, along with his lust he focused his depravity on her. No, Raven believed that Hawthorne was not stupid and not just someone to be "dealt with". He was to be avoided and kept at a great distance. Not to be let in. Not in her body, mind or soul.

And absolutely not one in whose hands she wanted those photos. *Get his hands off your life, no fingerprints, no traces at all.* She must accomplish this, before she left in the spring. Retrieve the evidence of her naïveté and put him in his place, finally, forever. Inwardly Raven growled and roared, as she opened the door to the Wild Shadows Café and searched out the crowd - on Sunday morning every table was filled - for the new poet.

She spotted Fiona Kelly right off, the romantical-ly-dressed, Celtic-looking one in the corner, trying to appear shrewd and detached, but looking everything like some poor witless slob who'd spent a few nights at the Fagans'. Yeah, the Green Man didn't waste any time initiating the poets over there. You walked in the door, down the hall of St. Francises and pagan characters - the Herns and those little female Sheila-na-gigs - and, whammo, you were in, and in deep.

The poet saw her, smiled and lifted her hand in a wave, apparently recognizing her from her book jacket. Raven grinned back at her, but it was more than a friendly acknowledgment. Raven knew the poor thing needed someone to grin at her. No one at that dour hacienda had shown the young poet their teeth yet, that was for sure.

At least, not in any benevolent way.

Fiona stood and reached across the table for a formal handshake with one hand, holding out Raven's book, *The Wounded Watcher*, in the other.

"Thank god, another poet in this wasteland," Fiona smiled. "Will you please sign this? I've read it twice this week."

"Twice deserves a well-conceived inscription at least."

Raven sat to sign the cover page. She paused, pen in the air, staring at Fiona as if searching for an answer. Fiona waited patiently, quite familiar with that "what's-the-perfect-inscription-for-this-person" look. Raven's expression changed to a half grin and she scribbled in the book, closed it and handed it back to Fiona.

"Should I look now?"

Raven smiled, shrugged and stood.

"I'll get the coffees."

Fiona watched the dark poet make her way to the help-yourself counter, responding with nods and waves to locals at the tables, welcoming her back and asking where she'd been. Fiona opened the book and read, "*May you find the Green Man before he finds you. Best wishes, RSC*".

"Interesting inscription," Fiona said as Raven returned with their coffees. "In fact, that was the first thing I wanted to ask you – Why do you paint such a dark picture of the Green Man in this book? Unlike your Green Man in '*Water Rites*'?"

"Has your experience of him been dark?" Raven countered, pulling off her leather jacket and sitting across from Fiona.

"My experience of him? You mean, my dreams, my writing?"

"If that's how he manifests for you, ok, your dreams."

Fiona leaned forward.

"Are you saying you've had actual *experiences* of him?" she asked.

Raven shrugged and sipped her coffee.

"It's all experience – I mean, *interaction* – whether with another human or an archetype or a vision or a dream. Our experience with what the world feels more comfortable naming 'the supernatural' or 'paranormal' is not all that rare or remarkable. I find the more I relax about it, the richer is my trip. You know, like sex."

Fiona sat back as the waitress brought menus. She puzzled over Raven's meaning.

"So...are you saying..."

"I'm saying, to answer your question, that it's all projection. Whether you meet the Green Man in a dream or walking in the woods in broad daylight."

Fiona blushed.

"The tone of the whole thing depends on you. If you see the Green Man as joyful and life-giving, then he's spring green," Raven continued. The Green Man was obviously one of her favorite subjects. "If you see him as malevolent and frightening, his leaves wither and fall. I've known him - and everyone else I've ever known at any level of intimacy – both ways. And a few variations in between. Red or green?"

"Pardon?"

"I recommend the breakfast burrito. Red or green chili?"

Four hours later, Raven was so relaxed and engrossed in her conversation with Fiona that she'd even taken out a cigarette and was smoking it at the table. Not that smoking in public wasn't still allowed in Ojo de Sombras, but this was Raven's first out-in-public cigarette since puberty. Something she hadn't planned to do. Something that would probably make it harder to give up smoking in time for Baltimore.

The two poets had stayed long past breakfast, sharing stories of Ireland, and trading survival manuals. Fiona was a careful listener and shared a common attitude with Raven about the dreaded-but-necessary world of "dwemp" academia (when Fiona first rolled her eyes and used the expression "D.W.E.M.P.", Raven slapped her knee and hooted, knowing exactly what it meant - Fiona had successfully used the secret password, Dead White European Male Poets). In Raven's presence, Fiona felt that sigh of relief she'd been longing for since her first night at the Fagans' - the company and perspective of another poet.

Fiona gave Raven the low down on the Baltimore Fine Arts Institute and warned her about Professor Bregman's tendencies (her watered-down version), while Raven filled Fiona in on the history of the Fagan Residency competition, Hawthorne's tendencies, and the few bits of gossip which were essential gear to function in the village.

It was getting close to three in the afternoon, and all the breakfast tables had been cleared away hours ago. The door that adjoined the café to the bookstore was closed, it being Sunday.

"Damn, wish Silver's was open today, I'd like to get you in there and show you some of the stuff from the earlier winners," said Raven. "Obviously there's been some sort of evolution at the hacienda. The work of the earlier poets has a kind of...innocence, I guess."

"I picked up Aisling Devlin's chapbook."

Raven shot Fiona a how-much-do-you-know look.

"So you've heard about Devlin."

"Just that she disappeared. Was maybe kidnapped, murdered."

"Yeah. That's another story... anyway, after Hawthorne started living there things changed. Not just him, there's something else going on over there. I don't know, something... dark."

"Connected to Devlin's disappearance?"

"Possibly. Do you feel like... like you're being watched? You know, in the woods, or in your '*casita*'?"

Raven emphasized the word "*casita*" with a twinkle in her eye, winking at Fiona. Talle was an ok broad, but Raven found her a bit pretentious when it came to using local jargon - choosing this word or that to add to her vocabulary, the way she added exotic bits of gourmet foods to the daily menu, or collected antique relics to display, yet couldn't tell you a thing about their history or significance. Raven had felt like she herself was an addition to the collection while she stayed there, and this was part of what fueled her need for those photos. She had no intention of becoming part of the permanent collection.

"Watched? Oh...no, not really."

"Well, it is soon, you've only been there a few days. Believe me, you'll begin to feel it."

"But I did have an... experience. In the woods. On my second day here. Did you - have you - ever seen Liam Fagan wandering around, you know, sort of spying on people?"

"Spying?"

"On people in the hot springs? Naked?"

"Oh, you poor back-East baby! Of *course* people are naked in the hot springs!"

"No, I know that. I meant - Liam was naked, while watching them."

Raven sputtered, inhaling ash and choking. She stomped her boots on the floor, caught between a cough and the biggest laugh she'd had in months.

"I'm sorry. It's just - my god, are you sure it was him?"

"Of course. I mean, he's very distinctive-looking. It had to be him."

Raven made a face and dragged on her cigarette, as if remembering something she'd rather forget.

"You mean...you don't find him...attractive?" Fiona pressed.

"God no! I mean...well, there is that hypnotic thing he does with his eyes..."

"Yes," Fiona said, feeling a little dismayed. She had thought the eye contact with Liam had been just for her, private, specific, personal.

"And at first I felt a certain vibe coming from him. But, hell, I'm not the one to ask about attractive! I'm the one who thought Hawthorne was sexy for a while, if you can imagine. Something about the place made me horny all the time."

Fiona noted that Raven's face took on a dark scowl at the mention of the sculptor, and wondered again what the other night had been all about. Though she wasn't ready to admit that she'd seen and heard the argument in the courtyard.

"I can imagine women would be drawn to Hawthorne," mused Fiona, "From a purely physical standpoint. But there's something about him I don't trust."

"Good for you! You must have good instincts, then. You listen to them! I don't regret anything else about my life, I've been the product of interesting times and perplexing genetics, and I've made all my own choices and can't blame anyone for the outcomes. But I do regret my interlude with that, that...person.

"As for Liam," she went on, now taking a calming drag off the last of her cigarette and leaning down to squash the butt under her boot heel, "There's a lot going on in that one, but I'm not sure he's worth pulling all the cactus spines out, you know? Although the *curanderas* tell me the juice of the prickly pear is big time magic medicine. Thing is, you have to pull all the spines out, cut it open, get the juice out and use it right away, the same day you do all the work to get at it. It doesn't keep well, loses its potency outside the skin."

"I saw that poem, in your *The Wounded Watcher* collection. I didn't realize it was about Liam, specifically."

"Yeah, well, that's our secret. As for him watching the bathers in the hot springs...I guess I can see it. It just cracked me up, because I used to model for Hawthorne, you see, and sometimes Liam would come watch."

"So *he's* the 'wounded watcher' in your poem?"

"Do you think so?" Raven asked with a sly look.

"Actually, I assumed it was the Green Man."

"Of course. Anyway, I always felt like Liam was fulfilling some kind of duty, he didn't really want to be there, it made him uncomfortable. Oh, he'd look me straight in the eyes and pretend he was cool about me being naked and all, but...I never once caught him looking at me otherwise, he's asexual or something. Or very wary of Talle. That might be it, really..."

Fiona's eyes couldn't help going straight to Raven's open shirt, the overt curve of her breast right there in broad daylight, in the middle of the Wild Shadows Café.

"Yeah, I can usually separate the men from the boys pretty quickly," Raven continued, sipping her coffee. "But those two - Hawthorne and Liam - they're tricky. Something goes on over there; I'm still figuring it all out. It has something to do with Devlin's disappearance."

Raven suddenly leaned forward, locking eyes with Fiona very intently. She didn't say anything for a long moment and Fiona waited, curious. God, she admired this cowgirl, this woman. No one would mess with this one, she was well defended. And there was reason for the armor; her poetry was raw, hanging-out guts, so vulnerable it hurt to read it. Fiona waited for Raven to speak; she felt she could trust this woman. Raven might inadvertently harm herself in her passionate way of immersing herself in a person or place or venture, but she would not intentionally harm another. Except in self-defense.

Finally Raven spoke, having apparently read in Fiona's eyes what she'd needed to read.

"Maybe you can help me."

"You name it," Fiona said, somberly.

"Hawthorne has some of my things. Part of my spirit is trapped over there. I need to get it back, get them back."

"What does he have?"

"You be careful if you ever model for him, you hear?"

Fiona was startled by the switch in Raven's tone.

"Model? Me?"

"Oh yeah. He'll ask you. I'm not saying don't, you'd be the first of the Fagan winners not to since 1979. You might want to be part of the tradition; it's not an entirely negative experience. I might even recommend it."

"For art's sake?"

"Right. Hah! You see through him, and since he bugs you, you'd be safe from Hawthorne. It's really quite erotic; the modeling for the mask, and that has nothing to do with *him*. You find out things about yourself you didn't know. Probably would never know, otherwise. It's a ritual, for sure, a kind of initiation. Takes you..."

"Where?"

"Somewhere with the Green Man. Anyway, that's not where I was going with this. Hawthorne's got some photos of me, when I modeled. He was going to take a mold with

175

plaster, of my face, which I never let him finish. So he might have done a mask anyway, from the photos. But if I at least had them back, I'd feel better."

"If it upsets you that much, I don't think I want to get involved. I mean, I'll try to help you get the photos, but this modeling thing doesn't sound like a good idea for me."

"No, no. It might be good. You should stay open to it, if it comes up. Experience everything over there you can, as long as you watch out for yourself. Grain of salt, you hear? With *everything* you hear over there. No, I'm not warning you *off*. Just...*warning* you."

"You think Liam is ok, then."

"He never did me any harm. Some of his critiques of my poems were dead on; I got a lot out of that. I actually believe the Fagan experience is quite valuable. For instance, did you know that Anthea Simone and R.J. Diver were Fagan winners?"

"I had no idea. Didn't Simone recently win the Golden Iris Foundation award?"

"Yeah. God, I'd like to get that one. Imagine enough money to just write for two years."

Fiona sighed. What had Talle said about every poet's dream?

"Anyway, the Fagan prize has quite a history. I searched for writings of the nineteen poets that won before me. I'd been housesitting for a professor in Albuquerque all summer, and I used her computer and the University of New Mexico English department's small press library. Through their publishers I was able to contact them by mail, email and phone."

"Wow. Sounds like quite a project you took on."

"It's my thesis."

"Ah."

"I found out that five of the poets became widely published – in all the right journals. Three of those have books with good small presses, regularly advertised in *Bards & Writers*. Two went on to teach in writer's programs. Not all the stories are happy ones, though. One gave up poetry to go into economics like his father. Pressure. One died three years after the residency of leukemia. Another gave up poetry to get 'a real job'. She was in the middle of a divorce, custody battle."

"Ouch."

"Another gave up poetry and went on to develop a good career in social anthropology."

"Certain logic there," Fiona smiled.

"But nothing on Devlin or O'Shea. You know what's really weird? It's that *all* the Fagan poets *write* about the Green Man. He has that much of an impact. Even the ones who came there before Hawthorne began carving those masks. I mean, the poems from before 1979 have a kind of naïveté. They're all about women's lib, LSD, peyote, flower children, references to Tolkien and Gibran and Jonathan Livingston Seagull for god's sake. Even those all have references to the Green Man. It's not until 1979 that the overt sexuality enters in. Of course, all the books are heavy on sensuality, but the out-and-out graphic stuff didn't start until Hawthorne. From then on, sex seems to be the main theme. An obsession, actually. Starting with Devlin."

"Yes, her poems were very erotic, from what I read," Fiona nodded.

"When the residency began, in 1972, the Green Man was more a frolicking-in-the-leaves sort of thing. With Devlin, the poems about him changed."

"Changed how?"

"She presents him as more ambiguous...yin yang...he's all about 'fertility', after all. And the world is dying, you see. He's about 'fecundity' when the times are anti-life. That sort of makes him the anti-Christ."

Raven lifted one eyebrow and winked at Fiona on the words "fertility" and "fecundity".

"And there are other things," she went on. "Disturbing things."

Fiona waited for her to continue, but Raven stopped talking, seemed to go off somewhere in her head, alone. The dark poet tapped her pack of smokes against the table top, dug out another brown cigarette, and lit up.

Fiona stood to stretch her legs. Suddenly she needed to create some physical distance between herself and Raven's intensity. To contemplate how much she really wanted to know, how involved she wanted to be. Had she really agreed to sneak in and retrieve things from Hawthorne's studio? Hawthorne seemed a dangerous sort, not someone who would take kindly to prowlers in the night. Not only that, but Fiona was a guest, she had her stature as the honored poet to consider.

By the time Fiona returned with fresh coffees, her sense of foreboding and chagrin at getting involved in Raven's problems with Hawthorne had been overcome by her intense curiosity to find out what else Raven knew about the Fagans and Devlin. She felt herself brimming with questions, and almost ran back to the table.

"Let's go to my place," Raven said. "There's a lot more I want to tell you, and I'm afraid big cooks have big ears."

For the first time, Fiona realized that the café owner had been at the register, no doubt taking in every interesting syllable. Not again - every time she came into the village she seemed to leave a trail of erotic rumors! Last time it was the fax about sex on the chessboard. Now nude modeling, erotic masks, voyeurism. Well, at least she hadn't spilled her guts about her own part in that little woodsy adventure. At the thought, Fiona blushed. After all, it had been the spines of Aisling's and Raven's books that she had shoved into her blue jeans' crotch that afternoon.

Fiona gathered her things, pulled on her duster, and followed the smoke blowing, leather-clad cowgirl out the door. Surreptitiously, she checked out the café owner to see if his expression might reveal what he'd heard. But he had turned his back disinterestedly, pulling down water pitchers and glasses off a shelf for the impending dinner crowd. Fiona breathed a little easier. Of course he heard it all, every day. Probably knew every little secret up and down this highway, and none of it made much of an impression on him. Perhaps the Fagans had a strange reputation down here in the village. Orgies, murder - what was it Professor Bregman had asked her?

"Have you had any weird, pagan-esque experiences there yet? Wood sprites, divas, bacchanalian rituals, sex orgies, strange herbs in your evening tea, the usual?"

The two women walked in silence, intent on all they had discussed, eyes to the ground, hands in pockets. Both wondered if they'd told each other too much, if their initial instinct to trust and tell all had been wise. Both tested the air currents between them. Fiona wanted to say, "Listen, I'm not so sure I can really help you." Raven wanted to say, "Look, all that stuff I told you, it's probably just my over-active imagination."

But neither of them said anything. Because the one thing they both kept thinking about was the Green Man who came to them in dreams. That they'd both had the dreams. As had, apparently, every other poet who'd ever stayed at the Fagans'. And finally they each had someone with whom they could really talk about this.

They turned into the low-slung gate at Raven's cottage and stepped their way through the mud. Dingo roused himself and shook, his tags clacking and the crows over-head cawing. It was getting quite cold, as the sun withdrew. Fiona realized it was close to dinnertime at the hacienda, and felt guilty, recalling that her one obligation was to show up for that every night. As if reading her mind, Raven spoke as she opened the unlocked door to her cottage.

"Stay for dinner if you want. I know Liam probably expects you, but I broke that rule a couple times myself. There were no repercussions. I'll give you a lift back later if you want."

Fiona put down her bag and took off her duster as Raven headed for the kitchenette. The two-room cottage was warm from an earlier wood stove fire, and perme-ated with the mixed scents of brown cigarettes and lemon polish. Raven kept a very orderly place, Spartan, everything arranged in neat forty-five degree angles. Through the bedroom door, Fiona could see a bearskin on the bed and, along one windowsill, an arrangement of various stones, feathers, candles, rattles and smudge sticks. The main room mostly contained books - poetry, anthropology, Southwest anthologies, and literary classics. There were three large cacti in old terra cotta planters, prisms at the windows, and a few pieces of mis-matched, utilitarian furniture. On one wall between book shelving hung a rawhide drum embel-lished with a blue spiral pattern, and on the opposite wall hung a wooden carved Celtic cross.

The only thing seemingly out-of-place was a very large pile of empty tequila bottles in the corner behind the wood stove. Fiona stopped to look at some framed photographs on Raven's desk, which was strategically placed near the wood stove with a window view of the back woods. There was a photo of Raven, her arm around a woman who appeared to be her mother - an older, wider, white-haired and braided version of the poet. One of Raven crouched in a wedge-shaped, stone tomb, an Irish *dolman* - Fiona recognized the landscape of the West Coast Burren in the background. Finally, there was a tattered black & white photo of a young man in priest collar and garb, leaning in a doorway. Fiona picked up the simply-framed picture for closer inspection. He had Raven's eyes, but his smile, unlike hers, was sad and apologetic. This must be her biological father. She imagined that, however Raven had come by this photo, there was quite a story there. As she replaced the photo, she noticed that Raven's word processor was on and some green words were spread across the screen in 24-point bold Arial.

"You always leave your computer on, mid-document?" Fiona laughed, calling out to Raven. "I can never do that, my cat Lady Gregory always walks on the keyboard. And I worry about thunderstorms."

"Huh?" Raven asked, peering around the corner of the kitchenette to the computer. Her eyes grew large and her mouth opened, then narrowed into suspicious slits.

"What the-?"

Raven put down the coffee decanter and stalked over to the desk, barely giving Fiona enough room to avoid a collision. She stood glaring at the screen, reading the words. Fiona moved away, keeping her eyes averted from the monitor.

"Shit."

Dingo had nosed his way in and Fiona closed the door behind him, feeling a draft sweep across the room.

"Anything wrong?"

"Someone's been in here. Again!"

Raven sat before the computer and clicked the mouse, checking on the last opened file.

"Damn! I haven't opened this file in a week; someone's been reading my poems! Stupid teenagers around here, have nothing better to do than bust into people's homes. I'm going to have to start using a password, I guess."

"Or lock your door?"

"There's no lock. Never had to worry about that before. I know it sounds crazy to you, coming from a back-East city. But that's the way it's always been around here. Not anymore, I see. Guess it's time to put in a deadbolt. Damn. Hate that. *Hate* that."

Raven slumped down in the desk chair, staring moodily at the words on the screen.

"Is that your poetry on the screen?"

"No. It's a message," Raven growled. "They never left a message before..."

Fiona sat down gingerly on an old overstuffed chair, scratching Dingo's ears and trying to be polite. Finally Raven read the words on the screen out loud.

"Grind our flesh and bone to gruel
Feed it to the fiend inside
Set our tortured souls as fuel
Upon the altar of our pride."

"Teenagers wrote that?"

Raven sat, brooding, staring into the screen.

"I guess it wasn't teenagers."

"It sounds familiar."

"It's the twelfth stanza from Liam's Green Man poem. I hadn't put it in here yet, but I was going to use it as the intro for the book I'm working on, *'Pride's Altar'*."

"Wow. Who knew that?"

"I hadn't talked about it with anyone. Not even Liam. But I suppose it was easy enough for someone to figure out."

"Why?"

"Because I quoted him in the last book. But how would anyone know which of his stanzas I was going to use next - if any? I've barely begun this new book, it's not all in the computer, it's…"

Raven indicated the stack of crumpled poems under the river rock.

"So they read the poems?"

Raven sorted through the stack, seeming to panic. She started at the beginning again, sorting very slowly, as if counting.

"There's one missing. Oh god, not that one."

Fiona sat quietly, continuing to scratch Dingo's ears, to his great delight.

"Of all the poems they could have taken."

"What was it about?"

Raven turned and looked at Fiona. Her eyes seemed to be carved more deeply into her face now. Tears were forming and the skin around her sinuses was reddening. It was distressing to see such vulnerability and fear in the face of this strong one, the one who had hurled karate kicks and verbal epithets at Hawthorne in the courtyard a few nights ago.

"I didn't even want to write it down in the first place. It was the tequila talking. But it's the truth about what happened. *The truth.* I wasn't going to publish that one. *NOT EVER!*"

Raven stood suddenly, her fists clenched. She looked around the cottage wildly, like a trapped animal.

"Raven? Are you ok?"

Raven seemed not to hear her, seemed to have forgotten Fiona's presence entirely.

"Not *ever*," she whispered hoarsely to the room.

She grabbed her jacket and stormed out into the dusk, the door slamming behind her.

Fiona waited a few minutes, then set out into the growing darkness. Dingo trailed into the yard behind her. Raven was nowhere to be seen. The dog stood in the porch light, looking forlorn and confused as Fiona made her way through the open gate and closed it behind her.

Looked like a long walk home in the dark.

Chapter 8 - Entry

*A*t least Fiona seems to have recovered from her curiosity - or finally found my journal to be dull reading. When I retrieved it from under the tree in the courtyard last night, it was exactly as I had left it. She would have had to walk right past it on her way.

It just occurred to me. Did I do that intentionally? Did I leave it to trap her? Perhaps there is some secret thing in these pages that I want her to find. Or maybe I hope to prove she isn't worthy of my trust. Or both?

Am I telling truth here, Fiona? Or pretending? Am I pretending I didn't leave a trap? Or pretending I did so unconsciously?

Perhaps I should give up on this book, put it away, find myself a new blank book and begin again. And keep that new book in a secret place.

If I hadn't caught her reading my journal, what would I think of her?

She's so quiet and secretive, not exactly warm and generous of spirit.

But neither is Liam and it isn't a problem for me. And Hawthorne, he is the soul of ice! Yet we cohabit very well with him, of necessity.

She's so young. That thing of youth - her kind of youth. She's the center of a vortex; all exists in relation to her, is either drawn into her or repelled away, by her beauty, her intensity. That is what is so aggravating about the beautiful and soulful young, when we, the elders, look on them. It is the power of their beauty coupled with our vision of all that they haven't yet seen. The blankness of their faces, the lack - that incredible lack - of lines.

Their eyes are not innocent, no, their eyes are filled with everything that compels, that creates desire. Longing, anger, avarice, lust. They are so hungry. And our egos are tempted to try to fill their hungers. They suck from us what little dignity and knowledge we have left. Willingly, we let them. They are like monsters that we nurture, we encourage their crimes. In this culture, we are obsessed with their youthful beauty.

I suppose that is the thing that is most aggravating about the young, the beautiful young. That they have all the time in the world and don't realize its value. Time is like a million-dollar trust fund and they fritter it away on...

On exactly the things we wish we had time to fritter away now. And maybe we should just do so. Long afternoons of passion, luxuriously slow mornings in coffee shops, and evening walks along the river. Never sleeping, up all night with wine and books and pens.

Wasted on the young, as the saying goes. Not "youth" but "time".

And what else about her?

How Liam looks at her. The way I knew, first I saw her that he would look at her. How his ego is attracted by her hunger and his rage is drawn to her rage. How he would suck from her, like a vampire, her sensory experiences of her world. What she sees, touches, smells, and hears. The keenness of all that, it becomes pale and faded and far away in age. Intimate knowledge of her "firsts". As a parent wants to be there for the first word, first crawl, first step. So the aging male wants to eat, like birthday cake, the beautiful young woman's first passion, first inkling that she has power, that she can do anything, that her simple presence in a room can move objects, start fires, drown sorrows.

It is competition so unfair I can't join in, I can only observe and wait it out. He can't look to me for firsts, in anything. He and I are equals in experience; we approach everything from knowledge together. For each "new" thing, we already have a point of reference.

"Oh, this is like that other time/place/person/thing, from before...Remember?"

Is that why I yearn and search, waking in the night, longing for Him, longing for the green forest? Is it that some new youthful part of me is budding, wanting new experience?

*A new experience **not** necessarily shared with Liam? Something secretly mine?*

Dare I believe so? Dare I allow it? Could anything new and green awaken in this aging body?

It is time for the ritual again. I need to talk to Hawthorne.

Isn't it just a trick of perspective, though? If I say I am "aging", then that is my experience. But if I ignore the cultural implications, and say that being in my mid-fifties is not "aging", but is a new beginning? Can I make it so?

I am supposed to call myself a crone. That is what Silver told me, she showed me the new books on crone-ness. It's the New Age baby boomers thing, to embrace our fifties as self-consciously as we embraced our twenties. But I grow weary of exerting all this exuberance! I don't like the word "crone", if I have wisdom, I don't feel like sharing it! It's my own, hard earned, and I can only now begin to use it. I won't be giving it away!

I also hate being called "Ma'am" in the stores. Even strangers on the telephone call me "Ma'am", not "Miss". I am not aware that my voice has changed over the years, but obviously it has. Now this voice has the rough edges of cynicism, is now a sound that has passed over and over the larynx so many times it's worn the tissue down and the new, fresh rush is gone.

I would rather be water. Water rushes over and over the same rocks century after century. Does the sound of it rushing, then, change? Become grating and hard? I think not, I think the soothing, lively sound of rushing water over stones stays the same through millenniums. Water has an eternal quality. It is perfect and alive. I understand that, in space, away from earth's gravity, water forms a perfect sphere. It isn't just an inert substance that fills whatever container we put it in. It has its own life, perfect and round.

I feel like that. Held down by the gravity of my life - my roles as wife and provider, queen of the hacienda and keeper of the traditions. I seem to be passive as a glass of water, or water pouring from a faucet, or rain to cool the courtyard, or snow to complicate our driving to and from outer civilization. I am all these things. But, in truth, alone and away from all the expectations and needs of others...I am a perfect reflecting sphere, suspended in eternity. I use that image in meditation. What a relief it is to see it! To let go and feel suspended and clean and simple that way.

If only Raven could have seen me that way. I don't know how she saw me, actually. Except that, whatever she saw, it enraged her. If I didn't know better, I might think that Hawthorne has told her things – but I do know better.

I wonder what Hawthorne and Raven were fighting about. I thought she was out of state; Silver had given me that impression. That she had flounced off and was never to be seen again, angry with us all. I still don't understand why she reacted so vehemently last year. I think Hawthorne knows why, but he evades my questions about all that. Raven has such anger in her. Just like Fiona.

Anyway, there was no light from under Liam's door, so I assumed him asleep through all the noise this morning.

Something happened between her and Liam, too. I've never asked him about it. I don't have to; it's in his poems of that period. As are each of his young beauties, each year of the competition. Raven, Arlene, Brenda, Rose, Leslie, Aisling - all of them. Even his innocent idol-worship of O'Shea. Anything I want to know, it's all there, in the books. I have had my late nights with a bottle of wine, the reading lamp, tears and rage.

Those nights always end in laughter, helpless and hopeless laughter. Because he always comes to the same conclusion in the poems. He always finds himself pathetic and laughable and vain - harder on himself than I could ever be. He is very self-aware. I could not love a man who was not so, could not have stayed all these years. He chastises himself, rages at his folly, knows his weaknesses enough...for the both of us. And his health is such, the last couple years, that there is not much he can do, with the young beauties, except secretly long for them. And watch Hawthorne with them.

Like those sessions with Raven, where she would lie about naked, writing in her books, modeling for Hawthorne's sculpting and sketching. And Liam would be there, "sketching with words" as he calls it, watching her and writing in his book. I passed by a couple of times and saw them all in Hawthorne's studio.

That was when I began taking my walks in the woods; on the days I knew Raven would be modeling for them. Looking for my Green Man visions, doing my water-sphere meditations. Partly so that I would have a reason to pass by on my way to my private place in the woods, and look in without them knowing I was there. Partly to stay away and occupy myself, lose myself, and forget about them.

Liam was welcoming and loving that one time I stopped in. He called me to him, put his arms around me, asked for his wife's kiss. Very reassuring. He invited me to stay, to sit by him. But I couldn't. Raven turned her eyes toward me and they were so dark and cold. I was embarrassed to look at her nakedness. Although, god knows, I should have been at least accustomed to seeing her breasts, the way she wears that white shirt always opened up, even on the coldest of nights. What a strange one she is, using her nakedness as a weapon. Her eyes always measure a man's reaction, and challenge a woman's. As if she's saying, "I'm naked and desirable, and what are you going to do about it?" I felt that in the studio, certainly, but it wasn't anything new. I always felt it in her presence, no matter the time or place, whether her jeans were on or not.

*I should write of this. I haven't, before. It was...is **so** distressing...*

Ok, then...There was that one day I felt particularly uncomfortable. I stopped by the studio on my way to the woods but only paused in the doorway and left immediately. I didn't want them seeing me, that day. Raven was lying in Hawthorne's usual nest of vegetation - leaves, branches, flowers; things from the woods nearby. He had brought out the green ropes to effect vines, wrapping her arms and legs in them. She held branches in her teeth, so it appeared they were growing out of the sides of her mouth and spreading around her head, like the Green Man. Raven was wearing only her cowboy boots. Her arms were pinned behind her and her back was arched. Her head was thrown back, her black hair spread around her head, woven in between tendrils of the vines and leaves. Her eyes were closed.

*Her eyes were closed and, for once, I felt I could really look at her nakedness without her judging me as I did so. It frightened me. She was flushed and moaning. Ok...write it down...she was **coming**. Hawthorne was there, watching, from his corner. I was so afraid to look and see if Liam was there, but his place was empty. The room was still... Hawthorne's hands were spread across his sketch pad, his eyes were on Raven and - well, it would have been ridiculous for me to enter at that moment, to act nonchalant, to ask did anyone want tea or cookies. I had intruded on her private moment - and was stunned, at the strangeness of it, because it didn't seem that Hawthorne had intruded. He was part of it. He watched her come with a familiarity.*

Up to that point, I had told myself that they didn't have a sexual relationship, they seemed so cool and detached in their dealings - at dinner and passing in the courtyard. In fact, I had been waiting to see if anything would develop between them. (Later I would find them with their hands inside each other's clothes, sometimes naked, everywhere on the property - in the woods, at the pool, in the back hallways. Sometimes they obviously knew I saw them, but didn't stop.) Watching them that afternoon, I felt frightened and angered and betrayed, and yet puzzled at my reaction. It was their business; after all, I had not truly been "betrayed" at all. Of course I knew that Hawthorne did have affairs with the poets, usually in the days right before our Green Man nest rituals, toward the end of each poet's stay. But this afternoon with Raven was so early on, during her first few weeks with us. It took me by surprise.

I was greatly troubled and needed to consider my reaction and what did it mean about my relationship with Hawthorne. I remember leaving, barely able to walk, my cheeks in flames.

Later, after Raven left us, Hawthorne gave me the mask he made of her, from sketches. Like the others, it is a mask of coming. I haven't shown it to Liam, I keep it hidden in my office. Sometimes I take it down from the closet shelf and look at it. Again, I see her arched on the nest of leaves. In my mind, I can enter with Hawthorne into that act of creation, the lust and godlike power of it. I can see why the Green Man requires it. I can find no fault, but only perfection in the act. This capacity in myself - the willingness to play my role in creating these offerings to the Green Man - once unnerved me. I see in myself a wisdom change: I can still be angered, but I can't imagine what it would take to unnerve me. I have crossed some line, there.

It is interesting to me that the privacy of the sexual expression is taken away in Hawthorne's masks. Especially the ones that have no eyes. Unlike the other Green Men I have seen in the art history books, some of his Green Men masks have only sockets. With the eyes gone, the mask is not really a mask of Raven. It is a mask of coming. Everywoman's coming. Necessary for the ritual, of course. Yet it troubles me that the individuality of one's passion may be an illusion. It is unnerving to be shown that we are all alike, that a man can create that same mask - that loss of self - from any woman's face. That he can have that power.

Although it is a power we can take for ourselves, coming, alone - as I myself have so often done in the woods, during my Green Man dreams.

I suddenly realize...there is hypocrisy in what troubles me about these young women: Raven has no respect for the privacy of sexuality and Fiona has no respect for the privacy of inner life. They both assert the privilege to intrude, to see, touch, feel, smell, hear all that they want to - behind any door, within any book cover. And yet, so do I, by facilitating the nest ritual. It seems we all have crossed some barrier, some boundary of decency. That which is private - because it is an act of losing *oneself to ultimate vulnerability - is made eternally public in the mask.*

Anyway, I began to wonder whether Liam had ever been alone with Hawthorne and Raven, like that, watching her pleasure herself. Or whether Liam ever watched Hawthorne touch her. Had my husband seen her face in her coming? Did more go on, between the three of them than I ever knew? Hawthorne and I have kept our secrets from Liam – he knows about the sketching sessions in the nest in Hawthorne's studio of course, and sees the final product of each poet's mask. But he knows nothing of the actual ritual in the kiva. It was very troubling to imagine that Liam and Hawthorne might have their own secrets from me.

That was when I began reading back in Liam's volumes, not admitting to myself that I was seeking clues. And I found them. A series of poems, the ones he calls the "Nest" series. Images of women, naked in leaves, one for each season we have had a young female poet here. They are very powerful erotic poems. The voice different from his usual "ancient bard". As if he is familiar with the ritual. Yet I know he is not. Of course, he knows that Hawthorne works from the rehearsal nest in his studio, to do the sketches. We have let him believe the masks are made from those sketches. I always make sure Liam is working in his studio, or asleep before the true mask-making ritual begins. I set up the materials for the mask, light the fire, the candles, burn the incense, leave the oils and scatter the sacred herbs, finalize the cords in the nest. Then I exit and watch

Hawthorne and the poet enter the kiva. I stand guard above. Liam is never present, yet, somehow, he has sensed the ritual - or dreamed, imagined it. Could it be that he, too, has seen Him? Has my Green Man shared visions of the ritual with Liam?

I fear those poems of his. When I read them, alone with my wine. There will be another in the series, no doubt, starring Fiona. There is a distance in them, almost a coldness. As if he is laughing, not only at his own lust, but at the sexuality of the women, laughing at their belief, individually, in the unique- ness of their sexual power. I choose not to know the extent of his feelings, his experience, his lust. I already know too much. I hide in my dreams, in the woods, in my belief in the function- ality - the good, honest functionality - of our marriage. Such messy things as passion and longing for the young, flaunting mares like Raven on my property - these do not fit into our world here. Yet they are exactly what we have always invited in, exactly what Liam has needed to have around him, to write. And what the Green Man needs, to be satisfied. These are simply the unpleasant side effects of what I must do to keep this desert land alive. To protect our world here. Without the young mares, the masks can't be made. Without the masks, the Green Man is not satisfied. And He must be satisfied.

I must admit I need all of it, too. The sense of mystery, suspense, sensuality. Knowing that, at any moment, I may turn a corner and see something I am afraid to see. In my own home, on my own property. Something that will push me deeper into the abhorrence of self-knowledge. Of truly knowing that of which one is capable. I have read that the Green Man knows no deceit, and that looking into his eyes may be too much for some.

Chapter 9 - The Missing Poet

aven moved through the muddy yard in her cowgirl boots as if they were combat gear, leapt over her three-foot gate, and angrily rushed into the Fagans' woods behind her rented cabin. In her rage at the invasion of her privacy and the theft of the poem, she completely forgot that she had abruptly abandoned her guest, Fiona Kelly.

A boot-worn path led through the woods, past the valley hot springs, up to the Fagan hacienda. Raven and Hawthorne had used this path many times last year, during the heated period of their relationship. She had just moved to Ojo de Sombras from Santa Fe the previous summer, having decided that these mountains, known for their hot springs and low-key community of artists - in contrast to the high-profile world of Santa Fe - were where she would spend her last New Mexico year (and the rest of her grant money), whether or not she won the residency prize. Meanwhile, she would apply to various Master of Fine Arts programs.

When she found out she won the Fagan prize, she decided to keep the rental cabin, even though, as the prize poet, she had the privilege of residing in the Fagan *casita* - the same one in which Fiona now stayed. During her two months at the Fagans', Raven had used their *casita* to hide from the villagers and to write during the daytime. To keep their sexual relationship a secret from the Fagans, she and Hawthorne had been careful not to meet in the *casita*. That had been part of the magic. Their midnight rendezvous took place in her village cabin - except for a couple of times in his studio, when modeling for him led to other things. And except for a couple of nights at the hot springs. And that one time in the secret place, when he had blindfolded her.

Her favorite times had been when, long after she had gone to sleep, Hawthorne would come into her cabin from this woodsy back way. She would awaken to the clink of his belt buckle dropping on the brick floor beside the bed, and feel his night-chilled nakedness crawl in behind her, wrapping around her, under the warmth her body had made of the bed sheets. She would pretend to be asleep, so that he would do everything he could to arouse her. He would leave before daybreak, to avoid village rumors.

The last time they made love - by then Raven was calling it "having sex" - was a year ago October, when she accompanied Hawthorne on a buying trip to a plant nursery in Farmington, New Mexico. Driving back to the Fagans' in a moody silence, he suddenly pulled the van into a rest stop outside of Counselor. In the back of the van, on a dusty sleeping bag, crowded between boxes of bulbs, bags of fertilizer and stacked planters, Hawthorne proceeded to exercise the animalistic rights of mutual consent the two had established with each other over the previous month. Raven was disinterested but too tired to resist, although various karate moves occurred to her when he began to tug at her clothes. To her chagrin, despite her diminished feelings for the man, she grew inordinately excited at the shifting of the sleeping bag underneath her, the cold metal floor against her spine, the occasional shower of freeway traffic lights across the van's vibrating interior, the snow starting to fall outside the van windows, and the sexual rage in Hawthorne's eyes.

But that was then and this was now. Now her mode was absolute resistance. Not only to Hawthorne, but to what she thought of as "the whole Fagan experience". The last thing Raven wanted to do was hike through the woods to their compound, but she must get her things back. The thought of Hawthorne breaking into her cabin enraged her again, and she moved even faster along the path, kicking rocks out of her way and growling under her breath.

After that night in the van, she ended her relationship with Hawthorne - no explanations, just stopped meeting with him one-on-one, didn't even give him a chance to suggest it. Walked the other direction if she saw him coming, locked her cabin door at night. Their only conversations after that point were a few intentional dinner discussions in the presence of Talle and Liam, in which Raven subtly tried to verify certain facts and events of the past, while Hawthorne stared at her darkly, creating uncomfortable silences which Talle rushed to fill.

A week after the Farmington trip, before the residency was finished, she had left the

Fagans'. She and Dingo had been traveling ever since. First they spent the winter holed up in a friend's Chicago apartment, finishing *The Wounded Watcher*. Raven stayed long enough to proof the galleys and take a few copies with her of the small press limited edition. She spent the spring on the road from Chicago to Denver - sneaking Dingo in and out of motel rooms, or staying on fellow poets' sofas - a modest reading tour to promote her book in independent, feminist-based book stores. Over the summer, she housesat for a University of New Mexico English professor who was taking a third-world sabbatical. In a state-of-the-art home office, Raven had access to the university library by modem and the professor's Compu-net account. Dingo had access to daily city-dog leash walks at the Rio Grande Nature Conservatory. For three months, Raven worked on *Pride's Altar* and continued the research on her thesis proposal. That was the part of her application to the Baltimore Fine Arts Institute, which, according to Professor Giles Bregman, practically guaranteed her a fellowship next fall.

Finally, to clear the cobwebs of civilization, publishing and academia from her brain, and the frustration of a leashed existence from Dingo's, woman and canine had taken a three-week tour of Chaco Canyon and Mesa Verde National Park in the truck, driving and hiking with no plan, camping wherever a tent could be pitched and a dog could pee.

Yet, despite the justifiable reasons for her past ten months' travel, Raven had to admit that she had simply pulled off a series of good excuses to avoid facing her dark suspicions about the goings-on at the Fagans', and Hawthorne's role in those events. As long as she was on the road, she kept her mind focused in the present, on what needed to happen to get her from one day to the next, until the coming December when she could leave New Mexico for good, for Baltimore and graduate school. As if, by putting the Fagan experience in a corner of her mind to gather dust, it might cease to exist in the world.

However, the morning after her late-night return to her Ojo de Sombras cabin, with no justifiable road trips ahead of her for the next four months, she had to ask herself *"Why did I come back here?"* That's when the Saturday night tequila binges, cigarette smoking and all the tension and anger began again. It was not good for her to be here, but there were things to wind up - the cabin to pack and vacate. Decisions about which belongings to take to Baltimore and which to put into storage. The new book to finish. That nagging feeling that she was somehow morally bound to find out if her suspicions were true and, if they were, to do something about it.

Did she really want to risk her neck about something that may or may not have happened to someone she never met, a very long time ago? Based only on a curious encounter, some weird dreams, some vague feelings?

Only, the feelings were no longer vague. It seemed the further away she drove, the longer away she stayed, the stronger in her psyche grew the Green Man's visions and dreams. Any idea that he only dwelled in the Fagans' woods had been proved wrong months ago. Even in the suburbs of Chicago, the St. Louis motel, on a Denver sofa, even in a tent in Mesa Verde, the same, reoccurring Green Man dream pursued her. He would pull her from her bed into the woods with a sense of urgency, dragging her by the arm with one hand, while his other hand pointed the way into the dark woods with a finger bone he had taken from a skeleton. It was because of that dream that she had returned.

Now it was time to deal. Even if Fiona Kelly hadn't looked her up, not only providing a possible ally but also reminding Raven that, if her suspicions were true, any Fagan poet might be in danger. Even if someone hadn't broken in to her computer and stolen that poem, it was clearly time to deal. To Raven, the events of this afternoon had simply been the universe – through its damned tour guide, the Green Man – nudging her, reminding her to get to it.

It was almost night as Raven made her way along the tramped-down, pine-needled path, but she knew where she was going, and was too angry to be leery of the woods. She was enraged that this man would enter her cabin, uninvited, and read her private writings. It had to be him. She had thought it was neighborhood teenagers, that first time she came home to find someone had been in her cabin, drinking her tequila and smoking her cigarettes.

But now she was sure it was Hawthorne. While they were lovers, she had talked with him about her planned series, about using Liam Fagan's Green Man verses as intros. It was coincidence that he knew which one she would use next; she hadn't even known that herself when last they spoke, months before *The Wounded Watcher* came out with the first quote. But they had grown close those first few weeks, closer than she cared to recall or admit. Based on that closeness, his guess had been educated.

She believed it would be in his character to look inside her computer to get inside her head. Raven thought he might suspect that she knew something, but he wouldn't know what.

Now, by leaving the Green Man quote on the screen, and by taking her poem, he had let her know he was watching. He wanted her to be forewarned. To be afraid. To back off.

What Raven suspected was that he had something to do with the disappearance of Aisling Devlin, the winner of the 1979 Liam Fagan Residency Prize for Emerging Poets - or, rather, as it was called back then, The Liam Fagan Bardic School. Raven was convinced that, somewhere in these thousand acres of Fagan land, the remains of Aisling Devlin lay, buried or exposed. She had no proof that Devlin's remains were here, only a gut feeling, the memory of a pink slip of paper, a series of nightmares, and the incessant ranting of the Green Man in her head.

When she decided to do advance work on that thesis topic, this was all brewing. It was a topic she had been certain would be unique and intriguing enough to catch the eye and approval of the thesis committee at the Baltimore Fine Arts Institute, despite the fact that university creative writing professors rolled their eyes at the mention of the unpublished Liam Fagan. The history of the Liam Fagan prize poets, where their careers were when they came to the hacienda, where their careers went, after was something to look into. Liam Fagan might not be an academically respected poet, but at least a quarter of the past Fagan winners were now established writers, well-published and even teaching in those same academic MFA programs that rejected Fagan's importance. Was it just coincidence, or might the poetry world have to give a serious – if begrudging - nod to the Fagan prize?

Of course, given Aisling Devlin's disappearance, Raven couldn't exactly encourage emerging poets to enter the competition. She realized she might not be the right objective researcher for this project. But she really thought Hawthorne was the problem. He was nothing more than a temporary employee, an unfortunate choice the Fagans had made but could un-make.

Of course, Raven would need to do a statistical analysis of the percentage of poets attending other, better known and respected residencies, to compare their success rate with the Fagan poets. Her project would also look into the intriguing reoccurrence of Green Man imagery in the works of the Fagan poets.

At the thought of the Green Man, Raven suddenly thought she saw something moving through the trees along her path. A low-flying bird? She stopped and looked again, but only saw the ordinary movements of the leaves in the wind. She continued, walking faster, remembering a line from an essay by the poet Chahil O'Shea, about the Green Man, that Aisling Devlin had quoted in her chapbook. About how, when you thought you saw a movement in the woods out of the corner of your eye, that was he.

Thinking of O'Shea's line reminded Raven that one of her next tasks was to follow up on the correspondence with her Dublin writer friend. Raven felt sure O'Shea had returned to Ireland and that she would find him through some Galway small press or Dublin publishing house.

Continuing through the woods, Raven recalled when her research on Aisling Devlin had led to the unexpected realization that the poet was still missing, after thirteen years. She'd done a media search on the computer at the UNM library and came up with articles about her disappearance in The Albuquerque Journal, The Denver Post, and The Durango Herald. Ojo de Sombras' monthly newspaper had not been around in the '70s, when a seat at the local watering hole sufficed for newsgathering. As she read the articles, Raven recalled some vague, stale gossip she had heard during her first couple of months in Ojo de Sombras, before she won the prize. The kind of quick-scan of the past twenty years one was fed in the saloon when one first moved into the village.

"And then there was the time that..." and "Watch out for so and so, he's..." and "Oh, did you know we had a disappearance here 'bout thirteen years ago? Oh yeah, one of those poets from up there at the hacienda, no sir, never did find her..."

Of course, Silver had been eagerly helpful, filling in the better-known details when Raven asked, three weeks into her residency. One of the details was the openly sexual relationship between the poet and the artist who had first came to stay at the Fagans' in 1979, and had never left. Back then, Hawthorne and Aisling Devlin used to come down regularly to the *Extranjeros* bookstore and the Wild Shadows Café, arm-in-arm, kissing and laughing.

But, after Aisling's disappearance and the investigation, Hawthorne hardly ever came into the village anymore. Kinda cute, though, Silver had shrugged. For all the good it did any of the available women. She'd see him, now and then, walking one of the poets home. But he didn't want to have anything to do with any of the locals. Only the ones working at or visiting the hacienda.

"He might go for you," Silver had giggled, sliding Raven a sly look. Raven smiled and kept her thoughts to herself.

The night before this conversation with Silver, Raven and Hawthorne had shared their first kiss, a very long and hot one as they passed in the woods, she returning from the hot springs, he heading in that direction. She thought, at first, that he was one of those Green Man hallucinations she was always having, that male figure leaning against a tree in her path. But, on second glance, it was Hawthorne, in a dark green t-shirt and jeans, watching her approach.

Not only did Raven find Hawthorne to be devastatingly good looking - in a pouting, little boy sort of way - but she had used the metaphor of a sculptor in one of her poems about the effects of the Southwestern landscape on her psyche and sexuality. Long before she ever came to the Fagans' or saw Hawthorne at the dinner table. Between her hormones and finding out that Hawthorne was a sculptor, that old female it-was-meant-to-be mythology kicked in big time.

She had on her usual silk shirt and jeans, and was rubbing water from her hair with an oversized towel as she walked. He stepped forward. Blocked her path, and grabbed the other end of the towel, looking her in the eyes with that same nonverbal question he'd been asking since the day she'd arrived at the hacienda - at dinner with the Fagans, watching her from his *casita* door, passing in the courtyard in the afternoons. She'd already decided the answer, just hadn't yet had proximity to give it.

She yanked on the towel, surprising him with her strength, pulling him toward her. They pressed up against each other, denim on denim, everything they could do - staying vertical and dressed - they did. And then parted, both out of breath, both gesturing "no more" with their hands, turning from each other. He walked down to the springs, she walked back to her *casita*. They never said a word. And, later, at dinner with the Fagans, gave no indication.

Raven had said nothing about any of this to Silver. Just smiled and changed the subject.

That was probably when her smallest first suspicions had set in, when Silver suggested Hawthorne had previous dalliances with women staying at the Fagans'. Right at the get-go, as her adopted dad used to say. So it wasn't some kind of fated soul thing between she and Hawthorne, she thought, leaving the bookstore that day. Not that she truly expected it to be. So Hawthorne had a habit of the lady poets, did he? How convenient, one-a-year, fed to him by the Fagans. How long had he been there now? 1979, Silver said, was his first year. The year of the disappearing poet, thirteen years ago. Thirteen lovers? No, not unless he was into men.

Mostly, at that point, Raven had found it amusing, thinking of the dark, wordless sexual heathen, Hawthorne, bedding all the fine young ladies of verse. *Ok*, she had told herself recklessly, *I'm game. I'll show him something none of them have shown him before. And I'll break him, in the end. I'll just be leaving, and no tears. Bet he's not used to that.*

This was one of the things about herself that had led to her Saturday-night, solo tequila parties. That she had welcomed it: the dark, unhealthy sexual connection with such a womanizer.

The other reasons for the tequila were the reoccurring nightmare of the woman tied up in the Green Man nest, and to escape from and avoid dealing with her suspicions that this not-so-long-ago lover was capable of murder. Murder of one like her, a lover, a poet. The dead poet had been a dreamer, no doubt. Whatever facade Raven presented to the world, she too, was a dreamer.

Raven had made references to Hawthorne concerning Aisling, in order to observe his response. Still, she doubted that he realized how serious her suspicions really were. Except now that Hawthorne had the poem she had written last night, he would know more about what was in her head than she wanted him to. God, she hadn't meant to write that poem. And, once written, meant to burn it. It was just that - after all these months - finally something had to come out, she couldn't hold it in entirely anymore. All these months of Saturday nights spent alone with her chagrin at having bedded a possible murderer - alone with her dark, brooding suspicions, the ensuing nightmares, and those visions of the Green Man. It was all too hard to handle. Hence the tequila.

How could her judgment have been that off? Raven stuffed her cold hands in her jacket pocket as she stalked through the woods. In her impetuous rush to confront the poetry thief, she hadn't thought to grab her gloves. It was incredible how immediately cold this high desert became as soon as the light left the sky. But Raven shivered not only at the cold. How could the hand of a murderer caress her skin, and she not know his true nature? It was so in keeping with the whole Fagan experience. *Santos* housed next to satanic images. The abnormal masquerading as normal.

Well, no, that was not fair. The pagan images were not satanic. She had loved them at first, the replica reliefs from the Gundestrup cauldron, the genuine artifact stone carving of the horse goddess Epona, the copper etching of the hero Cu Chulainn, the bronze stags and bears - and Liam's never-ending history lessons on their significance. But, eventually, her over-all experience of her time at the Fagans' was so overshadowed by her obsession with the disappearance of Aisling Devlin, that everything associated with the place began to seem evil to her. Even the eccentric but innocent older couple.

A rock caught on the heel of Raven's boot. She paused to flick it away and stood a moment, staring into the dark tree shadows, feeling her cheeks burn from the cold. Should she keep on going?

She hadn't thought this through. Confronting Hawthorne at dinner in front of the Fagans would not be a good idea. She didn't want to bring anyone else into the picture until she was clear about what to do.

After all, she only had suspicions, she had no real proof.

No. There could be no more hesitation, no more legitimate excuses. Raven kept moving, heading toward the valley and the hacienda, remembering the night she first began to form her suspicions about what had happened to Aisling Devlin.

Raven and Hawthorne had driven up to Farmington late in the day on October 12th last fall, and checked into a motel for a night of animal sex. The next morning they gave a repeat performance, slept in until noon checkout, had a long margarita lunch and browsed some pawnshops, looking for turquoise jewelry. Around four o'clock they drove to Lam's Nursery on the outskirts of Farmington to pick up the gardening tools, seeds, fertilizer and planters for Talle's greenhouse, things that she had ordered ahead of time. A gaunt Japanese man at the front counter nodded to Hawthorne with an owner's air of dignified familiarity. Raven followed Hawthorne to the back, where the doors opened out onto a large greenhouse. From there, a young man began loading boxes and planters into Hawthorne's van.

When Hawthorne stopped to sign for the items, the young man opened the Fagan account file and commented that Hawthorne had signed for a similar set of gardening supplies the year prior, on October 24th.

"We come here every fall," Hawthorne replied, pulling Talle Fagan's pre-signed check from his wallet. The young man flipped back through a stack of pink carbons in the folder.

"I'll say...look at this! October 5, 1990, October 18, 1986, October 2, 1982...shit, man, this goes all the way back to...October 6, 1979! Why do you do that, come here the same time every year all the way from Ojo de Sombras?"

Hawthorne looked irritated at the young man's naivete and over-enthusiasm. He leaned on the counter, placed the check on top of the open account file, and poised his pen to write.

"Mrs. Fagan prefers this nursery. You have..."

Hawthorne glanced around, gesturing with his pen to the pottery stacked at the back of the greenhouse.

"A line of Southwestern pottery there that she prefers. And your nursery has a long-term contract?"

"Hell, those pots? Those are made in Ponderosa, I drove down and picked up the last load myself. Ponderosa's just fifteen miles down the road from Ojo de Sombras."

The young man chuckled, pleased with himself, shook his head and threw a conspiratorial grin at Raven while Hawthorne wrote out the check. During this exchange, Raven had been standing nearby, flipping through a how-to book on Japanese gardens. She smiled politely until the young man dropped his gaze to her open shirt and tight black jeans then raised his glance to meet her eyes. The predictable leer. His attempt to put Hawthorne in his place had been a show for her. She also noticed that, when Hawthorne straightened up and capped his pen, her lover surreptitiously pulled the bottom pink 1979 carbon out of the account file and wadded it into his denim jacket pocket. The young man broke his gaze from Raven's - being no match for the cold disdain in her eyes - cleared his throat, picked up the check, ripped the customer's copy from the current invoice and handed it to Hawthorne. Hawthorne pursed his lips and spoke icily while he tucked the invoice into his wallet.

"The thing Mrs. Fagan has always been most impressed with at this nursery is your discretion."

The young man looked puzzled - at both the word and the tone.

"You're new here, aren't you?" Hawthorne asked.

"Yes sir, started a week ago."

"Have you noticed the owner, Mr. Lam, keeping thir-teen-year-old account files on *every* customer?"

"Uh...no sir..."

"Exactly. If you plan to keep your job here, you'll make it a point to familiarize yourself with your regular custom-ers. If you review this file, you'll see that Mrs. Fagan orig-inally hired this nursery in 1979 to landscape her historic estate."

Raven's eyebrows lifted at the increased agitation in Hawthorne's voice.

"Yes sir!"

"And that there is a long-term contract by which your nursery staff travels periodically to Mrs. Fagan's estate to do whatever she sees fit, at *her* preference and direction."

The young man looked nervously up to the front of the store, where Mr. Lam was watching with folded arms and without expression.

"Have I made my point or do I need to be so crude as to remind you how much revenue Mrs. Fagan brings to your employer?"

The clerk nodded, then shook his head, uncertain how to respond without incurring further wrath from Hawthorne, his eyes wide and his cheeks crimson.

Hawthorne turned on his heel and walked briskly to the van. Raven replaced the gardening book back on the shelf and turned to follow Hawthorne, puzzled at his heated reaction. The young man touched her elbow as she passed.

"Hey, I didn't mean anything by it, ok?" Raven shrugged him off, as she rushed to the van that Hawthorne was already backing up, as if he might leave her there.

She and Hawthorne drove an hour before either of them spoke. During that hour, she observed his rage, realized he was in no mood to talk, and hoped his driving would slow down to a safe speed. She watched out the van window, wondering what had angered him, wondering at the significance of the annual October visit to the far-away plant nursery. What the young man said was true. The pots were made in Ponderosa; she saw their labels when she helped Hawthorne rearrange things in the greenhouse the previous week. Why *did* Talle insist on using a nursery and a land-scaping service that was so far away - eight hours round-trip from Ojo de Sombras - when there were several excellent ones in Santa Fe and Albuquerque, half the distance in either direction? More importantly, why had Hawthorne secretly taken that invoice carbon from the account file?

October 6, 1979, the young man had said. Raven puzzled and mused on it, watching the changing landscape slide by, knowing there was something familiar about that date. Suddenly it came. The newspaper article, the photo-copy she'd made for her research file on the Fagan poets. Aisling Devlin disappeared in Durango on October 6. 1979. The last day anyone had seen the poet.

A witness had seen her in her olive VW Beetle with the "Nuke the Wales" bumper sticker at dawn, driving out of the Fagan compound, passing through the village of Ojo de Sombras, onto the highway heading toward Cuba, New Mexico. They recognized her by the familiar purple and black bandana tied around her hair and her oversized, rose-colored sunglasses. She had been wearing her sheep-skin jacket. The last anyone saw of her was several hours later that same morning, at a gas station on the outskirts of Durango, less than a mile from the apartment she shared with a boyfriend. Her car was found at the station, apparently abandoned. The journalists and the police finally decided she must have been abducted - or otherwise disappeared - from the gas station. The boyfriend checked out - he had been at work at a ski shop on Main Avenue all morning - and the investigation came to a dead end. Or, rather, she was still listed as a missing person, thirteen years later, but any active search had long since ceased. Her family hired a private detective, but eventually ran out of money. The investigation now sat dormant, its tires flat, like the abandoned olive VW.

Raven needed to see the pink carbon in Hawthorne's pocket.

She had her chance. As the van heated up, Hawthorne shrugged out of his jacket and tossed it behind the seat. When he stopped for gas and to use the bathroom, Raven waited in the van. Keeping her eye on the bathroom door, she found the pocket of his jacket and quickly scanned the invoice. The 1979 supplies were similar to the ones they had picked up today.

She almost kept the pink carbon, but feared he might suspect her of taking it. Who was he, really, after all? Was she in danger, in his company? Had he taken Aisling Devlin on a similar trip, thirteen years ago, in this same van? No, calm down, this van was new, a recent model.

She had to find out more. Meanwhile, she had to act as if nothing had changed. She wadded up the invoice and put it back in his pocket. She couldn't wait to get back to her Ojo de Sombras cabin, safe and sound, alone and quiet, to think all of this out. Only two more hours.

As Raven sat in the van waiting for Hawthorne's return, she thought of the shift in her reaction to him over the past few weeks. Something was going on, subliminally. She had thought it was because of the brevity of the residency - their sexual liaison would not endure her departure from the hacienda. He wouldn't want to continue, she knew, and she would keep her promise to herself - to walk away, and to not cry. She would show him something he'd not seen before, with the other sensitive poets.

Raven didn't kid herself; it wasn't passion or love that she shared with the sculptor-gardener. It was a very powerful lust. Not even habit, but addiction. She hated herself for it, and began to want to resist. She posed for him, he drew her, and he put his hands on her. Her body reacted, urgently, but her mind began to remove itself. To watch, dispassionately. Coming was no longer pleasure. It was something her body needed, craved, something she had to make sure was available to her, daily. At any time he asked. Things were out of control, she even felt afraid of how much. She and Hawthorne had become less and less careful about their sexual moments on the grounds of the Fagan hacienda. More than once, Talle had come upon them, pinning each other against an adobe wall or a tree.

It was this loss of control, this connection with a possibly dangerous man, that had everything to do with her current tequila binges, the increasing craving for brown cigarettes.

Raven had a feeling whatever Hawthorne had done to Aisling, it had nothing to do with the kind of immortality poets hope to have. Her Green Man dreams clearly led her to believe that Devlin's bones were somewhere on these Fagan acres.

Raven's memories were interrupted, as she found herself at the end of the woods trail, which opened out onto the valley. She needed help with this. It was too much to take on alone. The private investigator Devlin's family had hired, the one mentioned in the newspaper clippings, would be the place to start.

Raven stepped out from the woods into the valley's edge, chamisa brushing against the tops of her boots. Dusk vapors rose from the hot springs, behind the tall boulders beyond. Someone was there, just emerging from the steaming water, flinging a towel around herself. The towel's edge just barely missed the kerosene lantern, perched on a boulder, which illuminated the bathing area. Raven stopped and strained her eyes to see who it was.

At that moment, Talle Fagan spotted Raven, recognized her in the faint purple moonlight, and waved in an overly enthusiastic way.

"Raven Shane Cordova!"

Talle beckoned dramatically, pointing to the ground in front of her, the gesture saying, "You come right here!"

Raven absolutely did not want to talk to Talle right now. She was too angry about Hawthorne, she didn't want to have to explain her emotional state, and she didn't want to have to come up with a story about what she was doing on the Fagan property.

Talle beckoned and called again. Raven shrugged and proceeded toward the hot springs. Talle continued smiling and waving with one hand, while pulling on her clothes with the other. As the night washed away the last pink smears of sunlight from the horizon, a bat swooped down over the water. A fat raccoon scurried across the path. Walking toward her half-dressed, former hostess, Raven put aside the disturbing memories and questions, and brought her attention back to the here and now, trying to think up a good explanation for her presence in the woods.

Chapter 10 - Talle's Salon

iona had no idea that she could access the Fagan property from Raven's door, so she walked the long way around, back through the village, to the dirt road turn-off where she had followed Hawthorne and the cook the other day.

The path seemed clear, and, as the purple and pink sky blackened over, the moon lit Fiona's way. The hacienda's lights were in the distance and, behind her; the occasional sounds of cars and slamming screen doors were comforting. However, when she reached the same place in the woods as last time she'd walked here, the village sounds stopped and the hacienda lights momentarily disappeared through the thickening trees. The branches, again, slammed into her forehead and chest, and grabbed at her coat and bag. She maneuvered her body between the trees that grew closer and closer together. Twice she almost lost her footing, catching on fallen branches. Her teeth clanked together and jarred her sinuses when her foot mis-stepped into a hole in the path.

Suddenly Fiona heard a crackling and looked sharply to her left. Someone was there - or something -a large, dark shape, leaning against the trunk of a pine about twenty yards away. Fiona's heart thudded inside her duster and she stopped moving. As if on cue, the click and flare of a cigarette lighter illuminated the face of a man as he lit a cigarette and squatted down, his back against the tree. He looked the other way, didn't seem to see her. Hawthorne?

Although less certain of her direction, she kept moving. She glanced back; he was barely visible to her now, only his red cigarette coal moving from his lips to his knee. She breathed in sharply as she realized he was dark green in color. A trick of the light?

The male figure bent down to crush out the cigarette, his long white hair falling over one shoulder. He stood and stretched, shook out his arms, picked up a backpack and began walking into the deeper part of the woods, heading away from Fiona. She breathed easier, but stood there for a moment, perplexed. It had been Liam again, she was sure of it. Wearing a dark sweater and jeans. So Liam was a smoker? She hadn't seen him smoke at the hacienda - well, of course, she'd only seen him there a couple times; so what did she know? She felt less frantic to get back; if he was just starting back there himself, he would be as late for dinner as she. Late, because he was out taking one of those walks he said he never took. Apparently the true message had been that he didn't want to take walks with *her*.

Even in the woods, he was a loner. Just as well, he was obviously one of those complicated, self-absorbed (and married) men with whom she would be smart to not get involved. Just like Professor Bregman. Despite the fact that he compelled her in a way Bregman never could. What exactly was it that drew her to Liam? Was it his outdoor sexuality? Or his indoor persona: that vaguely erotic, aloof, mixed message? Best she never solve that mystery.

As she walked on, the trees cleared out and the steam from the valley hot springs became visible. She thought back on her day's conversation with Raven. Fiona felt frustrated that they hadn't gotten to discuss whatever Raven brought her to the privacy of her cabin to discuss. The dark poet seemed to know something about the missing poet, Devlin. Who was the intruder who had destroyed their illusion of privacy? Wasn't it time these people started installing dead bolts? Fiona certainly wished she had been given a key to lock her own *casita* door when she was out. Leaving one's secret writings lying about seemed less and less a good idea. Fiona blushed at that thought, recalling her own disrespect of Talle's privacy.

As if on cue, Fiona saw Talle, backlit by a lantern, talking with someone. Parts of a heated conversation floated towards her.

"…privacy! How dare…"

"…friends, after all…"

"…protecting him! Anyway, you tell him that I want to talk to him. But to call me, on the telephone, like a civilized person. And to keep the hell out of my house!"

It was Raven, gesturing angrily, her back to Fiona. Talle finally noticed Fiona and raised her hand.

"Fiona! I was *hoping* to see you before dinner. Have you met…"

Reluctantly Fiona approached the two women. Talle pulled Fiona in close to her side, as if they were the dearest of friends, and held her firmly by the elbow.

"Raven Shane Cordova. Your predecessor. Raven was last year's winner. Raven, this is our current prize winner, Fiona Kelly."

Fiona blushed and smiled, expecting Raven to do the same, about to laugh and correct Talle's misunderstanding. But, to her astonishment, Raven kept her face set in cool anger and reached out to shake Fiona's hand.

"Glad to meet you. Congratulations."

Without hesitation, Raven looked back at Talle.

"Anyway, I'm sorry to bother you, but…please give him the message."

"Of course I will. But I do think you're mistaken… Please come visit, Raven. It would do Liam so much good to see you. He asks about you, he worries."

Raven nodded, her face grim, turned and walked briskly back toward the woods. Talle bent down and turned off the lantern. She gathered her towel and the ubiquitous velvet journal; still gripping Fiona's elbow, as if she feared the young poet would bolt. Which was exactly what Fiona wanted to do, to bolt after Raven, to ask her "Why the hell didn't you acknowledge me?" What was this? Her new-found friend walking away, coldly, as if they'd never met? Her hostess, with whom she held a distinct and mutual mistrust, clutching her near like a long-lost daughter? Dutifully, and filled with confusion, Fiona accompanied Talle along the path toward the hacienda. This side of the hot springs, the path was lined with hand-set river rocks and small foot lights every few feet. Fiona looked back and, to her relief, saw Raven's white shirt against the trees – the dark poet was standing at the edge of the woods, watching their departure. Fiona didn't dare wave, but the fact that Raven had waited and watched seemed some kind of signal. Raven had a reason for pretending not to have met her today.

"Raven is a strange one. But a very talented poet. Have you read her work?" Talle was babbling, breathlessly, her hand on Fiona's elbow causing them to crowd two-by-two along a path meant for single file. Fiona kept in mind today's lesson about unlocked doors, recalling the two books of Raven's, sitting in plain view on the table in her *casita*.

"Actually, I bought a couple of her books the other day."

"Oh? Then you've made your way to our bookstore, and met Silver?"

"Yes, she was helpful. She said I'm giving a poetry reading there - which surprised me."

Fiona couldn't pass up the opportunity to chide her hostess.

"Didn't I tell you about that? Oh, surely I did. We'll present your award that night; the whole village will be there. And the Los Alamos crowd usually comes, too. They are starved for culture, up there with all those bombs, poor dears."

Fiona stifled a laugh. Cooks, physicists and cowboys! Fiona was used to urban audiences: bespectacled, crew-neck-sweatered literature students, long-haired musicians from Charles Village, professors and their dutiful spouses, Fells Point poets who felt obligated to support a fellow poet. This must be part of her "adventure in the desert" about which Professor Bregman had forewarned.

"I'm sure I'll be honored."

"There you go again. Listen, Fiona, I feel I have neglected you terribly. Liam's not been well, he's still recovering from pneumonia, you see…"

Fiona flashed on Liam's cigarette. Did Talle know he smoked? And after pneumonia?

"…between caring for him and - well, I've hardly had a moment to myself. Would you join me tomorrow for a picnic? There's so much of the property I want to show you."

Talle proposed it in a tone of gaiety as she and Fiona passed through the woods onto the hacienda grounds. Fiona wanted to say no, she needed a day alone, to think, read and write. She looked at her *casita* with longing, as they entered the courtyard together. But this was a first overture from her hostess. Something needed mending between them, and it might be a good opportunity to ask Talle about Aisling Devlin. Fiona accepted the invitation.

"Let's just go on into the dining room," said Talle, gripping Fiona's arm harder than ever, guiding her toward the mansion. "They'll have to put up with our blue jeans tonight!"

"Let me at least drop off my bag," Fiona insisted. The older woman shrugged and let go of Fiona's elbow, following her through the *casita* door. She sat on the sofa folding her towel as Fiona put down her bag and removed her duster. In the bathroom, Fiona washed her hands and splashed cold water on her face.

"I think you'll enjoy this dinner, it's *tres* Americana," Talle said brightly as Fiona came back into the room. Fiona took a moment to unpack her books and notebook from her bag and place them in orderly fashion on the table. A gesture toward getting some writing – or at least reading – accomplished later.

So it was that Fiona and Talle entered the dining room, arm in arm in denim and sweaters. Liam looked up from his plate with a vaguely startled expression.

"My dear, we were just about to give up on you. Where have you been?" he asked in soft, cultured, husbandly tones, standing when the women entered.

Talle guided Fiona to the head of the thirty-foot table, then relaxed her grip, indicating that she should sit at Liam's left and herself at his right, enabling the two women to face each other across the table. Liam helped his wife with her chair and waited until the women were seated before sitting back down himself. Hawthorne's plate was already half-empty. Fiona watched him as the cook brought to her what appeared to be a very simple meal, yet elegantly arranged on an oversized, sage-colored stoneware plate: rare roast beef sliced as thin as crepes, mashed potatoes and green beans. As the cook reached over Fiona's shoulder to set down the plate, Fiona wondered, did Hawthorne look like someone who had run through the woods from Raven's village cabin to make dinner on time, clutching a pilfered poem? He did seem preoccupied, but, then, when did he not?

Liam had freshened up. He was no longer in sweater and jeans from his cigarette break in the woods, but had taken extra care in his dress, wearing a loose-fitting, blue-black silk shirt and vintage slacks of the same color, cinched with a black leather belt. The buckle was a well-polished bar of silver knotwork. His hair was neatly combed back into a silver knotwork clasp. For an anti-social mountain man, he "looked his Sunday best" as her dad would say.

Fiona was distracted from these observations by a wonderful mouthful of potatoes, permeated with strong garlic and sharp Romano cheese.

"Hawthorne, don't rush off after dinner, please, stay and visit with us," Talle asked, nudging him with her elbow. "I ran into a friend of yours tonight. I have a message for you."

"He might prefer to get back to his work, my dear, " Liam gently admonished his wife.

Fiona listened as she forked two green beans and deposited them delicately into her mouth. Garden fresh, honey, mustard, balsamic vinegar, toasted sesame seeds. Incredible.

"No! I miss his company in the reading room. Don't you miss it? Remember the good old days, when we all would sit and drink those bitter brandies you like, and you two would smoke those horrible cigars..."

Cigars! So Liam *did* smoke, thought Fiona, chewing a rich and tender mouthful of roast beef while she buttered her hard roll. She stopped in the middle of the act, stared at the slab of yellow she had piled on the bread. Butter? She hadn't used butter in over a year! She had to get herself back in control. She put down the knife and roll, and sipped her wine. Tried not to look at the food. Desires and addictions certainly had their own momentum. Here was Liam, barely recovered from pneumonia, *smoking*.

"...and talk about art and philosophy? That's why we bring the poets here! We've been neglecting Fiona, Hawthorne, *neglecting* her, I say...Oh my, Fiona, aren't you feeling well? You haven't touched a bite!"

"Talle, really!" Liam murmured.

Fiona sipped her wine, trying to look weary, hoping the matter was settled. Talle frowned, cutting her meat. Hawthorne swallowed, staring at his plate, then looked up, directly at Fiona. He actually smiled, exuding warmth, staring her boldly and directly in the eyes.

"It's true. We have neglected her. I'll stay."

Down again went his blond head - had he, too, combed his hair? Fiona again felt that sense of confusion. She finished her wine and poured a second glass. Roles were shifting, before she could even figure out what hers was supposed to be.

"If you're in the middle of work, please don't let me interrupt," she murmured to him.

"No, I need a break from it."

Again he smiled, straight at her. His voice was different tonight. Not so gruff. Real words instead of his usual silence and grunts. Something about his eyes changed, briefly, a light flickered on. Then off again, back to his plate.

"Armagnac and cigars it will be, then!" To Fiona's surprise, Liam actually bellowed. "And a game of chess, dare I hope?"

Fiona didn't know whether to mention their agreement about the Green Man dreams in front of the others, but before she could respond, Liam continued.

"Have you got a move for me?"

Fiona looked at Liam; he was cutting his roast beef meticulously, but watching her, waiting for her reply. Eagerly, like a young boy. Apparently his walk had done him good, there was even color in his cheeks. He was acting downright boisterous.

"I'm sorry, not yet."

Who had time for dreams, with the lack of sleep and strange goings-on?

"We'll meet nevertheless, we'll discuss it," Liam nodded to her, chewing on a piece of beef. "After the reading room, of course," he nodded to Talle, who had visibly bristled. Liam winked at Fiona. She blushed and earnestly studied the contours of the wine glass in her hand.

"Chess jargon, my dear," he answered his wife's unasked question.

Fiona concentrated on finishing her second and third glasses of wine.

The plates were carried away by the new cook, a grey-haired woman with an expression of infinite patience - or apathy - whom Talle introduced as Mindy. Apparently Dolores had quit yesterday morning, announcing suddenly that she had to go back home to El Paso to care for her ailing mother. As Talle explained this to everyone at the table, Hawthorne showed no reaction, just continued eating.

Four chairs were pushed back and, obediently, three adult children followed Talle to the reading room. Apparently this was a familiar ritual: while Liam opened the humidor to select the cigars, Hawthorne stepped to the corner bar, a masculine oak sideboard carved with an elaborate vine-&-grape motif which twined up into the lips of yet another Green Man's face. This one bore the laughing features of the bacchanalian family. The sculptor/gardener was as focused as a geisha, warming four large, crystal, amber-filled snifters of Armagnac over a Sterno flame, then setting them on a silver tray for presentation.

Despite the tension in the room - coming off of Talle, mostly, and Hawthorne, some - Fiona welcomed the lulling, *pinon* scent of the corner *kiva* flame, the large, irregular patchwork of sheepskin, seemingly thrown casually across the gleaming brick floor, and the warm fragrance of amber, adult alcohol. Despite her usual disgust at smoking, the cigars smelled agreeably sweet. Liam offered one to her with a questioning look, and she accepted it, just to hold it and smell it. She'd give it to Raven when she saw her next, the cowgirl poet would appreciate it.

Fiona wondered when that would be, and how Raven would explain her odd, unfriendly behavior at the hot springs earlier. Perhaps Talle invited that same dishonesty from Raven that, for still inexplicable reasons, she invited in Fiona?

But Fiona didn't want to delve into the complexities of other people's relationships tonight. It had been a long day, she had absorbed about all the gossipy information she could handle for now, and the dinner wine had done its work. She huddled into herself at one corner of the long, white sofa, appreciating the luxurious sounds and sensations of its leather. Soft music was playing in the background. The Fagans' taste was eclectic: Peter Gabriel, Eric Sati, Gypsy Kings, Edith Piaf. Tonight Fiona recognized the culturally-diverse Ottmar Liebert, an appropriate choice to compliment the hacienda's eclectic ambiance.

Again, Fiona took in the elegance of this room of books and stunning artifacts. At night, it had an entirely different quality than it had during the intense afternoon sunlight of her arrival. Less than a week ago? It seemed longer. The hacienda warped one's sense of time, condensing the sense of a history that was more significant than the span of one small individual's single day. Despite its casual/sophisticated decor - a complex display of European, Celtic and Southwestern icons - the room exuded an arrogant disdain for the world outside its walls. Fiona noted that there were no televisions evident in the house. As if the external business of the planet itself was trivial, compared to the history encrusted within the mud walls of this castle.

Feeling fuzzy from the dinner wine, Fiona watched Liam. In the dark green leather recliner that was obviously his personal chair, the aging poet closed his eyes and blew intricate smoke rings. Smiling softly, he seemed oblivious of his companions, apparently listening carefully to Liebert. He was in his self-created element, bolstered on one side by the book shelves - that leather-bound wall of his own history, spelled out in his own hand-written stanzas - and on the other by the double-paned wall of glass that kept out the wild night. Large bronze sculptures of Apollo and Zeus were positioned across the room, as if guardians to an enormous, and apparently quite old, painting of the Virgin Mary.

Softening the hard edges to the room were Talle's vivid dried arrangements of bristling, long yellow stalks of desert vegetation, and dark red water reeds, mingled with massive bunches of sage and eucalyptus, all potted in large, copper kettles. Liam seemed to entirely relax and expand into this verdant environment that was worthy of his spirit. Whatever his physical ailments, tonight there was a vibrancy about him. There had been buoyancy in his step when he handed out the cigars.

In high contrast to Liam's, Fiona noted that Talle's energy was restless in this room. Impatiently, Talle had turned down the brandy snifter offered by Hawthorne and, while he handed the others around, she went to the bar to make herself an over-sized martini, poured into a large soda glass with six extra-large stuffed olives, which sank to the bottom. She moved around the room, surveying her domain, sipping her drink and munching on the olives, which she harpooned with a long swizzle stick. She stood in front of the shelves, which held Liam's forty-two identical black leather volumes, scanning them as if there were titles on the bindings, as if she could actually discern one from the other. Fiona was certain that, if one of them was missing, Talle would be able to tell.

"Hawthorne," Talle spoke loudly from her position in front of the books, her back to the room. "I ran into a friend of yours today."

"So you said," Hawthorne quipped amicably, seating himself on the sofa and placing his brandy snifter on the blue-tiled table. While he clipped his cigar, Fiona stared at the blue tiles, remembering how she had read Talle's journal here.

Talle turned, drinking her martini as if it were water, and fixed her eyes on Hawthorne.

"It was Raven."

Hawthorne put his cigar in his mouth and lit it, closed his eyes and settled back into the white leather. He apparently had no response. At the mention of Raven's name, Liam's eyes shot open. He stared at nothing, and then closed them again. Fiona watched Hawthorne, fascinated. How would he react to the accusation that he'd been snooping in Raven's cabin?

"She thought you had come calling when she was out."

"Fine cigar, Liam," he said smoothly.

"Saint Luis Reys. Churchill," Liam's contented smile was waning. "I thought Raven had moved on."

"She was gone for a while," Talle enjoyed her position as news-bearer. "Traveling alone. Poor dear, she so much needs a family."

"We tried to provide that, she was not interested," Liam answered, sipping his brandy.

"I wasn't referring to surrogate incest."

That poem about Liam, what Raven said about the juice of the prickly pear - that she'd not been sure it was worth pulling out all the spines to get at its potent medicine. Fiona watched Liam's reaction sharply. He grimaced slightly, his eyes still closed.

"Anyway, Hawthorne, Raven wants you to call her."

Hawthorne sipped at his brandy.

"She said that?"

"Whatever disagreement you two had - aside from whatever mess my husband, the great mentor, made of things with her - *you* are the one depriving us of her company. You need to make amends."

Talle took another long drink from her martini and moved across the room, standing in front of the painting of Mary.

"Did I tell you about this one, Fiona?" she asked.

"Uh, no, I don't think so," Fiona responded, but kept an eye on Hawthorne. He didn't appear at all guilty.

"This came with the house, it was painted hundreds of years ago by a Mexican artist - It's *'Nuestra Senora De Soledad',* Our Lady of Solitude. Did I tell you about the former owner of this house?"

"Only that you inherited all this."

"She's always quick to point that out," Liam added. "My dear wife thinks it makes it less embarrassing that I married her for her money, that she would stoop to 'keeping' a man. It's not her fault if she *inherited* it, rather than *earned* it and then was foolish enough to squander it on an old gigolo."

"He's right, Fiona. I only explain so that *he* won't have to feel guilty for exploiting *me*."

Fiona watched their faces, uncertain whether to laugh or keep silent. Liam opened his eyes and winked at Fiona, a gesture Talle couldn't see from where she stood. But, no doubt, could feel, even with her back to the group.

"I didn't exactly inherit the hacienda. I inherited the money, and used it to buy the place. Lock, stock and artwork. A very old Spanish Catholic family owned it. The last descendent - a young man who'd gone to Hollywood to make his fortune - had massive debts and no appreciation for his family history, nor his cultural heritage. He put everything up for sale after his mother died, was going to auction off the antiques and art back in New York City. Fortunately I stepped in before that happened. I - we - gave a lot of the old artwork to the local Spanish community, to the church, donated some to local museums, some to friends of the old couple, some back to the original artists. Then began to collect our own things. We have more of an affinity for the old Euro and Celtic pieces. But I - we - felt the original guardians of the hacienda should have their place, so we kept many of the *bultos* and *retablos.*"

"So it all fell into good hands, then," Fiona smiled.

"Too bad Talle's not as concerned to preserve *our* history as she is to preserve that of some old family she never met," Liam grunted, his good humor wearing thin.

"Meaning?" Talle asked, standing behind him and glaring at the back of his head.

"You know what I mean."

"You're referring to our marriage?"

"No, our marriage is fine. Always has been, always will be. We weather the storms, that's what we do best."

"Oh really?" Talle spoke into her martini glass again.

"He's talking about the Bardic School," Hawthorne explained, as if it were obvious.

"I know what he's talking about, and it's a subject we agreed not to discuss," Talle spoke directly to Hawthorne. Fiona had the curious impression that the "we" referred to the young sculptor and herself, not Liam and herself. Hawthorne stared at her, his look unreadable. Talle met his look with a sudden harsh mask, all traces of civility falling away. The subtext, whatever it was, was quite familiar to them, and a source of great discomfort.

"The Liam Fagan Bardic School for Emerging Poets was what we originally called the residency program," Liam spoke to Fiona, leaning forward in his recliner, elbows on his knees. "You know about the Bardic Schools of Ireland? Also referred to as 'the dark schools'?"

"From my Irish literature courses, yes. I stumbled upon a fourteenth century one in County Galway. All that's left is a bit of a ruined castle and a gatehouse covered with vines, filled with broken bits of slate. Now the grounds are a cow pasture. I fed them treacle bread over a stone wall."

"It's sad how they are all to ruin. That was a fine tradition. I tried to keep it going here in our small, New Mexican bastion of Celtic culture. We had a Bardic Cabin, an old log one back there along the river. The poets had to stay there overnight without candles at least once during their residency, and compose without paper and pen..."

"And they had to dress in twenty layers and bring Arctic sleeping bags with them!" Talle rolled her eyes and swigged her drink. "He was such a stickler for 'the purity of the classical form' that he didn't even want to give them fire wood, for fear the flames might illuminate the cabin! But, of course, I insisted they have fires."

"Yes, my dear, ever careful of the comfort of your guests," Liam nodded and lifted his glass toward her.

"So why did you discontinue the school?" Fiona smiled.

Liam sat back, his look of disgust making him look every one of his fifty-seven years.

"Talle discovered the foundation was deteriorating. The roof was caving in. The walls were dry rot. Bats in the attic, snakes in the fireplace, that sort of thing. She declared it a danger zone, posted warnings, shut it down."

"I didn't, the village did."

"Yes, but you dragged them out here on our private property and showed them where to look! I said, let's at least keep the name, we can refurbish the cabin, or build a new one, hell, we can afford to do that. But she wouldn't have it. Said it was too archaic of a concept, we needed to keep up with the times, 'residency prize' was the right jargon; it would look better in the *Bards & Writers* ads. Damned shame, the end of the Bardic School. At least then we had something *unique.*"

"Oh, believe me, dear, the Fagan residency is still unique."

"When was it, the change?" asked Fiona.

"Oh, let's see…"

"1977," Talle interrupted. "We always fight about this, but I checked, it was 1977."

"The year of Cynthia O'Rourke? I don't think so. It was the year of Brenda Rayne, I remember distinctly."

"It had nothing to do with Brenda Rayne."

"I didn't say it 'had anything to do with Brenda Rayne', it's just that I recall it was that same year. Or wasn't it 1981? Or, rather, wasn't it actually the same year as…"

"The history is so important to Liam," Talle interrupted quickly, smiling at Fiona. But her smile was thin. "Hawthorne, here, though, is very much like the disloyal Spanish descendant who wanted to auction all this off to the New Yorkers. He has no regard for history, for keeping bridges in repair."

Hawthorne laughed.

"Because I won't go begging to an old lover?"

"Your stupid, *stupid* pride!"

Talle spat the words out vehemently. Liam turned in his seat.

"Now dear, if the boy doesn't want to see her, that's really his business…"

"It's not just his business. You have no concept, Liam, of what it takes to run this place, to keep peace with the community. You live in your tower up there, writing your own myopic version of reality, you are completely disengaged from all matters of life and death."

"Aren't you being a little melodramatic? We're not talking life and death here."

"*OH YES WE ARE*! I *KNOW*! And there are two things a person should *never* know, Liam Fagan. To be bound to someone you loath, and to long for someone to whom you are bound! Oh, you are so...so...*SPOILED!*"

To Fiona's astonishment, Talle's face turned beet red and she began to cry, throwing her martini glass to the floor where it shattered. Shards flew to every corner of the room. Hawthorne put out his half-smoked cigar in the large brass ashtray on the coffee table, set down his brandy and stood.

"She went too fast with a strong drink, I think," he murmured softly to Fiona, out of earshot of the older couple. He had a surprisingly gentle and embarrassed look on his face, as if he was responsible. "Please forgive her, there is some history here, some grieving..."

Hawthorne moved swiftly to Talle's side while Fiona and Liam rose, looking about for something to clean up the mess. Fiona shook off her alcohol-induced dizziness and picked up the larger chunks of glass while Liam left the room, calling out to the new cook. He returned with a dish-rag, Mindy following quickly behind, carrying a broom and dustpan. Fiona had the sensation that she was witnessing an often-rehearsed play, for which the cook and her props of rag, broom, and dustpan had been waiting, on cue, in the wings. Liam beckoned to Fiona with a tilt of his head as he carried the martini-soaked dishrag to the kitchen.

Hawthorne had his arm around Talle, who was sobbing softly and murmuring, "He just doesn't understand, he just doesn't appreciate..."

Fiona ran to keep up with Liam, whose long legs carried him swiftly down the hall.

"Please forgive all this, it is so embarrassing," he called back over his shoulder. She followed him through the swing doors into the kitchen. He opened a trashcan and handed her the lid while he shook out the glass pieces onto coffee grounds, banana skins and onion peels.

"You needn't apologize. That was a pretty tall martini."

"She's used to that. She has one of those every night. No, there's more than that going on. Frankly, I had second thoughts about running the competition this year, Fiona. Don't take this wrong, I am very..."

Liam paused, looking into Fiona's eyes with a grave expression.

"...*very* pleased that you have joined us this year. Do *not* misunderstand."

"Yes, ok," Fiona felt flustered at the sincerity of his gaze. That rush was beginning again, like the one the other night in the chess room. Completely inappropriate, she knew, this was a family crisis, her hostess, his wife was in great distress, they needed to get back to the library room and help assuage whatever it was that needed assuaging. But that rush was undeniable, and it moved with alarming swiftness from her throat to down between her legs.

Liam seemed unaware of his effect on her. He leaned again to his task, picking out tiny slivers of glass from the dishrag. He held it as if it were the most delicate living thing, as if the glass shards hurt the fabric. She watched in fascination, half expecting the dishrag to start bleeding.

"What I mean to say is, my wife has not been herself for some time."

"I think running the household, the competition, all of that is really more than she can handle, with the menopause," he continued, carrying the dishrag to the sink.

"And yet she insists, it's like a religion for her, this poetry prize. It's always been her idea. I just want to be left alone and to write. But...supposedly I do some good, for the poets."

"Raven says everyone's poetry is stronger after working with you."

Liam folded the dishrag, saying nothing. Mindy quietly returned to work. Talle's voice boomed suddenly, from the doorway.

"Raven? You spoke to Raven? But I just introduced you two, only this evening!"

Fiona froze, afraid to face Talle. But she had to, Liam came to her rescue, moving to his wife. Fiona turned to see Hawthorne lingering behind Talle in the doorway. His face had lost the empathy and concern of moments before, and was haggard and pale with despair. Fiona realized for the first time that, for a young man, his demeanor was that of one much older. Lines cut through his narrow cheekbones, down the sides of his mouth, which was set in a permanent frown. His brow was a spider web of worry lines and, around his temples, grey hairs mingled with the blond. Yet, he could not be older than thirty-five.

"You misunderstood, dear wife."

Fiona exhaled the breath she had been holding, turned her gaze on Talle, and started to speak. But Talle was shaking her head, waving her arms as if irritated with the subject.

"You two go on and play your chess game," she said, her words slurring. "I'm going to bed. Sorry about the mess."

Hawthorne stepped forward again.

"I'll take her upstairs," he told Liam. Liam held the kitchen door open, watching the younger man escort his wife.

"So what is this about you meeting and not meeting Raven?"

" I read her books and then arranged to meet her."

"To find out more about your mysterious captors?"

"Captors?"

"Forgive my off-base humor. Go on."

"It's not off-base. Or, if it is, then I am. I enjoy your humor, Liam."

She heard herself say the words; she heard the infusion of warmth in her tone. Where did this come from? But it was true, what she felt in his company. Whether or not she should.

"Well, I thank you. At least, then, I may be safe from unintentionally shocking you?"

"But not safe from doing so intentionally."

Liam looked at her in surprise, saw that she was teasing, and laughed. Then he looked over her shoulder, nodding to Mindy who was finishing up at the kitchen sink.

"Thank you for your help, Mindy. I apologize for – all this."

Mindy smiled and shrugged. Liam and Fiona walked out into the hallway.

"So, about Raven?" he prodded.

"Well, we met today for breakfast and had a wonderful time. I really like her. Later on, I ran into her with Talle and Raven pretended we'd not met."

"Ah." Liam nodded as the two moved down the hall of icons, toward the chess room. "Yes, people do behave strangely around Talle, they hide things from her. They resist her need to know everything, to control everyone. It's the dark side of her talent. The talent that allowed her to purchase this place, to fill it with beauty as she does. To keep me contented. That is, after all, her hardest task. I am very difficult."

Just as Fiona felt a sense of guilty disappointment that the subject was veering toward a husband's loyalty to a wife, Liam stopped so suddenly that she, following closely at his elbow, stumbled. He turned quickly and grabbed the moment, taking her by the shoulders and stopping her fall, then pulled her toward him and took her mouth into his. The kiss became wonderfully confounded with the illicit taste of him, of beef, brandy and cigar. She felt hot with confusion, yet could only respond, and return his kiss with moaning hunger, as if she had forgone dinner for this, instead. He wrapped his arms around her thoroughly and pulled her against the length of his body. She panicked, what if Talle or Hawthorne returned? She tried to pull away, but he kissed her harder. His hands did not move over her body, but held her in place. Finally the kiss ended, and he held her near, his hand wrapped around her head, pressing it into his shoulder as her breathing returned to normal. Their hearts thundered through wool and silk. Rationality tried to return to Fiona, but she let the scents from his silk-shirted shoulder intoxicate her. *Surrogate incest.* The phrase suddenly reared itself in her consciousness. *Black velour for chess*, Professor Bregman's warning. At the thought of Bregman, Fiona pulled away. No, not that again, she would not let things go there again.

Sounds from upstairs - Talle's voice, crying again, shouting, Hawthorne's voice soothing, comforting. Fiona and Liam stared at each other, listening. Fiona was concerned, what was going on up there? But, to Liam, it was apparently a too-familiar scenario, and the significance was only that his wife was safely upstairs, and he could continue to hold Fiona. He pulled her to him again, and continued his kiss, with renewed urgency.

"Liam, sir," Hawthorne's voice thundered from the upstairs balcony. Fiona pulled away in shock. Hawthorne appeared at the railing. "She's insisting on taking her sleeping pills but...with the martini, I'm afraid..."

Liam rushed upstairs immediately. Fiona's knees were rubbery and she found her way into the chess library, collapsing in the window seat. She needed to get out of here, get out of this situation, before he returned. She didn't even know if she was that attracted to him, and yet she responded to him as if she were, urgently so. The wine, the brandy, the cigar smoke, not eating - these had all clouded her faculties; Fiona felt exhausted, heavy. She closed her eyes for a moment. Just a moment, then she would get up and go to her *casita*.

While kissing her, Liam walked Fiona backwards until he had her pressed against a glass doorway. He opened the door and turned her to face outside, gently pushing her forward by her shoulders. He walked her out into the night, through the courtyard, into the woods where they would be hidden from all eyes. Except the eyes of the Green Man.

In the dark woods, her heart pounded mercilessly as he kept his hands on her, now sliding up and down her spine. She moaned, feeling no control whatsoever. She looked into his eyes. He WAS the Green Man. Vines protruded from the corners of his mouth, wrapping around his neck and head, the leaves on his brow shimmered, the sound of crackling twigs and rustling greenery, the strong earth smell of green enveloped her. The

Green Man pushed her against a tree trunk. He was ancient and eternally young at the same time...

"Fiona. Fiona," Liam was shaking her. Fiona's eyes opened and she was back in the chess library, staring into Liam's eyes. Over his shoulder, the Green Man mask stared at Fiona, stern yet compassionate. "Talle's ok, she's sleeping now."

Fiona pushed herself up off the window seat cushions.

"Liam, we shouldn't."

"I know, I know," Liam bowed his head, remorseful. "We are drawn to each other, but..."

Was she drawn to him? *Was* it really so hard to resist him? Right now she wanted *out* of this evening's situation, to be back in her room, to throw up, brush her teeth, do whatever it took to shake off this physical malaise. Liam took her by the elbow and walked her down the hall of *santos* to the large wooden door.

"Talle and Hawthorne have a relationship of sorts," Liam explained. "It's been going on for several years. I try to look the other way, if it's what she requires. God knows, I understand the need to have the beautiful young around oneself."

Hawthorne and Talle? Was he mad? She realized that, in a form of twisted emotional logic, Liam offered this information by way of explaining his own illicit behavior.

"Are you sure?"

Liam nodded. "I don't entirely understand it, but it's been going on for a very long time. And I, well, I have not always been faithful myself. Perhaps it's her way of keeping things balanced. She is a very proud woman, you know."

Liam and Fiona had reached the door and were staring out into the courtyard.

"Well, we have shown you more tonight than you ever wanted to know of us. I apologize and hope you can forget it all. And I am truly waiting for your Green Man to give you a move."

Fiona nodded.

"Fiona, you are so, so beautiful to me."

Fiona wished he would stop talking. She didn't want to have to respond, to say it was nice or it wasn't or why did we do it or why can't we do it again. Her Green Man dream was still wrapped around her. Had he given her any moves? No chess moves.

Nevertheless, Liam waited for her to respond.

"We'll play chess," she said, lamely.

Liam waited for her to say more. Then smiled sadly and nodded. He understood he'd crossed a line. He moved back inside the shadows and closed the door to the fortress.

Fiona stood in the night, looking toward the row of *casitas*. The crisp air held the keen scents of juniper and pine. Hawthorne's light was on. At some point, he'd returned to his rooms. It was as if a storm had rushed through the place, disturbing and shattering everything. Displaced, that's how she felt. Perplexed at the spell this place seemed to cast, where her waking and dream realities were blending and blurring around the edges. She didn't belong here, was all she could think. Yet now she was so immersed in questions, her former instinct to pack and leave was completely gone. As she moved across the courtyard, she shook out her shoulders, trying to rid herself of the evening.

The relief at being alone, once she stepped inside her *casita* and slid the cast-iron bolt across the door, was short-lived. A lamp was lit, and she knew she'd not left one on. Something was different about the books on her table. And there were cigarette fumes, a tea cup stained with ashes, a stubbed-out brown cigarette. One of Raven's books was not as she had left it, propped with the others against the lamp base. The book that Raven had signed - the latest one, *The Wounded Watcher* - lay in the center of the table, with something tucked into it. Fiona opened the book and found a page from her own notepaper. On it was scrawled:

"F: Hot springs. After midnight. R."

Next to the book was a flashlight. She smirked. Raven probably figured she was such a city girl, she'd never find her way, even on a moonlit night, even with Talle's footlights along the path.

Although Fiona was exhausted and still shaky from her evening with the Fagans, she was greatly cheered at Raven's note. Now she would find out why Raven had pretended not to know her earlier, and could ask the growing list of questions she had about this place, her hosts, and Aisling Devlin. She checked to see what poem was on the page where the note had been tucked. As a poet, she knew enough to not take the note's position as coincidence.

He kept them there/His green web whispered along their spines...

Fiona looked at the kitchen clock. Ten thirty. The idea of tramping through the woods this late was a bit unnerving, but Raven apparently did these things all the time. She decided to go now, to test her courage and have some time alone in the hot springs. Fiona grabbed a towel, an extra sweater and the flashlight, made sure the cigar Liam had given her was tucked in her jeans pocket, put on her duster and opened the door to leave.

As she turned to close it behind her, she saw that Talle had left her towel and the velvet journal on the sofa when they stopped by before dinner. Another test. She'd deal with the book later. No doubt Talle was very much asleep at this point and wouldn't miss it until morning. Fiona crept past Hawthorne's cottage and along the path leading into the woods. She played the flashlight ahead of her, following the path of the footlights down to the water.

Chapter 11 - Hot Springs

The mountain night air was chilly and the bubbly hot water only came up to Fiona's breasts unless she crouched. Closing her eyes, she slowly bobbed up and down, alternating the sensation of wet chill on her shoulders with up-to-her-ears submersion in the natural cauldron. She found an underwater stone ledge inside the rim of the pool to sit on. Directly below the ledge was a hole deep enough to dangle her feet into invisible watery space. Leaning her head back against the earth, she stared up at the stars that were beyond counting. She had folded her clothes neatly on the dry stone ledge at the other end of the pool, next to the ever-present kerosene lantern. Fiona had lit the wick with matches she found wrapped in plastic inside a soapstone box under the ledge. Another of Talle's considerate and careful touches. The lantern's soft glow dimmed and radiated hypnotically, keeping time with the wind, which moved through the surrounding trees, stirring the leaves and needles, pushing vegetation across the ground. Fiona closed her eyes and the scattering, rustling sounds continued, changing from a random cadence to one specific in its rhythm. What was that rhythm? It seemed familiar.

Like the rustling of a dress – a sound like a woman's long skirts as she lifted them to sit. Then there was silence, and a scent filled the air near the pool. That of mushrooms and spores and thick, shiny plant leaves coated with dust. Not the sweet perfume of flowers. The dark musk of insistent, green vegetation. Fiona heard a soft laugh, and opened her eyes.

There he sat, having trailed the vines and debris of the floor of the forest – tonight it seemed more a primordial, European forest than a desert mountain woods – and gathered it like a cape, draped across his lap. Fiona let her gaze follow the greenery back into the woods from where he had emerged. It was as if he was a spider and the green threads of the woods were his web, attached to his body. He laughed again, leaned back on his elbows, and also watched the sky (as had the nude Liam that day on the rocks).

Fiona was amazed at how calm she felt with this fantastic, mysterious creature sitting so close by.

"Do you have any more moves for me?" she asked, making circles on the water's surface with her hands.

The Green Man stopped laughing, but kept his gaze on the sky. There was a long silence while he pondered his response.

"B5 knight to 4d," he finally said.

His voice was deep and warm. Fiona closed her eyes to visualize the chessboard and concentrated, memorizing the move he'd given her. She frowned. What piece was on 4d? Would her knight take a pawn there? She couldn't recall it. Then she smiled. The move would at least put Liam's queen in check. A quick rustling movement broke her concentration and she opened her eyes. But it was too late to see anything. The Green Man had moved swiftly behind her on the bank and covered her eyes with his tendril-wrapped fingers, so fast it made her gasp and flail in the water. She regained her balance by clutching at the large stones at the water's edge. Leaves and twigs pressed into her cheeks and scratched against her forehead and eyelids, a not entirely pleasant sensation. But his hands were very warm.

"What—?"

"Shhhhhhhhhhhh," he whispered into her ear, his breath hot and smelling of something like parsley, a touch of rosemary. "Something you must see. Open your eyes."

Fiona obeyed, although she couldn't open them entirely, with his vegetation fingers pressing against her lids. He began to hum, a low animal sound like a purr from deep in his throat. Images began to come through, whether through her eyes or imagination, she wasn't certain. It seemed she was dreaming, yet awake.

"What do you see?" the Green Man whispered, then continued to purr.

Fiona squinted and the vision was clearer. Vegetation, a mound of it, an impression in the center, a woman's body, a naked woman. What was she doing? Arching her back, aroused. Her wrists and ankles were wrapped in green straps or vines, she was secured into the vegetation. What did this remind her of? Ah, the nest images in Liam's and Raven's poems! Was this it, "the Green Man nest" of which they had written? She strained to see the face, whose face was it? But it wasn't visible, it seemed covered with – she peered closer. A mask. A mask of leaves and vines, with openings for the eyes and mouth. Fiona couldn't tell where the woman's features began and the mask left off. Vines seemed to protrude from her mouth and wrap around her cheekbones and eyelids, spreading back like hair against her earlobes and throat. Or was the woman chewing, swallowing the vines?

"What do you see?" the Green Man repeated.

"A woman, a nest, a mask," Fiona found it hard to speak, the words seemed like dry pebbles working their way up her throat to spit themselves out from between her teeth.

"How does she feel?" he whispered. Again, the herb scent of his breath, warm in her ear in the cold night air, his purr vibrating against her neck.

Fiona strained again, trying to see the woman's eyes behind the mask. It was hard to tell...did they gleam with pleasure or terror? Pain or rapture?

Something shifted. Fiona began to feel that the Green Man held her down, beyond just pressing his hands against her eyes. She suddenly felt her naked skin exposed to the air - as if she was no longer floating in warm water. She gasped at the sensation, then cried out, as she was crushed uncomfortably against twigs and thorns and dried leaves. She moved her arms and legs and found they were bound with something that cut into her flesh.

The Green Man's hands became a mask through which she viewed her dark and vague surroundings. She smelled damp earth, a scent oddly like turnips or parsnips. And what was that other smell? Fear began to spread through her entire body like an electric charge. She was shivering uncontrollably. She cried out but no sound would come. She felt a cold hand on her leg, moving up her thigh, cold fingers like a spider creeping...

"Fiona! Wake up! Fiona!"

Fiona heard a scream and her eyes shot open. She gasped and flailed in the water and would have slipped under, but warm hands under her armpits pulled her up.

"It's ok, you were having a dream, you're ok," a voice of empathic sanity brought her into the present and she regained her footing on the bottom of the slippery pool. She was hyperventilating and slapping at the water. The scream had been her own, she realized, as she felt the rawness in her throat.

"Take a slow, deep breath."

Fiona did as she was told and the world of the woods and stars and water began to reorient her. Raven let go of her arms, apparently assured that Fiona was now thoroughly awake.

"What happened?" Fiona whispered, staring at Raven. "When did you get here?"

"Just a few minutes ago. You were out, looked like you fell asleep there. I was taking off my boots and then, all of a sudden, you were gasping and struggling and sliding under. Guess I got here just in time. You must have been having a bad dream."

Raven hadn't had time to undress before she'd been called upon to play lifeguard. Now she returned to the shallow end of the pool and peeled off her soaked shirt and jeans, tossed them onto the bank, next to a red blanket and pack of cigarettes. In the inky night, her body was sleek and strong, muscles along her back rippled like shimmering silk in the moonlight.

As Fiona watched the poet undress, she shivered and crouched in the water up to her ears. She felt like a stick of ice melting in the bubbling water. A wind came up, sifting through the leaves all around the pool. She stared at the trees, then the stars, trying to remember what she'd been dreaming. Ah yes, the Green Man. Fiona stood up in the water, staring into the woods.

"What? What are you looking at? Are you ok?" Raven asked as she glided through the pool to Fiona's side.

"Didn't you see him? When you got here, didn't you see him - the Green Man?"

"Really!" Raven stared out into the woods. "I didn't see him. But I have, before. Several times. He's in these woods, for sure."

"Then it wasn't a dream after all," Fiona whispered, more to herself than Raven. She lowered herself back into the hot water. "Oh god, it was terrible! I was tied into this thing, made of tree limbs and vines and leaves and..."

"The nest? You've been in the nest? But I thought you said you were having nothing to do with him."

Fiona looked at Raven, puzzled.

"*You've* been in that nest, then?" Fiona whispered. "You've seen it before? The one in your poem, and Liam's - that's a *real* place?"

Now it was Raven's turn to be confounded.

"Ok, start from the beginning, " Raven demanded, gliding back to the other side of the pool to get her cigarettes. "You have or you have not been in Hawthorne's Green Man nest?" Raven clicked her butane lighter against the tip of a brown cigarette between her lips as she walked through the water back to Fiona's side. The lighter's flare momentarily illuminated Raven's face - which bore a very serious and worried look - and her large, pear-shaped breasts. The ones that were usually only half exposed by daylight.

"Hawthorne?" Fiona asked, looking and yet not looking - the way you glance to the side of a star in order to see it more clearly. As an only child with no sisters, Fiona never quite knew how to handle other women's nakedness. Or how to handle the fact that Raven's body was so beautiful - As she glided through the water, Fiona could easily understand why a man would be compelled to her. "What does this have to do with Hawthorne?"

"He made that nest, that's where he takes the impressions for the masks," Raven exhaled smoke, set the pack of cigarettes on the ground near the pool and settled back into the water near Fiona. As she did so, Fiona noticed the woman had a black tattoo of a flying raven on her hip. "So, *have* you?" her tone was as dark as the woods.

"Have I what?"

"Good grief, Fiona! Been in Hawthorne's studio, in the *nest!*"

"Hell no! I told you I don't really like him. We've hardly spoken."

Raven sucked her cigarette, giving no indication whether or not she was relieved.

"So what's this about masks?" asked Fiona.

"You know, I told you, the Green Man masks, the ones in the Fagans' house. Like the one over your bed. He uses the poets' faces as prototypes, takes a plaster mold to work from."

"Ah. So that nest, it's not really the Green Man's place, then, it's just Hawthorne's thing. It's not – magical."

"Oh, it's magical all right. Something happens when you're in there. It was the most erotic experience I'd ever had. And then it turned into something else. Sex and terror, Hawthorne's unbeatable combination. I think he is a very sick man. But…"

"Yes?"

"Oh…it just bothers me how much I enjoyed it. I mean, when I think back on it, I know I was afraid, I know

261

I shouldn't have a good memory of it, I feel guilty that I remember it as an incredible sexual experience. I can't say I wouldn't let him tie me in there again, if he wanted to. And it has nothing to do with him, with Hawthorne. I loath him, I have no desire for him anymore. I mean, I would never get into his *bed* again. But the *nest*...It's like it has a life of its own. I believe I really met the Green Man there, in the nest."

"And what happened?"

"He made love to me!" Raven's voice was impatient, as if she resented having to state the obvious to a stupid child. "Or copulated with me. Whatever!" She inhaled deeply on the cigarette, leaned back, closed her eyes and exhaled smoke to the stars.

"Who, Hawthorne?"

"No! I mean, yes, but...the Green Man took over. Then I made love with the Green Man. At least, that's how I remember it."

Raven slapped her hands onto the water's surface. "It really pisses me off, too! He changed me and it really, really *PISSES ME OFF!*"

Fiona watched Raven in the moonlight, her dark hair trailing like angry water snakes around her shoulders. Who angered her, Hawthorne or the Green Man? Fiona decided to just accept the ambiguity, and stared back into the woods. Were they sharing hallucinations? Or was the Green Man real?

"The Green Man - made me feel I was in the nest," Fiona finally said, speaking more to the woods than to Raven. "Or I dreamed it, a vision, whatever. I think he was trying to show me something. I guess that's why I was freaking out, that's what woke me up. It seemed so *real*. He began touching me, and his hand was so cold. Yet, before, when he covered my eyes, his hands were so warm."

"I've had that dream, too," Raven stubbed out her now damp cigarette against a rock.

"Really?"

"Yeah. Only...maybe it wasn't him. The cold hands, I mean. Maybe it was Hawthorne in your vision. It's a mixed experience being in the nest. It's Hawthorne, but more than Hawthorne. It's like he's invoking something or someone." Raven sighed, ran her hands through her hair to pull it back from her forehead, and moved out to the center of the pool, squatting to bring the water up to her chin. "We did it everywhere, let me tell you. We were out of control. But when we did it in the nest, that was something different than the other times. It took me over some edge. I wasn't sure I wanted to go there, I'm not sure I should have. But it's too late now. Anyway, that's why I wanted to talk to you." Raven looked at Fiona. "Thanks for coming here tonight."

Fiona shrugged and gazed into the woods again, trying to see the Green Man there. But, whether he had been real or a dream, it seemed his theatrics were over, he wasn't going to make himself visible again tonight. Then she remembered the events earlier in the evening.

"Why did you act as if we hadn't met, with Talle?"

"Because I need your help, Fiona." Raven glided back to Fiona's underwater ledge and sat, leaning her head back against the stones. "There are things I need your help to retrieve from Hawthorne's studio. It will go better for you if no one knows we've spoken. I know it's a lot to ask, but I just need you to trust me on that. For all you know, I'm Ms. Loony Tunes and you don't want to get involved. I'll understand, if that's so."

Fiona didn't know what to say, so said nothing, just watched her new friend's profile as she spoke.

Raven told Fiona everything - about her research, the trip to Lam's Nursery, her suspicions about Hawthorne's part in Devlin's disappearance, the pink invoice she hoped to find in his things, the negatives of photos he had taken of her in the nest that she needed to retrieve. And about the contents of the missing poem from yesterday afternoon, the one the intruder had taken.

"To anyone who knows about Aisling's disappearance, it should be obvious what the poem's about. But if Hawthorne has it, I think my life may be in danger."

Fiona's reaction to all this was an unexpected anger. Not at Hawthorne, but, oddly, at Raven. Before these disclosures, the personal lives of these people were already too much for her to deal with. Now she *really* felt overwhelmed. She wished Raven had not told her any of this. She began to question the poet's sanity. Believing that Hawthorne had murdered Aisling Devlin, and hidden her body somewhere on the Fagan property? That the annual trips to the Farmington plant nursery were diabolical in some way? Fiona recalled all those tequila bottles behind Raven's wood stove. Why had she looked this woman up, gotten herself involved with all this? What would this do to her standing at the Fagans'? Obviously Raven had alienated herself from them.

Fiona thought back to the conversation in the hacienda, over brandy and cigars. Talle had encouraged Hawthorne to reconcile with her. Liam had seemed distinctly upset at the mention of Raven, as if she had hurt him somehow. "*Surrogate incest,*" Talle had said. Fiona truly could not say they had expressed anything malevolent toward Raven, only a kind of sadness and perplexity. They genuinely seemed to miss her. Although there was something more - some nonverbal exchanges between Talle and Hawthorne. However, that might be explained by Liam's news that those two had been, or were still, lovers. Which Fiona still didn't believe.

Her reaction to Raven's story was, in fact, not different from her reaction to Liam's story about Talle and Hawthorne - she thought these people were all delusional!

But, she wondered, how many delusional people did one expect to encounter in one day, in one town, at one hacienda? Maybe she needed to open her mind a bit, she thought, looking again to the incredible stars. Perhaps Liam had been right after all; presumably, he knew more about his wife than anyone. As for Raven, until this moment,

Fiona had been all too willing to help her, had not for one second considered Raven out of touch with reality. Had, in fact, admired her tenacity and sense of balance. Her guts. Perhaps it was that simple: Raven's courage led her into situations that Fiona, in her caution, would never even see, much less *look* at, much less *go into*.

"You look overwhelmed," Raven's voice cut into her musings. "I've said too much."

"No, it's ok. I mean…"

"You don't believe me. You think I've imagined it all."

"It is a pretty incredible story, you have to admit."

"Even for a poet, huh?"

Fiona looked at Raven. The dark poet gave her a strange smile, lit another cigarette and took a long drag.

"Well, if you don't feel you can get involved, I understand," she said. "I mean, hell, you didn't come all this way for this kind of shit. You won an award, you've got a poetry reading to give, you have work to do, a master's degree to think about," Raven waved her cigarette around, the tip flickering like a red firefly. "I understand all that. Look, I'll find a way to get into his studio myself, no big deal. And the trip to Durango, I'll just go get that over with."

"Trip to Durango?"

"I need to go up there and look for that private eye Aisling Devlin's family hired. I hoped you might want to come along, but that's ok, it's not as if I'm not used to solo road trips. I'd like to compare notes with this guy. I'll go on Tuesday if I can set it up."

Now that sounded interesting. A road trip with Raven – even just a day trip – sounded very intriguing. To escape this place, see more of the Southwest, two writers on the lam. That sounded like good old-fashioned fun! Keroac, Ginsburg, Whitman, Nin – all would approve.

"I'll go with you."

"Yeah? Would you?"

Raven sounded unexpectedly relieved. She guessed Raven was more nervous about all this than she liked to admit.

"Sure, a road trip sounds like fun. I mean, of course, it's serious business, but...still..."

"You're chomping at the bit to get outta Dodge. I don't blame you, place gives me the willies. We could leave early Tuesday morning, spend some time with this private eye, be back at the Fagans' by six; they'd never miss you."

"Sounds great. And..." Fiona paused, wishing fervently she wasn't about to say what she was about to say. "And I'll help you. I'll look for your stuff in Hawthorne's place."

"Hey...I know you're skeptical. Hell, I would be if it were me listening to you tell this crazy story. So...I appreciate that."

"We poets have to stick together."

"True. If a poet won't stand up for another poet, who will?"

Fiona reached over, took the cigarette from Raven and treated herself to a drag. She coughed sufficiently to turn her face purple in the moonlight, slapped herself on the chest, returned the cigarette, and leaned back in the water. Then she remembered the cigar.

"I have something for you," she said, and glided across the pool to her clothes near the lantern. She retrieved the cigar and walked back through the water, holding it high and dry. Now it was Raven's turn to observe another woman's beauty, a beauty quite different from her own - frail and watery, like she'd slip through your fingers if you didn't hold on tight. Fiona would be a shy lover, she suspected, the kind who would be "taken" like the heroines on those supermarket paperback covers. Ladylike on the outside, a wild woman on the inside. If the right kind of man came along to bring her out of her shell. Not someone like Hawthorne. He was too self-absorbed, he expected his sexual partners to take care of themselves. Fiona walked like a woman whose main preoccupation was self-protection, unaware of the erotic impact of those long crinkly curls dangling over her pink nipples, and could only think of how to put one foot in front of the other without slipping on the algae.

"Here!" Fiona handed Raven the cigar.

"Ahh! I see Talle held one of her salons!" Raven laughed and drew the cigar under her nostrils, inhaling with a grin. "The Churchill?"

"You know?"

"That's Liam's favorite. Thanks, I'll save this for a special occasion." Raven set the cigar next to her cigarettes.

"You said it would be better if no one at the hacienda knows you and I have met."

"Right."

"Liam knows we met this afternoon. But I asked him not to tell Talle or Hawthorne."

Raven gave Fiona a sideways look as she stubbed out her cigarette on the stones.

"So you and Liam are becoming tight, are you?"

"I don't know if I'd say 'tight'. But I think we sort of understand each other. Anyway, I thought you should know that. If you think it's a problem..."

"Probably not. I think if Liam agreed not to say anything, you can count on that. But don't underestimate Talle. She doesn't let much go unseen. She's lady of the manor, after all...So I bet Liam has the hots for you?"

"Oh, I..."

"Kissed you yet?"

Fiona blushed.

"That's pretty typical. He tries that with all the women, at one point or another. He always feels too guilty, though, to let it get anywhere. I think he just likes to find out if he could. Bolsters his ego."

Fiona was feeling ambivalent again. One minute she would feel such kinship with Raven, the next minute Raven would say something that made her want to bolt and run. The dark-haired poet seemed to inadvertently keep taking Fiona's treats away. Things that Fiona hoarded as secret treasures, private moments - suddenly Raven would be there, belittling them, as if saying, in an offhand way, "Oh yeah, I have one of those, too, got it at the flea market for a quarter."

"I think you're being hard on him. He's a very interesting man. A sad man, I think."

Raven glanced sideways at Fiona again. Maybe that was it. Fiona would need an older man, someone to be respectful and gentle and... grateful. After all, hadn't she hinted at having had some interlude with that professor on the graduate committee? Someone at distance – too old, too married. A good way of keeping herself protected, by choosing the unavailable, dysfunctional father figure. Not that Raven could criticize. Picking men like Hawthorne wasn't exactly a sign of mental health either. Or the best way down the path to sacred matrimony.

That's one more thing she and Fiona had in common, aside from being poets. They both had worked out a temporary, complex way of holding men at bay while they pursued their true love: poetry.

"Well, you may be right."

"He has another side, you know. I've seen him."

"That's right, you told me, the naked voyeur!"

At the memory of their previous conversation, Raven laughed out loud.

"I saw him again, last night before dinner, in the woods. He was smoking a cigarette."

"Liam doesn't smoke. Except cigars and them only occasionally, only as a social thing."

"Like I said, he has another side. In the woods he runs around naked and smokes cigarettes. Carries a backpack, too. And spies on his own house through his own windows!"

"Really? That's a little spooky. You sure it's Liam? You sure it's not the Green Man?"

Fiona giggled at the idea of the Green Man wearing a backpack and smoking a cigarette.

"No, seriously, I think you've confused him with someone else," Raven continued. "There are a lot of long-haired men living in Ojo de Sombras. You probably just saw a hiker. They're not supposed to come on this land, but they do, all the time. Hard to control a thousand acres."

Fiona frowned, remembering the three encounters. No, it had to be Liam. He was so distinctive-looking, that man couldn't be anyone but him.

"We need to figure out a safe time for you to get into Hawthorne's studio. I can tell you how to get there, but the best way would be to get yourself invited."

"Maybe Talle can show me. I have to go on this picnic with her tomorrow, she wants to show me the grounds."

"Excellent. Get her to show you where the studio is. Hawthorne's chopping firewood this week, I saw him driving up to Cat Mesa. That will detain him about three hours usually. He keeps the studio locked."

"What? A locked door in Ojo de Sombras?"

"Yeah, probably the only one. He's so paranoid, yet he'd never think to check those old, cobwebby, crank-open windows in back. I noticed the crank is broken on one of them. I'll lend you a pocketknife; you'll need to cut through those prehistoric grape vines. I wanted to ask you..."

Raven pulled out a folded piece of paper tucked between her cigarette pack and the cellophane wrapper.

"I found this inside a Yeats collection Liam lent me last year, from his personal library upstairs."

Fiona carried the paper over to the kerosene lantern, set it on the ledge and got out of the water, pulled on her jeans and sweater, shaking so hard her upper and lower teeth rattled against each other. She put on the extra sweater she had thought to bring, and wound a towel around her hair, and then sat on the ledge to read by the lantern's light. It was a hand-written, erotic, Green Man poem. Signed "from A.D. to L.F." and dated October 4, 1979.

"Is this what I think it is?" Fiona asked as Raven joined her, climbing out of the pool and pulling on her clothes. The dark poet wrapped herself in a red wool blanket and sat, shivering.

"Your clothes are still wet from rescuing me," Fiona noted. She took off the extra sweater and handed it to Raven, who didn't object. Fiona put on her duster.

"Yeah, one of Aisling's poems. To Liam, it seems," Raven pulled on the sweater and bundled back into the blanket. "See the date? That's two days before she disappeared."

"What do you want me to do with this?"

"Read it out loud at your poetry reading."

"What? Why?"

"'The play's the thing…'"

"'Wherein we catch the conscience of the king,' right. Wow. That's pretty…"

"Overt?"

"At least!"

"I just want to see Hawthorne's reaction when he hears it. I think it would tell us a lot."

"How do I explain where I got it and why I'm reading it?"

"You're writing Green Man poems, right?"

Truth be told, she wasn't writing *anything* since she'd arrived at the Fagans', other than a few notes about poems she *should* be writing.

"Well…"

"So you say you are interested in the history of Green Man poems being written by Fagan poets?"

"Yeah, but how am I supposed to know about that? *You're* the one who's done that research, not me."

"You don't have to let on you know the whole history. But those three volumes of Liam's in your *casita* - Talle herself gave you those to read, right?"

"How did you…?"

"She did the same thing to me. When I first came, she handed me the volumes he wrote the previous year - from the fall and winter of the previous poet's stay, and from the summer after she left, leading up to my arrival. Just pulled them off the shelf as if it was random. But it wasn't. I always suspected that, but when I saw the three she handed you, I knew it for sure. She's got her little games, that one. Wants you to know, for some reason, about Liam's relationship with the poet before you. She knows everything about Liam's poetry; she's really the one who keeps up that collection. You could pretend you found it tucked inside one of Liam's volumes of poetry, and that you happened to notice that not only yours, but Liam Fagan's and Raven Shane Cordova's poems made references to this Green Man. Say that the poem was written by 'a former Fagan poet', and give the initials - A.D. If Hawthorne has a reaction, I'll know I'm on the right track."

Fiona stared at Aisling Devlin's handwriting. She had a very bad feeling about this idea of Raven's. It could backfire terribly. The Fagans might feel betrayed, that she had overstepped some boundary by bringing up the missing poet in public like that. Yet, on the other hand, she could act completely innocent. After all, Talle had handed her the books herself, it wasn't her fault if one of them contained this poem.

As for Hawthorne, she might be setting herself up as a potential target – if Raven's theory about him was right. At best, she would read Aisling Devlin's poem and no one would think anything of it, because Raven's suspicions were ridiculous. At worst, she would read Devlin's poem and earn the wrath of her benefactors and become Hawthorne's next victim.

The images from her earlier vision of the Green Man's nest came back. *What do you see? How does she feel?* he asked. He had shown her a woman's fear, in the nest. Was that woman Aisling Devlin? Was it a sign Fiona should try to help solve the mystery of the missing poet?

"I know I'll regret this...but I'll do it. It's a beautiful poem, anyway. The world at least owes it to her to listen to her poems now and then."

To Fiona's surprise, Raven reached from the depths of her red wool blanket and hugged her close and hard. It seemed uncharacteristic of the tough cowgirl poet. Fiona was reminded how vulnerable and alone Raven must really feel, underneath her black leather.

"So..." Raven pulled back and grinned at Fiona. "Durango here we come, eh?"

Back in her *casita*, Fiona rubbed her damp hair and, trembling from her cold and wet adventure, lit a three a.m. fire in the *kiva*. She stood in the middle of the room, scanning the walls, looking for the safest place to put Devlin's poem. The Green Man mask smiled down at her invitingly from the wall above the loft bed. She climbed the ladder and slid the folded poem between the mask and the wall, then pulled the comforter from the bed, tossed it over the railing to the floor below and climbed back down. She wrapped herself in the comforter and curled up on the sofa in the dark, staring into the flames until she was warm. She fell asleep.

Her dream was dense, in the primeval forest. She was walking up a trail carrying a backpack filled with stones. At each tree she stopped, withdrew a stone and dropped it on the path. Yet the backpack grew heavier and heavier, and the path deeper and more complicated with under-growth. As she dropped the stones, they disappeared under the tangled vines, then the vines transformed into snakes, then into ripples of water. She began to swim, freed from the pack of stones, exuberant and happy in a river that went on forever.

After the brisk hike back to her cabin, Raven lit the wood stove, which she had preset with kindling and paper before going to the hot springs. She peeled off her damp clothes, wrapped in her father's blanket, and curled on pillows with Dingo. He smelled like he'd had a great day in the ditch chasing rabbits, and would need a serious bath in the morning. Despite the stink and his oily fur, he was warm and his snoring made her smile.

Raven's dream was light and airy, she leapt from a mesa as if she had wings, and flew over acres and acres of verdant grass. She landed and began running, barefoot, through the grass, feeling a freedom she had not felt since she was a child. Maybe not even then. As she ran, she began to realize that, parallel to the field was a dark cemetery filled with gravestones. Poets' graves. She ran all the faster, trying to escape the vision. But it went on, forever. The incredible freedom, the damp and soft green grass, and the unending graveyard.

Chapter 12 - Trespasser

Talle commentated while she worked, "... plus a teaspoon of red currant and a pinch of cayenne. There, that should set me right." She finished filling the muslin tea bag and clipped a piece of string from a roll suspended on her work board. "Let me just put these things away and we can go. Mindy packed us a lunch of poached salmon and basil and tomato salad. I hope you like salmon? It's all I could think of having when I woke up with that hangover," Talle babbled breathlessly as she tied the muslin bag and straightened her workstation. "I think my liver is craving the amino acids. I shouldn't drink those damned martinis. I really apologize, Liam says I made quite a scene last night; I hope I didn't offend you. Anyway, this remedy will set me right, always does."

"Salmon sounds wonderful," Fiona said, closing her eyes and inhaling the wonderful, sun-warmed scents of Talle's greenhouse.

The discovery of Talle's *curandera* talents and amazing greenhouse were a genuinely delightful surprise to Fiona.

She was impressed at the organization of the room. The peg board on the wall at Talle's work station held orderly rows of twine, shears, tape, labels, a roll of brown paper and various tools. A shelf next to the work bench was filled with a comprehensive library on gardening, gathering wild herbs and edibles, guides to the art of the *curandera*, recipes for herbal teas and tinctures, and several notebooks labeled with Talle's now-familiar handwriting. *"Colds & flus"*, *"Love Potions"*, *"Skin Ailments"*.

"I had no idea you had this greenhouse. Silver showed me your herb sachets in the store, and I knew you used a lot of herbs in our meals here, but I didn't realize how serious you are about this."

Talle gazed up into the rafters of the greenhouse. She looked very much the farmer today, in denim overalls, a raspberry shirt, and a wide-brim straw hat that tied under her chin. "I come down here at sunrise with my mug of coffee, and feel it warming up, see my beauties in that light. I mail order some of the dried herbs and medicinal plants, some I prefer to grow-like the lavender and golden seal. Others I gather locally, such as sage, *flor de Santa Rita*, Mormon tea, *cota, yerba santa* – I've studied for years with some local *curanderas*. I still have a lot to learn – You have to know what to gather and what to leave alone. The plants that grow along the interface are my favorites. "

"The interface?"

"Between land and water. Things from the interface have a special potency. Some are best gathered in the morning, others by the moon. I love to forage along the river."

Fiona nodded, drinking in the smell of rich soil from the beds, the view of roses and rosemary plants, flowering cacti and basil basking in the soft light of the solar panels. Somewhere in the room was a bubbling fountain. There was even beauty in the simplicity of the watering can and collapsed pair of muddy rubber boots next to the doorway. A room that was both industrious and soothing.

"This is so obviously *your* room..." Fiona mused out loud. "Oh, by the way, you left your book on my sofa. We mustn't forget to pick it up on our way back."

Fiona casually stuck her nose into a hanging basket of yellow blossoms.

"Careful, those bruise easily, best not to touch them," Talle said over her shoulder. Did she have eyes in the back of her head? Talle closed the jars of herbs and dried flowers from which she had mixed the hangover remedy. She said nothing about the journal. Fiona hadn't opened it when she returned from the hot springs last night. She had placed Talle's folded towel on top of the book to keep temptation out of sight, even though she suspected it was left for her to read from again. Inwardly, she shrugged. Obviously Talle intended to leave the subject hanging in the air, and over Fiona's head.

"This is my apothecary – the herbs are dried and stored where it's cool and shady."

Fiona followed Talle as she carried the herb jars into the adjoining pantry. Each jar was labeled and placed alphabetically along wooden shelves that lined the walls. Many labels were in Latin, others in Spanish, a few in English. Bunches of dried flowers and herbs were tied in twine and hung in careful rows from the rafters. Others were spread to dry on a workbench. A chiffarobe door was ajar, revealing more supplies and baskets of dried and pungent vegetation.

"Oh God, this is wonderful, what is this?" Fiona inhaled a suspended bunch of silvery green leaves.

"It's ok to touch those, go ahead, feel them," Talle smiled as if to make up for the off-limit yellow flowers.

Fiona did. They felt like the softest suede.

"That's a white sage from California, my favorite. There are many sages; depends whether you're putting together a culinary, medicinal or ritual treatment. I'll have Mindy brew me a thermos of this and we'll be off."

Talle left and Fiona wandered through the greenhouse, walking quietly up and down the rows of plants, reading the names on the tags. *Anethum graveolens,* Dill. *Primula officinalis,* Primrose. *Datura stramonium,* Jimson Weed.

Back in the pantry, she stood before the rows of jars. Some of them she recognized from her favorite herb-and-tea store back in Baltimore. Ginseng. Arnica. Pennyroyal. Others were new to her. *Canutillo. Flor de San Juan. Jarita.* The shelves of jars were so tall, a ladder leaned next to them to access the top rows. Fiona strained to read the labels on the topmost shelf, and realized the jars and small vials of variously-colored liquids and oils were embellished with the traditional skull-&-crossbones warning. Dog's Mercury. *Cicuta maculaeta. Mandragora officinarum.*

"Sorry it took me so long, I had to run upstairs for my shawl, it might get chilly in the woods. You wore layers, I hope? So...if you'll carry this, I'll carry the blanket and thermos," Talle stood in the pantry doorway, watching Fiona's explorations.

"Looks like some dangerous stuff way up there!" Fiona smiled and reached to accept the picnic basket. It was slightly heavy; Fiona hoped the picnic spot wasn't too far away.

"That's why I keep those 'way up there'. Some of those bottles can't even be handled without gloves. You have to know exact proportions; you have to know what you're doing. "

"I see," Fiona murmured, again feeling like an adult child, obediently followed Talle out the door, through the greenhouse and onto the path through the courtyard. As they passed Hawthorne's *casita*, he appeared in the open doorway.

"Good morning," he greeted them, uncharacteristically cheerful. "And where are you ladies off to?"

"Giving her the tour. I thought you were going to check along the river this morning?" Talle looked slightly irritated to see him.

"On my way. Guess I partied too much last night – and how are *you*?"

"I have my remedy, thank you," Talle gestured to the thermos.

"Ah yes, you know, I have a theory. It's getting up the courage to drink that stuff that sobers a person up, not actually drinking it. Ugh!"

Hawthorne seemed determined to be entertaining and gave Fiona a rakish smile. She nodded, neither wanting to encourage his friendliness, nor wanting to give away her new Raven-induced perspective of the man. Talle waited, watching Hawthorne expectantly. He cleared his throat and smiled at Fiona pointedly.

"Fiona, I'm glad to run into you actually," he began, stepping out onto his front stoop.

"I was wondering – I like to sketch each of the poets who stay here. Would you be willing to let me – just an informal portrait?"

Although the idea of spending any time with the man was an unwelcome prospect, it would allow her the access she needed to Hawthorne's studio, and hopefully the opportunity to search for Raven's photos and the pink invoice. Fiona nodded.

"Oh, good," Hawthorne seemed inordinately relieved that she had not resisted. "We can discuss it at dinner then."

"Why wait that long?" Talle prodded. "Her calendar is filling up, she has a reading to prepare for, you know. I think you two should get to work on the portrait this afternoon. We'll be heading across the meadow after lunch, I'll bring her to the studio."

A shadow of irritation crossed Hawthorne's brow but he masked it with a thin smile. "Fine with me if it's ok with Fiona."

"Fine," Fiona shrugged.

"See you then," Hawthorne showed his teeth again and stepped back inside.

"He has a lazy streak, so I have to push him sometimes," Talle explained as they walked into the woods. "The portraits are part of his obligation to us, but if he had it his way he'd wait 'til the last day to do them. You know how artists are, it's their own projects that inspire them, and anything on commission is a necessary evil. I mean, if he took it into his own head to sketch you, then he couldn't get to it fast enough. But since it's something we commission, he resists. It's the curse of the artist, balancing creative passion and discipline. Hawthorne doesn't know how good he has it, living here with us. With all that pot he smokes, if it weren't for us, he'd never accomplish a thing. Not that he isn't good, mind you. His masks – have you seen them?"

Fiona grabbed a chance to get in an edgewise word as she shifted the picnic basket to her other arm.

"I know all about the Green Man. I did a research project on him last summer, for a series I'm writing."

"Ah...So I suppose you know about our ritual?"

Earlier, Fiona had decided that, should the subject arise, she would pretend that Raven hadn't told her anything about the mask ritual. Talle pushed aside branches and gestured for Fiona to go ahead. The narrow path they had been walking opened out onto a wider one covered with soft pine needles. They walked on side by side.

"The sketches, you see, are preliminary for the making of the masks. You may have seen them, in the hallway? And there's one in your *casita*. Since the year Hawthorne came to us, we've had him do a mask for each poet. There are thirteen of them now. We would like to do one of you, if you will agree. You don't have to agree, of course, and if you don't, there will be no pressure. The Green Man only accepts conscious and willing subjects."

"But most of those mask faces are masculine. Haven't the poets been…"

"Women, yes, all but Chahil O'Shea. The Green Man prefers the masks to originate from feminine or creative energy, for balance. Then we leave it to Hawthorne whether the final product is depicted as female, male or androgynous. It is a truly free, creative process for him."

"So how is it a ritual - and why the Green Man?"

"You really don't know about this? I would have thought Raven filled you in," Talle asked slyly. So she hadn't been drunk enough last night to not remember the slip Fiona had made to Liam in the kitchen. However, Fiona had thought this one through in the wee hours, on her way back from the hot springs. She agreed with Raven that it would be best if they kept their budding friendship as clandestine as possible for the time being.

"Filled me in?" Fiona asked innocently.

"I believe you and she have met? Or so you were saying to Liam."

"Oh, that. I was telling him about the proposal she sent the Baltimore Institute of Fine Arts. My professor mentioned it when we spoke the other day. How complimentary she was about Liam's impact on the poets who have come here."

"Well, that is good to hear. So she's applied to the Baltimore Institute of Fine Arts? I wasn't aware."

"She's been accepted. They loved her thesis proposal."

" Which is?"

Fiona paused before answering. Would Talle welcome or be angered at the prospect of having the history of the Fagan poets looked into? A tricky subject to open; however, it would ease the transition into the subject of Aisling Devlin. She answered cautiously.

"I'm not privy to the details, but I believe it's something about the publication careers of the Fagan poets."

"That truly amazes me. The academics have been notably insulting in their comments about our residency program; yet they would find such a thesis worthy of their attention?"

"Perhaps they can no longer ignore the correlation between good publishing results and the Fagan residency.

It can take time for residencies to be accepted as part of the tradition. You know, so much is about classical training at the universities."

"So much is about snobbism, you mean," Talle sniffed. "You couldn't ask for a poet more appreciative of the classics than Liam." But she did seem pleased at Fiona's compliment.

"And there is, of course, some curiosity in our department, about the missing poet."

Fiona slid a glance at Talle as they moved along the path deeper into the ponderosa grove. Talle frowned and looked down at the tops of her shoes. Today she wasn't wearing the Chinese dragon slippers, but a pair of sturdy hiking boots. Fiona looked at her own feet as she waited for a response. She'd forgone her stylish boots for a pair of Reeboks that she hoped would be sufficient for the terrain on Talle's agenda.

"Yes, I can imagine there is," she finally spoke, her voice subdued. "I'm sure you've heard the local gossip. Aisling Devlin disappeared. But she did so <u>after</u> she left here; people tend to forget that part. It was unfortunate that the Fagan residency was ever implicated in her disappearance. As if we have any control over what happens once a poet leaves our program, in either her publishing or personal life!"

"But she did leave before her residency was completed."

"Yes, about two, maybe three weeks before. It's so long ago, I have tried to recall why that was, what she told us.

Something about her boyfriend in Colorado, wanting to have some time with him before he transferred to a new job. Something like that - younger women often give up career opportunities for the sake of love."

"I hear she was an interesting talent. Silver told me about the harp."

"She built the instrument herself, she modeled it after the hand-made harps of the Irish bards—the mask in your *casita*, that was Aisling."

The hair on Fiona's arms stood up. She had tucked Aisling's poem behind that mask for safe-keeping. The women walked in silence for a few moments.

"So...was she here during the Bardic School?"

"I really don't recall, the years get blurred together. Oh, here we are!"

Talle suddenly stopped in a semi-circle of ponderosa grove that didn't look much different to Fiona than any other group of trees they had passed.

"Here, let's spread the blanket. I really need a swig of that remedy."

Talle shook out the blanket with a sharp slap of the air and settled it in a patch of noonday sun. Fiona thought the woman would smooth out the wrinkles before they sat, but, instead, she took the basket from Fiona with a brusque gesture, and sat down cross-legged, a nervous Buddha. Fiona straightened the blanket herself, watching her hostess. Talle was visibly shaken by the discussion of Aisling Devlin.

Fiona wondered for a moment if the thermos of "remedy" might not include hair of the dog, the way Talle was swigging it from the thermos cup.

"I'd offer you some of this, but it contains my personal menopausal arsenal. Probably not a good idea for you to partake at your age. I didn't forget you, though – "

Talle opened the basket and handed Fiona a cobalt blue bottle of imported mineral water. Fiona accepted it gratefully and sat cautiously on the edge of the blanket.

"This is a lovely spot."

"Yes, as lovely as any. We have an eternity of lovely spots on this property," Talle closed her eyes and swigged again, throwing back her head and swallowing to the sky. "If you look over there, you can see a great view of our mountain."

"You own an entire mountain?"

"A couple," Talle laughed. The subject of her real estate instantly cheered her, even if the property deed did stipulate that her "ownership" was in fact a 99-year lease from the Native Americans. "And a dormant volcano, some Anasazi ruins, quite a bit of river front. It all increases in value by the hour, if we ever decide to sell anything. Which I don't anticipate. So!"

Talle took a deep breath, centered herself, and dug into the picnic basket. Out came a set of lightweight, red laquer plates, pewter flatware wrapped in turquoise linen napkins and tied with bits of red silk cord. A flat bundle wrapped in muslin, a wooden Japanese box filled with foil-wrapped salmon, more mineral water, a paper-thin bowl made of shell, filled with salad, and a small, fancy white box of chocolates. Talle laid each item out along the blanket - Ralph Lauren, Fiona now noticed - with an eye to display, opening the containers and slipping pewter serving spoons into each. Fiona - now understanding why the basket had been heavy - watched in amazement at the artistry displayed in a simple picnic for two, and listened in dismay at the hungry rumbling in her stomach. Had she really thought she could get away with just drinking water on this picnic?

"What's that? It smells incredible!" Fiona pointed to the muslin bundle. Talle unwrapped layers of muslin to reveal a round, Navajo basket cradling a loaf of flat bread imbedded with nuts and herbs. She broke off a chunk and placed it on one of the lacquer plates, then added a serving of salmon.

"My own recipe. I call it 'Desert *focaccia*'. It's an Italian bread, wine-infused dough. I add a touch of blue corn meal, *pinon* nuts and sage."

Fiona sighed and accepted the red lacquer plate Talle handed her.

"I want to ask you about your work," Talle said, spooning salad onto Fiona's plate. "But I am sure, first, that you have a few questions, now that you have been with us – how long has it been?"

"A week and a half."

"Time is mysterious, isn't it? Now, I suppose you have questions about Liam. The poets always do, after they've met him. And, of course, he is my favorite subject. So fire away," Talle dug into her plateful of food.

Fiona hesitated. She had imagined all sorts of ways to slip into the subjects about which she wanted to quiz her hostess; to be invited to ask head-on had not been in her plan. She took a deep breath and slowly exhaled, spearing a piece of the pink fish to help her focus.

"Ok. I do have one question. Is Liam perhaps a touch agoraphobic?"

"No, he's just a touch poetic. He's a recluse; he must be, in order to create. The classic artist, that's Liam. Almost the stereotype, actually. Why do you ask?"

"So...it is really true, he doesn't walk in the woods, back-pack on the property – "

Talle laughed and swigged her remedy.

"Now there's a picture I'd like to see! Liam in hiking boots and a backpack!"

"Well..." Fiona swallowed her fish and sipped her water, "The reason I ask is...I thought I had seen him, several times now, in the woods. With a backpack and smoking cigarettes."

"Liam? Oh no, you're mistaken. Last night, Hawthorne told me that he'd seen someone camping on the property, that's probably who you saw."

"Talle, I *know* it was Liam. It was his hair, his build. How many Liams could there be, walking on the planet? He's very distinctive, you know."

Fiona surprised herself, pushing the subject. What if Liam really didn't want Talle to know about his double life? But how could she truly not know? Talle had an eagle eye on everything that happened in her domain. Fiona felt that, if she pressed the subject, Talle would be forced to reveal something by her reaction.

Talle gave Fiona a perplexed look. Fiona could detect no pretense in her gaze.

"Fiona...have you seen the Green Man? Some say they've met Him in our woods. Perhaps this person you've seen..."

"I've had dreams about the Green Man since I came here."

"There are those who claim they've actually *seen* him. Maybe this man you saw..."

"He isn't the Green Man. The man I've seen has long white hair and Liam's build and face. Only - he's different. He walks more energetically, wears his hair down, dresses in jeans and sweaters, and smokes cigarettes. And he looks in your windows at night."

Talle frowned and set down her plate and fork.

"Now this is serious. Someone is looking in our windows?"

"The chess library windows. Talle, it really is Liam. You don't know about this?"

Talle stared into the trees, then looked at Fiona.

"Fiona, I must ask you something. I promise I won't be upset by your answer. But I must ask...has my husband made advances to you?"

Fiona didn't have a moment to decide how to counter the alarmingly direct question. The blush across her freckles told Talle everything.

"I thought so," Talle said calmly. "He is always enamored of the young poets. It helps him create. As long as you understand he doesn't mean anything serious by it. I just don't want you getting hurt by his attentions, misinterpreting them."

Talle sipped her secret brew and continued.

"No, to answer your question, Liam rarely leaves the house - only on occasion to visit with Hawthorne in his studio, once a year to attend the reading at the *Extranjeros*. He doesn't even own a pair of jeans. He never has - not even in the sixties. Now, he did smoke cigarettes when we first met, but he quit a long, long time ago. The man you saw – you imagined him, I suppose. Because of your fascination with Liam – perhaps you even have a bit of a crush? It's entirely understandable...Although there may be another explanation."

"Another explanation?"

Talle took the blue bottle from Fiona and poured the water out. She replaced it with half of her remedy and handed it back. She poured herself another cup and raised it to toast. Fiona followed suit.

"To truth."

Fiona sipped from the bottle. Menopausal remedy, indeed. Hair of the dog. Bourbon, vermouth, cherry juice, and a hint of herbs. Not entirely pleasant but not entirely awful either. It reminded her of the Manhattans her father made to toast in the New Year.

"The other explanation for what you have seen could be Jungian in nature. Archetypes can manifest if there is enough psychic energy focused to bring them up. That is why, I believe, so many of us see the Green Man here. Simply because we need to, we want to, at this time in the history of the earth. If you are to take part in the Green Man mask ritual, you will need to be fully informed."

Talle gave Fiona a significant look.

"*Fully.* You should accept all information offered you on the subject, however it comes to you. I hope you understand my meaning."

Fiona nodded as if she understood, but she didn't.

"Anyway, as archetypes relate to your visions of my husband wearing a backpack and smoking cigarettes – I think you might be seeing the manifestation of Liam's desire - his desire for his double. His twin, if you will."

"Liam has a twin?"

"It's a joke between us, about his lost twin. I began teasing him about it early in our courtship. He was always off in his head somewhere, as if talking to the other half of himself. There was a part of him I could never see, his shadow side, the missing twin. The first time I made this joke, Liam was so startled, he couldn't respond. Later I realized that he must have almost felt hurt, and unnerved, that I had figured it out. He was the only one who's ever known about the missing twin; he still has never admitted it to me. It's just something that I know about Liam, about his longing."

"So he really has a twin?"

"It's not that simple," Talle bit into a dark chocolate square. "I think it's one important reason why he married me. Because, somehow, I knew. He always knew yet always kept that knowledge secret. He knew he was adopted before his parents were killed in that train wreck and he found the papers, when he was sixteen. He told me that the day he was digging in that trunk and found the letter from the Irish priest, he had no strong reaction. He simply sat back and thought to himself, *so that explains it. Why we were separated.* They never spoke of his having a twin or any siblings at all. They never said, and he never asked. But he knew. And, when I met him, so did I.

"His cousins later told Liam that he was born in Ireland, that the Fagans adopted him from there. No doubt that is where the wet forest is, the one I envision - perhaps you've read that part in my journal?"

Talle sorted through the chocolates. Fiona frowned, sipping the remedy. She was not about to admit to that. She gave Talle a quizzical look, but it was lost on the storyteller, who was gazing off into the woods again, sucking on a chocolate-covered cherry. She continued, as if she was talking out loud to herself.

"Perhaps it was such a place in which the twins were born. Perhaps it's a memory, not just a longing of an aging man. Perhaps we've created our life in the desert in order to get back to his birth in the rain. It would be just like us, to do it the round-about way."

Fiona resigned herself to Talle's convoluted story and chose a piece of fudge.

"Our computer wizard told us you can find lost people on the computer. Adopted people find their real parents, parents find their lost children, old flames, soul mates, chess partners find each other. I watched Liam as our friend said this. He didn't react - except to the idea of a chess partner. And, for a while, he had one. But as for the twin, no, we never speak of him. He allows me the joke about his missing twin; it has become part of our marital language. Part of the dictionary of our interaction. But he has never spoken of the missing twin, or how real his long-ing is. He believes it's a secret thing - the fact and the ache - and it has always seemed that it must remain so. To dilute it with others' misunderstandings, about the nature of his knowing, would be like discovering the soul and poking holes in it, just to see what would happen. That's why our mysteries must remain mysteries. We can't trust ourselves with them."

Talle was finally silent. She had stopped drinking and held her hands open on her knees, sitting Buddha-style again, staring into the woods.

"That was quite – eloquent."

"I know. I wrote it last year and memorized it. I try to memorize my writings. I don't know why, exactly. It's just something I do when I come out here by myself, to pass the time, to remind myself...of who I really am, who we really are. The Green Man likes it, likes to hear the words of creation in His woods. It's a form of prayer for me."

Fiona chewed the fragrant, still-warm bread. Talle was a strange woman; either very complicated or very mixed up, but what else could you expect from one whose creativity was so immense? Did it have any boundary at all? Her house, her land, her herbs, her food, her writing, the nurturing of artists and writers, her devotion to Liam. Fiona wished she could like the woman as much as she admired the physical manifestations of her talent. But she just could not. The remedy was like Talle herself; a strange mixture that didn't quite work. Too heady, too bitter, too sweet. Fiona shook her head, trying to clear away the herb-&-alcohol fog.

"Do you drink much of this stuff?"

"I have my moments. I'm not an alcoholic, if that's what you mean."

With that, Talle began to giggle, her giggles turned into raucous laughter, so hard she fell backwards on the blanket, squashing her elbow into the salmon and her knee into the salad. She laughed all the harder. Suddenly her laughter turned to crying, and she covered her face with both hands and rolled over, wailing and shaking with anguished sobs. Fiona stared, appalled at the immensity of her own lack of compassion. Still, she felt socially obligated to make at least a pretense of caring. She patted the woman's shoulder, murmuring "There, there." The way her mother had done for her when she was a child. Talle went limp and let herself cry until she was exhausted with it.

After a few minutes of silence, Talle lifted herself up and looked away, embarrassed, wiping her face with one of the turquoise napkins.

"I'm not myself these days," she said softly, about to break into giggles – or further tears – again. "I'm very tired. I didn't sleep last night, then was up so early."

"This was a beautiful feast, Talle," Fiona said quietly. "You are so talented. Thank you for all the trouble you went to."

Talle looked at the mess she'd made as if seeing it for the first time, and began wiping salmon from her elbow and picking bits of tomato from her knee.

"I didn't do it. Mindy did. Except the bread, I made the bread."

"And the remedy."

Talle smiled, accepting Fiona's joke. "Oh yes, the remedy. I do make good remedy."

Fiona began packing up the picnic. Talle could only sit and watch, depleted.

"So...do you think this man I've seen *is* Liam's twin?" Fiona asked, stacking the plates.

"What? Come to spy on us? Found us somehow out of the blue and, instead of calling or writing like a normal, long-lost sibling, comes to camp out and spy on us on our own property?"

"Something like that, yes."

"That's a very strange idea. Why would he do that - even if he did exist?"

"But you said there *was* a twin."

"I told you, Liam's never admitted it outright."

"But you believe there is."

"Oh, all right, yes, I do. Whether Liam admits it or not. Because I *knew*, I knew it from the moment I met Liam. I trust my instincts, my visions. I don't trust anything or anyone else - well, except Him, of course. So you may be right."

"Does it seem like something Liam would do? I mean, if he were the long-lost twin, if the tables were turned? They say separated identical twins are still identical, their personalities, likes, dislikes, habits. So if it's something you can imagine Liam would likely do – find his twin, check him out first before revealing himself - then why wouldn't his twin do it, too?"

Talle sighed, "I can imagine Liam doing it."

Talle got up unsteadily and held her forehead. Fiona rose and closed the lid on the re-packed basket. Talle stood still for a moment, then seemed entirely sobered up all of a sudden. She had a look of determination in her eye.

"We should go on back," Fiona offered. "I think you could use a rest."

"Oh no, I still have to give you the tour. I want to at least get you to Hawthorne's studio.

I'll head back to the house after you two get started. Really, the remedy actually works, you see. Don't you feel better now yourself?"

To her amazement, Fiona felt no lingering effects of the remedy. The *focaccia* had apparently grounded her intake of Manhattan. The reminder that she had promised to spend the afternoon in Hawthorne's studio was also sobering. Especially if Talle was going to leave her alone with him.

"We can leave all this, I'll pick it up on my way back."

The women placed the picnic things under a tree and headed toward the valley. Talle pulled her shawl across her shoulders as a breeze followed the women through a shady patch. Under her layers of camisole, T-shirt and the bulky, wool sweater she'd bought in Ireland, Fiona shivered – and not entirely from the breeze.

It seemed Raven had beat them all to Hawthorne's studio. Talle and Fiona found the studio door ajar and Hawthorne in the middle of the room, distractedly lifting and putting down the tools of his artistry, which were thrown and scattered in every direction. Furniture was overturned, cans of paint and turpentine were spilled across the floor, papers were strewn. Hawthorne looked lost, he seemed to have no idea how to turn the chaos back into his own sense of order. Fiona was quite shocked at the damage the angry poet had done - trying to retrieve her photos seemed a reasonable mission, but all this rage was not going to help them find out what had happened to Aisling Devlin. Even given the suspicions Raven had successfully planted in Fiona's mind about Hawthorne's involvement with the poet's disappearance, the violation of his space seemed overkill. Fiona made a note to - very gently - broach the subject of anger management with Raven.

"Hawthorne, what the…?"

"Someone broke in. This is how I found it."

"My god but she's angry!" Talle said, staring at the wreckage.

"Who's angry?"

Then realization dawned in Hawthorne's eyes. He threw down the jar of brushes he had just retrieved from a corner and the brushes scattered across the floor.

"Shit! SHIT! What is *with* that god-damned woman?"

"Retaliation, I would figure. Come on, pull yourself together!" Talle was apparently more at ease throwing fits than observing them. She slapped Hawthorne's shoulders in a big sisterly way and began to gather and replace items. Fiona hesitantly joined her, taking her cue as to where things belonged. Hawthorne just stood there, in shock, watching.

"Quit feeling sorry for yourself and pick up all those papers," Talle scolded him.

Hawthorne picked up a folder of photos and plastic sheaf of negatives strewn across the hearth of his wood stove. He spread the prints on his worktable, slipped the negatives under a stack of papers, and began to wipe away the soot.

"I should have explained to you last night...Raven believes you broke into her cabin yesterday and stole some writing," Talle spoke over her shoulder as she blotted a slick of red paint on the floor with some old rags. "I tried to convince her it wasn't you but she was in a blind rage. That's why I told you to give her a call, to smooth things over. Was it you?"

"I haven't been near her place for about a year. She knows that damned well."

"Well, obviously she *doesn't* know that," Talle said as she pushed a heap of broken glass together into a neat pile with two pieces of cardboard. "So...aside from paying you back, do you think she actually took anything? I mean, is there anything she might *want?*"

Talle looked Hawthorne in the eye from across the room. He glanced at Fiona, who pretended not to observe them and bent to gather the paintbrushes from the floor. As usual, there seemed more behind the surface conversation between these two. Fiona flashed back to Liam's story about their relationship.

"I know you and Raven had a confrontation the other night, I heard it from our deck," Talle continued. "I distinctly heard her shouting 'Give them to me' in Navajo, along with a few colorful adjectives."

"I forgot. You're a linguist, on top of your other multitude of talents," Hawthorne responded in his characteristic sullen mood.

"One should embrace the culture into which one finds oneself living, it behooves one to take an interest. Which, as you know, I have tried to tell you more than once."

"Perhaps one feels differently if one has *chosen to live* in a particular culture, than if one has been *forced to*."

"You've made your own choices, Hawthorne. No one has forced you. You can walk out of here tomorrow morning if you want, it's just a matter of choosing your own consequences."

Hawthorne stopped and stared at the photographs on his table. His jawbone moved as he ground his teeth, but he said nothing. Fiona glanced over his shoulder as she settled the can of brushes down on the table. Spread before him were the photos that Raven wanted back. He had captured her sullenness, even though she was blindfolded - in the nest, from every angle. Bound in vines, her hair woven into the branches, images on the wall behind her - like pictographs or cave paintings. Lightning. A corn stalk. A bear.

Fiona glanced at the wall behind the nest in the corner of his studio to see the actual images, but the wall was bare. Beautiful, erotic, black and white photographs, the artist's interplay of shadow and light evident, despite the layer of soot. Apparently it hadn't been Raven who broke in here after all - she would have taken the photos with her.

Talle moved near the table, settling a chair into place. Hawthorne quickly pulled the photos into a stack to hide them from his benefactress, but he was too late. Talle pushed his hands aside and pulled the folder toward her. As the woman opened the folder, Fiona instinctively moved from the line of fire, as if she had seen nothing. She heard the shuffling of photographic paper, heard a sharp intake of breath, then a long silence.

"I thought you said you did her mask from the sketches," Talle spoke in low tones.

"I did. These weren't for the mask, I never took an impression."

"You took her *there?* When?" Talle whispered.

"I don't remember exactly. It wasn't for the mask, it was just, we were only..."

"*You don't just take them there!*"

Fiona felt Talle glance at her from across the room.

"We'll discuss this later," she whispered venomously. "And we *will* discuss this."

Hawthorne said nothing, but closed the folder of photos and slid it into a drawer.

The three worked for an hour, reassembling the studio in silence.

"So...what's missing?" Talle asked again, in a lighter tone. "Your marijuana?"

Hawthorne frowned, opened the desk drawer and pulled out an old metal ammo box.

"No, it's here. Nothing's missing," he shuffled through baggies of marijuana, envelopes and papers. "Maybe we interrupted her before she could get what she came for."

"Which would be?"

"I told you, I have no idea—wait a minute. Shit."

"What's gone?"

Hawthorne covered his momentary panic and frowned again.

"Nothing, never mind."

Again, Talle attempted to cover her emotion with a light, curious tone. "So...how do you think she got in?"

Hawthorne closed the box, preoccupied.

"Huh? Oh, the door was open, it was ajar."

"But you keep it locked."

Fiona suddenly remembered Raven's description at the hot springs of how to sneak into the studio. She glanced around the room, then saw the back window as Raven had described it. She went to it. Yes, there it was, the vines were snapped, the window was cranked open.

Fiona fought the instinct to take in a sharp breath when, through the vines, she saw Raven's white shirt, only yards from the cabin. She was crouched behind a rock. Apparently she'd been waiting because as soon as she spied Fiona, she pressed her finger across her lips, pointed west, gestured for Fiona to follow her, and vanished.

"She came through the window," Talle's voice in Fiona's ear made her jump.

Fiona's hand flew to her mouth to cover an uncontrollable gasp.

"Are you alright?" Talle asked.

"Y-yes, just, a little jumpy."

Talle reached to touch the window crank.

"This crank is broken, see?" Talle turned back to Hawthorne. Had she seen Raven? Was she just pretending she hadn't?

"I still think you should call her, go see her, fix this mess. You two are acting like adolescents. Of course, you always did! Couldn't keep their hands off each other," Talle smirked at Fiona. "So...are you too emotionally distraught to work?"

Hawthorne was obviously not in the mood, but he responded to the edgy voice of authority. He brushed the tangle of hair from his eyes, gathered his sketchpad and pencils with a scowl, his shoulders bent with the weight of an indentured servant. Without words, he led Fiona to a stool in the corner. Fiona felt a panic setting in. She needed to leave, right now, follow Raven before the poet was too far into the rocks for her to track.

"Uh, before we begin, is there a bathroom?"

"There's an old outhouse out back…"

Fiona nodded and walked toward the door, trying to move slowly and nonchalantly.

"…but it hasn't been used for years. Floor boards are probably rotted."

As Fiona made her escape, Talle was tinkering with the window crank and dusting cobwebs from the glass - no doubt seeing the post-break-in clean-up as a rare opportunity to do a little housecleaning. Hawthorne was collapsed in his chair, wearily running his hand over his eyes. Fiona walked quickly around to the side of the cabin, careful to stay out of Talle's line of vision at the back window. She looked out into the red rocks where Raven had gestured, and saw the familiar white shirt again. Raven gestured urgently and Fiona climbed as fast as she could, looking back to be sure she wasn't being followed.

"My god, what did you do?" Fiona whispered when she got to the poet.

Raven was bent over, gasping for breath from the climb.

"It wasn't me. I got there and the window was open, the door was open, someone had come and gone. I left my canteen in there. You can't let him find it, he might recognize it."

Fiona recalled having picked up a canteen, encased in a distinctive embroidered pouch, and setting it on a shelf.

"Ok, I'll get it."

"I grabbed a folder, then I heard him coming. I dropped it and climbed out the window. I didn't have a chance to see if they were mine."

"They're yours."

"Can you get them?"

"That could be tricky. So...you didn't do all that? They're convinced you did."

"No. Someone's either got it in for him or just random vandals or..."

"Or someone else was looking for something."

"Can you get away? We need to check out the Bardic Cabin, *now*."

"Why now? Go home, we can do that together later. Tomorrow."

"Tomorrow we go to Durango."

"Ok, so Sunday."

"No, we have to do it now. I saw something in his studio, about Devlin. I'll explain later. We've got to get into the cabin before sundown."

"It's boarded up, it's dangerous. You shouldn't go there alone."

"So go with me. I want to check it out before we see Hank Walker - the private eye in Durango. I spoke with him this morning. He sounds like a real curmudgeon - but curious to talk with us - we have an appointment with him at ten in the morning. Listen, I'll go on to the Bardic Cabin.

I won't go inside 'til you get there. Just bring my canteen, and the photos if you can."

"Raven, if I take the photos now, he'll know it was me. He saw them scattered; Talle got upset about them, I watched him put them back in a drawer."

"She got upset? Why?"

"Something about him taking you somewhere he wasn't supposed to."

"Hmm...Just get the photos. He knows what he did, he knows he deserves it. He's got too much to hide, he can't act like the victim here!"

Raven reached into her back pocket and pulled out the pink invoice. Fiona grinned.

"My first real evidence. He signed this. Proves he was there that day, the day Devlin disappeared. It was there with his pot, in an ammo box in his desk drawer."

"He knows it's gone."

"He mentioned it?"

"No, just looked pissed, even a little scared." Fiona brushed her hair back, trying to think. "Ok, here's what I'll do. I'll go back, pose for about twenty minutes. Then I'll make some excuse and get out of there. If I see your stuff, and if I can grab it, I will. But I can't take any chances – if he finds out I'm in on this with you, we're screwed."

"Ok, do your best. The cabin is that 'a way, less than a mile. See that dip in the hills there? Pass through there, then head north about fifty yards, just past the old ruins."

"Ruins?"

"Anasazi. You can't miss the cabin, it's the only building there by the river."

"If I'm not there in an hour, come find me. By the way, I have something really amazing to tell you about Liam."

"We'll talk at the Bardic Cabin. Don't worry about Hawthorne. He's not going to try anything until after he's cast your face in plaster. That's weeks away."

"How can you be so sure?"

"They take the impression on your last night. There's a mask for every poet for the past thirteen years, except me, of course."

"No, there's one of you."

"What?"

"I heard them saying he did one of you from sketches, after you left."

"Damn. I was afraid of that. Well, anyway, you're in no danger until they get your mask. Even Devlin didn't disappear until after the ritual, obviously."

"Gee, thanks, that really makes me feel safe," Fiona scowled. "And what if he comes on to me in the meantime?"

"Oh, he will, guaranteed. Just don't do anything I wouldn't do. See you in an hour!"

Raven grinned and scrambled off into the rocks heading west. Fiona rolled her eyes and turned back toward Hawthorne's studio. Teamwork obviously had its drawbacks. Raven had a lot more guts – or lack of discretion –

than she did, that was for sure, and no compunction about leading Fiona into dangerous situations. And there seemed to be a touch of superstitious beliefs in Raven's character; she was more concerned about her likeness hanging on a wall than about placing her body in danger.

When Fiona came around to the front, Talle was standing outside staring toward the grazing meadow beyond Dragon Rock.

"There you are...I'm going back, I want to talk to Liam about all this."

"Are you going to call the police?"

"Oh, no. Hawthorne just needs to deal with Raven. Cause more harm than good to get the locals worked up, it's just a lover's quarrel. He gets overly dramatic about his women."

Fiona kept a straight face, thinking back on Talle's own recent theatrics.

"Just let him get down the first rough sketch. Try to cheer him up. I'll see you two at dinner. I apologize for the tour having to end this way. I can show you more another day."

"Thanks for the picnic, Talle," Fiona said, "And for telling me about Liam's twin."

"Twin? Oh yes, we did have quite a talk, didn't we? You'll tell me if you see that man again, won't you?"

"Sure. I'm going to try to talk to him, next time."

"I don't know if I'd recommend that. Hawthorne says he found remains of another campsite on his way over, down by the river. He's going to find the guy and get him off the property. Or we *will* call the authorities. I will *not* have strangers snooping around like that. So...you be careful, we don't know what this guy's really up to."

"Sure. Don't forget to stop by my *casita*, your book and towel are still there."

Talle shaded her eyes and gazed into Fiona's. Fiona kept her smile carefully fixed in place. The day's adventures had taken them down quite an intimate path together, yet Fiona still felt the need to keep careful walls erected with the strange, rather volatile, woman. Finally, Talle just smiled enigmatically, turned and headed toward Dragon Rock.

What was it with the woman's journal? If the velvet book was still on her sofa when she got back to the *casita*, Fiona would have to assume that her hostess really wanted her to read it, for whatever reason. Talle's earlier words now echoed: *"Accept all information offered to you...I hope you understand my meaning..."*

As for Hawthorne, hopefully he had enough on his mind – between the break-in and Talle's anger - and would postpone any ill intentions he might have against her own well-being.

Chapter 13- The Riva

Fiona found Raven stretched out under a cottonwood tree next to what the locals called "the river", the Rio de Sombras. Fiona was used to looking out over the water from Fells Point, this was nothing more than a half-dried-up creek. She wondered if these desert-dwellers were having a good one on visitors when they called it 'the river'.

What Raven had referred to, as "the Anasazi ruins", however, had been impressive. Fiona had encountered them on the other side of the red rocks as she approached the sound of the river – to her amazement, it did make quite a lively sound for its size. If Raven hadn't mentioned the ruins, Fiona would not have noticed them. The remnant indentations, mounds and rubble in the red earth were so worn and grown over with weeds that they were barely visible. But, if you knew to look for it, the man-made pattern became evident. The eye began to pick out a couple of foot-high walls built of rounded red clay bricks, and crudely-shaped bits of black obsidian scattered in the rubble. Fiona was hesitant to call the ruins "Anasazi", however. She had read enough to know that word was losing some popularity; that it was the Navajo word for the Ancestral Pueblo people and meant "enemy ancestors".

Raven's arms were folded over her chest and her legs crossed at the ankles, a desert-scape in black and white. Fiona tiptoed up to her and waved the sheaf of photos under her nose. Raven's eyes shot open.

"Fantastic! You did it!"

"It wasn't easy. You owe me big time. It's just the negatives, though. I didn't have time to get the photos."

"The negatives are more important. How'd you do it?"

"I acted like I was fascinated with the nest, asked him to let me lie down in there while he sketched me – I think I'm having an allergic reaction, my back is itching like crazy." Fiona sat next to Raven, panting and scratching, and handed her the folder. "Anyway, when he went outside to get more branches, I slipped them under my sweater. I was a nervous wreck; sure he'd hear the plastic crackling! He had this weird look in his eye."

"That 'hey baby' look?"

"Yeah. Anyway, so when he came back in, I said I'd changed my mind. I was afraid he was going to jump me or something and find those! You really owe me!"

"Is he still there?" Raven asked, holding a row of negatives up to the sunlight.

"Yeah, I said I wanted to walk around a bit, he said he'd be leaving soon. We're expected for dinner."

"You might not make it for dinner...we might be a while...Did you get my...?"

Fiona handed Raven the canteen and watched her guzzle.

"I didn't have time to look for your poem."

"That's ok, we've done damn good for one day," said Raven, wiping her mouth on her sleeve. "Anyway, maybe he doesn't have it after all, maybe the same person who broke into his place broke into my place."

"But you were so certain it was Hawthorne."

"Now I'm not so sure...So what was it you wanted to tell me about Liam?"

"He's got a twin. Talle told me about it. They were separated at birth. I think he's here."

"What do you mean?" Raven stared at her.

"I've been seeing this man, I thought it was Liam, in jeans and a sweater."

"Is this that same guy you told me about, your naked voyeur?"

"Yeah, same guy. Talle said someone's been camping on the property for a couple months. I think it's his twin, he's come to find Liam."

"So why would he lurk in the woods?"

"That's the part I haven't figured out. I'm going to try to find him, try to talk to him."

"Careful. Could be a weirdo."

"Weirder than these folks?" Fiona laughed. "I don't think so!"

"True. But watch out, just the same."

"I will. So...what's the big rush to get into the Bardic Cabin?"

Fiona drank from the canteen herself.

"I was looking at Hawthorne's portfolio this afternoon, before he got there," said Raven. "He's kept sketches of all the poets and their masks. There's one that has to be Aisling. It's dated, 9-79. But the background, it's not like the others. There are symbols behind her. Lightning, a cornstalk, a snake, a bear - like in a *kiva*, you know? Have you ever been in one?"

"No, but I've pictures in my books back home. Hey, wait a minute, I just saw those! In the photos he took of you!"

"The symbols are there?"

Raven held the negatives up to the sky again, squinting.

"Yeah, the corn stalk, I remember that," said Fiona. "And the bear, with an arrow pointing to its heart."

"You're right. There they are." Raven put the negatives down and lit a cigarette, shaking her head. "That night when Hawthorne blindfolded me..."

"When was this?"

"Oh, didn't I tell you? We had sex this one time, in the real Green Man nest...that's what he called it, 'the *real* nest'.

He said we weren't supposed to go there until the ritual, so I mustn't tell Talle - as if I would - anyway, we got so horny with the blindfold in the practice nest that he got it into his head that he wanted to take pictures of me in the real nest."

"So that's what Talle meant...She got upset when she saw the pictures of you."

"Yeah, see, that's what I'm thinking. He crossed some taboo. Anyway, so he led me through the woods, about a mile walk, blindfolded. We went inside a building, and then outside and around, several times. I guess he was trying to confuse my sense of direction. Then we went down a ladder, like into a cellar...that was tricky...and he put me in this nest and we did it with the blindfold on. It was pretty intense. Total lust situation."

Raven stopped a moment, inhaling on her cigarette and remembering. Then shook her head and continued.

"Then he walked me back part of the way, before he took the blindfold off. We were walking along the river by then, it seemed we'd gone about half a mile. So...I got to thinking, Aisling disappeared in '79, the last year they used the Bardic Cabin."

"Are you sure? Talle seemed confused on that point."

"Oh please! You know she knows the exact day and hour! This is her domain, remember?"

"True."

"Anyway, I'm sure, I researched it. So there's got to be a connection. It makes sense, from the distance of the cabin from his studio. This is where he took me. The clatter of the leaves in these trees - you hear that? The sound of the river. I remember all of this. He must have sketched Aisling in there, too. I figure we were in a basement under the Bardic Cabin. It was cold and smelled real earthy, the floor felt soft. He built a fire to warm us up. It was such a sensual experience; back when I still felt good about him...I remember all those details. Maybe there's something in that basement that will tell us about Aisling. It's a hunch but..."

"A good one. Especially with those pictures of you – those symbols are definitely there in some of those shots. So how do we get into the cabin?"

Raven motioned for Fiona to follow her. Beyond the grove of cottonwoods, an old log cabin, similar to Hawthorne's studio cabin, with the windows boarded over. Raven hadn't spent the last hour just napping. Boards and yellow warning signs had been pulled away from the door and were stacked on the front stoop. The door was pushed ajar.

"I haven't gone in yet, I wanted to wait for you. Watch out for spiders."

Raven pulled a flashlight from her jacket pocket and directed the beam through the front door. The room reminded Fiona of the description of Thoreau's cabin. The fireplace looked as if it hadn't been used for at least a decade except by the spiders. A set of dusty iron fireplace tools from another time was propped on the hearth, anchored to the wall by a large cobweb. A table and one chair. On the table was a candle burned to a stub, a cup and a water jug, the contents having long since evaporated. There was a cot; the bedding in disarray as if someone had recently slept there, yet the blanket was obviously well-seasoned with a layer of dust.

Fiona smiled. The Green Man had no doubt visited a few poets here - Raven's flashlight illuminated piles of old, dried leaves in every corner, held in place by dust-caked webs. She closed her eyes and imagined the poets spending their nights here, casting metaphors across the dark walls, working hard to capture those illusive lines of verse before dawn. Forming, editing, shaping, all without pen or paper. Catching a fleeting image, holding it in place, wrestling with it, trying not to lose it - and yet here came another, how to hold them both down at once? Fiona suddenly remembered the Yeats poem, *I dropped the berry in a stream/ And caught a little silver trout.* Yes, the process was probably a lot like night fishing. She made a mental note to talk to her father about that next time she called him. She felt a wave of sadness, standing in the cobwebby dark, watching Raven's light move along the time-worn walls and abandoned objects of the cabin. Sadness because she missed her father, sadness that Liam's beautiful vision of the Bardic School had come to an end.

"Hmmm... all the walls are logs. No cave paintings up here. We've got to find the ladder to the basement," Raven said, stepping cautiously inside.

"Keep the light on these floorboards," Fiona whispered, following her friend closely and wondering why she was whispering. "I'm really spooked about falling through."

"Hey, look at this...it's stone!"

Relieved, Fiona watched the flashlight beam as it played across the floor.

"And these beams look pretty solid," Raven tapped on a beam. "It's not that old a cabin, probably built in the '50s, another hunting cabin like Hawthorne's studio."

"So why did Talle have it condemned?" Fiona wondered. "This place looks better-preserved than Hawthorne's, even."

"Aside from the mouse droppings. Smells like one or two of them died in here. I think something happened here to freak her out."

"It's really a beautiful cabin," Fiona sighed. "I like the idea of the Bardic School, don't you?"

The romance of writing was the last thing on Raven's mind as she flashed the light in every direction.

"Something bad happened in here - I can *feel* it," said Raven. "Perhaps while Devlin spent the night here. Maybe it had something to do with her disappearance. Whatever happened, it scared Talle enough to close it up...There's no basement. Damn! I was so sure this would be the place."

"Have you checked for an outside entrance?"

Raven and Fiona went back out into the waning daylight, circled the cabin, but could see nothing, other than a low stack of firewood and some trees that had been felled nearby.

"Wait, I remember this," Raven stopped in back of the cabin and lifted her nose, inhaling sharply. " Some kind of mint? Smell that?"

Fiona inhaled. The scent was strong, like the spearmint that grew near the kitchen porch at her father's Oklahoma farm. She nodded.

"That night, I smelled that. Spearmint. It's *got* to be here."

Raven walked a few feet into the miscellaneous shrubbery, scuffing at the dirt with her boot heel. Suddenly her heel hit something that sounded like metal. In an instant, both poets were down on their knees, digging with their bare fingers. Two inches down, they could see a metal surface, scratched and rusted. They grabbed rocks and dug quickly, revealing a small, three-foot square metal-and-wood hinged door set into a very old, wooden frame in the ground.

"My god, this is it! We need something to pry it with."

Raven jumped up and rushed back to the Bardic Cabin. She returned with the fireplace poker and ash shovel. The women poked and pried until they lifted the door. The hinges creaked and dust rushed up, sending Fiona into a sneezing fit. Raven covered her mouth and nose against the dust and smell of more dead mice - rats, maybe. She turned on the flashlight, shining it down into the darkness.

"Here's the ladder! You hold the light, I'm going down."

Fiona bit her tongue on all the warnings that piled in the back of her mouth, knowing there was no way to stop

Raven now. She leaned over the edge and shone the light while Raven climbed down.

"The ladder's sturdy. God, it's damn cold down here...! Hey, this is a cinch, it's only about ten feet down."

Fiona could just see the top of Raven's head and heard her boots hit dirt.

"Can you play that thing in the corners? It's pitch dark down here."

Fiona angled the beam, but it was too awkward to direct it into the corners.

"You'll have to come on down, I need the light."

"I could toss it to you," Fiona suggested hopefully.

Raven looked up and her expression was unmistakable. Fiona sighed, clutched the light like a lifeline, and began her descent down the ladder. At the bottom, the two poets stood, inhaling the smell of earth and rot in fear and amazement at what they'd found.

"This is the place. I remember this smell. We burned incense, to keep it at bay."

Raven took the flashlight from Fiona, who now held her nose, and played the light slowly along the walls. The structure was about twelve by fifteen feet and ten feet high. At one end was a tiny clay fireplace with a rectangular ventilating hole in the wall behind it. There were paintings - pictographs - on the walls, faded colors of ochre, black, white and blood red. A red hand, a brown bear with a red arrow, ears of corn, lightning. In one corner were a cluster of old clay pots, some whole, some broken. In the walls were *niches* similar to the ones in the Fagans' hallway, filled with artist's supplies. Plaster, rags, brushes and carving tools. Similar to the supplies in Hawthorne's studio. Against one wall was a small work table and a tall, narrow cabinet. More supplies, jugs of water, bottles with labels. Packages of incense. Leaning against the cabinet were planks, a shovel, a pick and other tools.

Finally, filling the opposite corner was a platform built of wood, a crèche piled with dried branches and leaves. Identical to the Green Man's nest in Hawthorne's studio. Fiona stepped up to the nest and reached to touch the dried leaves.

"Watch out for mice, they carry lovely diseases out here," Raven warned her. "There are droppings all over, a few dead ones. And recluse spiders, be careful, they jump."

Fiona pulled her hand back, but saw something gleaming in Raven's flashlight beam. A thin piece of wire, caught between the platform of branches and the wall. Fiona tugged on the wire until it came loose. Attached to the other end was what seemed to be a small wooden peg.

"Just like I thought," Raven whispered. "It's a *kiva*. It's – very old. Looks like it was used for something else later, some kind of cellar...but it was originally a *kiva*. We shouldn't have entered this place without asking permission."

"Of Talle?"

"No. There's always a guardian. A spirit. We need to make an offering. It's not right for us to just come in here. We have to go back up and come back down."

Fiona stared at Raven, then shrugged as she realized how serious she was. She tucked the bit of wire into her jeans pocket and followed the flashlight beam, as Raven quietly ascended the ladder again and stood above the opening. Fiona hadn't realized how bad the rodent smell was until she was breathing above ground air again. Raven looked around, perplexed.

"What's wrong now?" asked Fiona.

"I don't know whose *kiva* it is. This one might not have been a place for ceremonies. It was obviously a pit structure, probably built in the thirteen hundreds. Since we have ruins over there, this was probably part of a small village, just a dwelling."

"How do you know all this?"

"I dated an archaeologist for a while. He was too enchanted with my genealogy, made me nervous. But we explored a lot of ruins together. Great moonlight sex on the mesas, too. Anyway, I think someone fifty years ago or so removed the fill from this pit to open it up. The family who owned this land had it for generations, they had the bucks to renovate this."

"Wouldn't they have to disclose its presence to the government or university archaeologists? Isn't there some legal requirement of excavation or preservation?"

"No. Private land is sacred. You can do whatever you want with any resources you find on your land. The only thing is, you can't mess with Native American burials. If you find a skeleton, that's when you have to contact the authorities and the tribe. You can't touch the remains or the objects buried with them. You wouldn't want to anyway."

"Why not?"

"Very bad medicine to mess with that. My archaeologist friend told me one of the biggest problems in his field is the pothunters, people digging up artifacts to sell on the antiquities market. It's big bucks. One prehistoric community he was working on down state was so badly 'potted' that he thought maybe eighty per cent of it had been dug into before he got there. Both by the old Anglo ranching family that owned the land and the pothunters sneaking in. He said entire buildings had been bulldozed - a crude but efficient technique for finding artifacts. The previous owner, or maybe their ranch hands might have excavated into this structure, looking for pots to sell. But ranchers can't leave open holes around for their stupid cows to fall into, so they would have had to fill up the hole afterward. That's probably when they re-built the ceiling and decided to use it as a cellar – Or there's another possibility."

"What's that?"

"Maybe they tried to renovate the *kiva* to show it off, like a tourist thing. That's been done before."

"Or maybe Talle had it opened up."

"Possibly. Sounds like something she would do, all right. That might explain where she got most of the artifacts in the hacienda. But who built the original pit structure? Could be Anasazi, could be immigrants from the San Juan/Mesa Verde area. If this was a *kiva*, I don't know what the guardian spirit would be."

"Is it ok to call them 'Anasazi'?"

Raven gave Fiona a complicated look.

"I mean," Fiona continued, blushing, "Isn't 'Ancestral Pueblo People' more accepted?"

"Call them whatever you need to, Fiona From Baltimore," Raven grinned.

"So...this guardian spirit...could it be the Green Man?"

Raven laughed and looked at Fiona again, then looked back at the *kiva* trap door.

"I guess that makes as much sense as anything, in this place and time."

Fiona watched Raven move through the junipers, gathering fallen branches. She sprinkled water on them from her canteen and reached for a cornmeal pouch in her day pack.

"Is this from your...religion?" Fiona asked shyly.

Raven smiled. "No... it's just...my mother would say it's '*what must be done*'."

Admittedly, Raven didn't affiliate herself with any religion or spiritual practice. Writing poetry was her form of worship, and the desert and woods were her cathedrals. She carried the cornmeal because it was what her mother would have done, whose father had been a traveling Navajo medicine man, what was called a "road man". Raven remembered watching her mother use cornmeal to bless the doorways and windows of their home in Santa Fe.

"Only the men are supposed to do this," she would whisper to her daughter as Raven followed her from room to room, carrying the basket of meal, *"But your father doesn't practice this way. So this is what must be done."*

Her mother had been referring to her adopted father, Orlando Cordova, who was very much Catholic. By marrying him, she had disconnected from her people. But, then, that had begun to happen long before Orlando, back with Father Shane. Since there were no men from her family to bless her Santa Fe home, Raven's mother did it herself. She burned the sage and smudged herself and her daughter, she even shared the pipe with Raven.

"Empty your mind and pay attention, Raven, when we bless the house together."

When Raven's mother died, the dark poet had poured the last of the cornmeal from the hearth basket into her mother's leather jewelry pouch. She carried it with her until the mealie bugs invaded it. Then replenished it with new cornmeal. She also kept the small, worn, Celtic cross she had found in the pouch with her mother's beads and earrings. She believed the cross had belonged to her father, the Catholic priest. Her mother never spoke of the man, which gave Raven a lot of room to imagine what had occurred between her enigmatic mother and the Irishman whose vows had obviously been troublesome.

Raven laid the water-sprinkled branches at each corner of the trap door, tossed cornmeal into the four directions, and sprinkled more in a circle. She stopped, hands on hips, staring down into the entrance. Her mother also would remind her, at this point, that it was taboo for women to climb down that ladder. Then she would hoist her skirts and begin the descent, admonishing Raven: *Empty your mind and stay alert, child.*

"My mother was quite an amazing woman, Fiona."

"I hope you'll tell me about her sometime."

"Ok, we can go in now," Raven said.

The two women solemnly climbed back down the ladder.

"Oh hell, I left the flashlight up there," said Raven when they reached the earth floor.

"Let's just leave anyway, it's going to be dark in a few minutes," said Fiona, holding her nose again. "We can come back another day–"

"Wait, I saw candles here–"

Raven fumbled around and found two white candles on the shelving. She lit them with a butane lighter from her jeans pocket, and handed one to Fiona. Raven began to walk around the room, scanning every surface. Fiona reluctantly followed.

"What are we looking for?" she asked, shivering. It was almost icy down here.

"The *sipapu,* if this was truly a ceremonial *kiva.*"

"What's that?"

"A hole, a symbolic passage to the third world, where the living can communicate with the spirit world. It should be in the center. Some bodies of water and places on the land can be *sipapu* too."

"What kind of ceremonies would go on in here?"

"My mother's people would tell you 'You don't need to know' if you asked a question like that, and in a not-too-friendly tone."

"Sorry!"

"I just mean, it's sacred, only initiates would know. And they wouldn't tell you. All I know is there would be a guardian at the top during ceremonies," Raven flashed the light along the wall on the other side of the room from the nest and moved closer, running her hands along the surface.

"Interesting...looks like someone touched these up at some point."

Fiona joined her and peered at the images of a lizard, a handprint and a spiral like the ones Fiona had seen at Newgrange in County Meath, Ireland. These pictographs did look a little different than the ones behind the nest, the colors were brighter, the lines more distinct. And yet there were areas faded out, the thumb was missing on the hand, half the tail gone from the lizard.

"Reminds me of the preservation work at the monuments," said Raven. "They'll leave one area as is, then paint in another to show you how the drawings looked originally."

"Well, you know Talle. She probably hired some artist to come do this."

"Yeah, probably. Maybe even Hawthorne."

Raven moved along, scanning the rest of the room. Fiona held the candle closer to the drawings. There was a tiny crack in the adobe work, running like a miniature arroyo between the lizard and the spiral.

"Hey, have you seen Talle's apothecary?" Raven called out from the other side of the *kiva*, where she was holding her candle high to illuminate the niches in the wall in which the mask-making supplies were stored.

"Yeah, just this morning. Why?"

Fiona traced the line of the fissure in the wall, and a small piece of the reddish-beige adobe broke off under the pressure of her fingers. Crumbs of dirt and plaster fell away.

"These look like those little blue bottles..."

Suddenly the room went dark with a sharp, slapping sound from above. Simultaneously, a last rush of outside air extinguished both poets' candles. Fiona gasped as hot wax dripped onto her fingers. She instinctively dropped the candle and leapt backward, lost her balance, then caught her fall by slapping her hands into the wall she had been inspecting. A large clump of adobe fell away and her right hand hit a smooth surface underneath.

"Shit," hissed Raven. "What the...?"

"Oh god, Raven, was that the wind?"

"Shit. Where's my damn lighter?"

Fiona stayed where she was, waiting for the sound of the butane click. The *kiva* was absolutely dark now, as if layers of dense, black fabric were pressed against her eyes, nose and mouth. She began to feel she wouldn't be able to breath – that the loss of light would also mean the loss of air. Images of rodents and jumping spiders instantly filled her mind.

"Hurry!"

"I can't find it. I must have set it down somewhere."

Raven held her hands in front of her and moved slowly in the direction she'd last seen the ladder. She reached it and began to climb carefully. Fiona stood still, straining to hear the hopeful sounds of her friend ascending the ladder in a silence as ultimate as the darkness. Raven reached the top of the ladder and shoved the door. It was heavy and wouldn't give.

"Hurry!" whispered Fiona, now shivering, certain she felt things crawling up her legs.

"It won't open."

Raven leaned her torso against the top ladder rungs and braced her knees and ankles into the ones below, then shoved her arms upward as hard as she could against the wooden surface. This time the door gave way too easily, as though a weight had suddenly been removed. Raven grabbed at the doorframe to keep her balance. A wind had started up and grains of desert sand stung her eyes.

"Wow, weather change up here," Raven called down as she climbed out onto the ground. "Looks like rain, it's getting very dark."

"Let me outta here, now!"

Fiona rushed up the ladder, and hoisted herself to sit on the edge of the doorframe. She dangled her legs into the hole and gratefully inhaled the about-to-rain desert air. The luminous and golden pre-dusk light spilled out along the ground from under a large, black thundercloud overhead. Raven was dusting off her jeans and buttoning up her jacket. Fiona reached behind her where they had left the fireplace tools and Raven's backpack and canteen.

"Raven...did you leave your backpack down there? And the canteen?"

"No, they're right there behind you, with the tools."

Fiona scanned the area between the cabin and the *kiva* door. The greens were still placed around the *kiva* opening, but the tools and backpack were nowhere to be seen. She felt a rush of fear up her back and looked quickly along the darkening horizon in all directions. No one.

"Raven...our things are gone."

Raven searched in the junipers, finding nothing. The two poets stared at each other. Someone – not the wind – had been here and closed the *kiva* door. Had that someone tried to lock them in? They looked toward the Bardic Cabin. Maybe that person was still here, inside the cabin, watching.

"We have to check in there. They've got the damned photos."

Raven strode toward the cabin. Fiona had no choice but to follow.

Inside the cabin, they found the iron tools had been replaced on the hearth. Raven's backpack and canteen were set neatly inside the doorway, leaning against the wall.

"What the?"

Raven dug into her backpack. The negatives were still there.

"Someone trying to be helpful?"

Not so far away, thunder rumbled and a cold wind rushed through the Bardic Cabin, whistling and rattling between the boards nailed over the windows.

"Helpful? Raven, someone tried to lock us in. We could have been left there to die, for god's sake. Let's cover the doorway over and get the hell out of here."

Raven hoisted the backpack over her shoulder and Fiona strapped on the canteen. They closed the door to the cabin and replaced the boards and signs, pounding the nails back in with rocks. They walked around to the back of the cabin and toward the *kiva* door.

Only to find it was gone. Or at least covered over. Slowly they walked to the exact spot where they'd left it, again scanning the bushes, the horizon, but seeing no one. They stood over the site of the door and stared in disbelief. The earth had been smoothed over. The greens they had left in blessing were gone. Someone had accomplished the camouflage thoroughly. Fiona gasped and pointed. Directly over the site of the *kiva* door, scratched into the earth, was some kind of message. Fiona bent to read it.

"ex4d."

"What the hell does that mean?" Raven asked, irritated with this search for clues that had taken on a life of its own due to someone else's intervention. She was certain that that "someone" was Hawthorne, pulling one of his little power plays again.

"It's chess notation," Fiona said, staring incredulously at the scratchings. "A move for my game with Liam. And a damned good one....

Raven...I think the Green Man has been here."

Chapter 14 - The Chess Game

Liam frowned, staring at his checked queen, sat back and rubbed a finger across his lips.

"Sorry...but that's the move the Green Man gave me," Fiona apologized as she placed his pawn - which had been one move away from queen-hood - on the table next to the board with the other pieces previously captured by her predecessor, the mysterious computer partner.

"Oh, never apologize for your gains – ill-gotten or honestly earned!" Liam teased as he leaned forward to move his queen out of danger, and capture Fiona's last remaining rook.

"Hmm. Well, I was feeling a bit guilty stealing my moves from the Green Man, but it seems he doesn't necessarily have my best interests at heart," Fiona laughed as she watched Liam deposit her rook into the gathering cluster of pieces on his side of the board.

"He gave you an interesting move. Of course, since this game sat dormant for so long, I'd had a lot of time to contemplate my opponent's next move. I figured he would either put my queen in check and risk losing his rook, or take my rook over here."

Liam indicated the other direction Fiona's knight might have jumped.

"Actually, that was the move I had thought to make," Fiona said. "But you said to go with the Green Man, so I did. And now I will again. He gave me two moves."

Fiona's heart began to pound faster as she realized that the move the Green Man had left in chess notation on the *kiva* door, "ex4d ", was a brilliant response to Liam's protective relocation of his queen. Liam hadn't noticed that he had placed his bishop in jeopardy. She made the move and lifted Liam's bishop off the board.

"Oh my. Did he tell you to do that?"

"Afraid so."

Liam raised his eyebrows, watching her set his bishop down with her takings.

"He knew what I would do after your first move, and what you should do next?"

"Apparently."

Liam and Fiona stared at the board. The only sound in the room was the crackling of the fire in the corner.

"I think I need a little something," Liam finally said, and rose to pour two glasses of vintage Macallan's single malt from the decanter on the library table. He handed Fiona hers. The two players sipped, still staring at the board.

"Charles Dickens said 'Love that has a game of chess in it can checkmate any man and solve the problem of life,'" Liam mused. "Now you must tell me how the visions come to you."

Fiona stared up at the Green Man mask. What was his expression tonight? Every time she saw this mask, it seemed to have a different mood. Tonight it was a smirk, as if he dared her to speak. How much could she really tell Liam? Given the investigation she had entered into with Raven - and not knowing how much of what was said in this room was relayed later to Talle, maybe even to Hawthorne - she had to choose her words carefully.

She was also reluctant to talk about anything so private as her inner visions and fantasies with Liam tonight. She had intentionally dressed down - jeans and a cardigan, Reeboks, no jewelry, no perfume. She didn't want any reoccurrences of hallway kissing.

"Or..." Liam was obviously trying to interpret her reticence. "Perhaps you find it too tedious to play it this way? Obviously you are a skilled player. We could forego the Green Man and play our own game. I wouldn't be adverse..."

"Oh no, it's not that. I don't mind doing it this way, really. It's...fascinating...But I'm not sure how much I can tell you about... my visions."

"Of course, they're private. I understand. It's just... so curious to me. Forgive me, I have gone and trampled on boundaries again. It's a bad habit I have, Talle is always chiding me about my social skills. I speak when I should be silent and I'm silent when I should speak."

"You don't need to apologize."

"However he reveals these moves to you, you can rest assured the Green Man has a plan. Those were not isolated moves," Liam scrutinized the board. "That was the thing that was so compelling to me, playing my computer partner. He was so good that I wasn't able to see where he was going and then, suddenly, it would be obvious. We were matched. He couldn't see where I was going either and then he would see it and counter me perfectly. It was like playing myself...Well, so I have one more move and then we are done for the night."

Liam sipped his scotch, and then set it down to focus in earnest on the pieces before him. Fiona sipped and glanced around the room while she waited. A courtyard lamp outside the window illuminated the colors of the stained glass, Book of Kells window. Again, she admired the twisted and intertwined figures of the four Evangelists - the lion, ox, eagle and man. She looked up at the Green Man mask. Still that smirk. She heard the clicking of pieces and looked down at the board. Liam had already sat back, satisfied with himself, and was enjoying his scotch.

"I missed it, what did you do?"

"Guard."

Fiona examined the board. Now her queen was a move away from danger from Liam's queen. Yet she had to leave her queen in peril until the Green Man spoke to her again. She didn't like the feeling. Easily she could get her queen on a safe track. There were two pieces she could move in Liam's path of aggression. But this was not her game; it was the Green Man's. Liam caught her expression as the two sipped their drinks.

"Hopefully he will visit you again soon," he murmured sympathetically.

"Hopefully."

"Has Hawthorne begun to sketch you?"

"Yes."

Liam lowered his voice to a husky whisper.

"Did you undress for the dear boy?"

Fiona blushed and averted her eyes.

"No, I didn't."

"Was he upset when you wouldn't undress?"

"The subject never came up. He was just sketching my face."

"Ah. Well...the subject *will* come up."

Fiona still avoided his eyes, staring into her glass.

"And when it does, what will you do, Fiona?"

Fiona's heart was pounding hard again. She felt her expression seal over in anger, an unexpected reaction to the sudden chill in his voice. Yet she was so aroused. What was this? She wasn't even looking at him; they hadn't even touched. They had been innocently and pleasantly playing chess. Why was he doing this? And how?

"I don't know why I do this, Fiona," he whispered, as if reading her mind. "I can't help it in your company. Oh please, dear girl—"

Liam was swiftly at her side, kneeling and wrapping his arms around her, almost upsetting the chessboard. He moved his lips to her ear.

"He will unbutton your sweater, like so...he will pull it down...he will touch you, here..."

Liam's fingers found her breast, his lips brushed her neck. Fiona moaned and, despite her resolve and confusion, closed her eyes and felt her spine arching.

Suddenly panicked that Talle might find them, her eyes shot open. She gasped at a dark movement outside the Book of Kells window.

"Liam, someone's out there!" she whispered, pushing his hands away and rising, straightening her clothes. She moved quickly to the window and stared out through a clear panel, but it was too dark to see anything. Liam readjusted the chess table and pushed his hands through his hair. He moved to the open doorway and listened down the hall.

"Everyone is here - I hear Talle and Hawthorne talking. You must have imagined it. Oh god," Liam placed his hands over his eyes. "I am so sorry."

"Liam," Fiona moved quickly to his side. "You must, you *must* stop this. *Please.* I don't know what it is you are doing, but it is so upsetting. I mean, you're an attractive man, but..."

"I am 'doing' nothing. It is you, your presence, I can't help myself."

"Yes you can. Liam, listen to me," Fiona pulled at his arms and led him to the love seat. "Someone was at the window. Someone saw what we were doing. And it's not the first time."

Liam looked confused and distraught.

"I know about your walks, Liam. I need you to tell me about that," Fiona amazed herself with the adult-to-child tone she took with him. But she felt a sense of urgency. "Why do you tell me you don't take walks, that you rarely leave the house? I've seen you now, several times. At the window here, I saw you one night, as if you were spying on your own house. And once I saw you watching Hawthorne and that woman in the hot springs…"

"I don't know what you're talking about, dear girl. I don't take walks. I have never watched Hawthorne in the hot springs. Why would I spy at my own windows?"

Fiona scrutinized Liam's face. He seemed genuinely confused. Liam was many things, most of which she hadn't yet figured out, but a liar didn't seem to be one of them.

"So if it's not you, who is it?"

"Honestly, Fiona, I have no idea what you're talking about. You were just nervous, you saw a shadow, maybe the wind, the trees–"

Fiona shook her head. They were already in dangerous territory; there was no reason to hold back now.

"Talle says you have a twin."

Liam's eyes darkened. He set his jaw and looked away.

"I'm sorry, I didn't mean to—"

"That is private," he said emphatically. "Talle had no right to speak to you about that."

Liam rose and poured himself another scotch. He was so distraught that his usual good-host manner had evaporated, and he forgot to refill Fiona's glass. He swigged the drink and then set the glass down. He pulled a white handkerchief from his pocket, rubbing his fingers with great concentration. Fiona realized he was wiping the scent of her from his hands. His spine had stiffened and his face was set in its puritanical pose. The sexless man had returned.

"I will retire now," he said, moving toward the door. "It's been a very long day."

Fiona sat, frozen. The chill in his tone was devastating. His acceptance and then his rejection of her had more impact than she could begin to understand. Yet, she felt a sense of urgency, that she should press the subject, regardless of rousing his anger.

"Liam, please talk to me about this. I've seen your twin, on several occasions. He's here, in your woods. He's watching you."

Liam stopped wiping his fingers. He seemed to stop breathing. After a long moment, he carefully folded the handkerchief into a neat square and tucked it back into his pants pocket. He picked up his glass and went to the Book of Kells window.

"Do you know why I commissioned this?"

Fiona shook her head. Suddenly she felt drained and wanted all of this to be over.

"I resonate to the knotwork. To the illuminated manuscripts. To the fact that the Book was resurrected from the bog where the thieves had thrown it to its grave. To the fact that the bog preserved it. This is the work of my ancestors, from a place of true magic. This window represents a heritage I was denied."

Liam traced a thin line of lead along the lion's mane, golden glass against a royal blue background, and continued.

"I was born in Ireland, in 1936, adopted to America, out of the basinet. It was pre-arranged, my biological family was poor and hoped I would fare better in America with the Fagans, a third-generation Irish family in St. Louis, Missouri. When I was sixteen, my adoptive parents were killed in a train accident. After their death, I found some papers. A letter from a priest in Ireland, commending my adoption. Unfortunately, the letter was only signed 'Fr. Paidric', no address, no county. My adoptive relatives were no help, they only knew I had come from Ireland. I could find no birth certificate."

Liam turned, putting his hands in his pockets, smiling sadly.

"None of this surprised me. Somehow, I had always known they weren't my true parents. They were Irish Americans who strove to be more 'American' than Irish.

"I was sent to live with my adopted uncle. At the age of eighteen, I finished high school and left. I was, I suppose, disenchanted. Perhaps even depressed. I had no family to speak of; I was cast alone in the world, not knowing my true family, in another country.

"I was sensitive, highly impressionable. I always had a longing, a sense of loss. Even as a young child, I was melancholy. That was how my adopted mother described me."

Liam gazed at the books surrounding him in his chess library as he continued.

"In my early years I worked odd jobs, I took courses at different times, almost finished my degree, but never could settle on any field of study or line of work. The closest I felt to satisfied was one brief job clerking in an antique bookstore. But the owner lost his business and I lost my position.

"I always felt lost, truly disconnected from all humans. Which only underscored this ancient ache, this hole in my heart. I thought of myself as 'a missing twin'. I couldn't articulate that at the time, but now, looking back, I understand that was my truth."

The older poet put the glass of single malt to his lips, realized it was empty, poured another. This time he added an inch of liquid to Fiona's glass as well.

"Anyway, then it was the sixties. There were others like me, disenfranchised, alienated. It was easy to blend in and become lost in the counter-culture. Until I met Talle, I roamed with the hippies. Oh, it's a long story, but what

I'm trying to tell you is..." Liam leveled an accusing look at Fiona. "...That when you come into my home and make light of this part of me, this part that has cried out forever to be awakened, nourished, acknowledged..."

"I am not making light. I believe your twin is here. I have thought, all this time, it was you in the woods. But if you tell me it wasn't you, I believe you. This man is identical to you. If you have a twin, this must be him."

"It makes no sense, Fiona. How would he find me? And if he did, why wouldn't he just come to my door, present himself? You're mistaken; it's some other stranger – or maybe your Green Man. After all, you are prone to visions, are you not?"

Was he being condescending? Fiona decided to present her theory.

"Liam, you've told me more than once that when you played chess with your mysterious computer partner, it was like playing chess with yourself. So, what if your opponent was your twin?"

Liam gave Fiona a look of incredulity and shook his head. She continued, regardless. "What if the fates brought you two together through the computer? Maybe, unlike you, his family had told him that he was a twin. Maybe he was searching for you. He somehow found you, discovered where you lived, and came to find out what you had become. But perhaps he's a poor, uneducated man, embarrassed in comparison to your wealth. Perhaps he doesn't want you to misunderstand his motives."

"I don't know what to think, Fiona. I simply don't know."

"I'm going to try to find him and speak to him."

"Leave it to Hawthorne. If there really is a trespasser, he's the one to deal with it."

"Talle has told him to run the man off the property. He's apparently camping near the river. I think Hawthorne is still cutting wood at Cat Mesa tomorrow, hopefully he won't have time to find the man and make him leave before I can talk to him."

Liam stared into the fire, realized it needed a new log, and stood to add one.

"My belief in my twin is like a legend, a myth of my life. An unreality in which only I believe. The way one says one doesn't believe in heaven and hell, but secretly fears they may be real. That is how I believe - and don't believe - in my twin. Do you understand?"

The new log flared, and then settled into a comfortable, slow burn.

"I think so."

"And for him to become real, flesh and blood – how could that possibly be?"

"It happens all the time today, people find each other."

"So our computer man tells us. He is the one who showed us about playing virtual chess. In fact..." Liam stopped, staring into the flame.

"In fact?"

"Now that I recall, Talle first found my chess player. She connected to an Irish-American bulletin board and discovered this chess player and hooked us up. But she didn't tell the player any details about our life, where we live, who we are. They only communicated briefly. Their correspondence ended. But our chess games went on."

"See? An Irish-American bulletin board! That might be a place your Irish twin would look if he was searching for you."

"It seems unbelievable."

"Not really, not in these times. And, Liam, I have *seen* him."

"Well, perhaps I'll take a walk tomorrow...It seems that you and I are incapable of a simple little game of chess, Fiona."

Liam turned and left the room without a further word, his final mood unclear to Fiona. Perhaps he was simply exhausted. Fiona sat on the love seat, taking over his task of fire gazing, perplexed at the range of emotions the evening had brought on. What were these complex feelings Liam raised in her? Not quite lover, not just friend...it was his immense sadness that pulled at her, despite herself. He seemed much too regal, too beautiful to be so sad and without hope. He reminded her of the caged panther in the Rilke poem.

"From seeing the bars, his seeing is so exhausted/that it no longer holds anything anymore..." she whispered to herself.

But perhaps she could see for him. Yes, her theory about his twin was fantastic, she knew that. It was just the kind of thing a poet would dream up. But it might just take the fantastic to free Liam from his cage.

Back in her *casita*, Fiona noted Talle's journal was still there, un-retrieved. Again, the woman's words echoed from this afternoon's picnic: *"If you are to take part in the ritual, you need to be fully informed...You should accept all information offered to you on the subject, however it comes to you. I hope you understand my meaning."*

Three hours later Fiona had read the entire book, which spanned about nine months. Talle never dated her entries, but Fiona was able to piece together the time frame because the book's first entries were about taking down the greens from the doorways and crunching pine cones into mulch after last winter's Yule and Christmas celebrations. True to form, Talle's household celebrated both.

This time the reading was not so fascinating. Fiona had to force herself to continue from page to page. She yawned and fidgeted. She was tired and wanted to go to bed, but she needed to get this over with, once and for all.

Her reaction to the book puzzled and amused her. Could it be that once the taboo text was allotted her, in the tone of a homework assignment, it was no longer titillating? Could she be that transparent, and Talle that manipulative? If so, Fiona felt even more embarrassed at her previous snooping. New entries which mentioned Talle's reaction to knowing her journal was being read made Fiona blush.

What were of real interest to Fiona were the passages about Talle's encounters with "Him" and the Green Man in the woods. She skimmed everything else, stopping to read those parts slowly. Something had changed over the course of the year, from the earlier passages where Talle described her longing for the elusive "Him" in the woods.

As the summer had passed, the Green Man seemed to have become more like a deity to Talle. She saw him as having some kind of power or control over her life. She also saw him as the steward of her land. A gatekeeper. A guardian. (*He is inseparable from the woods...the manifestation of the woods, in human form...He already knows...everything.*)

Talle also seemed increasingly concerned not to "displease" the Green Man. It was puzzling to Fiona that the woman seemed to feel her ownership of the thousand acres was tenuous. Talle's concerns about how the Green Man reacted to her attempts to placate him seemed increasingly urgent, as if something was veering out of control. Was it something internal, in Talle's mind? Or was it some real threat, from the outer world?

Fiona looked up at the Green Man mask in the loft. The one Talle had identified as modeled after Aisling Devlin. From where she sat on the sofa, the mask's expression was immensely sad. It hadn't seemed so, before. Fiona turned back to Talle's pages again, and read:

"He wakes me up in the middle of the night, standing by my bed, holding out His leafy arms and crying. It is terrible to see Him cry, He who is all-powerful. His crying mouth is a dark opening, foul-smelling, it is horrifying to me. The sound of His cry is grating, like dried winter branches scraping against a window - a demented sound. I feel chills across my whole body. What does He want from me? What more can I give Him?"

Several pages later:

"I went to the kiva tonight, so excited to see Him. I brought a poem to read to Him, about the wind in the trees being the sound of His cry of longing for us. I thought He must be inside, waiting for me. I went down the ladder. I felt arms grabbing me from behind, pushing me into the nest, tying me down.

It was not what I thought it would be. Something was pressed against my eyes and nose, I felt leaves crammed into my mouth. There was a smell of parsnips, I couldn't breath, my skin was burning, I tried to scream...It was not what I thought it would be."

Parsnips? That was what Fiona had smelled, in her vision at the hot springs.

A recent entry:

"I fear He is angry with me, that I have misunderstood His directives. And then He smiles, unexpectedly. I am like a schoolgirl with a crush. His every gesture lifts me or brings me to my knees. And yet I must continue in my daily world, tending the plants, running the errands, as if He, who is everything, does not exist."

Were these Talle's real experiences? Or visions? This didn't seem to be the benevolent Green Man of Fiona's encounters. Nor did the voice of this woman seem the same voice Fiona had first read in this journal, only last week.

Reading these pages disturbed Fiona. She put the book down and stood, restless. Not knowing what else to do, she went to the kitchen, put on water to boil. Carried the journal from the sofa to the table and turned on the lamp. Sighing, she sat to continue her task.

More recent passages were about Talle's walks, at night, in the woods. Looking for the Green Man, references to "appointments", then disappointed notes:

"He never came. . . ."

"I waited until dawn, then had to get back before I was missed at the hacienda. But I felt terrible giving up...why should His timetable be contingent on such mundanities as the serving of breakfast? I felt I should wait for Him longer, I felt so keenly the rift between the demands of my 'real' life and the vibrancy of His reality, which I embrace. . . ."

"Oh Lord, I want to be with You, to go where You are and not return to this world...yet I realize the sacrilege of that longing in me...You need me to be where I am, to do Your bidding here."

These passages had a dual nature. In part, they reminded Fiona of an unrequited lover who read meaning into her love object's every non-response. On the other hand, it was as if Talle had reached a spiritual crisis, as did the saints at times. She wanted to *meet* her lord, to *see* him, to have tangible, sensory proof of his existence. She teetered on an edge now: she either required a sign, or needed to resign herself to absolute, blind faith. Faith for faith's sake, much like art for art's sake:

"*Life, to me these days, is tinged with an irreparable sadness. I wake in the morning drenched in the sense of loving someone who is close and intimate but does not feel passion for me...the desire to cry, for no reason. Then there are those moments of longing. Longing is the motivator, the norm, the way things are and should be.*"

Fiona rolled her eyes. Even as a poet, there was a limit to her patience when it came to the Romantics. And was this passage about the Green Man or Liam or Hawthorne? Or even anyone in particular?

The teakettle whistled sharply, startling Fiona. She went to the kitchenette and fixed a pot of lemon tea.

Sitting again, she turned back to look at the velvet cover of Talle's journal. It occurred to her that the book's spilled blood color was appropriate. The spilling of blood was compelling, yet abhorrent. The spilling of Talle's mind in these pages created the same reaction in Fiona: it drew her in, yet she compulsively shuddered as she read.

Fiona paced the *casita*, sipping her tea. She turned off overhead lights, lit candles, turned on lamps. She wished she had some music or news - or even TV commercials - from the outside world to temper this experience. There was another reality out there, she reminded herself. Only a couple of hours away in Albuquerque, people were coming out of movie theaters, going into bars. Even the local villagers were putting their children to sleep, washing dinner dishes. Normal life.

She still felt puzzled over Talle's wanting her to read the journal. If she was interpreting her hostess right, if reading this was in order that she becomes a "fully informed" participant in the mask-making ritual, then it seemed the education process was a failure. All she could figure out from the journal was that the ritual was tied to the Green Man's stewardship of Talle's land, and her feeling that she must placate "Him".

The final passage, written prior to the evening Fiona ran into Talle and Raven at the hot springs – was enigmatic:

"I wanted to believe that no one could think ill of me, of Liam, of our work here. I wanted to believe we were Protected, that my serious efforts had accomplished that. That we were Invincible, under His guidance. But I now see that there is no Protection from the minds of others, from their interpretations. Not even He can control Thought. But He has, at least, taught me that the power of Thought lies in the vessel. Mine is the stronger vessel. Mine is not glass or pottery, but a vessel of iron. Casting a metallic taste to the wine within, but a necessary taint, if the wine is to be Preserved, Potent and kept Sacred. For, once Sacred, it cannot be spilled upon the ground. I will not allow a false mind to spill His wine. No more than would

I offer Him a Cup of common brew - nor have I ever! I once thought hers would be the most potent of all. I see I was terribly misled. It is imperative that I speak with Him, before..."

The passage was apparently interrupted before she could finish it. Then she handed the book over to Fiona's sofa that same evening. Something had obviously happened that upset Talle. And to whom did the female pronoun refer?

The masks were of the poets, thought Fiona, running her forefinger over the velvet cover. Creative creatures...an offering to Creativity in the larger sense?

"Without the masks, the Green Man is not satisfied. And He must be satisfied."

A sacrificial offering?

Fiona closed the book and yawned, stretching her arms and legs.

Despite the odd emotionality of the writing, Fiona found it difficult to attribute any real malice to Talle. Eccentricity, yes. A touch of unconscious racial supremacy, possibly - the motives behind the wealthy woman's fascination with owning artifacts from so many other cultures was unclear. An aggravating queenly attitude, yes. A blatant case of menopausal depression. And one mustn't forget the effect that Talle's home brew "remedy" must have on these writings.

But if Raven was right and the mask-making ritual had any malevolence to it, how could it be at Talle's hand?

She seemed too much of an earth mother, too emotionally out-of-control.

Hawthorne, on the other hand, was the cynic who seduced the poets, took the impressions of their faces, created the masks as a ritualized offering to the Green Man. She could easily imagine him having a malicious streak and commandeering a sacrificial scenario.

As to the necessity of the poet being "fully informed", Fiona could see the logic. The ritual would be superficial, false or dishonestly gained if the poet whose face was being copied didn't herself really understand or believe in it. As it was Hawthorne's task to sexually seduce the poets, it was Talle's task to turn the poets into willing participants.

"He must be satisfied."

Back at the table, Fiona shook her head in frustration. She picked up the velvet journal, realizing her thinking had become as loopy as Talle's handwriting. She couldn't expect to resolve any of this now, it was two in the morning and she was truly exhausted.

She set the book on the sofa, folded Talle's bath towel across it again, and climbed up to the loft bed. Only four hours until she needed to meet Raven, down by the highway for their trip to Durango. When was she ever going to get any writing done?

Chapter 15 - The Curmudgeon

September 7, 1993

The office of the 'curmudgeon' - as Raven had irreverently referred to him during the drive up from Ojo de Sombras to Durango - was housed in a grim-looking, older residence. Covered with dark wood siding that almost looked burnt black, the building seemed to be mostly empty, with some of the second-story glass panes cracked. More than enough red and yellow "For Lease" signs were attached to the office directory in the front lawn-gone-to-seed, on the front door, and upper windows. Aside from "Walker's Private Investigator Services", the only other occupants seemed to be an accountant and an insurance agency.

The two poets found Hank Walker's office in the basement, at the end of a labyrinthine series of hallway turns, which seemed far too complex for such a small house. His name was on the door, carved into a western-style, rustic plaque. The door was ajar, so they entered. The back door to the tiny one-room office led up a set of concrete steps outside to the rear of the building and it, too - despite the cold - was ajar. Cigarette fumes wafted in. Assuming the PI had stepped out for a smoke, Fiona took a quick and polite glance around and then sat like an expectant customer on one of the visitor chairs near the door.

Raven remained standing, restlessly moving from one corner to the other, skeptically eyeing the walls which were full of framed photos, Native American paintings, small shelves filled with Native American pots, *kachinas*, clay figurines and several feather-&-bead objects. On the wall hung a scenic 1982 Colorado calendar, courtesy of Rudy's Pick-Em-Up Gas & Groceries on 9th and Main Avenue. Next to it was a framed movie poster from "Butch Cassidy and the Sundance Kid". From a ground-level basement window, she could see the mountains.

On the vintage oak desk was a state-of-the-art computer system, the only high-tech object in the room, looking a bit out of context. An old, sixties, avocado-&-gold plastic turntable and speakers - tweedy brown ones - graced a corner table. A battered metal bookcase against the wall behind the computer held a multitude of file folders, the contents spilling out. The bottom shelf held about two hundred old LPs. Raven pulled out a couple of them, to check the guy's music taste. Country Joe & the Fish, Frank Zappa. On a scratched metal side table was an old-fashioned rotary dial telephone and a black leather DayTimer, opened to the current week. The appointment slots were mostly blank.

"Looks like crime investigations are at an all-time low," whispered Raven, sitting next to Fiona. His appointment book is blank."

"Yeah, but look at his terminal screen."

Raven stood and peered around the front of the desk at the computer screen. It was covered with seven small, pink, Post-It-Notes, each bearing a tiny scrawled message. The edges of the screen were covered with about thirty more of the same.

"'Reynolds Tues 9 am-dognap'," read Raven. "'Bkfst @ Slim's/DV', 'ins prm due 11-2'."

"What does he do when he needs to work on his computer?" Fiona wondered.

"I don't think the curmudgeon is computer literate. I bet that thing isn't even plugged in,"

Raven smirked, sitting back down next to Fiona. "And god, I hate it when there's all this kind of stuff around," she indicated the abundance of Native American artifacts.

"Why? He seems to have good taste, I think. Looks authentic, those pots."

"Yeah, well. Do you even begin to understand the spiritual significance of these objects?

Raven had bitched the entire trip from New Mexico: about Talle's affectedness, Liam's passivity, the traffic, Hawthorne's womanizing, the roads, Silver's attitude, the weather, her lack of expectations regarding Hank Walker's investigatory skills, the gas station coffee - on and on. At first it had been amusing, Raven made complaint an art form. But, after half a day's drive, Fiona had finally had enough.

Before she could answer, she saw something move outside the basement window. She nudged Raven and the two poets strained to get a better look. A tall man with well-combed salt & pepper hair had moved into the low window's view, standing with his back to them, staring out toward the La Plata Mountains, smoke gracefully rising from his left arm. His broad shoulders and otherwise well-defined form were clothed in a Western-cut suede sports coat and linen trousers of matching beige. Bending down, he crushed his cigarette under the heel of a cream-colored, reptile skinned, and Western boot. He turned, hoisting his belt - black-tooled leather with a large turquoise-&-obsidian inlaid silver buckle - and walked toward the basement door, carrying the crushed butt. His eyes were covered by impenetrably black sunglasses. Around the neck of his crisply ironed white shirt (Fiona detected the scent of starch mixed with tobacco and cherries as he came down the steps into the room) hung a black leather bolo tie, clasped with a simple silver disk, in the center of which was another turquoise stone. He deposited the butt into an ashtray inside the doorway, looked up, saw the two poets and smiled.

"Curmudgeon?" Fiona whispered under her breath.

"Well, he *sounded* like one," Raven whispered back. "How was I to know he was Harrison Ford!"

"Paul Newman, you mean," said Fiona.

Hank Walker entered the room, closed the door, removed his sunglasses, and held out his hand. Fiona and Raven stood and extended theirs. The three exchanged names, and the PI gave the women good, old-fashioned, word-is-my-honor handshakes and a level, penetrating gaze.

"Sorry I'm late. Got it down to two cigarettes a day now, doc's orders. I have to smoke them exactly at the same time each day or I lose control of the thing, you know? My last appointment ran over, so I was five minutes late for my ten o'clock drag. So, how was your drive?"

Hank Walker's fast-talking voice didn't fit his face or form. It was as Raven had said; a curmudgeon's voice - gravelly and medium-pitched, slightly nasal - no doubt induced by years of smoking. But the content was not at all cranky. Fiona closed her eyes for a moment, listening without the visual cues, trying to hear it as Raven had on the phone. An interesting mix of aggression, anxiety and humor. As if he had a lot to prove to someone, and knew it and found it laughable, but had to keep on pushing anyway.

"'Scuse me a sec," he paused and scribbled in an appointment book with one hand while, with the other, he uncapped an oblong object hanging from his neck, lifted it and squirted something into his mouth. The scent of cherries drifted Fiona's way. How oral was this guy, anyway?

"I have to keep this DayTimer for the IRS, but I hate the damn things with a passion - I always forget to open them up and *look* in them. So I put my appointments there cause that's where I'm going to be *looking* every day, see?"

He gestured to the pink slips on the computer terminal.

"And then *after* I've actually had the appointment, I go write it in here. Saves a lot of erasing and all. Oh yes, the Devlin file. I found it down in storage in the old building I was in back then."

Raven sat forward, crossing her legs. Walker's eyes strayed for a second to her opened shirt, then quickly back to her face, where he kept them steady. To Fiona's amazement and interest.

"Yeah, I did a lot of work on that one." Walker reached behind him for a file, seeming to randomly grab from the center of one of the shelves without turning to read the file name. He *did* have his own system, as Fiona had suspected. No doubt it was one no one else on earth would be able to decipher. Probably why this elegant curmudgeon didn't have a secretary.

"Her uncle spent all he could and then ran out of money about the time we ran out of ideas. Really frustrating. I pride myself on solving every case I take on, or I wouldn't take them on, see. But this one evaded me entirely. Damn, damn shame, whole thing. Aisling Devlin grew up right here in Durango, over near Needham Elementary. Anyway, I got the family's permission to show you what I have here. Her mother died a couple years ago, the girl never knew her dad, all that's left is the uncle and a second cousin."

Walker handed Raven the folder and she sat back, opening it across her knees. She gave half the papers to Fiona and began reading the ones left in the file. Fiona pulled off her duster and sat back to read her stack.

"Listen, you two go ahead there, I gotta make a couple phone calls. Just keep your questions in your heads and then - say, you had breakfast?"

Fiona shook her head, focusing on a set of newspaper clippings. A high school photo of Aisling Devlin stared back at her. A poet's eyes - expectant, wounded, serious, yet wanting to laugh. A soft and slight smile.

"No, just awful coffee," Raven answered, also absorbed in something she had picked up from the file. "So you checked this out, too, I see."

"What's that?" Walker craned his neck to see what Raven was holding up. It was a business card from Lam's Nursery. "Oh yes, the plant nursery over in Farmington. Yeah, thought there was something to that, the poet's wife…"

"Talle Fagan."

"Yeah, Talle Fagan, and that young guy…"

"Hawthorne."

"Never could get a last name on that guy, then I finally figured out Hawthorne *was* his last name. Oh, he gave me another one, but it didn't check out. The police questioned him at length but never made an arrest or anything. I did some digging, found out a few things. I'll tell you more about that at breakfast, or, hell, by the time - that'll be lunch. Great little place down the road, the Renegade, if you don't mind pool halls. You gals like burritos?"

"How about something more Colorado?" Raven grinned back at him.

"Oh, like steaks? The Renegade's about it, though it makes a mean Rueben sandwich."

"Ruebens are Colorado?"

"Ruebens are ubiquitous."

"Sounds great. So Hawthorne is his last name, huh? What's his first name?"

"Uh...James, John, Jake - I'll check the file."

Raven grimaced, reminded again of her ill-advised affair with the sculptor. She couldn't fault the private eye for forgetting Hawthorne's first name. Hell, she'd never known it and she'd slept with the guy!

"There was no real connection with the nursery trip that day, just a weird coincidence."

"You still think so?" Raven asked, frowning into the folder.

"If there is a connection, I couldn't find it. Mrs. Fagan and Hawthorne showed up, bought some supplies. Signed a landscaping contract, made a healthy deposit and left."

"Hawthorne still goes there. Every October, same day."

Hank Walker stared at Raven, his mouth open. "No shit?"

"No shit. I saw the file at Lam's."

"Wow...Same day, huh? The sixth?"

"No. Not same *date*. Same *day*. I checked '*The American Ephemeris*' on a hunch. He goes to Lam's the day after the full moon."

Fiona looked puzzled. "The American?"

"*Ephemeris*. It tells you daily positions of the planets from the past, present and future. Silver lent me her copy," Raven explained to Fiona. "You know, she does astrology."

"So...the full moon every year?"

"There's some connection with that nursery trip, I just know it," said Raven.

"Maybe they buried her along with the new landscaping job," said Walker.

"I've wondered about that...I suspect Hawthorne did something to Devlin."

"But his alibi is tight. The day Devlin was last seen in Durango, Hawthorne and Mrs. Fagan were in Farmington, New Mexico picking out indigenous shrubbery. Witnesses and all."

"You didn't tell me about the full moon," Fiona pouted.

"I just looked it up last night, didn't have a chance to mention it. Let's go to breakfast."

* * *

The decor in the Renegade Pool Hall was as ubiquitous as its famous Rueben sandwiches. Situated at the entrance was the long, leather-trimmed bar, requisite stained glass mirrors and heavy wood shelving filled with every kind of alcohol. Hank, Raven and Fiona inhaled the usual cigarettes-&-beer blast of air as they pushed their way in against a heavy, dark, windowless, wooden door. The pool hall's dim corners were illuminated by neon beer slogans, and the rustic-wood walls were filled with semi-nude photos of Marilyn Monroe, the owner on various hunting trips, and an assortment of antlers, animal heads and skins mounted high. A video arcade and juke box lined the back wall and three sturdy pool tables filled the center of what had apparently been a 1950's auto-mechanic's garage. Dark red Naugahide booths flanked the pool tables on either side of the large space. Hank and the two poets had to speak at a semi-shout level, and lean close across the table to hear one another, to compete with the cracking and rolling sounds of late-morning pool and juke-box rock & roll.

"But this doesn't make sense to me, Hank," Fiona frowned. Half way through their first Bloody Marys (Hank had insisted), the three fell into a comfortable first-name basis. Fiona was so engrossed in the conversation with Hank and Raven that she forgot to be appalled at the high-fat, high-sodium and downright greasy, cheesy lunch that Hank had ordered for her to eat without asking her first, or at her lack of self control in consuming it with such gusto. She rolled a fat French fry in a puddle of generic ketchup. "If Aisling's car was found in Colorado-if she was really abducted here-and if Hawthorne had something to do with that-then why would he keep coming back to the same nursery an hour away, the day after the October full moon every year? You'd think it would be the last place he'd ever come again!"

"For that matter, why did he go there in the first place? Why not just do the kidnap, and get the hell away?" Raven added.

"It's like some weird anniversary thing," continued Fiona. "I mean, if Hawthorne followed Aisling and killed her..."

"No, he *kidnapped* her," Raven insisted. "Brought her back to the Fagans', then killed her. Her body is there."

"That's a strange theory," said Hank. "Why not just kill her in New Mexico?"

"I don't know the whys and wherefores. I just know that's what he did."

"And how do you know that?" Hank wrinkled his eyebrows at Raven, removed his jacket and rolled up the sleeves of his starched white Western-cut shirt.

"She has visions, the Green Man tells her, " Fiona said, licking ketchup from her lips.

Hank nodded as if this was to be expected.

"Oh yeah, I forgot, you two are from New Mexico. So who's the Green Man?"

"I'm not, I'm from Oklahoma. I live in Baltimore."

"Thank god, at least one of you is grounded."

"The Green Man is an ancient figure – usually you see him as a mask with vegetation coming out of his mouth, making a wreath around his head," explained Raven. "His image is carved onto church walls throughout England and Europe. You've probably seen pictures and didn't know it was him. I've had visions, he's trying to show me where Aisling's buried."

"Watch out for that vision stuff, Raven, you can't go figuring out murders that way," Hank took a man-sized bite from his Rueben. "Bad things happen, horrendous things are done, but objects and observers are left behind. Every time. It's false pride that gets them. Someone out there will come along and see one little hair, one little paper clip that the murderer forgot. There's always a trail made up of tangible stuff. Not dreams. Now, hunches, yeah, you can get good old-fashioned, American hunches."

"Well, I have a hunch. Hawthorne makes a Green Man mask every year," said Fiona.

"Talle writes about him in her journal, as if he's a real life man."

"And how do you happen to know what this woman writes in her private journal?"

Fiona blushed.

"Just trust me, I know," Fiona went on. Raven stared at her, a French fry suspended halfway to her lips. "Whatever you say about visions," Fiona continued, "We've both had them."

"Frankly, I think every person who has ever spent time at the Fagans' has seen the Green Man," Raven interrupted. "Including Devlin. We found a poem she wrote just a couple days before she disappeared." She turned back to Fiona. "You read her *journal?*"

Raven felt a measure of satisfaction at the incredulous look on Raven's face. *Didn't think I had it in me, did she.*

"Maybe this Green Man killed her?" Hank thanked the bartender with a wave of his hand and got to work on his second drink.

"No. The Green Man doesn't kill," said Fiona.

"I only know of one legend where the Green Man kills anyone," said Raven. "In 1100 A.D. ..."

"1100 A.D.? How old is this Green Man anyway?"

"I'm not sure, but there's Cernunnos in the first century, Dionysos in the fifth century. He's been around all through antiquity, the Dark Ages, the Gothic period, then off and on up to current times. He's here again today, associated with ecological concerns mostly."

"The Druidic, Celtic version is hooked in with their preoccupation with death, metamorphosis and rebirth," Fiona told him. "They revered the human head; attached to the body or not, it carried inspiration and prophecy for them, and was a guardian against evil. And the fertility thing. They put skulls everywhere for protection, an easy link from heads to masks."

"So, oh great authorities, tell me the gruesome Green Man story," grinned Hank.

"He's not gruesome," Raven defended. "Ok, anyway, in 1100 A.D., this guy Rufus, son of William the Conquerer, was murdered while riding in the woods. The locals had predicted that he would invoke the wrath of the lord of the forest, because he was letting developers rent the land he had taxed so highly. One day they found Rufus pinned to an oak tree by feathered arrows - crow feathers - made of rowan wood with flint tips. The peasants swore it was the work of Herne – the hunter and guardian of the greenwood, a form of the Green Man or 'the Jack' as he's also called. The legend of Robin Hood comes from this, too. So, you see, that was a case of justifiable retribution. The Green Man is a highly moral being. Now there are legends of the Green Man *being* killed, but, as a rule, he doesn't kill."

"Tell me about him being killed," Hank leaned forward, making a note on his pad.

"There's one pagan legend where, at Beltane, the Green Man goes through a courtship with the May Queen and is then killed by her and her handmaidens. Then he's reborn as a new Oak Lord and gets it on with the May Queen. It's a fertility rite. They say the winter Green Man's death is necessary for the rebirth of the summer Green Man. Also, the Green Knight in the Arthurian legend is a Green Man, and his head is always being cut off and resprouting itself. The Green Man is all about regeneration, fertility, mystery, natural honesty."

Hank nodded, then returned to the subject of Hawthorne. "So, back to your question, Fiona, about why Hawthorne would keep coming back to Lam's Nursery every year at the same time. I did some digging on this guy. Something happened in 1972 back in Kalamazoo, Michigan. A sequestered court file naming Hawthorne as the defendant. Juvenile court, I figure he had to be about sixteen, seventeen."

Raven stopped squirting mustard on her sandwich and stared at Hank.

"Meaning...?"

"We don't really know what it means. But, given the case caption, state versus, my hunch is it was something sexual. I checked the local newspapers, nothing in the microfilm. Possibly a rape allegation, or he had sex with a minor and her folks raised a stink. Hell, *he* was a minor. It's just a hunch but when a teen file is sequestered like that – stands to reason. He never did any time."

Fiona watched Raven light a brown cigarette, her hands trembling.

"This is quite a piece of information," Raven finally said after blowing smoke.

"It's something to keep in mind," Hank agreed. "Whatever happened, he had trouble with the law at a tender age. We just don't know if it fits what we're looking at."

"Oh, it fits all right," said Raven bitterly. "He's got strange sexual habits."

Hank cleared his throat. He was too much of a gentleman to ask how she knew.

"Well, anyway...Let's say he drives up to Durango with Aisling in her car."

"No. A witness saw *her* leaving in her car from Ojo de Sombras, about six a.m. that day," Raven insisted.

"Humor me. Maybe he's lying down on the back seat, sleeping. Maybe she picks him up down the highway. Maybe the witness is wrong. Whatever, play with me here."

Raven looked dubious but nodded.

"In Durango, he kills her or kidnaps her at the gas station."

"If he kidnapped her, he needed another vehicle," said Fiona. "According to your file, they found hers there, the gas station attendant remembered her getting the bathroom key."

"Yeah," Hank shuffled through the notes in his file. "That was out at the old Link's station on 160, south of town below the Animas River. It's long gone now, burned down in '83. Partly why the attendant recalled was she was in the bathroom so long...here it is...He said he could see her car in the parking lot and half an hour later it was still there when the cleaning lady showed up for the key. That's when he checked the women's room, found the key in the lock and no Aisling. Her car was unlocked. Her suitcase and purse and stuff were there. I'd say the kidnapper had an accomplice."

"Still, why couldn't he have simply followed her there and kidnapped her in his van? Doesn't that make more sense?" Raven asked.

"Except the way the gas station parking lot is set up, the attendant would have seen the van. The attendant was adamant that it was a slow morning, not one single other vehicle came into the parking lot while Aisling's car was parked there. That is, until the cleaning lady."

Raven frowned. "So you're saying that Hawthorne follows Aisling into the bathroom, kidnaps her, and some accomplice is – what? – not in the parking lot but...?"

"Nearby," Hank went on. "Maybe the accomplice waits down the block in the kidnap vehicle. It's not so crazy. Hawthorne makes her 'take a walk, go get a cup of coffee'."

"It would have to be Talle, then," said Raven. She tapped out her cigarette into an ashtray bearing a Renegade Pool Hall logo. "Waiting in the van."

The combination of late-morning vodka, city smoke, and trying to follow Hank's logic was making Fiona dizzy. She took a bite of her sandwich, trying to ground herself with food.

"Maybe he coerces Talle into becoming his accomplice. Blackmail, whatever," mused Hank, speculatively stirring his Bloody Mary with a celery stick. "So let's play with this idea. We have Hawthorne and Talle in cahoots on this."

"That would explain..." Fiona mused.

"The weird tension between them," Raven interjected, lighting a second cigarette.

"Power stuff," said Fiona. "Complicated."

"Yeah, I'd like to see Hawthorne's job description," Raven grimaced and blew smoke.

"Ok, ok, we're onto something here," said Hank, scribbling enthusiastically on his pad. "So Hawthorne and Talle do in Aisling, for whatever reason, Lam's the alibi… If there is a connection to these annual trips to the nursery, if Hawthorne is the perp – with or without Talle – then I'd guess it's to hide something in broad daylight."

"Maybe it's the God thing, like you said. Maybe he's thumbing his nose at the universe, figures no one would think he'd be that stupid to keep showing up the same day as the murder for fourteen years in a row."

"Thirteen," corrected Fiona. "He hasn't made the trip this year. Yet."

Raven frowned, as if something had just occurred to her. She jotted the number "14" on her notepad.

"Ok, so show me what you have there," Hank said, pushing his plate away.

Raven drew a large manila folder from her knapsack and plopped it down in the center of the table. Fiona wiped away the cigarette ashes that scattered in its wake.

"This shows the careers of all the Fagan poets, from 1972 to date."

"'72? There's that year again."

"Yeah, weird," Hank made a note.

"Anyway," Raven continued, "I was able to find all of them – or at least their work or a reason for the lack thereof

– except for two. Devlin's last publication was a piece in the Colorado Quarterly in 1978, her chapbook was from 1977."

"Chapbook?"

"Oh, it's a little thing poets put together to show their work, before they're published. Aisling never made it to book form, unfortunately."

"Ok, go on."

"I couldn't find any new work from Chahil O'Shea, the 1986 winner from Ireland. But I've been corresponding with a writer friend in Dublin. Actually, Hank, maybe you could help me there. I got this in the mail a couple weeks ago and haven't been able to follow up..."

Raven spread out a tissue-thin, airmail envelope from the folder.

"He says he's heard of Chahil O'Shea but isn't sure what he's doing these days. There's a rumor he went back to Galway. He said I should see if I can locate his work through this computer bulletin board that features Irish artisans and writers, but I don't have computer access from Ojo de Sombras, we're still stone-age there."

"But the Fagans do," said Fiona, puzzled.

"They can afford a long distance bulletin board service," Raven explained. "Anyhow, Hank, can you follow up on this? I'd really like to talk with Mr. O'Shea; I have one of those hunches. He left a few days early, skipped the honorary dinner. I wonder if he didn't suspect things like I did, and decided to get the hell out."

Hank skimmed the letter and nodded.

"Yeah, shouldn't be hard to find this guy. What else you got here?"

"All the articles from The Denver Post, The Albuquerque Journal, The Durango Herald."

"I have all that. Girls, I have to tell you, I really went down every alley on this one. It was a stone-cold trail back then and now fourteen years later..."

"But you said there's always something to trace," Fiona pleaded.

"Oh yeah, it's there. Somewhere there's still a bit of old dust and in that old dust there's a footprint. The Devlins ran out of money, and I ran out of time. Got to keep food on the table, you know," Hank looked genuinely regretful. "Another case came up and I had to follow my paycheck. It's feast or famine, doing PI work in a small tourist town."

"We don't have any money. We can't hire you."

"I figured that, coupla grad school poets. Look, this case really bugged me, there was something staring us all in the face and it just wouldn't come up out of the water. Maybe enough time's gone by now that the ropes tying the thing to the bricks have snapped and the body's about to float up. Maybe we can be there just at that moment. So... yeah, I'm in. Don't worry about the bucks. I was just about to take a couple weeks off, but, hell, who needs a vacation, huh?"

"Hank Walker, you're a poet yourself," Raven grinned. "Listen to you!"

"Yeah, colorful, that's me. So what else have you found?"

Hank sipped water and squirted a shot of cherry spray down his throat from the vial hanging on the cord around his neck. Raven reached over and grabbed it.

"What is this stuff, anyway?"

"Vitamin B12. Keeps me going without the cigarettes."

"Oh? Maybe I need some of that," Raven teased, leaned across the table and squirted it into her mouth. "Mmmmm, cherries!"

Hank blushed at the whole ordeal and sat back, putting the cap back on the vial.

"Ok, anything else?"

Fiona and Raven explained to Hank about the Green Man nest, the mask-making ritual. About the *kiva*, and the sketches of Devlin that had the same pictographs in the background as behind the *kiva* nest. About their investigation of the *kiva* the day before. Catching each other's eyes during the telling, they skipped the part about someone closing the trap door on them.

"So you say this place is behind the Bardic Cabin, where Aisling spent her last night?"

"Yeah, just a few yards back."

"I checked out that cabin, I know where that is. So... this is Hawthorne's ritual, then?"

"His and Talle's."

"Is this common knowledge?"

"No. It's just between them and the poets. They've done a mask of every poet since 1979. They were getting me ready for it but I left," Raven smirked. "Now they're grooming Fiona."

"Why did you leave? If I may ask?"

"Vibes. Whole thing started giving me the creeps. I... got kind of involved with Hawthorne. I had to break it off. Had to just get out."

Hank nodded, sipping his beer.

"I was young and stupid, back then."

"A year ago," he smiled at her.

"Yeah, a year ago."

"That list you read us, of what they found in her car at the station," Fiona changed the subject. "Her suitcase was in there, right?"

"Right." Hank sifted through his briefcase and pulled out a timeworn spiral pad, flipped through it until he found the page of notes he'd taken during his 1979 interviews with the police.

"Suitcase full of clothes – there's a list of those here – jewelry bag, purse, stuff in the glove box – sunglasses case, auto papers, half-eaten bag of sunflower seeds, lots of pennies. Buncha books, a sack of New Mexico souvenirs she bought like a Route 66 coffee mug, some roadrunner stationary, a little pottery turtle from Taos Pueblo. And a bag of dried herbs. The label on the baggie read 'Talle's Love Potion: Gathered with Love by the Full Moon.' There's that old moon again."

"Talle Fagan sells stuff she gathers and grows in her greenhouse," Fiona explained. "Medicinal and cooking herbs, bath oils, that kind of thing."

"That full moon stuff, she some kind of witch?"

"She says she's a *curandera*. She told me she likes to forage by the river mostly."

"But no poems," Raven interrupted suddenly. "Aisling's book of poems! Every poet has a book they're working on, carrying around with them – what were the books in her car?"

"Let's see, Adrianne Rich, E.E. Cummings, something called *Uranium Poems.*"

"Yeah, the Yale Series of Younger Poets," said Fiona, "Go on..."

"...Some novel called *I See/You Mean* by a Lucy Lippard."

"Lip*pard*," Raven corrected him. "See? She was right on top of it. That came out in '79. There's some pretty eclectic stuff on this list...What else?"

"The 1978 issue of Colorado Quarterly, the one you said she was published in."

"Damn," said Fiona.

Raven and Fiona grew quiet, sipping their drinks, sobered by the list. Fourteen years later, Devlin's list was not too different from what was on their shelves. In fact, Raven had an autographed copy of the Lippard book and Fiona had an almost complete collection of the Yale Series in a bookcase at home. The list of books that the poet carried in her car struck a sensitive, personal nerve.

"Her poems would have been with those books," said Raven. "A folder of typed poems or a handwritten notebook. *Something.*"

"Oh my god," Fiona's eyes widened. "The harp. What about the harp?"

"Harp?" Hank looked up and down the list. "No harp. What's that about?"

"Of course!" said Raven. "Devlin had made this lap harp thing she used to play at her readings. That harp was her signature. They didn't find it in her car?"

"No harp in the car, no one ever mentioned that to me."

"I can't believe her family didn't say something about it," Fiona frowned. "You'd think at least they would have wanted it as a keepsake. I mean, she *made* that harp."

"Well...her family...they weren't close. Single mom, father unknown. A lot of animosity between Aisling and her mother. Anyway, I got the impression she wasn't thrilled about Aisling going off and being a poet. Aisling was off at college in Boulder, on a student loan, supposed to be getting a business degree, and then dropped out to be a waitress and write poetry. I got the sense Aisling was doing the hippy thing, judging by her clothes and jewelry. A little stash of pot in her jewelry bag in the car. She was in her twenties, it was the seventies, hell, we all know what that was about."

"*You* know, Hank," teased Raven. "*We* don't."

"Thanks hon, remind me I'm an old codger. Ok, *I* know. Anyway, I doubt her mother knew about the harp or, if she knew, cared. I mean, her mother was all broken up about Aisling's disappearance but...I think she'd been long gone to her already. She'd really wanted Aisling to do better than she had, go to college."

"So where's her poetry? And where's her harp?" Raven pressed. "Don't you think that's odd? All her stuff in her car but not the two most important things in her life? She was a serious poet."

"You're saying this is our proof of foul play?" asked Hank.

"Aisling would not have left her poems and harp behind," Fiona stated.

Hank made a note in his steno pad. "Probably important. Now it's a damned shame this didn't come up before, fourteen years ago. I mean, now that you mention it, I seem to recall someone – a bookstore owner maybe?"

"Silver."

"Yeah, in my notes, she mentioned something about Aisling Devlin playing an instrument at her poetry reading, but I never understood it to be her signature. Damn."

"Don't feel bad. Poetry audiences are pretty select, if you weren't in those circles, there's no way you could have known her harp was important," Fiona told him.

"Still," Hank was clearly upset at himself. "Might have been a help back then, someone might have seen her note-book or the harp somewhere and made a connection."

"That's why you need us. Only fellow poets would know that was important, see?" Raven grinned at Hank to lighten things up, and shifted in her seat just enough that her shirt opened a bit more. Hank blushed and concen-trated on his drink. Fiona rolled her eyes and put her chin in her hands, gazing around the pool hall. Something else was bugging her. But she couldn't quite put her finger on it.

"In fact, we poets have a plan," Raven went on. She liked this Hank Walker and felt pretty good from the two Bloody Marys. "Fiona has a poetry reading to give a week from Friday night. She's going to read the Green Man poem we found from Aisling to Liam Fagan, a kinda hot poem."

"What? Was there something between them?"

"We don't know, but Liam is always sweet on the ladies. He was sweet on me, he's sweet on Fiona, as a matter of fact."

"I never said that," Fiona said hotly. "I just like him, he's ok. We relate."

As she said this, Fiona felt a flash of heat.

"Anyway, we'll watch and see how Hawthorne reacts. I figure he'll keel over. I'm thinking the time to follow him will be after the reading, he might lead us right to the body."

It was Fiona's turn to stare at Raven. She hadn't realized a late-night trailing of Hawthorne was part of the plot. Was

Raven really planning to do that alone? Or...Fiona put her head in her hands and groaned softly, unheard in the din of pool cues cracking against pool balls and the bells and whistles of the video arcade. The Bloody Mary wasn't feeling so good all of a sudden. Now she realized the full extent of Raven's plot: they were *both* going to follow Hawthorne that night, after the reading. A little detail Raven had cunningly forgotten to mention. Fiona didn't think she was up to this.

"This sounds like a bad plan to me," said Hank. "Can I convince you to shelve it?"

Fiona looked up hopefully, ready to entertain his objection, but Raven laughed.

"No, it's going down."

Hank and Fiona exchanged glances.

"Ok, so when and where is this again?" Hank asked Raven, slipping Fiona a sly wink.

"Week from Friday. *Extranjeros*, middle of Ojo de Sombras."

Fiona watched as Hank scribbled in his note pad. She breathed an inward sigh of relief. She had a feeling Hank Walker would attend her poetry reading. Maybe he packed a gun.

"You'll keep me posted on the results, right?" Hank asked Raven.

Raven beamed at him. She liked this man who showed compassion and concern – and interest in her body – but was wise enough not to try to impose on her his maleness in any intrusive way. She got the impression he would be subtler than the younger men she'd been with. She might just have to take another road trip to Durango sometime soon to find out more about that.

"And as for Liam Fagan, maybe it's time to re-interview him. I believe my meeting with him was abbreviated at the time. He was ill, if I recall..."

"Interview? You're going to come to Ojo de Sombras and talk to people again?"

"At some point. Let's see what we find out in the next few days."

"Don't do that before next Friday. I don't want to tip our hand before the reading," said Raven. "So, uh, how will your wife feel about you using your vacation time to work on this?"

"She died four years ago."

"Oh, I'm sorry..."

"So, anything *else* weird I should know about?" asked Hank, to change the subject.

"Only Fiona's naked voyeur," Raven grinned.

Fiona frowned. "It's not a joke. Liam Fagan's doppelganger has been hanging out..."

"So to speak... in the nude, no less," Raven leaned forward, pressing her breasts against the edge of the table and smiling warmly at Hank. He blushed and tried to look more serious.

"I saw him nude once, near the hot springs. I've seen him looking in the Fagans' windows, smoking in the woods, he carries a backpack. He's absolutely Liam's double. And now both Talle and Liam have admitted to me there might be a twin somewhere in his background."

Hank tried to ignore the effect Raven was having on him, and made another note. Fiona went on to tell everything she knew about the trespasser, and said that she would try to talk to the man as soon as they returned to the Fagans'.

"I don't really recommend you go traipsing in the woods looking for this guy. Could be he's involved in this whole thing somehow," Hank gave Fiona a stern, authoritarian look. "Seriously. We don't really know anything yet. We need to look at everyone and you gals need to be *careful*. If you do find out anything, you call me immediately. "

Raven grinned and rolled her eyes at Fiona. Fiona shrugged and nodded. She still felt agitated. What was it? Something she'd heard? Something she'd seen? No...it was something Hank had said earlier, about footprints in old dust. A memory was trying to emerge, but it was overcome by the smell of Raven's cigarettes, the odor of stale beer and the wafting scent of pine sol from the nearby ladies room. Too much pool-hall alcohol and grease. Fiona felt queasy.

"You look like you could use some air, honey," Hank said. "Let's head back to my office."

Hank left a thick, crumpled wad of bills on the table, dumped Raven's cigarette ashes into a coffee cup and emptied his pocket change into the ash tray. The handsome curmudgeon left the darkened pool hall, flanked by the dark-haired sultry poet on one arm and the fragile red-haired poet on the other, all of them burdened with briefcases and folders about a long-missing, harp-playing poet. Hank grinned; pleased at the eye-brow wiggling the bartender gave him as they pushed their way out into the sunlit, chilly afternoon. Fiona and Raven smiled at each other as he unlocked and held open the doors of his rusty-brown, Volvo wagon. They both had a good, old-fashioned American hunch that they had found an invaluable ally.

Chapter 16 - Liam Takes a Walk

The evening of his chess game with Fiona and her theory about the identity of the trespasser, Liam retired to his studio, telling Talle he would be writing through the wee hours.

However, he didn't feel like writing, he just needed to think, to sort out all the feelings and information with which Fiona had left him. He changed into his evening gear – an old velvet smoking jacket, loose cotton pants and sandals over navy Irish wool socks. He prowled, restlessly but quietly, in his studio until after midnight. Then, to his amazement, found himself getting dressed for the outdoors. Apparently he was going to take an unprecedented walk.

Liam's writing studio was Spartan – a desk, chair, bookshelves and day bed. There were no curtains at the windows, which gave him a good view of the mountain. The rug on the oak floor was very old and worn; a brown and black one from Egypt that he bought at a flea market before he ever met Talle. It had been the flooring in his old

386

school bus, those long ago days of another kind of freedom. Talle had wanted him to throw it out but he refused. She wanted to put artwork and regal office furnishings in his studio, too, but he said no, explaining to her that no one but himself would ever be in the room, so it should be exactly as he wanted it.

Aesthetics were secondary to comfort in his private room. A rugged oak desk, purchased for fifty dollars from a Santa Fe schoolhouse auction. A comfortable chair. Above the mantel of the corner *kiva* fireplace was tacked one of Hawthorne's preliminary Green Man mask sketches, one that Liam had salvaged from the sculptor's garbage - Raven in profile. Its abundant erasures showed it had given the artist a lot of trouble. On the mantel was a thick beeswax candle in a pewter holder and a box of matches. A coat tree in the corner held Liam's writing uniform - the comfort-able Irish sweater Chahil O'Shea had given him. The only sign of Talle's influence in the room was the presence, on its own table in a corner, of the computer she purchased, that allowed him to play chess with strangers. Or used to. Since he lost his partner he hadn't even turned the thing on.

Moving slowly and methodically, as if some part of him had planned this earlier, Liam pulled open the desk drawer and found a flashlight, checked the batteries, tucked it into the pocket of a tweed sports jacket hanging in the closet. He then stood in the middle of his studio, listening. Talle had retired earlier, the house was still.

He surveyed his room. It was very different from the rest of the house, which, to him, at times felt graced, and at other times overwhelmed by Talle's extravagant taste. Sometimes Liam would wander through the halls and rooms and marvel at the echo of his footsteps, and that the artifacts, artwork and oversized furnishings were really his domain. The hacienda was certainly large enough to sustain the presence of such an opulent and rich collection. Talle assured him their finances were also large enough to sustain it all, and more. He let her take care of all the money matters, since he had brought nothing tangible to their union.

When they met in 1966, he was thirty and she was twenty-eight. In their circles, it was stylish to travel light and not be slave to a job. Liam lived in a small, fourth-hand school bus, painted over with large, psychedelic images of the planets, moon and sun. Due to a frozen engine (a friend had taken it on its last voyage while tripping and, instead of stopping when steam began to boil up from under the hood, had tranced out on the steam particles) the bus was parked with an assortment of vans and tents next to an arroyo in Placitas, New Mexico, where Liam made a daily and conscious effort to not worry about what would happen next. *Be here now.* Until the bus engine died, Liam had spent two years traveling from St. Louis to San Francisco, and was slowly working his way through the southwest. He found encampments of modern day gypsies in every ranger park along the way, and visited a few communes he'd read about in counter-culture magazines. There were always free vegetarian meals, pitchers of sun tea and highly sexualized women in gauze tunics, embroidered jeans and delicate India jewelry embellished with tiny, tinkling bells. And marijuana and various hallucinogens.

However, it wasn't so much the drugs or free love or even the politics that drew Liam to this subculture. It was simply that the hippies provided him an easy way, accountable to no one, to spend his time doing only what he wanted - writing poetry. He was quiet, stayed out of everyone's way, smiled peacefully and retired to his room - or corner, or mattress - to write. During that time, Liam owned a sleeping bag, a chess set, a copy of the I Ching, an African gourd rattle, a Native American drum, a cooking stove, a tea pot, an iron skillet, and a collection of Big Chief tablets to write in. For the in-between communal meal times, his fruit-crate pantry in the school bus consisted of various herbal teas, rye crisps and tins of processed meat. He spent as much time alone as he could, although the bus usually contained two or three bodies in various states of bliss and recuperation. It was hard to find chess partners, but he always asked when a newcomer arrived, and often ended up teaching, just to have someone to play with.

Then along came Talle, a traveling gypsy with the kind of style afforded by a trust fund.

Her strong presence and sense of "anything is possible" drew Liam to her side immediately. And the fact that she played chess. She drove a new rust-orange VW van, tastefully embellished with New Grange spirals painted in silver and black. The interior was covered with real sheepskin, stacks of mirrored pillows, bedspreads and sandalwood boxes of incense from India, which she sold at flea markets. (Even with her trust fund, she was always enterprising.)

Thinking about Talle in those days, Liam opened the desk drawer and pulled out the most vintage of his bottles of Macallan's, a glass and a pewter flask. He filled the flask and then poured a glass, and sat on the day bed, leaning back against the wall.

When she had first arrived in Placitas, the others had been wary of her, suspecting she might be a narc, since her resources seemed unlimited and her attitude a bit condescending. She read books none of them had heard of – except Liam Fagan - and had very strong opinions about the correct way to garden organically and organize the shelves in the communal kitchen (located in a squatter's geodesic dome, around which the encampment had grown). Talle kept her van interior too neat, and wouldn't lend out her clothes. She insisted the others boil water for washing dishes, but always managed to be off taking a walk by herself when it was time to wash them. She used exotic scented lotions on her skin and washed her long, tangled hair very often.

But she won them over after three communal meals. Talle carried a sophisticated collection of organic herbs and grains and was a fine and daily bread-maker. She always had gallon jugs of wine stashed away and was the purveyor of large, decorative tins of imported cheeses, olives and fancy cookies sent by her New York City family, in care of whichever post office was nearest her route. Her van's extras included a state-of-the-art tape deck and a well-stocked library of Van Morrison, Bob Dylan and the Doors. Talle always had the largest and best stash of pot and was generous with it. The group also grew to accept her in their midst because Liam did. He was such a gentle, quiet man, that his trust of her was good enough for the rest.

Liam got up, poured more scotch and returned to the day bed, smiling at his memories. In those days, Talle was enamored of reading the romantic poets, mythology and gothic mysteries - *The Hobbit, The Golden Bough, Wuthering Heights* and *The Turn of the Screw* - and was drawn to anything Irish or Celtic - books, artwork, music, iconography. She was disinterested in her own mixed heritage, which she called "white bread".

"I'm the product of the union of a New York City stock broker and a high society neurotic who lives for the opera," was all she would say, and would refuse to discuss it any further.

When she discovered that Liam was Irish, a poet and a tender and attentive lover, she gave no further attention to the other sexually willing men in the commune. When he finally trusted her enough to tell her the story of his adoption, and alluded to the possibility that he was a separated twin, she was hooked.

"You are my Heathcliff and my *Cu Chulainn*."

This monogamous devotion to Liam was the first indication that she might be having a parting of the ways with her chosen lifestyle.

Talle and Liam soon became the surrogate parents of the makeshift commune. Eventually the owner of the dome left to go to hotel management school in California. She bequeathed the dome to Talle and Liam. Talle took it over and made it extraordinarily homey. Liam moved in with her there and used the psychedelic school bus as a writing studio. They began to spend their evenings like an old married couple, playing chess after dinner, reading out loud to each other by the wood stove and oil lamps, gardening and hiking the nearby ruins during the daylight hours. Between trust fund disbursements, Talle would pack up the van with her India wares and head to a flea market to make a few dollars. Liam would travel with her, writing in his tablets inside the shaded van and guarding the cash box.

By 1970, the rest of the Placitas encampment had deteriorated - a few bad trips and one drug raid while Talle and Liam were on one of their flea-market trips were its demise. (The times were changing, as Bob Dylan had predicted.) Talle and Liam no longer allowed drugs in the circle, so no one stayed on for long anymore. Just as Talle was in the process of negotiating her squatter status with the new owner of the property - to stay on in the dome for a nominal rent and unending supply of homemade bread - the news came that her father had died and that her mother was "not handling it well". Talle immediately flew to New York, entrusting her rust-orange van and stash of incense-scented bedspreads to Liam, and promising to return as soon as possible.

Liam lived in the van for six months, found his way up to Taos, visited the hot springs in Ojo de Sombras, and located a pay phone every Friday night for a touch-base, collect call to Talle. Finally the estate was safely in the hands of an attorney she trusted, her mother was "being cared for", and she was able to return to New Mexico.

Liam was left breathless in the wake of Talle's activities from the moment they left the airport. First, she didn't arrive in her usual gauze and knapsack. Instead, she wore a New York chic version of a Santa Fe fringed suede outfit, from head to toe, and heavy silver jewelry. She'd permed her brown hair and was even wearing make-up. She got behind the wheel of the VW, now crammed with very expensive Italian leather luggage Liam had helped her load onto a cart at baggage check – Talle had even enlisted the help of a porter and given the man a twenty-dollar tip, to Liam's astonishment. Using porters was akin to using slaves in his mind, it was just not something a self-respecting hippy ever did. Talle drove straight to Santa Fe, checked them into a fancy adobe hotel off the plaza, ordered an elaborate meal and champagne, and treated Liam to twenty-four hours of hedonism like nothing he had ever experienced in his life.

Too many memories tonight, Liam felt too restless to sleep. The branch of a tall tree outside the window scratched at the glass like a finger tapping. As if to remind him of something he must do. He tucked the flask of scotch in the tweed jacket pocket, pulled a pair of new, soft-soled walking shoes down from the closet shelf - they were still in the box. Talle had bought them for him several years ago; he had never even tried them on - nor had he thrown them out.

The morning after that Santa Fe hotel night, Talle was on the phone with realtors and car dealers. By evening she had traded the van for a Jaguar, which would be delivered the following week - "Just 'til we figure out what kind of truck we'll need," she'd laughed - and lined up seven properties to check out the next morning. Liam followed her around, listening and watching in amazement and admiration. That evening, after an elegant meal at the hotel restaurant, Liam and Talle sat with brandy snifters at a copper-and-stone fireplace in the hotel lobby. There, Talle explained how things were going to be.

"You will never need to worry about money again, Liam."

Liam didn't remember ever having really *worried* about it before, but smiled and listened. He had never seen Talle so pleased with herself.

"You can devote the rest of your life to writing."

He nodded. That was what he had intended to do all along.

"I learned a few things from my stockbroker father, and one of them is to invest my money in real estate. I'm going to find us a huge hacienda, preferably out in the country, where we can live as we want with no interference from anyone. I... we might even open a school or resort of some kind eventually. I'll finally have my own greenhouse and the kitchen of my dreams. And you can have the writing studio of your dreams and whatever kind of library you want. The only catch is that we need to get married, Liam."

Married? He didn't even know any married people. No one he spent time with anyway.

"I want things as clear and stable as possible. A solid commitment to me and our hearth, no more communes, no more domes and outhouses. No flea markets."

Liam thought he would miss the flea markets, but kept listening.

"A clear line of inheritance, so if anything happens to me, you'll be the legal inheritor of our estate, and my relatives back east can't take anything away from you. We are very fortunate, Liam, we can create our lives. We are free now, we don't have to wander anymore."

Liam remembered that moment very clearly, even now as he rose, testing the shoes. He had nodded, staring into the hotel fire, sipping a rare cognac he would soon begin to buy by the case, and turned the word "free" over and over in his mind. There were those who might have had a lot of intellectual and moral adjusting to do, before accepting what Talle was offering. After a young adult life devoted to a very specific definition of "freedom" - that was, to wander without commitment, to travel light, to eschew ownership of material possessions and partners, to practice the religion of the starving artist, with the ingrained concept that a writer must suffer in order to write anything of value - to his puzzled and delighted amazement, he found himself quickly adapting to Talle's new definition of "freedom". By the second cognac, he was holding Talle's hand, nodding and listening to wedding plans. In the space of twenty minutes, Liam Fagan had ended his vagabond youth and entered his resplendent retirement.

All of which had led them to this hacienda (which they bought a month later, using a Santa Fe law firm to negotiate the long distance deal with the disloyal Spanish descendent in Los Angeles) and the poetry residency. Twenty-three years of a most interesting and comfortable life. Yes, there were his unexpected health problems - "weak lungs" Talle called it - her odd and secretive fascination with religious, spiritual and pagan iconography, her menopausal moodiness and drinking problem, her increasing preoccupation with her "Green Man religion", his mostly un-acted-upon flirtations with the young poets (his "crushes" he called them to himself), and the constant longing he accepted as the price he paid for his freedom. Still, it was not a life about which he could justify complaint.

He didn't realize how much the longing bore him down, like a weight that grew heavier on his shoulders, causing him to walk slower, his head hanging down, a beaten man. It was just age, he thought, a natural course. He didn't realize that not all men carried this weight of longing. Because not all men had a missing twin. A "better half" as Talle teased him. Not all men had felt, their whole lives, that an arm had been severed, or that every word they uttered was spoken into a void that should have been the ear of The Other. That some part of them was existing, simultaneously, in an alternative world, like the Irish *sidhe*, who lived in sunken ships or off in the woods, eating the same food you ate, wearing the same clothes, thinking the same thoughts as yours...but with an invisible and impenetrable wall keeping the two worlds separated.

Sometimes he thought he should travel to Ireland. He should try to find his brother, even if he didn't know where to start looking. But he never pressed the subject with Talle. He was afraid that if he did go to Ireland he would never return, and he owed it to Talle to stay. He owed everything to her. Where would he be, now, if not for her? A street person, no doubt. He couldn't work for a living, he could only write. And even that he could only do for the sake of doing. He couldn't publish, compete, nor present himself in the literary world. He had always felt this sense of powerlessness, of "going with the flow", as his generation called it.

Only here in solitude, in his writing studio, in the words from his pen, did he feel anything akin to power. Thinking about that sense of power, Liam removed his smoking jacket, put on Chahil O'Shea's sweater, and pulled the tweed sports coat from its hanger. At some point, he mused, that power had become equated with rebellion against his wife.

As had the dalliances with the young poets. They were mostly emotional. A few soulful kisses here and there, adolescent-style heavy petting. It never went any further. There were a couple of times when the young women were willing – especially when he himself was younger – but he stopped before clothes were taken off, avoided situations where there was any real privacy. He preferred his kisses stolen, in hallways, at dangerous moments. He told himself, after each poet left her residency, that he would not have these feelings again, would not allow himself the attractions. Would renew his devotion to Talle, would bring himself back to the marital bed. But, with each new young poet, the feelings emerged again. He fought the desires, in his studio, in his way. He avoided as much contact with the poets as he could.

Evenings like this evening, conversations like the ones with Fiona – he felt ruefully reminded why he tried to avoid them. The scratching of the branches at the window intensified. An urgent wind had come up. Nevertheless, Liam slid his arms into the tweed jacket. It had been years since he'd worn it, it felt loose even with the Irish sweater underneath.

Yes, he mused, Talle was always pushing him, forcing him, making him be there, be present, be visible with the young poets. He was Liam Fagan, the founder of the Bardic School. Except she had a way of giving a thing and taking it away with the same gesture.

He loved the Bardic School, it was his brain child when Talle first spoke of opening a school or resort. He came to life in a new way, when the Bardic School began. He oversaw every detail – the advertisements, the publicity, the arrangement of the sparse furnishings in the Bardic Cabin, the mentoring sessions. On the first night, Liam would recite Yeats' *The Song of Wandering Aengus - I went out to the hazel wood /Because a fire was in my head -* and give his lecture on the traditional Romantic symbolism of fishing for the trout of language in the waters of inspiration. He instructed the poets about the Bardic tradition, prepared them for their night alone in the cabin without light, their recitation the morning after. At each residency's end, the honoring dinner was always the same menu: broiled Rio de Sombras trout with a hazelnut sauce. That was Talle's little joke.

Then there was that business with Aisling Devlin. Her reaction to him was so strong.

She wasn't intimidated by Talle, she wrote him erotic poems and tucked them into his books where he would find them later, alone in his studio.

He used to walk with her in the evenings. She was the first poet to play chess with him; afterwards, he made it a requirement that the winning poets be chess players. He came closest to sleeping with Aisling than any of the others.

She came to play chess one night in a long, filmy dress, and guided his hand, under the chess table, letting his fingers realize her absolute vulnerability. After she left that night, he cried, silently, in his studio. Cried that he wanted her so, that he would not let himself take her, that she wanted him. There was so much danger with Aisling, he could imagine himself becoming cruel and ungrateful. He fantasized leaving it all, his comfortable life with his wife, her adoration and devotion. Then what would become of him? He raged at his weakness - in lusting so after the young woman, and in not having the courage to throw himself upon his longing like the sword it was. To throw himself out into life and see what would become of him without his dependency on Talle, who seemed more and more a mother to him than a partner.

Then, so unexpectedly, Aisling left, three weeks before the ritualistic trout and hazelnut feast. She went to spend her requisite night in the Bardic Cabin, the next night she was to read to him what she had composed in the dark... instead, when he woke that morning - late, for he had been up all night writing a sonnet - she was gone. In fact, everyone was gone. There was a note from Talle explaining that she was irritated that Aisling had left early to be with a boyfriend in Colorado, and that she had decided to not let the day be wasted, but had left with Hawthorne on a buying trip for the greenhouse.

Liam wrapped a wool muffler around his neck and checked his pockets. Gloves, flask, flashlight. The tapping at the window was almost frantic now. He had to look, to assure himself that it was not some creature on the second story deck, trying to get his attention. He peered down into the compound. Was that someone down there, behind that tree? Perhaps the Green Man everyone said they saw in his woods? He rubbed his eyes and looked again. No, he smiled sadly, just the wind, playing tricks with the shadows. Did he really want to go out in such a high wind? He stared down, leaning his forehead on the cold pane, remembering that day, back in 1979 when he had been plunged into his longing at a new level. Suddenly snapped from his sweet, illicit interactions with Aisling, deprived of the closing ritual of her residency, abandoned by everyone.

Even the cook had been given the day off, since there was no evening meal to prepare after all. Liam had wandered the hacienda, went to Aisling's *casita*, hoping for something – a note, a message, a sign of her emotional state. A boyfriend? He hadn't realized she had a boyfriend. What had all the emotion between them been about, then? He felt embarrassed, his cheeks actually flushed. He had been *her* dalliance, then, there had never actually been any danger of him running off with her. They could have had their one night and then she would have left, back to her boyfriend, her real life. He had over-interpreted the importance of their connection. He was becoming a silly old man.

In her *casita* he found nothing. She had packed everything and Talle had already cleaned out the rooms and left the windows open as she did after each poet. There wasn't even a trace of Aisling's patchouli left. The bed was stripped, the laundry piled in the basket outside the door for the housekeeper. The waste baskets were empty, no drafts of poems there.

Although he felt the beginnings of a cold, he walked to the Bardic Cabin that morning - it was the last time he ever did. Surely she had left some sign there, perhaps written down her poem and left it for him. He found the door ajar and signs that she had at least spent the night. A candle burned to a stub. The bedding on the cot in disarray. Leaves scattered across the floor, probably blown in by the wind. A cup half-filled with water from the jug. Nothing else.

The rest of the day was dark, the sky filled with an impending storm that never broke. Liam stayed in his studio, sitting at his desk with his head in his hands, napping a couple times on the day bed. His dreams were tangled and grey, with the sense of someone present but not visible. He wanted to cry but couldn't. He understood neither the urge nor the inability.

On her return from the greenhouse-shopping trip with Hawthorne, Talle was moody, commented on the rudeness of Aisling's sudden departure. She and Liam ate a late and simple supper of cheese sandwiches and barley soup. Hawthorne didn't join them, retired without dinner, complaining of a sore throat.

"Did Aisling leave any compositions from her stay last night in the Bardic Cabin?"

Talle frowned and shook her head.

"Liam, I feel the Bardic School has seen its day, these young poets don't take it seriously. We need to change the nature of the residency, change its name," she said, ladling soup into his bowl. "In fact, it's time our life here had a face lift. I hired Lam's Nursery today. Mr. Lam will be coming down next weekend to confer on the landscaping project. I have some stunning ideas."

"I'm sure you do, my dear."

A week later Talle advised him that county officials had condemned the cabin as dangerous, it was now boarded up, so there was really no choice, they would discontinue the Bardic School and open the Liam Fagan Residency Prize for Emerging Poets. The longing set in again, in the wake of Aisling's departure. He went up to his studio and slept, off and on, for two days. Developed a fever. Funny, both he and Hawthorne had been sick together during that time, he had forgotten about that. Hawthorne had the flu and Liam had a bout with pneumonia, his first of many.

Then, three weeks later, all that business about Aisling being missing. Liam, still not fully recovered, had a couple of bed-side interviews with the local marshal, watched from the bedroom window as they questioned Hawthorne in the courtyard, and listened as they questioned Talle downstairs.

Liam shook himself from his memories of that time, left the window and checked the clock on his desk. Two a.m. He left the lamps on, so it would appear he was writing – Talle, if she was awake, would never disturb him then – and very quietly exited his studio. He paused near the bedroom door and could hear her snoring softly.

He began his descent down the stairs, his mind on Aisling Devlin. A couple of times he had walked with her after midnight, leaving the hacienda like this, telling himself he wasn't really sneaking out, that he and Talle understood each other. He never took such walks with any of the poets after Aisling, though. His emotional responses to them were never as intense. The closest he came was with Raven, but he kept that under control. Except for one stolen kiss. He supposed he was growing too old and unattractive for these things; Raven seemed more angry with him than interested. She was a different sort from the other young poets. She knew herself already, had found her voice, and had no need of a mentor. And seemed quite taken with Hawthorne. At least, at first.

And Fiona? He felt such a tenderness for her, yet a puzzled awareness that he was saying and doing things he shouldn't. He felt fatherly toward her and yet, in her presence, inappropriate urges came over him which he couldn't seem to control.

She was strong, though. And kind.

Something was definitely different. The flirtations with the young poets were no longer working to distract him from what was really missing. That inexplicable, ancient longing. Fourteen years ago, Aisling had nailed it in a poem she had written about him and the Green Man. He remembered the particular lines that had chilled him with their uncanny revelation:

I hide in the dark of the Green Man's woods
To watch you coming near
Yet when I call your name out loud
It is not my voice you hear
You are always slightly turned away
Watching shadows in the leaves
Whom do you really wish to see?
For whom is it you grieve?

What had happened to that poem? He had tucked it somewhere, in one of his books. He was always tucking papers into books and then forgetting about them. He should look for it.

And now this news from Fiona, about the man she called his twin, camping on the property, looking in the windows. It was an insane idea, he knew that, and he didn't believe for a moment that his twin had come to spy. Or that they had found each other through the miraculous synchronicity of a computer chess game.

But...what if it was true? Didn't miraculous things happen, after all, on this earth? After all, wasn't he - reclusive and almost agoraphobic Liam Fagan - headed down the stairs, down the hall past the candle-lit Green Man masks, the statues of the Virgin Mary, moving cautiously in quiet walking shoes, out into the dark wee hours? And, once he opened the heavy wooden door, and stepped outside into the wild night, didn't the wind die down? As if finally satisfied? Didn't the branches of the courtyard trees seem to wave and bow to him, as if guiding him along in approval? He moved across the flagstones, past the *casitas* - all lights were out - along the lighted path to the hot springs, heading into the trees.

As Liam moved into the woods behind the compound, all of his senses seemed to wake up – his hearing, sense of smell, even his skin prickled. His eyes widened to compensate for the new darkness, away from the lamps and path lights. As he breathed, his sense of taste seemed to intensify: he could swear he tasted one of Talle's herbs in the air. What was that? Fresh parsley? Sage? Rosemary? No... the taste was rosemary, but the scent was sage...he inhaled deeply. Yes, the scent of sage, burning, to the west, toward the riverbank. He headed that direction.

In all these years of resisting night walks – or much in the way of day walks - Liam had often looked out the windows of his second-story writing studio, into the dark edges of the ponderosa groves, thinking he saw a bear (an obsidian boulder), a napping cougar (a weather-worn log), a giant crow (a tree stump burnt to black by lightning). Once he did see a rattlesnake sunning itself just outside the compound wall. He thought to warn Talle of its presence, but what would be the point? Talle might go take a look, out of curiosity. On the other hand, she might kill it; with that gun she'd bought and taught herself to shoot. Much against his wishes.

"This is the Wild West, Liam," she had admonished him. "You should learn to handle a gun, too. Bear and cougar are seen all the time up here. They *LIVE* on our property!"

Over the past few years he had heard that she had shot lesser snakes within the compound, even though Hawthorne argued that they were helpful for the gardens - for instance, that the presence of a bull snake would keep rattlers away. Something in Talle had changed over the years, to the extent that her own husband couldn't necessarily predict her every reaction or move. As she had taught herself to shoot a gun, she also insisted on splitting the firewood herself. She had always been strong-headed, from the day they met. That strength had come to manifest itself in her physicality, also, through the years of their marriage. Liam watched her, from his windows, chopping wood, hauling sacks of compost and manure for the gardens. Doing things they paid Hawthorne to do, just because she apparently enjoyed it.

That day, he had simply watched the rattler as it rested in the sun, and kept silent. Finally, the snake had moved itself somewhere out of view.

Through the years after Aisling, Liam's interactions with the wilderness of his own property had been reduced to whatever he could see from his window, be it hallucination or real life. Walking now into the woods, it seemed his body was on alert, but his mind and emotions were having a different experience. A thrill ran through him, an exhilarated sense of power. He walked in the darkness as if he knew the way, not stumbling at all on the multitude of objects that could trip him - down and dead wood, cacti, rat holes, stones, low-lying branches. He felt as if there was a guiding hand at the small of his back, gently prodding him along in the right direction.   The scent of sage grew stronger and easier to follow. The night breeze stirred then became mischievous. Leaves began to lift and dance, tickling his ankles as he walked briskly toward the river. The leaves began to lift higher until handfuls of them tossed against the backs of his legs, his thighs, up across his shoulders. He turned to see, was someone there behind him? No, it was only that the breeze became a wind again, the dance of the leaves had become assaultive, the sounds of crackling vegetation and snapping tree limbs louder.

Liam realized he was walking into the center of a high windstorm. Dust devils swirled into the ponderosa and whipped around him. He hung on tightly to his jacket, wrapping his arms across his torso and keeping his head down, squinted against the grit. The sudden night-wind in the middle of his forest didn't concern him. Instead, he felt invigorated.

The power he usually felt only when at his desk, writing in his tablets, began to course through him, as if the wind carried that power and somehow rejuvenated the very cells of his body with it. He realized that he was grinning widely, and that he wasn't having his usual post-pneumonia coughing fit at the exertion. In his legs he felt the muscles tensing and loosening, tensing and loosening - as he strode to his destination, toward that smell of burning sage. He felt, for the first time ever, like the true steward of his property. The Proprietor. The Master. Landed Gentry. Liam's grin turned into a chuckle. He almost felt a gently-prodding finger at the bottom of his spine, keeping him moving.

There was the sage fire on the river bank, burning low in a careful circle of stones. Next to it were remnants of a recent meal, a blanket hanging over a tree limb, a tent. Liam stopped, listened. The wind died down, the flying leaves settled. Then silence. No wind, no audible signs of another human.

Liam stared all around him, saw nothing moving in the shadows. He retrieved his flashlight from his coat pocket, went to the tent and flipped on the beam, directing it inside. Sleeping bag, backpack, water bottle. A small stack of books, on top of which sat a miniature chess set. Liam stepped inside, shining the light on the game in progress.

It only took a few seconds for him to realize it was a reproduction of the same game he and Fiona were playing in the chess library. It even included tonight's new moves. He knelt, carefully lifted the chessboard – the pieces were magnetized – to check out the titles of the books. *A Book of Ireland*, Frank O'Connor. He opened the front pages.

Copyright 1959. A first-edition copy of *The Hidden Ireland*, Daniel Corkery, 1924. Liam whistled softly. *The Course of Irish Verse*, Robert Farren, 1948. A well-worn collection of Yeats. Hardbacks, all of them. A camper who carried first-edition hardbacks, Irish poetry. At the bottom of the stack was a leather-bound journal. Liam left it untouched, replaced the books and chessboard.

He listened to see if anyone was coming. The forest was absolutely silent, holding its breath. He reached into the camper's backpack. Tee shirts, shaving gear, maps. A puzzled look crossed Liam's brow and he pulled out a pair of rolled-up socks from the pack. These weren't just any socks. Talle kept him supplied in these, a special brand of navy blue wool socks from Donegal County, Ireland. Every Yule it was one of his regular gifts, a dozen of these, ordered from an Irish catalogue. Not only that, these were folded into a double roll, the way Liam rolled his own. He was so particular about that, Talle had to train the laundry staff to do it properly. Had this camper actually somehow gotten into the hacienda, gone upstairs, into his sock drawer and helped himself? Liam shook his head in amazement. That was just not possible.

Liam stood and stared for a long while at the outdoor bedroom of his trespasser. Could it be that Fiona was right?

Liam lifted his nose and caught the scent of a newly-lit cigarette. Funny, it smelled like the ones he used to smoke, in the school-bus days. He froze as he heard the unmistakable sound of autumn leaves crunching under foot. Somewhere behind him, a strong and distinctly Irish voice began to speak.

"'Twilight people, why will you still be crying /Crying and calling to me out of the trees?'"

Liam's heart thudded. Before he could think to turn and see the source of the voice – an all too-familiar voice except for the brogue – he heard himself continuing the recitation. He knew it well, the Irish poet, Seumas O'Sullivan's *"The Twilight People"*:

"'For under the quiet grass the wise are lying /And all the strong ones are gone over the seas.'"

Liam turned and found himself staring at the vision Fiona had described. His own image - in a wilder form - stood smoking a cigarette. The long white hair was loose, the man wore a white Irish sweater, like the one under Liam's coat, only well traveled, and jeans that needed washing. The two men stared at each other for a long, breathless moment. The trespasser then grinned and dropped his cigarette, crunched it out under his hiking boot, buried it with the toe, and stepped forward, his fingers outstretched for a handshake.

"Mack Magee at your service."

"Liam Fagan," Liam kept his hands in his pockets and stared hard at the man, trying to assert his role as proprietor of his property, to keep this trespasser in his place.

"Hey, now, " said the stranger, "Ye know who I am. Ye *know*." He grinned at Liam.

Liam was fast losing grip on his landlord pose. He was looking into a mirror-slightly tinted copper, for the skin tones of the man were darker than his own—but a mirror, nevertheless. The man smiled Liam's own smile back at him, then laughed out loud.

"Well, my brother, I have long awaited this day, yes I have!"

Tears filled Liam's eyes and the twins stepped forward, embracing long and hard. Every time they started to release the embrace, one of them held tighter. They stood that way for a long time in the middle of the dark woods. Tree branches around the campsite shivered, dropping leaves and needles.

They finally separated and stood back, staring at each other. Liam shook his head, his hand over his mouth in disbelief. Mack slapped his knees and gave a loud laugh. He beckoned Liam to the fire and the two sat across from each other on tree stumps set up like stools, the flame between them. Mack crumpled a bit of sage, dropping the pieces into the flame.

"I've been reading up on your local customs. Sage is a symbol for home, did ye know that? The old people in these parts used to burn a wee bit of it so travelers would follow the scent and know they had a place to sleep."

"Home," Liam echoed, staring into the fire. "Well, if you are who you are, then I suppose that's exactly where we are at this moment."

"Oh, I'm who I am, rest assured."

"You've been here a while, I'm told, camping on my land."

"I was waiting for the right moment, to introduce myself."

"And what moment was that going to be?"

"This one, obviously," Mack grinned across the flames.

"Ah!" Liam smiled at his twin.

"So, how've ye survived, Liam?"

"Shouldn't I be asking you that question? You're the one roughing it here."

"Not-a-tall, I have it easy here in your lovely woods. Ye, however, ye belong in Ireland. You're not of this world, this 1990's Ameri-kay. It's not in your blood, its harshness, its cynicism, its materialism."

"Then you haven't seen the accumulations inside my castle!" Liam laughed ruefully. He picked up a twig and snapped it into pieces, tossing them into the coals.

"Ah, but I have. You don't lock your doors at night. I've had my-self a look."

"Fiona said you had looked in the chess room window. So...you did more than that. Inside? While we slept?"

"Just once, to see is all. I found your poems. I read a while, sat there in your fancy green leather chair with the gods and goddesses and the Virgin Mary lookin' over me shoulder."

"Really! And what if we had found you there?"

"I took the chance. It would have made for an interesting reunion, wouldn't you say?"

"I would have thought you the *sidhe*," Liam stared at his twin, not so sure he actually wasn't. "And what did you think of my books? And my socks, for that matter?"

"Your socks?"

"I found them in your backpack. My blue Donegal wools."

"Those are mine, Liam. The cousins send me those from back home, now and again. What? Did ye think I'd be comin' all this way across the ocean to steal your socks? As for your books, your verse is out of time, my brother. I mean, out of the times in which you live. If there is such thing as reincarnation, perhaps you are Keats or Shelley."

"Two of my favorites."

"Of course."

"So...why? Why didn't you call, write, or knock on the door?"

"We share the reclusive gene. I'm an odd bird, is all. When I thought of coming here, I realized I had no one a-tall to recommend me to you. No witnesses to my character, no one who could say, 'Yes, this is your twin', or even 'Yes, this is a trustworthy stranger asking entry into your home'. I have been in this country for about twenty years. I'd wanted to come anyway, but when the priest finally told me my twin had gone to America and he wasn't certain but thought it was under the name of Fagan - he wouldn't tell me, you see, until after my...oh dear..."

"Yes?"

"Well, this is a bad way of telling you...but our dear mother passed on in 1972. So that's when the priest told me more of the story. And our father...well, he died when I was a lad, I never knew him, really."

Liam stared into the flame, trying to feel what he felt at that moment. It wasn't clear. He had never expected to find his biological parents, yet to hear that now he never would, left a strange, empty feeling.

"I'm sorry to tell it all to you this way," said Mack, watching his brother. "But of course, you had to know."

"Of course. So...you came looking for me twenty years ago?"

"I knew it was a big country but I thought, miracles can happen. So I came along."

"Twenty years you've been here?"

"It's true. I started out with the best of intentions, to become an American, to have the American life. I studied, I became a citizen, I found work."

Mack got up, pulled a log from a stash of firewood he'd gathered earlier in the day. He set the log in the center of the low flame and sprinkled kindling on top. The flame caught itself on the kindling and flared. He poked it with a stick, then sat on the stump again.

"I never married. I had, you know, girls, some. Lived with one girl for two years, in New York. Another for five in Boston. Broke their hearts, I suppose, left without explaining when I had to move along. Since the last one, I have traveled, mostly. Hitchhiked, buses, now and then an old car until it would die by the roadside. Worked the odd job – mechanics, construction, whatever would give me room and board as I moved around."

"But you are an educated, intelligent man. Why have you done this with your life?"

"Not really educated. I took some courses, here and there, into my thirties. When I found you through the computer chess, I was in Chicago, fixing cars, living with a couple co-workers. Using one guy's computer there. You see, I can't make a decision for myself, Liam. I can't decide this is where I want to stay, that is who I want to know, here is what I do best for a living. I can't find my purpose, is all. I have had such an emptiness within, at times."

Mack looked at Liam across the campfire, smiling sadly, before breaking into a full grin.

"Only now I'm full up."

He lit a new cigarette and continued his story.

"So when I stumbled upon ye, it was most amazing to me. There I am, sitting at someone else's desk, in someone else's life, at their computer, using their own password to get inside, even. Passing the time, lonely at the bulletin board. And Talle finding me there, it's just amusing, I have insomnia, don'tcha know. Up at night, tapping the keyboard with strangers across the universe. She tells me her husband plays chess and says we should meet in a chess room. So we did. As Naoise and Finn. It was so incredible."

"It was. A perfect match."

"Like playing myself."

"That's how I describe it."

"I couldn't wait to get home at night from the job, all nervous until my roommate was finished with his own email and off to bed. That was our agreement; I could use it after hours. I   began to realize there was something odd about it, about our connecting so purely."

"How did you find me? Was it through my old chess mentor, Professor Swenerton?"   Liam searched his pockets and came up with the flask. He handed it across to his twin. "Talle fussed at me for telling you about him. She said it was too big a clue to my identity."

"*Go raibh maith agat,*" Mack gratefully accepted the flask. "Yes. I started from there. It took a bit of doing, but I found out where he taught - in Chicago, in fact, where I was at the time. Which I took as no small omen, I'll tell you! I figured out in which decade you would have graduated and began searching in the campus library there. Took a month of Sundays as the saying goes. *Slainte!*" Mack took a sip and handed the flask back. "Ah, The Macallan."

"My favorite. But I never finished my degree; I wasn't in the annuals or on any graduate list. How did you…"

"Besides a good Guinness now and again, Macallan's the only one I drink."

The two men shook their heads, grinning.

"Although, I must say, this is a rare vintage! I've not had this one before," Mack closed his eyes, savoring the good

417

strength of it. "Anyway, so Father Padraic had at least told me the people who'd adopted you were probably Fagans. I looked at back issues of the old campus newspaper. You had a poem or two in there."

Liam smiled and shook his head. Ancient history. Those were probably the only poems of his to ever have seen print.

"So, once I had your name, I asked the librarian where an important poet might be published, and she told me the best bet was in 'Bards & Writers'. So I looked, and there was the residency prize listed. I found Ojo de Sombras on the computer, printed out a map and all."

"But I still don't understand. After all that, to then just come here and hide in the woods? Why didn't you reveal yourself?"

"Well, once I found out about your prize for the poets, I thought, my brother is this poet, in this egghead, highbrow world, how will I fit into that? And New Mexico! I thought it was the Wild West, you know, that I was going to! Then I come upon this article about this missing poet back in '79 - and how it put a bit of a curse on your residency here for a while. I thought to myself, this is odd, what has my brother gotten himself mixed into? Let's face it, how was I to know if you hadn't become some dark person? I mean, the potential for darkness – it's in all of us. I've felt it a time or two myself, the temptation to do whatever I pleased, and in situations of raw survival, you know, on the road."

"Living as you describe, I can imagine. But did you really think I might be - 'a dark person'?"

"No… but I did wonder what kind of company you'd fallen into. Or if you'd come to grief. I mean, the Wild West, I imagined everyone here carried a pistol and hung out in western saloons."

Liam smiled, drank from the flask and handed it back to his brother.

"So I thought to myself, ok, I'll just go hang out in the local pub, listen to the talk, get a look at my brother's castle, then I'll give a call, tell him I'm about. Of course, I still couldn't know for absolute certain that you were my brother. I mean, the coincidences were all lined up, but what if I was wrong? I couldn't know until I laid eyes on ye. All I really knew was we were supposed to be identical. The priest had told me that, at least. He said they'd never been sure which one of us was adopted out, especially given that they didn't name either of us until the deed was done. Ha!"

Mack rolled his eyes up and slapped his knee, laughing loudly. He took another swallow from the flask. Liam chuckled.

"I figured all the facts and coincidences in the book wouldn't mean much against the undeniable facts of whether we looked like each other or not, ye see. So I came on."

"And when did you first see me? And verify for yourself that I was your twin?"

"I've cheated a bit with the binoculars. I saw you on your deck, reading in the mornings. Couple months ago."

"Couple months ago!"

"I was going to come forward sooner. But I rather got caught up in watching the going's-on here, and didn't want to lose my vantage point until I had figured a few things out."

"What going's-on do you mean, Mack?"

"Oh…I'd rather not say, quite yet. I don't want to go pointing fingers unless I'm certain… And… well, there's the thing of the Green man, ye see."

"The Green Man?"

"He lives in your woods, here, ye know. As sure as I do, only more sure, because I'm just visiting, but he *lives* here."

Mack handed the flask back and Liam took a swig.

"Haven't ye seen him?"

"I've heard rumors that others have. Talle speaks of him. The poets, Hawthorne."

"I read in some of your books that night, you've written of him quite a lot."

"Yes…he's captured my fancy…but I can't say I've ever actually seen him."

"That's very strange. I see him all the time."

"He gives chess moves to Fiona."

"Is that what she's thinkin' then? Oh no, that wouldn't be him. That'd be me."

Mack uncoiled his long legs and stood, reached into his tent and pulled out the small chessboard.

"She said the Green Man gave her the moves," said Liam.

"Well...that might be so. I see she's made three moves since you began the game. I gave her that last one, though. Funny, those moves she made, they're the ones I would've. That's our game you two are playin' there."

"I don't understand. She didn't say you two had met. In fact, she said you hadn't met, she was going to seek you out. That was only this evening. And those moves, they're only from this evening too. How do you have them already?"

"No, Fiona and I haven't met. It's a long story – I'll explain all that. But it's connected to why I haven't come forth before. Liam, there's something I need to be showing ye. Come."

Mack stood and tossed dirt on the flames, putting out the fire. He rummaged in his tent, put a few things in his backpack, and shoved his arms through the straps.

"It'll be dawn in a couple hours. We'll need to keep an eye and ear out for wildlife, but I've had no trouble so far. Heard a wild cat one night, though. Gave me a bit of a scare, is all."

"Where are we going?"

"Just follow me."

Mack led Liam through the woods toward the red hills.

"We're going to the Bardic Cabin?"

"Yes. I thought that must be what it was. I read about the early years, in that one magazine, where they did the article about your Bardic School."

"My god, how did you find that?"

"In your own library the night I visited your castle."

Liam laughed.

"I haven't been to the Bardic Cabin since Talle had it closed down."

"Good lord, Liam, that's a far time ago!"

"I've become a recluse. Aside from occasional visits to Hawthorne's studio, I rarely walk out beyond the compound. The last time I was in the Bardic Cabin was the morning after Aisling Devlin left us. Otherwise, once a year I go into the village for our poetry reading."

"Why have you hidden yourself away like that?"

"I've been - depressed, I think the word is. The current vernacular."

"This girl, Aisling. You loved her?"

"I suppose, yes. I took it hard that she left without saying goodbye. I knew she had to go, of course, her residency was almost finished, there had never been any hope of her staying on."

"Or of you going off with her?"

"Between you and me...I had fantasies. But that was all they were. I would never leave Talle. I owe her too much."

"Talle, if you don't mind my saying, thinks she owes a bit herself."

"How do you mean?"

"She wouldn't be running this poetry school without your name, without your presence. You are the great poet."

"I'm no great poet. I'm a poet with a benefactress who has built up this residency out of a myth. The myth of the bards."

"The bards are no myth. Many of them died for their poetry."

"I know that. But in this country, they are just a myth. Of another country, another time, another world. They might as well be mythical heroes as real men and women."

"Anyway, yes, she owes you your name and presence, your creativity. But that wasn't actually what I was talking about. What I meant was, she fancies that she owes...to someone else."

"How do you mean?"

Mack stopped to pull back a low-lying branch while his brother passed through. He looked Liam straight in the eyes.

"The Green Man. She has made a religion of him, hasn't she? I've seen her in the woods here, praying to him, reciting to him and all."

"Praying?"

"Oh yes, it's prayers. Prostrate on the ground, 'Come to me oh lord', the whole bit."

Liam frowned. If anyone else were saying this to him, he wouldn't allow it. Yet, Mack's tone was one of solemnity, not ridicule.

"Is she a bit spare, do you think? A troubled soul? If you don't mind my asking."

"She's overabundant with creative energy. She has many outlets but never enough. I think this obsession with the Green Man has helped fill the parts that need filling. Perhaps also makes up a bit for what I can't give her. We are bound together by our history and our mutual values. We have a comfortable partnership. But...something is lacking. I believe young Hawthorne also helps her in that department."

The two men continued walking.

"Ah, Hawthorne. The young groundskeeper? The artist?"

"Yes. They have a relationship. I suppose you've figured that out."

"I never would have thought it was – romantic."

"I believe it is."

"Hmmm... I wouldn't have said so, not in all my life. You can read so much about people, you know, watching from a distance. It's what I have spent my life doing, after all. Being a rover, watching and moving on. What people say and what they do when they think no one is watching... are often quite different, don'tcha know."

"So what have you seen?"

Mack reached in his backpack and pulled out a water bottle, offered it to Liam, who gratefully accepted. His brother was clearly in much better physical shape than he.

"There is a lot of tension between them, but I don't believe it's sexual. They have heated words. She walks away, angry, rigid. He watches her go, his shoulders slump, he turns away. He seems beaten down for such a young man."

Liam handed the water bottle back to Mack, who took a sip as they continued on.

"I think you may misread them. She is his employer, after all. You see, he smokes a lot of marijuana. It makes him lazy sometimes."

"Ah."

"She has to ride him to do his work. The sexual... I don't know. I have always assumed it, between them. Perhaps the fire has gone out. But they are still close. He watches out for her, I trust him in a strange way. I trust his loyalty."

"Loyalty. Interesting word. Do you think, perhaps, his loyalty has been...purchased?"

"Purchased?" Liam put out his hand to stop Mack from approaching the cabin door. "Careful, it's not safe to go inside. The floorboards have rotted."

"There are no floorboards. It's a stone slab floor."

"Well, of course there are floorboards. Do you think I don't know my own property?"

"There are no floorboards."

"But that's why we had to shut it down. The floorboards were rotting, the roof, the whole foundation."

"The cabin is basically sound. I don't understand why it was condemned. Believe me, I've been inside. It could use some work, but there's no danger."

Mack focused the flashlight beam on the boarded-up cabin and proceeded to the front door, tugging at the two-by-fours, which, barely secured by Raven's make-shift rock hammer from the day before, came off easily.

Liam stood, his mouth open, and listened to the splintering of old planks in the dark of the autumn morning. He felt as if the air had been knocked out of his lungs, as if his knees were going to collapse. *Floorboards. The floorboards are rotting.* How was it so, that all these years, he had heard that phrase from Talle's lips, yet not once had he ever questioned it? Had, in fact, said it himself, like an obedient parrot, when asked. *Oh, we can't go in there anymore. The floorboards are rotted.* Mack was right; Liam knew damned well there were no floorboards in this cabin. He had spent nights in the cabin, had swept out leaves and twigs himself on more than one occasion. It had a stone slab floor. Yet he had seen the floorboards, in his mind's eye, when she told him the building had been condemned. Why had he done that to himself? Why had his own mind tricked him, and for so long?

Liam's legs were shaking and he began gasping for air. He lowered himself to the ground on one knee and tried to control his breathing. For the first time in fourteen years, a startling piece of truth was shouting inside his head:

Because I didn't want to know. I didn't want to know. He ran his hands over his chest, as if to soothe himself from the outside in.

Didn't want to know what?

The truth about Aisling.

"Liam, are you coming?"

Mack was inside the cabin. The light from his flashlight was causing random patterns of off-and-on yellow light between the slats of the boards at the windows. Liam stared, remembering all the work he had done to ready the Bardic Cabin for the poets. He himself had nailed the boards over the windows, to keep out the light of the moon and dawn. The Bardic School experience of total darkness was what he had meant to create.

"Did I help to put her into *permanent* darkness?" he whispered to himself.

The cottonwoods chattered overhead, and the pre-dawn breeze rustled the grasses underfoot. That prodding finger again at Liam's tail bone, the sensation of hands on his shoulders, gently pushing him in the direction of the Bardic Cabin. He needed to see, now.

Liam joined Mack inside the cabin.

"There's not much here. I had wanted to stay a couple of nights. But...I couldn't take it."

"Take what?"

"There is a presence here. A strong one. Like the *sidhe*. A sadness."

427

Liam closed his eyes to feel the cabin around him in total darkness.

"I stayed here a few times, in the early days before the residency began," he finally spoke. "I would catch trout in the Ojo de Sombras, cook it in the fireplace, my little tribute to…"

"But something rustled on the floor,/And some one called me by my name–" to Liam's delight, Mack caught the reference and recited the words from Yeats' *The Song of Wandering Aengus* in his gentle brogue. The twins finished the verse together, speaking to the cabin's walls of the trout that transforms into the muse, "a glimmering girl".

"Who called me by my name and ran/And faded through the brightening air…"

"Yes, I caught many a 'trout' here," Liam smiled at the memories. "Like the ancient bards, I composed some of my best work here. The modern critics would hate what I wrote here…but it was the most soulful of all my work."

"I'm sure it was." Mack knelt on one knee and drew designs in the dirt on the stone floor, while his brother spoke.

"Those were pure times. In the mornings, Talle would bring me scones and a thermos of coffee and my writing book. I would sit and write down my poem, in the doorway there, watching the morning begin. Then I would read it to her, we would sit and talk of our plans and dreams for the Bardic School."

Mack watched his brother describing those times. The lines in his face were softer in this mood of reflection. Outside, they replaced the boards in comfortable silence - using the same make-shift rock hammer Raven had left lying on the stoop - and Liam didn't speak again until the last board was attached.

"Why did you bring me here tonight?"

"I wanted you to feel it again. Your dream. And... there's something else... Come."

"I'm not sure I can really bear to see much more right now, Mack. Come back with me now, we'll set up a room for you at the house."

"Follow me."

Liam sighed and followed the strange specter of himself in jeans and sweater, hair flowing over his back. Liam suddenly felt as if he was outside his skin, watching himself. He knew that he and Mack walked the same, moved their shoulders the same, looked the same when perplexed, tired, at peace. Except...were they ever at peace? Had either of them ever known peace? Liam felt a catch in the back of his throat; whatever was happening, there was one new sensation that overrode all other impressions at this moment. The sensation of having come home. A gypsy having found his tribe. He was with his twin, and whatever was wrong with his world, it would now be righted.

"Here," Mack shone the flashlight on the ground and pushed aside desert sand with the toe of his hiking boot.

"Stand back a minute."

Mack bent down and yanked, and the earth fell away to reveal a door in the ground, which he opened to reveal a darkness below.

"What is this?" Liam marveled, kneeling to peer inside.

"Ah. I thought you didn't know about this. It's a Native American pit structure, maybe a *kiva*. Or once was – some kind of cellar, but it's been refurbished. Down the ladder with you now, it's safe," Mack shone the flashlight on the ladder and Liam, his heart beating wildly, descended the wooden rungs. Mack followed and the two men stood on the earth floor. Mack handed Liam the flashlight and waited while his brother circled the room in silent amazement, shining the light on the altar, the table, the fireplace, and the cabinet. The light lingered on the bottles of oils and supplies, then moved slowly into the corner, discovering the Green Man nest. Liam drew a sharp breath.

"What is this place? It smells so strange."

"I was hoping you could tell me. Yeah, over time I think some small animals have died in here. Rat's nests, too, have a bit of a smell. There's drawings over there."

Liam's light discovered the bear, the corn stalk, the lightning.

"It's the Green Man nest. There's one in Hawthorne's studio. He does the poets' portraits in it. It's a kind of game he and Talle made up, for inspiration. He creates the masks, you'll see in our hallway."

"Oh, yes, the Green Man masks. There's one in your chess room."

"He draws the poets, then makes the masks from his sketches. There's one for each poet. He does them in the nest so he can get the effect of the vegetation coming from the mouth, you see, twining about the head and all. He changes the features, some male, some female. But you can see a trace of each poet in them. A cheekbone here, an eyelid there. Quite amazing, what he does."

"I was wondering what all this might be for," Mack was now standing next to Liam. He gently took the flashlight from his brother and directed the beam back onto the cabinet shelves, playing it along the containers of plaster, water, packages of gauze, gloves, carving tools. And up along the top shelf, the tiny vials with crossbones-&-skulls.

"But why are his supplies here? Underground? I don't understand. He does all this work in his studio. And those little blue bottles look like Talle's, from her apothecary," Liam said.

Mack went to the nest and ran his fingers through the branches and leaves.

"Well...it would appear someone has been having a bit of fun here..."

Mack turned and lifted a bit of cloth into the beam of his flashlight.

"A girl's undies. Lace. Nice. Talle's?"

"No, I don't think so. Not really her style," but as he said it, it suddenly occurred to Liam that perhaps he didn't really know Talle's style. "Let's go."

Liam was overwhelmed with new information – other people's secrets, a growing set of questions, but no answers – and suddenly felt the need for fresh air of dawn. He didn't need the flashlight to ascend the ladder this time; the sky above was faintly purple with a wash of gold. Mack followed up and re-latched the door, brushing sand and leaves over it to once again hide it from view.

The brothers walked side by side, Liam's eyes to the ground and Mack's eyes on Liam. The brothers didn't speak until they reached Mack's campsite by the river. Liam sat on the ground, slumped over his knees with his head in his hands while Mack packed up his things.

"Brother, I think I've, as the Americans say, 'blown your mind' a bit here?"

"Yes, a bit. I finally take a walk in my own woods, and find my long lost twin and some rather strange goings on, apparently involving my own wife."

"Perhaps ye should walk on your property more often, is all."

"That would seem to be the lesson here."

"Maybe all that is part of Talle's Green Man religion, is all. If, as you say, that pile of debris in there has some-thing to do with the Green Man. Maybe that's her chapel, of sorts."

"The Green Man - I've always thought of him as a benign figure. He is, isn't he?"

"By most accounts. He can be a fierce protector, though, if need be. There are old stories."

"So if my wife has gone bonkers into some kind of pagan rites, at least it's for the good, not satanic or anything like that. Oh, how can I even ask such a question? Talle is the most loving, generous woman; she has done so much for so many of the poets. She has given so much of the artwork we purchased with the hacienda back to the church, to the families. She has lived her whole life for me, for my comfort and welfare, set everything up so I can write. She has given me incredible freedom. No one can measure or repay such a gift."

"Freedom?"

"Yes, to create, to not worry about the work of the world. I am very spoiled, Mack. Well, this will all make more sense by light of day - after a long morning's nap. Come, let's go up to the house."

The sun-tanned Mack studied his pale brother for a moment. He pulled out a cigarette and lit it, blowing smoke into the sky.

"Liam, I'm not going up to the house with you. Not just yet."

"But of course you are!" Liam lept to his feet and reached for Mack's backpack. "You don't think you're going to keep camping like this? There are cougar and bear out here. Such nonsense, my own twin finally here and living in the woods!"

"Liam, listen. Not just yet. I need you to trust me on this. Give me a few more days, let me find a new place to camp. I've been thinking I should go to Bandelier before the first snow."

"No, I won't hear of it. Anyway, Talle has instructed Hawthorne to run you off the property this morning. If you don't go to the house with me now, you may end up in the custody of the local marshal."

"She won't be calling the marshal."

"She has threatened to."

"The marshal is the least of our concerns here. Something is going on, Liam. Don't ask me to tell you everything I've seen and heard, not just yet."

"You mean there's more?"

"Let me put a few things together, then I'll tell you everything." Mack gently retrieved his backpack from Liam's clutches.

Liam frowned and stared at his twin. Again, that incredible sensation of union… reunion… completion.

"Is this about Hawthorne? Has he done something?"

"It involves him, possibly…that's what I need to find out. And the two young girls, Fiona and the other one…"

"Raven?"

"The dark-haired one."

"How are Fiona and Raven involved?" Liam asked.

"Give me a few days. You have a lot of questions now. And I might be able to bring you some answers. But I want them to be the right answers, is all. Just give me a few more days. I'll stay out of sight; I'll be off the property for a bit. There's things I have to do. Don't tell anyone you found me."

"Yes, I've *just* found you, after all these years of wondering, wishing, dreaming of my twin brother. You're not going to disappear on me again, are you, like you did with the chess?"

"I promise. Anyway, I didn't really *abandon* you with the chess. And now as I have the taste of my brother's company in me blood, I'm not likely to be going far away from him again."

Liam couldn't speak for a moment. But then he found his voice.

"There's still so much to talk about, so many questions. When can we talk again?"

"A week from Friday night."

"That's too long! Impossible!"

"I'll be back from Bandelier in a few days. Slip out at about nine a week from Friday and meet me...there, again, at the *kiva* entrance."

"That's the night of Fiona's reading at the *Extranjeros*. It could go on past ten before we're back, there's a reception and all. But I'll get here as soon as I can after that. Meanwhile, what about your provisions? I can't leave you here without food."

435

"I'm fine. I have all I need. Especially now." Mack grasped his brother by the shoulders and the two men looked each other in the eyes. Tears made each nothing more than a familiar blur. They blinked and the tears washed down their time-carved cheeks.

"You are being so mysterious, Mack. This is outrageous! You belong with me now, there's a guestroom in the hacienda we can prepare for you. You don't have to wander anymore, no more worrying about money, no more flop houses, no more hitchhiking."

Liam heard himself repeating a litany quite similar to the one Talle had recited to him in front of the Santa Fe hotel fireplace so many years ago.

"We'll see, my brother. But as much alike as we are, I think our definitions of 'freedom' are a bit different. We'll see, just the same."

Liam stared thoughtfully at his rover brother, the wildly loose white hair, the worn-and-torn jeans, the sweater stiff with the soil of the road. The scent of cigarettes wafted from Mack's sweater in the cold morning air and stirred an ancient longing in Liam. Again, he remembered his long ago, school bus, traveling days.

"Maybe not so different. But you're right. We'll see. Here, at least take this." Liam pulled the pewter flask of Macallan's from his jacket pocket and pressed it into Mack's hand.

"Ah, your *poitin*? I'll gladly put that in safe keeping for ye," Mack grinned.

The brothers clasped hands over the flask for a long moment. The morning sun was flashing between the trees and mountain range, when they finally parted.

As Liam walked back to the hacienda, the rest of the lines from Yeats' *The Song of Wandering Aengus* came to him. He could almost hear them in the rustling of the morning leaves, the gradual and sporadic twittering of the birds as they woke in their nests overhead.

...Though I am old with wandering...I will find out where she has gone,/ And kiss her lips and take her hands;/And walk among long dappled grass...

Liam walked quietly through the compound court-yard and into the hacienda, exhausted and exhilarated.

Mack buried his campsite debris, rolled his sleeping bag, folded up his tent gear and strapped it onto his back-pack, took one last look around his campsite and headed along the river toward the red hills. The finishing lines of the Yeats poem about the muse - the one he and Liam had quoted to each other - came to him as he walked past the cottonwood trees.

...And walk among long dappled grass,/And pluck till time and times are done/The silver apples of the moon,/The golden apples of the sun.

Chapter 17 - Voyeur

September 14, 1993

Mack sat at the Bandelier campground picnic table, writing by the light of the Coleman lantern the next-door camper had kindly lent him. The man felt sorry for him, making notes in the dim, wavering glow of a candle. Mack had been quite content with his own makeshift holder - the tin can from his meal of beans-and-wieners, cut out in part to shelter the wick. But he couldn't fend off the enthusiasm of his neighbor, an insurance salesman from the Windy City who was pleased to meet a fellow Chicagoan in the wilderness. The guy was all set up with a fine RV, grill, microwave and television, and couldn't bear to have such rudimentary digs right next door. Last night he had even given Mack a filet mignon from his grill - a bit of neighborliness Mack didn't mind accepting. He was happy to have a break from his usual camping fare. He'd poached and cooked a few trout and one rabbit out at the Fagans', but that had been a couple weeks ago. Since then it had been mostly beans, rice, sardines and crackers.

Mack had mixed feelings about pitching his tent in the Bandelier campground. Everything was so orderly, so suburban here, compared to his furtive encampments on the Fagan acres. Even the juniper bushes seemed like landscaped shrubbery. Here, he could trot down the path and fill up a jug of fresh water from a tap. He could stay for days on end, build as roaring a fire as he wanted - in his allocated pit - and keep it stoked all night, without fear of betraying his whereabouts.

Yet, in truth, Mack Magee was not this type of traveler. He preferred to rough it in Mother Nature, staying to himself - aside from the occasional chat with the Green Man - with only the nearby presence of deer and elk. He didn't even mind the dangers of the wild - keeping an eye and ear out for cougar, bear and rattlesnake. It all contributed to a lively feeling.

Still, it was good that he'd been able to get away for a few days, create the illusion for Talle and Hawthorne that their trespasser had vanished. This also gave him a chance to sort through his impressions, try to make sense of the odd events he'd observed over the past couple of months. He wondered if his brother was in some kind of danger, or if perhaps the two young poets needed looking after. That Talle, she was a bit gone, if he said so himself, and might need protection from her own self if she went much further.

As for Hawthorne, he didn't know what to make of the man. On the one hand, he seemed to be a loner like Mack, so the gardener/artist's behaviors didn't strike him as peculiar - as they probably would seem to some. On the other hand, the man brooded so much, seemed rough with the women, smoked incredible amounts of weed, and certainly didn't seem like someone you'd want to cross.

Then, coloring everything Mack saw, there was that business of the missing poet.

He had hiked part of the route from Liam's, keeping along the Rio de Sombras, making his way toward Bandelier. Once he was far enough away from the village to feel safe hitchhiking - without someone mistaking him for Liam Fagan - he'd begun his trek along the old highway with his thumb out. He got a ride from a Los Alamos engineer most of the way, then hiked the last two miles to the visitor's center in Frijoles Canyon. Picked up a handful of fliers about the ruins, and bought a couple of books on Anasazi culture and architecture. Walked the two miles to the campground, selected one of the numbered sites with tables - located within walking distance of the privies - and paid his fee.

He'd spent the last seven days hiking the ruins, climbing over a hundred feet of sheer vertical ladder to peer into the dwellings. He napped in his tent, read the books he'd picked up, and - mostly - thought about the Fagan situation.

It was amazing what a little geographical distance could do for your perspective. He'd almost come to feel like the things he saw and heard at the Fagans' all these weeks were ordinary, of no great consequence, meaning no harm to anyone. After all, he'd gone there to find out if Liam Fagan was indeed his twin, and then to determine his brother's situation before intruding himself into the fifty-seven-year-old man's long-established, twin-less existence. To get to know the humans that peopled Liam's world by spying on them was hardly an impartial way to gather information. He felt he owed it to them all to hold off judging or misinterpreting what he saw, from his unfair vantage point of relative invisibility.

By lantern light, at his Bandelier picnic table - several miles away from the world of Liam and Talle Fagan - he revisited his impressions of the past eight weeks. After seven evenings of this exercise, he had come to the conclusion that, indeed, there were strange and possibly foul goings-on at the estate. That he wasn't unfairly judging anybody. That some questions needed to be asked.

For one thing, he had seen several rendezvous between Talle and Hawthorne, in and out of the *kiva* over the past few weeks. They carried in shovels and backpacks of supplies. Talle was chopping firewood behind the Bardic Cabin. Mack went down into the *kiva* a couple of times, and found they'd left new items: packages of herbs, bottles of perfumed oils, towels, gauze, scissors, tape. A large supply of emergency candles, the twelve-hour kind. Jugs of water. As if they were setting up some kind of botanist survivalist camp. Only without food, nor a stash of weaponry.

He was there the day Fiona and Raven discovered the *kiva*, and overheard much of their discussion. When he saw Talle headed their way with more supplies, he did what he could to warn them off. (And took advantage of the moment to have a little chessman's fun with Fiona. He'd been keeping tabs on the game he and Liam had started, through the stained glass window, and wasn't ready to forfeit his hand in its progress.)

More than once he followed Talle on her early-morning - sometimes full moon - foraging trips along the river's edge. Mack had done a lot of survival camping in his time. He kept himself informed, especially in new terrain, which New Mexico was to him. He saw the woman gathering things he wasn't sure she should be gathering – plants he himself knew to avoid. After snooping in the greenhouse that one night he'd let himself in to the hacienda, he'd figured out that she ran some kind of herbal business on the side. Still, the little skull-and-cross-bone bottles on her shelves made him nervous.

Other things about his brother's wife made him even more nervous. All that business of Talle spreading herself out on the ground, mumbling prayers to the Green Man. Walking alone in the woods at all hours, as if she was looking for someone. Mack had no problem with people holding conversations with the Green Man, or even thinking they saw him out of the corners of their eyes. He'd grown up with bedtime stories about a lot of mythical figures, and the Green Man had been one of the ones about whom his mother had told the most fanciful tales.

But to worship Jack the Green like he was a godhead… Mack was stunned to witness such a thing. He wondered if his brother was wise about his wife's spiritual eccentricities.

"*Sure, the Green Man is part of our world. But there's no need of going on about it!*" he whispered out loud to himself, thinking on what he'd seen Talle doing one afternoon in the woods. "*I mean, the fellow has always been around! Americans seem to have a need of being the first to discover everything, it seems to me.*"

He chuckled to himself, shaking his head. Then, just as quickly, frowned into the flames, suddenly recalling his strange experience, at the hot springs. It was that day he was sunbathing in the raw, asleep on a flat, warm rock, like a lizard. He woke up to see that one, Hawthorne, naked in the water with a woman, and, to his astonishment, found himself aroused - and let nature take its course - right there in broad daylight.

All in all, an experience that made it pretty difficult to go judging Talle Fagan's weird activities in nature. He supposed it had something to do with how long it had been since he'd been with a woman; he seemed to be having more than his usual dose of erotic dreams, in these woods. Many of them starring himself as Pan.

Nevertheless, he still thought Talle Fagan could use a dose of reality. More, he was certain that Liam didn't have a clue about his wife's true nature, her spiritual leanings. Or about much else when it came to judging character. A good-hearted man, a trusting soul. Too passive for his own good.

That quality in Liam was familiar to Mack: had it not been for Mack's need to keep his own wits about him in a foreign country and rely on himself alone to survive – through some hard times at that – he would probably be just as moony. Liam was set up to indulge his creative side and completely neglect his survival skills, while Mack was set up just the opposite. If they'd been raised together, maybe there would have been more of a balance for the both of them.

Mack wasn't quite sure what it all added up to, these things he had observed, but he knew there was a missing poet, and that that fact had done some harm to his twin's enterprise. He also suspected the young women, Raven and Fiona, might come to grief, the way they were nosing around. He thought he'd keep an eye on them for Liam.

It was starting to rain. Mack closed his notebook and turned off the lantern, sat a few minutes breathing in the sharp perfume of wet juniper. Then he crawled into his tent and pulled off his boots, wrapped in his sleeping bag. It was a light rain, a good sound for falling asleep.

He would also sleep well because he had a plan now. Mack always felt better when he had a plan. He wanted to get an early start in the morning, hiking the Frijoles Canyon falls trail. A nice way to wind up his little Bandelier vacation. Tomorrow afternoon, he'd break up this civilized camp, hitch a ride into Los Alamos to pick up a few supplies and spend the night in a motel room. With a real bath, a Laundromat and a hot meal. On Thursday, he would hitch and hike his way back along the Rio de Sombras to the outermost, north western edges of the Fagan estate. There, he would set up a new camp, far and away from the well-traveled paths.

On Friday, he had a little reconnoitering to do. Before his rendezvous with Liam. An idea was forming - one that came through his eyes and hands. Partly from the reconstructed *kiva* walls he had touched here at the monument. Partly from the glossy photos of Anasazi petro glyphs in the books he'd purchased at the visitor's center. Partly from the dark chambers he'd visited over the weekend at the Tsankawi ruins, maneuvering himself along the cliff by putting his hands into ancient holds carved in the rock face. All of these moments had led him to contemplate the ways these desert-dwellers had dealt with the harsh realities of life and death.

Mack needed to get back inside the Fagans' *kiva*. If his hunch was right, he needed to do so before he saw Liam again.

Chapter 18 - Chivalry

September 16, 1993

Hank Walker squirted a blast of Vitamin B under his tongue, and sat staring at the last message he'd sent to the Irish student writer at University College Galway. What time was it there? He counted on his mental fingers...about nine-thirty in the evening. Hopefully not too late for a literature major to be checking his email in the student computer center on a weekday night.

Hank was seriously craving his second daily cigarette, for which he was now about a half hour late. This was not a good thing. There was a certain amount of superstition attached to the timing of his two daily smokes: as long as he stuck religiously to the schedule, he told himself he wouldn't slip up. He was only three weeks away from his long-term goal of going down to one-a-day. This was not the time to be getting sloppy. He had slipped up once this week, during a telephone conversation with Raven - lit up before he realized what he was doing. Stubbed it out after one puff. Meanwhile, he hadn't missed his two o'clock backdoor ritual in six months.

But, he mused, the nicotine recovery market was missing a big clue: searching computer bulletin boards and libraries was damned compelling! If you could cure the heroin habit by substituting methadone, why not the cigarette habit by substituting Compunet sessions? Or, better still, this new Internet stuff. He was in the middle of a transition - in his jargon, his thinking and computer browsing habits - from the 'Compunet' mentality to the 'Internet' mentality. Hank Walker tried to keep up with all this, realized that it was the wave of the here-and-now future for a private investigator. He drew a skull and crossbones on one of his little pink Post-it notes and stuck it to the frame of the computer screen. Not in reference to his idea, but to remind himself about one more item he should check in his research today.

He went outside for the smoke, leaving the back door open in case the phone rang, and stared out at the La Plata Mountains. They stood up to their name today. It had rained this morning and the rocks still glistened silver in the sunlight. He'd not put on his jacket, so he shivered through the whole ordeal - the smell of snow was in the air. Another part of his ritual, to make the smoke as physically uncomfortable as possible. He'd told himself it was the relative boredom of his current life that kept him smoking.

He'd been widowed four years, had no offspring and no dating life. He'd paid off the house - a humble 1970's wood structure on two and a half acres - with his wife's insurance money. His cases were almost entirely from the two big insurance companies out of Denver, with the occasional local process service for dead-beat dads on the lam from other jurisdictions. He supposed he'd reached the burnout stage long ago and was just going through the motions for sake of a paycheck here and there.

Yet here he was, less than nine days into what looked like a piece of cherry pie 'a la mode' compared to his usual stale Danish – this business of reopening the Devlin case. It wasn't so much that Raven and Fiona had presented him with any new evidence. But their intuitive approach to the subject, their passion – for life, for poetry, for righting the world's wrongs – their wound-up, angry, sultry, hot female energy – that had him a bit stirred up. Poets, he chuckled to himself. Who would have thought a couple of poets from the hills of Northern New Mexico would have been in the crystal ball of his immediate future?

Having met them also stirred up something else. A memory of who he was during the Devlin investigation. Someone he hadn't been since then, that was for sure. Someone who could feel that little catch in the chest, that little thrill-chill down in the gut, when he got close to a hidden truth. When he, Hank Walker, was about to become the guy who figured it all out.

But the guy who had investigated Aisling Devlin's disappearance and the guy who was waiting for email from Ireland this afternoon were quite different people. These days, as he took his usual Sunday stroll along the Animas River (his version of church services), where he'd sprinkled Loraine's ashes back in '89, he often speculated that it was appropriate he lived here. For those who knew and cared, the river was really called *El Rio de Animas Perdidas* – the river of lost souls. That's how he'd come to feel, between losing Aisling Devlin's case, and then losing Loraine.

Until the Devlin case, Hank had always fancied himself a pretty good detective - thorough, tenacious, shrewd. And, yes, intuitive, that most important quality that Raven Shane Cordova and Fiona Kelly had plenty of. When he had come up against a brick wall on the Devlin case, he had lost a piece of his edge and, therefore, some of his confidence. Maybe that was why he'd taken on more insurance fraud cases. More of a sense of control?

There had been that car, left right there at Link's gas station like an Easter bunny basket of brightly painted clues. But they led nowhere. There had been that character, Hawthorne, looking as guilty and dark as mortal sin, and with that mysterious old courthouse record to boot. But no way to link him. In fact, that whole New Mexico mountain village was full of characters worth checking out. But they all had alibis for the time frame of Aisling's Colorado disappearance, and, being a small village where everyone knew when you took your last pee and what you had for breakfast last Sunday...every alibi was fully verifiable.

Hank had closed that file with anguish and reluctance. He tried to tell himself Aisling had decided to disappear for reasons known only to her. That she had come to no harm. What the hell, he'd told himself; might as well paint an ending he could live with, since reality wasn't coughing one up.

This week's discoveries were ringing a lot of those old bells again. This last communication from the Galway student should be the last piece of the day's puzzle. Where was Chahil O'Shea, the 1986 Fagan poet? Hank had emailed a couple of writers he'd found through the Irish/American bulletin board Raven's Dublin contact had sent. Yesterday the Galway student responded, and said he had two of O'Shea's books from the 1980s in his personal library. He said O'Shea wasn't a very important Irish writer, but was listed in the course syllabus of one of his literature professors because the professor actually knew him, and because O'Shea was part of a particular movement from the 1980's. O' Shea had been in a lot of anthologies from that decade. However, once the poet left for America in 1985, the publication trail seemed to fade out and the student hadn't heard anything about him in recent years. The student said he'd check with his professor and get back to Hank. This morning's message was that others were looking for O'Shea also. "Who and why?" had been Hank's question.

Through the open basement door, Hank heard the cheerful tone and static that indicated that he'd been bumped off line and was about to be reconnected. He crushed out his cigarette - nothing left but the filter - and carried it back down the steps inside to the ashtray. He heard the cheerful announcement of "incoming mail."

The student said his professor would himself be very interested to know where O'Shea was located:

"Some years back, a letter was sent to O'Shea in America from the publisher of his last book - a friend of my professor's, that is, Prof. McNiff - offering a contract to do some Gaelic translations of certain Irish/American poets residing in the United States. O'Shea responded that he was definitely interested, returned the contract with his signature, and wrote that he would be coming back to Ireland for a visit in the early spring of 1987, and would bring some drafts then. In response, the publisher sent a small advance, in the form of an international money order. It has never been cashed and the publisher has not heard from O'Shea again. It all seems very much out of character, says Prof. McNiff - both that O'Shea never cashed the certainly much-needed money order, and that he never got back to the publisher about the book deal. Prof. McNiff says the translations would have been very good for O'Shea's career.

"The publisher last heard from O'Shea about mid October, '86, from some writers' colony in Mexico. That's where he sent the money order. In spring of '87, he wrote to him again, but his letter came back 'No Such Person at This Address'. Prof.

McNiff says O'Shea was thought to be an honorable man who kept his word and wouldn't take a signed contract lightly, but seven years is a long time to not hear anything. Let me know if I can help otherwise."

Hank leaned back in his chair, staring at the word "*seven*" on the screen. He'd seen references to the importance of the number seven on the pagan bulletin boards. Seven days a week. The seven seals; seven planets; seven wonders of the world; seventh son of seventh son; seven-year itch. The body even changed every seven years, at the cellular level, so he'd read in Scientific American. The pagans said seven-year cycles were magical. Number seven was obviously important and mysterious, for reasons beyond his understanding. Hawthorne's courthouse record dated back to 1972. Aisling Devlin disappeared in 1979. Now it was clear that Chahil O'Shea disappeared in 1986. Seven years apart, each event.

What was that about Mexico? O'Shea wasn't in Mexico at a writers colony in the fall of 1986. He was in *New* Mexico at a writer's retreat. It wasn't the first time someone from outside the states got that detail wrong. Hell, Hank even knew people in Colorado who thought New Mexico was south of the border.

So...if something was being done to every seventh poet at the Fagans', then...

Hank froze in his chair, chills running up his legs. "*...seven years is a long time to not hear anything.*" 1993. This was the seventh year after O'Shea's disappearance.

Fiona Kelly was a seventh poet.

He stood up abruptly, almost knocking over his chair. He ran his hands through his hair, staring at the Irish writer's email on the computer screen. He'd been planning to go to Fiona's poetry reading tomorrow night anyway, to keep an eye on those impetuous girls, but now he realized he had to stop those beauties from reading that poem of Aisling Devlin's at that event. He knew a simple phone call to Raven wouldn't do any good. The woman was too headstrong, she wouldn't listen to him. He didn't dare try to call Fiona at the Fagans', too risky; someone might listen in on the line.

He realized there might not be any way he could stop Fiona from reading that poem, but at least he could be there to whisk the two poets off somewhere safe. It would be better if no locals realized the PI was in town. It was time to pull out the old trunk of disguises he kept hidden under his bed.

As Hank reached to pull his "Aisling Devlin" list from the printer, the skull and crossbones sticker caught his eye. He logged on to the toxicology site of his old college buddy, Dr. Rorey Mercer. Ordinarily the materials at Dr. Mercer's site were encrypted and thereby available only to a select few in his field. Ever since Dr. Mercer had worked as a toxicology witness on a malpractice case a couple years ago - for the same insurance company that hired Hank - the two had renewed their old friendship. The doctor had entrusted a password to Hank for professional usage. Several keystrokes later, Hank was able to print out a detailed list of toxic plants of the Southwest, along with their specific effects on the nervous system and organs of the human body.

As Hank logged off and shut down his computer, the stirring of that little old-time thrill-chill down in his gut began again, very faintly. He shoved all the Devlin paperwork back into the file and stuffed it in his briefcase, and headed home. Tonight he'd put together his disguise, pack his bag, and sit on the back deck a while. A solitary beer while watching the sunset hawks circling sounded right. Then a good night's sleep.

Chapter 19 - Mummies

September 17, 1993

Fiona felt herself sink willingly into the warm passivity, the feeling of binding weight across her knees and ankles, her arms as if strapped to her sides. The scents of various herbs were strong in the room, the faint sounds of drum and flute overhead.

"Lavender or rose?"

"Lavender," Fiona said faintly, relieved from the wet heat by the application of a cool cloth that shut out the light, gently pressed against her eyelids. I'm a living mummy, she thought. Lavender water was spritzed on her cheeks, water brought to her lips through a straw.

"I'll check on you in a little while," the soft-voiced technician assured her. Fiona drifted off, vaguely aware of the sounds of wet towels being flapped in the air and settled onto the bed next to hers, the murmured instructions to "lie down, remove the towel", the sounds of tarp, blanket and towels being wrapped over Raven's torso and legs.

"Arms in or out?" the technician asked. As instantly as Fiona had answered "In" to the same question a moment ago, Raven answered an emphatic "Out". The two poets were left in the serene quiet of the sweat room, listening to the drumming tape playing through the speakers mounted on the walls. They didn't speak. Raven mentally tested her reaction to the mummy thing, and Fiona basked in the unfamiliar serenity of being a captive audience to pampering.

Before their wraps, during their mineral baths – in side-by-side tubs separated only by a cotton curtain - they had been talking, careful to use euphemisms and codes and no one's real name, due to the presence of bathers in the other tubs. Then the technician came through, advising them that this was a "whisper only area" and that there were others who would appreciate the silence. That put an end to Raven and Fiona's cryptic discussion. It was just as well; they really needed a respite from the subject matter of the Fagans ("the you-know-who's"), Aisling Devlin ("our lost friend"), Hank Walker ("the curmudgeon") and Hawthorne ("Mr. Wonderful").

They had each spent the rest of their session in the water lost in their own thoughts. Raven was trying to imagine what would happen tonight when Fiona read Devlin's poem at the *Extranjeros*. Fiona knew she should decide what else she would read tonight besides Devlin's poem. However, it was difficult, at this point, to get excited or even nervous about reading her own work, she was so overwhelmed with trying to piece together all the information and lack of information that made up the last few days.

The technician returned to Fiona's side, placed the straw between her lips again, then turned to Raven.

"Which *curanderas* do you use?" Raven asked from the depths of her mummy wrap.

"Oh, there are several. Ashley Ross, Jon Prieto, Morgan Moon, Talle Fagan."

"Is this Talle's rose water?"

"Yes it is. The lavender, too. And we used her mix for your herbal wraps today. You should also try her herbal facial mask sometime; she uses Irish moss in that. And her body oils are excellent."

Fiona thought about Talle's greenhouse and apothecary. So these flannel sheets wrapped around her had been boiled in Talle's herbs.

The technician spritzed them again and left, advising they had twenty more minutes. Fiona started to drift off again.

"Oh my god!" Raven suddenly whispered. Fiona heard her friend sit up and noisily twist herself out of her blankets, towels and plastic wrap with urgent maneuvers. She scrambled off the bed, quickly padded back to her tub-side bench. Fiona heard her pulling on her clothes, zipping up her jeans.

"Raven? What's the matter?" Fiona was so relaxed from the music, bath and herbs that she felt as if she was trying to speak from the inside of a dream; not being able to lift her arms out of the mummy wrap didn't help either.

Raven apparently didn't hear the question; she was rattling her keys and coins so loudly, rummaging in her knapsack. Fiona heard the door swing open and shut and Raven was gone. The poet lay there stunned, staring up into washrag cotton. What had gotten into her friend? Fiona sighed. Raven was much too high-strung. Should she follow Raven and find out what was going on, make sure she was all right?

No. She resented the dark poet for not being able to just relax and enjoy a few moments in between all these high-emotion encounters and dangerous liaisons. Fiona tried to enjoy what she could of the rest of her few minutes in the mummy wrap, closing her eyes yet bracing herself for the next interruption. But it was no use. The technician would be coming to unwrap her in a few minutes. She was actually ready, now. Her legs wanted to kick out from the binding, and her nose itched badly. To distract herself – it seemed embarrassingly mundane to undo the good magic of the herbal mummy wrap just to scratch her nose - Fiona mentally re-entered the *kiva*, watched the flashlight play around, along the ceiling walls, floor. Something kept bothering her about that visit to the *kiva*.

Finally the itching stopped and Fiona fell asleep long enough for the Green Man to guide her down the *kiva* ladder and back into the dark underground room behind the Bardic Cabin. As Raven had described from one of her dreams, the Green Man pointed with a finger bone that beamed like a flashlight, first to the drawings on the wall, then to the images on the wall behind the nest, then into the nest. Something shiny, she tugged, up came the piece of wire, tied to the wooden peg-

Fiona was startled awake. She panicked when she felt the restraints on her arms and legs, then remembered where she was. She stared into the soft blindfold covering her eyes and tried to calm her breathing. The piece of wire she'd found between the nest and the wall. It was still in her jeans pocket. That's what had been bothering her all week. That and the images that seemed more recently painted than others in the *kiva*. The background paint of that wall was different than the wall behind the nest, a darker shade of roseate earth.

"So, how are we doing?" the technician asked, coming to Fiona's side. "Your friend left so suddenly!"

"Yeah, I think she's claustrophobic."

"Some people have that reaction. But the way she tore out of here, I was worried that she might have had some emergency?"

"I'm sure she's all right."

The technician unfolded the layers of plastic, blankets and sweat-dampened towels and Fiona went back to her bench to dress, preoccupied by the images the Green Man had shown her. She and Raven should get back into that *kiva* with lanterns and tools.

Fiona reached into her jeans pocket and pulled out the wire and peg. What was this thing, anyway? Something about it now seemed vaguely familiar...she dangled the peg at the end of the string, held it up to the window light. It looked like a guitar string, and one of those pegs you turned to tighten the strings – except made of unvarnished wood, and snapped off. Broken.

Aisling's harp. Everyone said it had been handmade out of wood, rough and homemade. Fiona felt a chill crawl up her spine like a spider up its web.

* * *

As Fiona entered Raven's yard, Dingo welcomed her excitedly, barking and dancing on his hind legs, swiping muddy paw prints down the front of her duster. Raven opened the door a crack, her ear affixed to a cordless phone, and motioned Fiona in, holding up her forefinger over her mouth. Fiona entered quietly and Raven went back to her desk, nodding and "Uh-huh"-ing as she went. Still feeling irritated with Raven for her dramatic exit at the bathhouse, Fiona acted disinterested and went to pour herself a glass of water from the tap. She shook off her duster and took a chair, absent-mindedly stroking Dingo's ears. The dog sat attentively as if memorizing every stroke.

"So, she actually was there while you," said Raven into the phone. "Oh, I see, then she was just–uh huh. I see... no, just... comparing notes. For a writing project on pagan fertility rituals.... Yeah... Oh, it's still going strong... Yes, I was one of the poets... No, last year... Uh huh... Yeah, that is odd, isn't it? This year, too... Uh huh...Fiona Kelly..."

Even at the mention of her own name, Fiona feigned disinterest. She shuffled through her bag for a lip-gloss.

"...Well, thank you very much...Sure, I will...let me get your..."

Raven jotted down an address, nodding, clutching the phone between her shoulder and ear.

"Thank you very much, Nora. And I'll look for you at the Circus next year."

Raven hung up and sat staring at the phone, tapping her pen against the edge of the desk. The two poets continued in silence for a moment or two. Finally Fiona couldn't stand another moment of mystery.

"So...what's up?"

"That was Nora Reiner-Byrnes, she was a Fagan poet about four years ago. She'll be at the Taos Poetry Circus next year. I usually attend, myself."

"What did she want?"

"I called her...I had these numbers of some of the poets from my research...I've spoken to three of them since I left the bathhouse."

"And, boy, did you!"

Raven looked up, surprised at Fiona's tone. Then irritated at her expression.

"Yeah, I know, it was socially incorrect of me to tear out of there, but I had a revelation."

"Which you're just dying to share with me?"

"Which I'm just dying to share with you... It was that rose water... Talle's rose water. And all those oils she makes for the bathhouse. Suddenly all I could see were those damned little blue bottles with skulls and crossbones on them. *In the kiva!*"

"You mean..."

"Maybe I've been wrong about Hawthorne all this time. Maybe Hank's right, it's Talle - or they're in it together. That *kiva* has Talle written all over it. Anyway, as soon as I got here I called Hank, left a message on his answering machine to check toxicology on the Compunet But I haven't heard back yet."

"Toxicology...you mean...so now we're thinking poison?"

"Maybe."

"But how? How does that fit with the abduction theory?"

"I don't know, so much is spinning in my head. The three poets I spoke with just now, I asked them to give me details on the nest ritual, to compare notes for an article I'm writing on pagan rituals. So, get this: all three of them said Talle was present at the ritual."

"But I thought the ritual was a...sex thing..."

"Yeah, it is. From what they gathered, being blind-folded like I was, she was there, but up top...each poet heard her and Hawthorne conversing when they first began to climb down the ladder. She would tell him she'd built the fire to warm things up, that everything was ready; she would remind him to 'use the gloves'. The gloves seem important, because each of them mentioned that. He would take the poet down the ladder. Each woman heard noises up above, the trap door being shut. And then, when he took them back up the ladder - with the blindfold back on - Talle would be there. She would help them climb up out of the trap door. They each spoke about the scents — some kind of oil he put on their faces before the plaster. He would put on these surgical gloves and then apply the oil."

"Surgical gloves. Wow, that sounds real erotic," said Fiona sarcastically. "What for?"

"I asked them. He told them the oil was to protect their skin from drying out from the plaster, but if it got on his fingers it would interfere with the setting of the mask."

"You'd think they were sworn to secrecy."

"They were. All three of them said they weren't supposed to talk about it, but they all felt weird about it as time went by and didn't mind talking now, they didn't really want to be part of the secrecy."

"Weird how?"

"Like there was more going on, something about it gave them the creeps, that's how two of them described it. They said Hawthorne was real seductive and, at the time, they felt sort of in his power...that sexual mesmerization thing, you know."

"So..." Fiona frowned, "...he puts oil on their faces with gloves, and Talle makes a point of reminding him to do so. For each poet?"

"Yes. They said they remembered that because it scared them, being so vulnerable and then hearing Talle telling him to wear the gloves."

"You know, the more we find out about all this, the less inclined I am to go through that ritual."

"I'll be there, when it's your turn," said Raven, lighting a cigarette. "You make sure and tell me when it is. I won't let anything happen to you."

"That's reassuring. Why don't you go instead? You skipped your turn, after all."

"Yeah, but they still got my mask, remember? Now they'll want one of you."

"Ok, so then he puts on the plaster, takes the impression, does the sex…"

"Reverse order," Raven exhaled and tapped an ash into a saucer.

"Huh?"

"He puts on the plaster and then, while he brings them to orgasm, he takes the impression."

"*While?*"

"Yup."

Fiona sat in silence for a few moments, absorbing this detail.

"So the ritual has something to do with the orgasm."

Raven nodded.

"But why does he use gloves to put oil on their skin if the oil isn't dangerous? Did any of them get a rash or get sick or anything from that?"

"No. They said it was entirely pleasant on the physical level. They didn't mention any strange or bad physical reactions at the time. You're right, it doesn't make sense..."

The two sat again, Fiona sipping water and Raven blowing smoke. Dingo lay between them, panting and looking back and forth at their faces. He seemed to be waiting for their revelation, but then Raven looked at the clock and realized he was really waiting for his lunch.

She got up and poured a bowl of dry food, tossed in a few pieces of cheese from a package in the refrigerator, and poured him a fresh bowl of water.

"Reading's in about five hours. You ready?"

Fiona nodded, but she felt more and more like the sacrificial lamb. Ever since she had agreed that she would read the dead poet's poem for Raven, the impending poetry reading had become an ordeal she only hoped to survive. Raven had set them up for the bathhouse, Raven had chosen how many of Fiona's poems she should read before reading Aisling's poem, what she should say before reading it, the tone she should use. Raven was taking Fiona to the saloon to calm her down before the reading, having reminded her that there was a very long and ancient tradition of indulging and inebriating oneself before reciting one's poems in public.

465

"No self-respecting beat poet ever got up without at least a glass of Chianti," Raven scolded her. "Hell, the great bards of Ireland drank mead while they sang their poems. The great old poets of the sixties were hardened alcoholics; they drank martinis all afternoon and then had to be carried on stage! Why do you think they invented podiums? Haven't you done this research into your lineage yourself? You have a great literary tradition to uphold!"

This was Raven's event, orchestrated and directed solely for the purpose of unearthing Aisling's murderer. Fiona blinked and swallowed hard, the way she had been doing the last forty-eight hours, every time she thought about the outrageous situation in which she found herself. There was an unreality about it, being driven to devote all her waking hours, actions and thoughts to finding out who had murdered someone she never met - someone, frankly, she was not entirely convinced had been murdered in the first place. Aisling Devlin was probably off somewhere enjoying a normal life, just didn't care to call home.

After all, poets were a strange breed. Many of them were hobos, living in tree trunks or dumpsters or even bookstore windows, like monkeys in the zoo - "The Writer At Work". Or walking from one end of Route 66 to the other, just for the experience, with no money in their pockets and refusing to accept rides. Taking notes in blank verse. Anything a poet would do would not surprise Fiona.

She remembered the wire and peg, pulled it from her duster pocket and handed it to Raven.

"What's this?"

"I found it in the nest when we were in the *kiva*. I'd forgotten it until today."

Raven untangled the wire from around the peg and held it up, squinting.

"A guitar string?"

"Try harp."

Raven froze, staring at the peg, her mouth open.

"In the nest?"

"Unnecessary rituals," Fiona said. "Seemingly meaningless events that reoccur, every year. The gloves, the harmless oil. The trip to Lam's, just to pick up stuff that Talle can get down the road here."

"So...the gloves and the nursery, they're connected somehow and they're to hide something."

"Right."

Spoken out loud, it sounded totally ridiculous. The two poets slumped in their chairs, staring at Dingo as he ate, his rabies tags clinking against his food bowl.

Raven stood and stretched. Fiona took her water glass back to the sink, shaking her head. This useless little session had brought to light more questions than answers.

"Damn, I wish Hank would hurry up and call me back," Raven said nervously. "Hell, I can't wait on him. It's time for a little PI work of my own. A little herb-book buying trip at Silver's. I'll meet you at the saloon at six, ok?"

"Ok...I have to go back to the Fagans' to shower and change."

"And to pick up Aisling's poem."

"And my own poems, too, thank you very much."

"Of course! Hey, I'm *happy* you're giving a reading, you know that. You'll knock 'em dead," Raven grinned.

"That's what I'm afraid of."

Chapter 20 - Excavation

ack's pocketknife hit what seemed to be wood under the crumbling faux adobe. He tapped and scraped. Chunks began to fall away in his hands and at his feet. Yes, as he had suspected, this portion of the *kiva* wall was not solid adobe, as was the rest of the room. It was only a three-inch layer of plaster, covered with a coat of paint very close to the natural red earth color of the rest of the room. But not close enough - Mack had done his share of construction work in his time, he'd painted his share of walls, and he'd seen the difference right away, even under the limitations of flashlight. As for the paintings of the spiral (which he'd seen both at New Grange in Ireland and throughout the Southwest) and lightning bolts were more recent than the others in the room. Mack had decided to begrudgingly call this pit structure a *kiva*, as did Liam; although, he now suspected it actually was not.

He knocked on the wood beneath the plaster. It wasn't that thick, just plywood, there was give and a slight echo.

He continued to dig with his knife and fingers, gouging, prying and brushing away clumps of painted plaster, until he had exposed the left-most vertical edge of a plank. Here was where the real adobe wall ended and the concealed wooden wall began. If he removed the plaster down to the floor, and about a foot above his head, he would be able to pry the board loose and find out what was behind it.

Although he pretty well knew what he would find. He'd already discovered a fairly new, empty crypt hidden behind the tall supply cabinet on the back wall of the room, just the right size for one reclining body. It also had a fake adobe wall that was recently opened up, and crudely at that. Two-by-fours were stacked inside the back of the crypt. A pick, axe, crowbar, sledgehammer and shovel occupied a nearby corner. Mack chose the sledgehammer and crowbar to make the job go faster. He returned to the plaster wall and renewed his labors at a more aerobic pace.

After a few minutes, he paused, playing the flashlight along the results of his demolition efforts. He'd had the idea to do this while he was visiting the ruins at Bandelier Monument. There had been mention, in one of the books from Bandelier, of burials occasionally found in *kivas*. Elaborate burials of especially important people.

That's when he had begun to piece together the comings and goings he had seen, in and out of the *kiva*. The bringing of shovels and supplies. The chopping of firewood. The packages of herbs and bottles of oils.

Mack removed the bandana from around his neck and tied it over his nose and mouth, just in case. There was a smell that was getting stronger - rat's nests, probably. He raised the sledgehammer, but before he could strike, he heard a noise overhead. Of course the trap door was exposed if anyone came along. He'd tried to pull branches over the top before closing the door, but it was a makeshift job. Cupping the flashlight to a minimal beam, he moved swiftly across the room. The noise overhead stopped.

Then the unmistakable sound of someone's foot kicking the brush away. He crawled into the crypt behind the cabinet. He couldn't see anything from where he lay except, through the open back of the shelf, a small stretch of *kiva* floor and the bottom rung of the ladder. He flipped off the light and made himself as quiet as he could. He calmed his breathing and closed his eyes. It was easier than straining them in the absolute blackness.

The trap door opened and Mack opened his eyes again. He watched the soft sheen of late-afternoon sunlight illuminate the ladder. Then the beam of a flashlight playing down the rungs. The sounds of steps descending. From where he was hiding, he couldn't see who it was. Pants legs, hiking boots. The visitor reached the bottom of the ladder and stood a long moment, playing the light around the room, then walked over to the cabinet, standing only inches away from Mack's face. He heard the clink of glass against glass, then the hiking boots turned, facing the wall Mack had been excavating. There was a sudden, sharp intake of breath - whether male or female, Mack couldn't tell. Then the boots moved swiftly away from the cabinet and Mack heard footsteps cross to the other side of the room. He assumed the visitor had discovered his handiwork. There was a long, very distressing silence. The flashlight beam illuminated the bottom of the ladder, and the boots and pants legs ascended quickly. The trap door was closed.

Before Mack could breath a sigh of relief, he heard the sound of something being slowly and laboriously dragged and rolled across the trap door. For the next few minutes, he heard thuds above, silence, thuds, silence - it sounded like the visitor was piling things onto the trap door. Mack didn't dare shine his flashlight yet, but his nostrils and sinuses told him that a lot of dust was sifting down through the trap door and falling from the ceiling. He held his nose into his sleeve and fought off the sneezing urge. Then it was quiet for a very long time.

He waited until all was quiet, then pushed at the cabinet slowly and cautiously - the rattle of bottles on the top shelf was alarming – just enough to give him passage to crawl out of the crypt. He turned on the flashlight, keeping the beam low, and then slowly ascended the ladder. At the top of the ladder he waited, listening. Nothing. He tucked the flashlight under his chin and pushed on the trap door overhead. It wouldn't move. He pushed again. Not an inch. He clicked off the flashlight, dropped it into his jacket pocket and, unencumbered, and gave the strongest heave he could.

The door wouldn't budge.

* * *

Talle pushed open the door to Hawthorne's studio with the proprietary air of a landlady. She entered and closed the door against the chill, watched as the man rolled a joint at his workbench. Hawthorne held the cigarette to the light to inspect the seal.

"Ah, Talle, care to join me?"

"What are you up to in the *kiva*?"

"Up to? Getting the nest ready, like you said," Hawthorne put the joint between his lips.

"No, I mean the wall. *THE WALL!*"

"Talle, slow down," Hawthorne lit the joint and inhaled, squinting and pursing his lips. Still holding in smoke, he spoke through clenched lips. "What are you talking about?"

"The wall I had you paint the pictures on."

Hawthorne exhaled slowly. Scented smoke snaked through the room to where Talle stood in the doorway. She waved it aside and crossed her arms.

"I've done nothing to the wall."

"Someone's tearing down the wall. They've exposed the wood...You really didn't do this?"

"I have no clue what you're talking about. What wood?"

Talle put her hands to her forehead and closed her eyes. Hawthorne had never seen her look so pale.

"Are you alright?"

Talle shook her head, her eyes still closed. Hawthorne set the joint on an ashtray and went to her, guided her to a chair. He poured water from a jug into one of his handle-less, chipped coffee mugs, wiping paint spots from it on his t-shirt. He brought her the cup and pulled up a chair next to hers.

"What's going on, Tal? You look pretty awful."

Talle took the mug and drank: so distraught she didn't make a face or comment about the ugly vessel. She stared across the room for a long moment. Then she looked at Hawthorne. Her eyes were glazed.

"Someone's been in the *kiva* and is tearing down the wall where I put her."

It took Hawthorne a moment to register what Talle was talking about. Realization crossed his face and he, too, went pale. If he stood he would pass out. He stared across the room, at the same non-existent point on which Talle's eyes were focused.

"You put her in the wall? When did you do this?"

"The next day."

Hawthorne finally felt he could stand up and did so, wanting to move as far away from her as possible. Wanting to walk out the studio door into the woods and keep on walking without food or water until he passed out, until he lost consciousness, until he died. But as far as he could walk was to his workbench. He sat on his stool and leaned his elbows on the table, putting his face in his hands, blocking out light from his eyes.

"You...you built a...a crypt? The day after? You couldn't possibly."

"It was already built, you didn't know about it. I had it built in when the contractors did the original remodeling of the cellar years ago, before you ever came here. I put her in there the day after our trip, and plastered it over. I took care of it, like I told you I would. You didn't go in there for a year, remember?"

Hawthorne wished he did not, but he did remember. He picked up the joint again and looked at it as if he didn't recall how it got into his hand; he gently tapped it out in the ashtray.

"You had me paint those images on that wall. And you never told me what was behind there? You had me perform the nest ritual down in there, over and over again, all these years – these fourteen years – and never told me she was there, behind the wall? All that time?"

Talle's gaze moved to Hawthorne's form crouched over his worktable. His voice was odd. Strangely subdued.

"It was better that I be the only one to know where she was."

"Better for whom?"

"For you."

Hawthorne looked at her, blinking to clear his eyes.

"For me."

Again that odd, flat tone.

"All of that doesn't matter now. What matters is, someone has figured it out. We have to find out who it is. We have to stop them."

"Stop them? Meaning what?"

"Stop them. Meaning whatever that means. He would not like this, not at all."

"Who? Liam?"

"No, not Liam," Talle scowled in irritation. "*Him.* The Green Man, of course."

Hawthorne grimaced.

"Ah yes, the Green Man, to whom we are all eternally grateful."

Talle gave Hawthorne a sharp look.

"To whom we *are* all eternally grateful."

"For whom we have done all we have done."

"Exactly. Who else?"

Hawthorne turned to the row of plaster masks on the table behind him. The masks he had taken from his own face, for his series on the seasons. He ran his fingers over the white cheekbones.

"What does the Green Man have to do with her... body? With it being in the wall?" he asked, his back to Talle.

"Everything, of course. How can you ask that?"

Hawthorne turned and looked at his benefactress. For

a long time – for years – he had avoided this discussion. What did the Green Man mean to her, what did the Green Man mean to him? Was there any connection at all? Wasn't she getting a bit carried away with all this? Wasn't it time to stop? Stop the masks, the ritual, the whole thing. Stop the pretense.

"Talle...Aisling's death was an accident. A horrible, terrible accident. I'm grateful for what you did that night, the next day, all those months, all these years, protecting me as you have. But... her body in the wall? Why didn't you just ..."

"Bury her? You expected me to dig a grave by myself in the dark and bury her?"

"I would have helped. You wouldn't let me. You sent me away. You told me to go get her things from her *casita*, to wait for you in my apartment. You sent me away. And you never, ever told me what you did with her body."

"You never asked."

The two stared at each other across the room. Their faces wavered in the late afternoon light, their features grew grotesque. The masks they had worn between them, in every encounter no matter how significant or inconsequential – from performing the rituals together with the naked poets, to passing each other dinner rolls at meal times – fell away now, for the first time. Beneath those masks lay the naked faces of fear, loathing, absolute distrust. And a struggle for power that neither could afford to lose.

"You said not to ask," Hawthorne said, his gaze locked into hers.

"And you obeyed."

Hawthorne finally could take no more and looked away. It was true. He had obeyed. From that horrifying moment, fourteen years ago, he had become Talle's property. A slave to his own terror. Of course he had realized the body was in the *kiva* all this time. He hadn't gone back inside the *kiva*, or hiked anywhere near the Bardic Cabin for a full year because of this knowledge.

* * *

It had been the most unpredictable of accidental deaths. It was the first Green Man mask-making. Hawthorne had been swept up in Talle's enthusiasm for the ritual she had devised, to honor the ancient archetypal guardian of the forest. Things were going very well for Hawthorne since he'd come to reside at the Fagans'. He had never before had this kind of freedom to create and live without the stress of worrying about next month's rent. That period of darkness from his youth seemed so far away, in this dry desert, high country. He was painting and sculpting, tending the garden, chopping firewood, eating well, relaxing in the hot springs, checking out the women in the village. Life couldn't be better. He agreed, a ritual to honor and thank the guardian of this beautiful landscape - and all the bounty in his life - was in order. Whatever his benefactress wanted, she could have, as far as he was concerned.

"Why not include Liam?" Hawthorne had asked Talle once.

Talle had frowned. "He wouldn't approve. He'd make fun."

"Do you really think so? He seems to indulge you. And he is really into the Bardic School rituals. Why the big secret?"

"The Green Man has said 'Not Liam'. To make light, to even *question* the ritual, degrades the sacredness of it. It is only for us and the poets to know. I… also wouldn't want to worry him – with his health problems."

"Worry?"

"If he thought we *needed* rituals to ensure our presence on and ownership of this land, he would worry. I want him to always feel entirely secure in the physical world."

"And *do* you 'need' the ritual?"

"So says the Green Man," Talle had responded. End of conversation.

Aisling had been most eager, most willing. The young poet was in love with Liam, it was obvious to Hawthorne and, he was sure, obvious to Talle. But it was the experimental seventies. Talle seemed ok with it; she was even warm and affectionate toward Aisling. In her usual fashion, she even promoted Liam spending time with the girl. And promoted Hawthorne's advances to Aisling as well.

Aisling had her own ethics of romance. She had a boyfriend in Colorado - "an open relationship" she explained to Hawthorne at the hot springs on their first night of sex. She freely spoke of her affection for Liam, of her sexual frustration with him. She overtly used Hawthorne to keep things equal with her boyfriend - she knew he was sleeping with someone while she was gone, and by the rules of their arrangement, it was her duty to do the same - as well as to burn off some of the intense sexual heat she built up over Liam, whom she suspected of being celibate. Hawthorne was very agreeable to being used. Aisling was unabashed in her sexuality. She would come directly to his place after her chess games with Liam, crawl into Hawthorne's bed, waking him. She had no respect for a man's need to sleep.

She and Talle discussed the mask-making ritual often. In fact, the current ritual contained many aspects that Aisling had first suggested. During her semester in Ireland as an exchange student, she had learned of the Green Man, so she was enchanted with the idea of the ritual. Talle didn't tell her where the secret ritual would take place, other than that it was underground in the woods. Aisling insisted on the pre-ritual, blindfolded passage through the woods, and was thrilled at the underground aspect – "Better ambiance, closer to the earth, IN the earth!" she said, her eyes bright with anticipation. It was Aisling who suggested that Talle prepare an oil to keep her skin from drying out under the plaster.

Hawthorne believed in the ritual, was taken with the concept of the Green Man, about whom he knew nothing until Talle and Aisling educated him. He performed his own centering ritual before Aisling's arrival at the studio that night, smudging himself, burning greens and incense in the wood stove, smoking weed and meditating on the meaning of the archetype. Hawthorne felt empowered by the Green Man, felt joyous at the whole experience. This gig at the Fagans' was turning out to be more of a trip than he had ever expected. He felt very fortunate. Not to mention the healthy commission Talle had offered, for doing the mask. More money than Hawthorne had ever received for a piece of art.

It was a beautiful night; he guided Aisling through the woods, carrying a lantern to light their path. Talle had gone ahead earlier and prepared the nest and the fire in the *kiva;* she was waiting for them at the trap door. Hawthorne and the two women embraced at the entrance.

"This is a passage into the spirit world for you, Aisling. Tonight you go through the *sipapu*," Talle smiled, holding the young woman's hands between her own. Hawthorne resisted the urge to roll his eyes; he wasn't sure Talle's use of the word *sipapu* was correct, or if the *kiva* even had one, but he was cheerfully going along with the spirit of the ritual. Talle kissed Aisling on each cheek. Then Hawthorne and Talle helped guide the blindfolded, smiling young poet down the ladder. Talle handed him a pair of surgical gloves then, and told him the vial of oil was on the shelf.

"Put the gloves on now."

"Gloves? That's not very sexy," Hawthorne laughed.

"Put them on. Don't touch the bottle without the gloves on," she said in urgent tones. "The plaster won't work in your hands if you get that oil on you, I know, I've experimented to get this just right. Sometimes the oil spills on the outside of the bottle. So be careful. Keep the gloves on - wipe the oil off of them with the towel I left for you down there, before you do the plaster. But keep them on until you've finished laying on the plaster."

"Ok, ok," Hawthorne nodded impatiently. Talle's instructions made no sense to him and he hated it when she acted like his mother.

"After, when you remove the gloves, do it the way I showed you, so you don't get oil on your fingers. Remember?"

This time Hawthorne didn't resist the urge: he rolled his eyes.

"Listen to me! It's important for the ritual! Only put the oil on right before the plaster, so it doesn't dry out. I mixed it precisely for this; I've meditated on the details. Do *exactly* as I say. The ritual must go perfectly, we must have a flawless mask."

Hawthorne left Talle still talking at the trap door, gave her a little grin and a wave, and descended to the nest.

The *kiva* was warm from the fire; the intoxicating scent of *pinon* permeated the walls. Despite his irritation with Talle's precision, he took the ritual seriously and followed her directions specifically. He undressed himself and Aisling, tied her into the nest with the green nylon cords, and then removed the blindfold. He and Aisling kissed, he kissed her nipples, touched her. He put on the gloves, moistened the plaster strips with a spray bottle, and took the bottle of oil from the shelf. Aisling moaned softly in anticipation while he applied the oil to her forehead, cheeks, jaw and neck. He wiped the oil from the gloves with the towel, and began laying the dampened plaster gauze strips along her face. When the plaster mask was in place, he removed the gloves, turning them inside out as instructed, to avoid the oil residue on the slippery fingers. He then began to caress Aisling. They had agreed the mask should capture her expression in orgasm, that it would be most pleasing to the Green Man to do it that way. The ecstasy of creation. Hawthorne's breathing became as labored as hers.

Aisling moaned as the plaster hardened over her features, then began to writhe and struggle against the nylon cords. Her moans turned to screams, her neck arching back so the veins stood out. He ran his hands roughly up and down her hips and thighs, laughing low. He felt like a thrilled and untamed animal. He had never seen a woman respond so wildly.

Until he realized that her screams were not of pleasure but of unbearable pain. The mask was recording a horrifying grimace, her head was jerking from side to side, the plaster was slipping, strips of gauze coming loose. Her back arched, her legs and arms went rigid, trying to flail against the green straps. He grabbed her shoulders and tried to push her back down, told her everything was all right, but her movements were so erratic that he couldn't control her. She didn't seem to hear anything he said, she had gone somewhere else. Her eyes stared unseeing and she seemed to be choking - on her tongue?

Crying "*Oh my god, oh my god*," Hawthorne rushed up the *kiva* ladder, flung open the door, climbed out of the trap door and called out for Talle. She appeared instantly from the nearby bushes. She quickly descended the ladder, telling Hawthorne to wait above. He heard Aisling still screaming and thrashing.

"*Oh my god, what have I done?*" he murmured over and over, on his bare knees, staring down the ladder rungs into the undulating shadows of the *kiva* fire. "*What is happening?*"

There was silence for a few moments. Then he heard vomiting and choking.

"There, there," he heard Talle say.

"It's him! He's burning! He's on fire!" Aisling's voice, raw and strangled, cried out. Then she screamed and he heard her thrashing and struggling again. "His eyes! Oh my god!"

Talle climbed back up the ladder, carrying Hawthorne's clothes. She hoisted herself up onto the ground and closed the *kiva* door. The sounds of Aisling's violent anguish became dull and far away. Talle told him to get dressed and go to Aisling's *casita* and get her things, put them in his van, make sure no one saw him doing so.

"Why? What's happening?"

"I'm not sure. She's hallucinating. Perhaps an allergic reaction to the plaster, or some kind of seizure."

"We need to get her to a doctor, we need to untie her."

"If we untie her she will do herself more damage. She's convulsing."

"We can't just leave her like this!"

"We aren't leaving her. I'll stay and take care of her. After you put her things in the van, go back to your *casita*, wait for me there."

"What are you going to do?"

"I'll ride it through with her. Just trust it to me."

"I can't! I have to do something! I'll get a doctor!"

Hawthorne turned to run back to the compound for help, but Talle grabbed at his naked arm. Her grip was surprisingly strong.

"And what will happen then?" she hissed.

"She needs help!"

"By the time we get a doctor here, it will be too late. Anyway, when the local Christian doctor sees the situation, do you realize how this looks? Is Aisling in any condition to say, 'Oh, yes, dear doctor, despite these cords cutting into my wrists and ankles, I am a willing participant in this Pagan ritual?'"

Hawthorne stopped, staring at Talle through the darkness.

"How in hell does that matter? She may be *dying*!"

"It matters –" Talle dug her fingernails so deeply into Hawthorne's forearm that she broke skin. "– because of how it will look for *you*, James Hawthorne."

Hawthorne swallowed hard. He had never told her his first name.

"How it will look for me?"

"Hawthorne, rest assured I do not hire anyone without checking them out thoroughly. I know about your record."

"Record?"

"The sequestered files at the courthouse. Kalamazoo, remember? I was able to put two and two together, even though the clerk would not tell me what the files were about. I know what kinds of files are kept closed that way."

"Those charges were dropped. The girl admitted, later, it was not rape."

"It's your word against hers. The case was not dismissed. It was sequestered."

"Because she wouldn't admit under oath. And she was under age and I was only seventeen, so things were - muddy. She was afraid of her parents. She admitted it in private to me, to the priest. Just not under oath."

"The longer we stand here talking, the less likely I am able to do anything for Aisling." She handed him his clothes. "Now *go* and we'll discuss this later. Stay in your *casita* and wait, *do not* talk to anyone. Do you understand?"

Hawthorne stood frozen and naked in the blue-white moonlight, staring in desperation at Talle, at the *kiva* door, still able to hear muffled sounds from below. All the horror of that other event came back to him. It had been his first time with a girl. In a car, in the woods. They had both been willing. So he had thought. After, he had stepped outside the car, to pee. She had begun to cry, inside the car, pulling her clothes back on. This was like that time, standing naked in the woods, listening to a woman's muffled cries. When he came back to the car, the girl wouldn't stop crying. She said he had hurt her. His joy of only moments ago was already soured. He spent the whole ride back to her parent's trying to cheer her up. She became despondent, terrified that her Catholic parents would find out. After he dropped her off, he drove around, feeling confused. Finally no longer a virgin. But had he hurt the girl? She had said to stop, but it was too late by then.

A week later, the police showed up at his mother's door. The questions. The accusations. The girl, her parents, their faces. His mother's face. The courtroom. The last six months of his senior year. Everyone at school pulled away from him. The stares in the hall. The teachers became cool toward him, even the ones who had encouraged his artistic talent. His mother withdrew from him, became silent, so far inside herself she could not be spoken to. She went into a frantic, focused mode of cleaning and re-cleaning the house. Hawthorne had been terrified that he would go to jail.

Just before the trial, the girl felt the other side of guilt, and called Hawthorne, saying she was sorry he was in so much trouble. Saying it hadn't been his fault, that he hadn't raped her, she'd gone to the priest and told the truth in the confessional. Hawthorne told his mother about the phone call. His mother told the police and wrote a letter to the judge. But the girl wouldn't repeat her confession under oath - her parents wouldn't allow it. Hawthorne wasn't sure how things were left with the court. A week before graduation, he finally had all he could stand. He left one night and never went back. Left his mother there, in her very clean, bleach-scented house.

As all those old feelings came down on his head, the empowerment Hawthorne had felt earlier in the evening - the affinity with the Green Man that had felt so genuine and blessed - fell away. Embarrassing and childish, fantasy and play. Not the adult reality of retreat that was his true life. That event back in Kalamazoo had been why he had left there and had never returned. The town had been too small, he had no future there.

This town was many times smaller. His profile at the Fagans' was high, in only the few months he had come to work here. Every time he went into the village, people waved and smiled and called him by name. And he had no idea who they were.

That full moon night, Hawthorne ran across that same ground under which Aisling Devlin called out her death sounds, pulling on his clothes as he went. He ran to Aisling's *casita*. Tears stung his eyes the whole way. "*Coward! Fiend!*" he berated himself in a hoarse whisper as he ran. He stifled his need to scream and cry out; afraid someone would hear him and the whole situation would be exposed. Yet another Event in his life. He entered Aisling's rooms, gathered her clothes in the dark, and gathered her books and bags and New Mexico souvenirs. He carried them to his van, locked them in there. He couldn't find her book of poems; the one she carried with her at all times and wrote in, daily. Her wooden lap harp was not there either. For once, he was the dutiful housekeeper. He kept the lights in Aisling's *casita* off and opened the curtains for moonlight. He pulled the linens from the loft bed, the towels from the bathroom, and piled them in the hamper outside the door. Wiping down the kitchen counter, rinsing out the sink, he found himself sweeping and straightening, the way he had watched his mother do, maniacally, especially all those months during the ordeal with the rape accusation.

And when he couldn't think of another thing to clean, he went to his *casita* and lay down on his bed. He stared up into the darkness and, like a terrified teenager, waited for Talle.

Before daylight, she came in, pale and sweaty, shaking. "It's done. Give me your keys."

Hawthorne remained on his bed while Talle went out to the van. She returned with some of Aisling's things and closed herself into his bathroom. At daylight she came out, wearing Aisling's clothes, Aisling's purple scarf wrapped around her hair, her large, pink sunglasses.

"Wait half an hour. Then get on the highway. Don't stop to talk to anyone in the village. Tank up on 44. Drive straight to Durango, Colorado. Liam and I used to go there a lot. I remember there's a station called Link's on Highway 160, on the right, below Durango. Look for me in the truck stop parking lot about four blocks further in. It's the only one, you can't miss it."

Hawthorne stayed on the bed with his eyes closed during these instructions. He couldn't bear to look at her in Aisling's things. He didn't want to know what had happened, what Talle was going to do. Something with the body, he supposed. But, no, he couldn't even think that much, because to do so, he would have to admit that Aisling was dead. Talle left and he heard the engine of Aisling's VW bug start up and recede down the dirt road to the highway.

Hawthorne drove to Durango in a white blindness. No radio, no coffee, no food. For hours, no stops except for gas. He saw Aisling's VW bug in the parking lot at Link's gas station, but, as instructed, he kept on driving four more blocks to the truck stop. There, he waited for only five minutes before his employer, now dressed as Talle again, came out of the truck stop café and climbed into the passenger's seat.

"Drive to Farmington," she said. Her tone was gentle and weary.

She slept as he drove in silence. In Farmington, she awoke and quietly directed him to Lam's Nursery. It appeared she had called there earlier in the week to discuss a landscaping job. Hawthorne stood by and listened as she and Mr. Lam set up an appointment for his crew to visit the compound. He watched her sign a contract and write out a sizeable check. He trailed behind as she selected pots and gardening tools, packets of seeds for her greenhouse, bags of fertilizer. Then he helped load them into the van while she wrote another check.

Back in the van, Talle settled into her seat and said, "I think He was very pleased." Hawthorne was too exhausted to wonder why she cared what Mr. Lam thought about anything.

They drove back to Ojo de Sombras in silence, Talle sleeping again. How could she sleep? They arrived around eight p.m. Talle still showed no emotion.

"See you in the morning. Come to breakfast as usual," she said in subdued tones as he turned off the engine in the driveway outside the compound. She got out of the van and turned to head toward the hacienda, then paused. Her eyes were bright in the moonlight and she smiled softly at Hawthorne.

"I'm sure He was with her at the end. She was having incredible visions. I think He was very pleased."

She walked toward the hacienda gates.

Hawthorne went to his *casita* and lay down, his head resting in the pillow indentation it had left there so many hours ago. As if it had all been nothing but a daylong, horrible dream. He lit the rest of the joint from the ashtray by his bed, the one he'd been smoking twenty-four hours ago, before he'd begun his hike to the studio to meet Aisling.

Every cent he made the rest of that year, and the year that followed, went into keeping the coffee can under the sink fully stocked, at all times, with *cannabis*. Even though he could easily control the movement of his body and keep himself away from the *kiva* area, away from – perhaps – the place Talle had left the body; he could not easily control his mind from going there in dream and memory. Except by keeping himself in an altered state. For a solid year after Aisling Devlin's death, Hawthorne pursued the art of being stoned with the focus of a religious zealot, with the urgent fanaticism of a man who had been told that *cannabis* was his only hope to cure the disease that would otherwise kill him.

His intake of the herb decreased somewhat after that first year, but became a necessary way of life from that point on. Talle seemed to realize why he needed to keep himself stocked, and looked the other way. She gently admonished Liam to look the other way, also.

So, although Hawthorne had technically not known what Talle did with the body...in truth, in his inmost self, he knew.

Early in January of the following year, Talle brought Hawthorne the plaster mask of Aisling's face in a cardboard box and, while the box was still closed, carefully warned him of its contents. She gently reminded him that he had contracted to make a Green Man mask, and that, given the circumstances of Aisling's passing, she had waited until now to bring this to him and to remind him of his commitment. To give him time to recover so that he could do his best work. Perhaps, she suggested, making the mask could help him heal from the terrible Event. She suggested he use surgical gloves again when handling the plaster model. Since it hadn't been removed from Aisling's face right away.

He said nothing while listening to her words. Had he been less foggy from the marijuana, he might even have found her words - and her insistence that he still make Aisling's mask - shocking. But the marijuana was working very well as a buffer between Hawthorne and the external world. Without comment or visible reaction, he had begun the work on the mask that same day. Over the next week, he finished it, let it dry, then glazed and fired it in the kiln twice. He transformed the horrible look of anguish in Aisling's death mask to one of saintly awe, as if she beheld the face of God. He left the eye sockets empty.

When he brought it to Talle, his employer was very pleased. That evening there was a large cash payment in an envelope next to his dinner plate. Over cigars and brandy, Liam tearfully thanked him for commemorating their lost Aisling with such a beautiful work of art, and expressed his amazement that Hawthorne could create something so life-like, simply from sketches and memory. Talle hung the mask above the loft bed in the *casita* in which Aisling had stayed, the one in which every Fagan prize poet stayed from that point forward.

Hawthorne and Talle didn't speak any further of Aisling's death or her body or any other aspect of The Event. For the next nine months, Talle was very gentle in her manner with the sculptor. She went to great efforts to do special things for him – bringing him baked goods from the kitchen, providing art supplies without him having to ask, adding unexpected cash bonuses to his pay envelope. In no way did she pressure him during the nine months following the finishing of Aisling's Green Man mask.

In September of 1980, she began her campaign for the next mask. In Hawthorne's presence she began to describe the ritual to that year's poet, whose name at this point he couldn't recall. She began to arrange for him to sit next to the poet, to sketch her in his studio, to join her and the poet and Liam in nightly cigar-and-brandy salons. In private he let Talle know, clearly, that he could not, would not have anything to do with the mask-making ritual again. After what had happened, it was too traumatic to endure. What if this poet had the same reaction to the plaster? Or a heart condition? How could they take that risk again?

But the Green Man requires it, she told him. They had no choice; it was the only way to ensure the protection of the land. The Green Man required the mask making.

"I don't want to force you, Hawthorne, you know as well as I the ritual requires willing participants."

"Then don't force me. Find someone else to help you."

"There is only room here for one artist, and we only need one gardener."

"Bring someone in just for the rituals, then."

"No. I have thought this through very carefully, I have conferred with the Green Man."

"What? You have had conversations with him?"

"Yes. And He wants you to do the mask making. He will have no one else."

"Then I must speak with him myself," Hawthorne had grinned, sucking on a joint. "Make me an appointment."

That night he had his first dream experience with the Green Man. He appeared at Hawthorne's bedside, anguished and burning.

The next day Talle visited Hawthorne's studio with a thermos of English tea and a basket of freshly-baked blueberry scones, just in time for his mid-day attack of the munchies.

"I saw your Green Man last night," Hawthorne told her, chewing on a scone. "It wasn't the kind of experience I was expecting, from your glowing descriptions."

"Oh?" Talle buttered a second scone and placed it on his saucer.

"It was a nightmare, actually. I did not get the impression that I am his chosen one. You need to find someone else to do the masks."

"He seemed displeased with our ritual?"

Hawthorne looked at her. She spoke of it so matter-of-factly; it sent chills up his arms.

"He often seems so," she said. "I'm working out the kinks in the ritual. This one will please Him. I've spoken with her, the poet. She's very willing. She's had her own visions. His displeasure is not at you, it is at your unwillingness."

Hawthorne frowned, breaking the scone in half.

"I can't imagine myself doing any of that again. I try to keep those images away."

Talle put down her teacup and placed her hands over Hawthorne's, scone and all. She looked him directly in the eyes.

"Hawthorne, this is how it is. If you won't do the ritual with us, then you must leave. Your very easy and privileged existence as our resident artist depends on one thing alone. You must do the ritual with me, every year. Otherwise, you must leave."

Hawthorne withdrew his hands from her clasp and put back the half-eaten scone.

"Ok, then, I'll begin packing today. I'll be gone by morning."

Talle rested her hands on her lap, turning them over and inspecting the lines in her palms. She spoke without looking up.

"After you have gone – within the hour – it will be reported that a very valuable artefact is missing from our home. And certain facts I have kept confidential in your employment file will be revealed to the authorities. Along with certain suspicions. The file on Aisling Devlin is not closed. Her family sent that private investigator out here to meet with me again, twice in the past six months. The one who interviewed us all when Aisling disappeared, remember? He had more questions. I was very careful to keep the conversation far away from any discussion of you, but, of course, once or twice he brought up your name. I told him I already checked you out. And when he asked about the sequestered case, I defended you as if you were my own blood."

Hawthorne felt his last bite of blueberry scone lodge in his chest. Talle stood, gathering the tea things into her basket.

"I value our relationship, Hawthorne. You are a fine artist. Your mask of Aisling surpasses anything I could have hoped for. We have been through a terrible ordeal together. But I must abide by the wishes of the Green Man. All other relationships are subservient to that one. By the way, if you do decide to stay, there is one more requirement. You will need to drive to Lam's Nursery every October. There will be a standing order of supplies."

"Why Lam's?"

"We must establish an orderly pattern of events. A history. One that can't be questioned, should...well, one never knows what the future holds. Does one?"

Talle picked up the picnic basket and went to the door. She paused there, considering her next words carefully.

"It has occurred to me that you might, at some point, decide to make some kind of confession...which would, of course, involve me, involve my actions that day, to protect you."

"Talle, I would never…"

"I sincerely hope not, James Hawthorne. I risked everything to help you."

"I know that, Talle. I'm very grateful."

"As the saying goes, 'my word against yours'. You see my point?"

"Yes."

"Good. So...you will let me know your decision before morning?"

Hawthorne bowed his head and closed his eyes as she left. After a while he rose, lit a joint and lay back on his daybed, staring up into the wooden beams and cobwebs that formed the ceiling of his cabin studio. He listened to the birds at the window, felt the autumn breeze that took liberties with his doorway. A blue-and-green striped lizard, warmed by the wood stove, darted across the floor. The scent of juniper was strong in the air. Talle was right, his existence here was privileged. In what other situation could he focus this way on his work and live so close to nature, his favorite companion? The gardening chores were pleasant, the physicality suited him. His every need was taken care of.

After all, Aisling's death had been an accident. He had never meant any malice toward the girl, they had enjoyed each other. Perhaps there was solace in knowing that her last moments had been spent in orgasm. Before the death throes set in, anyway. He closed his eyes against the memory that fought to surface. Obliterated it by letting his mind dance into the lights and colors behind his eyelids, brought on by the very good weed. He exhaled and smoked again. He wanted to smoke enough to put himself into a deep sleep for the rest of the day.

As it turned out, the ritual was flawless that year, and had been every year since. So Aisling Devlin's death had been a fluke. The annual October nursery trips were even pleasant. The poets were pleased, Talle was pleased, the Green Man was pleased.

Hawthorne endured the annual ritual with a mixture of loathing and lust. Yet, he came to think of it as his atonement. Each year, as he delivered the completed mask to his benefactress, he felt a renewed absolution. The masks were good. Better each year.

Even the one of Chahil O'Shea, made from the rudimentary plaster cast taken by Talle herself. That one had been especially challenging. It was difficult to transform the amateurism of her mask-taking into something worthy. She had been embarrassed at the imperfection of her work, and had tried to compensate by adding a thick coating of plastic fixative to the back of the mask. Which only made it more difficult to work with. She explained that she hadn't let it set properly, making it particularly fragile. One cheekbone was sunken in. He humored her and even let her watch him do the clay reconstruction on that one. It actually turned out to be one of the best he had done - because he felt challenged to make it so.

Hawthorne came to understand - and to express in the masks - that the Green Man was masked by the foliage of his own making, that the Green Man *was* his mask. As was the role that

Hawthorne came to play with Talle Fagan a kind of mask. The innocent, employer/employee relationship that he and Talle presented to Liam Fagan every night at dinner was a mask.

Over time, Hawthorne told himself that he had nothing to confess, nor did Talle. At least most of the time that was his story. Now and then there were those moments when that inner dog went digging for that old bone. A little altered state always quieted down that aging canine. The beast would wander off somewhere, forgetting what he had been digging for.

Hawthorne put his prayers for forgiveness into the masks he made, into the plaster, the clay, and the glaze. He transformed his dark secret into a terrifying beauty.

* * *

Mack leaned against the rungs of the ladder and took a slug of Macallan's from the pewter flask. He was pretty certain the Scottish single malt was of a vintage much older than any he had ever tasted. His twin was leading quite the privileged life, here in the desert.

But at what price, he mused.

To preserve the battery in his flashlight, he partook of this ancient courage-getting ritual in semi-darkness, burning only one of the emergency candles he had found in the cabinet. By how things felt, he couldn't have said whether two hours or six had passed since the logs had been rolled over the trap door. Mack was not a watch-wearing man, and time was an entirely different experience when you were locked up in a hole in the ground. He had been in there long enough to have survived his first, second and third waves of panic. Long enough to have piled on all the clothes in his backpack and thanked god for his thermal underwear. Long enough to have thought things through.

And long enough to have found what he'd come looking for in the first place.

After calming his breathing and descending the ladder the first time, he found what he figured was supposed to be the *sipapu,* a small hole in the center of the *kiva* floor. He wasn't certain whether or not he was performing a sacrilege, although he seriously doubted it. After his tour of Bandelier and reading of the books on Anasazi ruins, Mack had decided that, even if this hole in the ground had originally been built by the Anasazi, Talle's and Liam's references to the structure as a *kiva* were in error. It was probably a pit structure, but not a *kiva*. Given its small size and remote location, it had not been the kind in which sacred rituals had ever been performed, but had been a place to store supplies. Secondly, he figured it had been refurbished - *sipapu* and all – not by anyone with ancestral claim, but by some very misguided "Anglo" as those of his race were called in these parts. Very misguided and very dangerous. Nevertheless, being one to believe that life was what you made it, Mack sat himself down right on top of the *sipapu* and focused on his breathing in a manner he had learned many years ago, from an old girlfriend who had taught yoga. And did some serious thinking.

He decided that whoever had log-piled him in here probably didn't realize he was in here. Perhaps they were trying to camouflage the place until they could return to deal with what was behind that wall. To make it more diffi-cult for anyone else to return and keep excavating the wall. Given what he'd found, he wagered the person who locked him in here would definitely be back. And soon.

Next, he recalled that Liam was supposed to meet him at the *kiva* entrance late tonight after the poetry reading at the village bookstore. If Mack could orient himself enough to estimate the passing of time – and he thought he had a trick for that – he could make sure to be at the top of the *kiva* ladder, beating on the door and shouting about the time Liam arrived. He could use one of the tools to bang against the door to make a louder sound.

Of course, the danger in that was, what if someone else, not Liam, chose to arrive about then? If they heard him shouting in here, they might decide to leave him to rot, or to come in and quicken his journey to the other side.

If for some reason Liam didn't show up tonight, Mack checked his backpack and figured he had enough camping food and water to survive about four days. If he rationed. Whether or not he would ration the whiskey was another consideration altogether.

Finally, of course he had to consider that none of these events might transpire. Perhaps no one would come and, if he couldn't figure out how to dig his way out, he would die in here. It wasn't the first time Mack had faced death. In his adventurous life, he'd had his share of near misses – almost drowned once, a serious rock-climbing fall, a bad car crash, fell from a scaffolding and broke his leg; almost killed a guy in a street fight outside a pub and suffered a sobering knife wound in the process; lived through a food poisoning, during which he was sure he saw the face of God.

It had been this final consideration that had moved him to action. If he was going to die in this place, at least he could do his part to expose the heinous crime that had been committed here. Someday when his body or skeleton was discovered, another discovery would also be made at the same time.

The two poor, stinking souls jumbled up in the crypt behind the wood panels.

Hard to determine which bones were which - or whose - all fallen and scattered through time amidst the branches of skeletonized tree limbs, rat's nests, cobwebs. One held - in what was left of its bony lap - a leather-bound volume that was dark with decay, essentially disintegrated. The other's notebook was reduced to black, compacted crumbs barely held together by a metal spiral. A rustic, wooden harp leaned against its shoulder - a harp that, in its better days, would have done Turlough O'Carolan proud. But, while O'Carolan's harp was preserved in a showcase in Castlerea, Ireland, this one was only blackened bits of wood and some tangled, rusted string. Wrapped around the skulls were splintered wreaths of vines, protruding from, or tucked into, their jaws.

The bodies had apparently been stark naked when deposited in the crypt. He was pretty certain the one with the harp was the missing lass; Aisling Devlin. Before his trip to the Fagans', Mack had done a bit of research and read enough of the gossip, among the online literary community, to know about the missing poet and how she had performed her poetry with a small harp. Were it still legible, no doubt the leather volume in the lap of the other skeleton would reveal that one's identity.

"Hopefully I'll myself be around to hear the telling of it," he said out loud, just to reassure himself with his own voice.

But, if not, he could at least rest in peace that he had done his part on the side of justice.

Assuming, of course, that whomever would discover this terrible thing would be someone who wanted justice. He shook his head. Apparently that ancient, horrifying and senseless tradition of the killing off of bards and poets had not yet come to an end.

In the pathetic light of one candle, against the absolute black darkness of the *kiva*, slugging the last of the whisky, Mack contemplated all he had - four days' supplies and a lot of assumptions. And, now that the exertion of digging out the wall was over, just barely enough layers to keep himself warm. He'd found a small fireplace and had searched the *kiva* for firewood; unfortunately, aside from the couple of planks that had covered over the crypt, the rest was piled outside, holding down the door.

For now, cold or not, it was time to work on tracking the passing hours. He dug into the side pocket of his backpack and found a worn, cloth bag. He opened it and pulled out a rosary, the metal links and glass beads softly clinking in the dark. It had been many years since he had prayed; he only carried the rosary for sentimental value, a memento of his long-dead mother. He figured it would take him about a half hour to say the rosary, once he wrapped his memory around the words of the prayers. He would make a finger mark on the dirt floor of the *kiva* after each round – he found a marking place with a quick flash of the flashlight. That way he could chart the hours until Liam should arrive. He figured, at this point, it must be about seven p.m. About the time the poetry reading was to start. Liam could show up in about three to four hours.

Given the unnerving presence of his two companions, the crypt's aroma, and his constant vigilance for any scurrying noises, Mack was not worried that saying eight rosaries might put him to sleep. Nor that the flask of *poitín* he'd just consumed would have much effect either. He had never felt more alert and awake in all his life.

Another wave of terror threatened to wash over him. He quickly made the sign of the cross and, holding the rosary's crucifix in his gloved hand, began his first prayer.

* * *

Talle watched Hawthorne in his long, silent, inward journey. Where had he gone? Was he remembering the night of Aisling's death? Was he plotting to leave? Was he truly not the one excavating the wall? If not him, who?

She sipped more water from the ugly coffee mug and calmed herself, thinking through the list of the possible curious. The trespasser, of course. Although he would have had to been watching them all very closely for quite a while, to even have located the *kiva* trap door, much less find reason to go inside and begin digging. How many months had she been hearing of his presence? Hawthorne had mentioned a trespasser camping about eight weeks ago, but he said he had left. It was only over the past few days Hawthorne and Fiona had mentioned seeing someone. The trespasser may have come, gone and returned – or never left. Could be someone who had read of Aisling's disappearance, someone playing sleuth. After all these years, who would come looking here?

Raven. That seemed very likely to Talle, given the folded piece of yellow-lined paper that was in her tunic pocket. It was one of those enigmatic poems; if you didn't know the story behind it, it could mean anything. But Talle suspected - from the moment she found it under the river rock on the desk in Raven's cabin - exactly what it was about.

Then there was Fiona. But Talle couldn't imagine when Fiona might have had a chance to get into the *kiva* in the past twenty-four hours. Only yesterday morning Talle had gone down the ladder and seen no sign of intrusion.

Talle was increasingly certain the amateur archaeologist was Raven, but she closed her eyes and scanned all possibilities. Liam? At the thought, a chill ran down her spine. No, not possible. Liam was complicated in his innocence. He wouldn't understand. His feeling of betrayal – that she had kept it from him – would be overwhelming. It would destroy him, and if Liam was destroyed, Talle was destroyed. Even the Green Man knew that she served Him only in order to serve her husband. To keep him safe, his creation pure – unworldly, even – Liam was a cause worth a lifetime of service.

This is what Talle told herself. Liam was her supreme, undeniable Cause. Her *raison d'etre*. Without such a Cause, her every action on the planet was suspect.

No, it was not possible that Liam would be the one to find the body.

Bodies, she corrected herself. And that presented a new complication. She needed Hawthorne's help now, to move the bodies, to find a place where no intruders would think to look. A place satisfactory to Him, where the bones would remain united with His Earth. Only Hawthorne could help, she couldn't accomplish the move alone.

He would have to be told, then, about the second body. After she explained, Hawthorne would have dangerous power in his hands – and the question would be, would he realize that, would he use it? Or stay in his marijuana fog, captive to his fear of consequences?

His reaction would be the price of her gamble. But she could see no other choice. Not right now, however. Later tonight would be soon enough. And it would have to be after the ritual. The ritual must take place tonight, she also realized. *Three* bodies, then, to be given a new home in the Green Man's care.

The more she thought this out, the better she felt. It was a good thing; actually, that she had seen what was going on in the *kiva*. It was the beautiful, ordered convenience of the Universe, orchestrated by the Green Man, that the time to do the ritual would accomplish not only the sacrifice, but would remove the young woman from their lives where she could do so much damage. Who knew what she was telling people? Yes, tonight was the night. It was, after all, the third mysterious and sacred seventh year cycle since the opening of the Fagan poetry residence again, that sacred cycle of nature's perfection, the preservation of harmony through the balance of all things coming and performed in sevens. Apollo's seven-stringed lyre, Pan's seven pipes, age seven for baptism, seven deadly sins. Whether one was Christian or Pagan, anyone would tell you, the seventh year was *the one*. Simply, the time was now.

Or, perhaps...Talle almost gasped out loud at the vision that suddenly filled her entire body, a flood of light and hot blood. She put her hand to her mouth, staring unseeingly past the threshold of the cabin door. No, she would need affirmation for that. She must go find the Green Man. There wasn't much time...Fiona's reading was only two hours away. She would need to make this decision before the reading. After the reading would be the best moment for the ritual.

"Hawthorne," she finally spoke. By now, Hawthorne's own reverie had ended and he had spent the last few minutes watching Talle, wondering what she was scheming. "It has to be tonight. Right after the reading."

"What does?"

"The ritual, of course. What else?" Talle said impatiently.

"That's precisely the thing, Talle...What else?"

The two stared each other down.

"That'll be difficult," he finally said. "I haven't even come on to her yet."

"No, not Fiona. Raven."

Talle's earlier thought raised its hand again. But she kept that one to herself; she needed to see Him first, and get a confirmation.

"Raven? Not possible," he said coldly. He re-lit the joint and took a deep drag.

"Not only possible, required. *Required.*"

A long and loud exhale. Talle held her hand over her nose and coughed lightly. This was not the time to be getting a contact high, she needed all her wits about her.

"May I ask why?"

"I think she's the one digging out the wall."

Hawthorne shot Talle an incredulous look. Then the look changed as he considered the possibility.

"It would explain a lot," he agreed. "Her breaking in here. She's been determined to get revenge or something. What for, I have no idea. But she's an angry woman."

He didn't mention that Raven had taken the pink invoice from Lam's Nursery during the recent break-in. Talle didn't even know he had that proof of alibi. He frowned, wondering again what Raven planned to do with it.

"Don't underestimate the feelings she still carries for you. The feelings *you invoke*. Under that rage is a lot of passion," Talle fed him the words as if they were buttered scones.

Hawthorne grinned and shook his head, indulged in a lengthy drag on his rolled smoke.

Then he frowned, confused.

"But what does that have to do with the ritual?"

"The power, of course. There is a dangerous imbalance right now. If the one causing the imbalance offers her face for this year's mask to Him, He will right the scales. And if we willingly bring her into the *kiva*, as if we have nothing to hide, she will forget about finishing her dig, she'll realize there is nothing to be discovered there and that we are not the enemy."

Hawthorne grinned at Talle.

"And who exactly is the enemy?"

Talle stood.

"I have a lot to prepare. After the reading I'll slip out as quickly as I can."

"Unless Silver gets hold of you first."

"Yes, I know," sighed Talle.

The annual reading was a big event for Silver, she made sure a reporter from the

Albuquerque Journal arts section was there, and she opened the evening at the podium with extravagant, flattering speeches about Liam and Talle and their generosity to the arts. The way Silver clutched at keeping control of the annual Fagan Poetry Reading, Talle sometimes suspected that, in Silver's mind, the economic survival and literary reputation of the *Extranjeros* hinged on the event.

"I'll get away as fast as humanly possible. You watch for that. As soon as I'm gone, you begin whatever it is you have to do to get Raven there." Talle turned to leave.

"Hey, Tal," Hawthorne's voice held a disturbing lack of respect. Talle looked back at him from the doorway, quizzically. "A moment ago you said something about doing whatever you have to do to stop the person who's digging in the *kiva*."

"Yes?"

"You wouldn't be planning anything...dangerous...or foolish...would you?"

"You've been smoking too much."

"Because if you are, and if you're planning on hurting Raven..."

"Why do you say that?"

"You're a powerful woman, Tal. We both know that."

Talle scowled. This conversation was going on longer than she had planned and she didn't like his tone.

"If you're planning to harm Raven, you can count me out. You hear me?"

Talle met his gaze. His eyes were unfocused from the marijuana. He was hunkered over his workbench, staring at her, trying to look malevolent. She smiled.

"If *I* harm her?" she asked softly. "Isn't it your *own* actions we should be concerned about?"

Hawthorne's face registered the blow.

"I never really told you how Aisling died, did I?" Talle continued. "It was a very long, horrible death, Hawthorne. Eight, ten hours. I left her after five that morning. *You* left her the *first* hour. Remember that, in case anyone should ever ask."

This was more than Hawthorne had wanted to know. He looked away.

"If you still do care about Raven, use that." Talle said, opening the door. "Get her to come willingly. That's always best."

Talle smiled, turned and left. Hawthorne watched her go until he could no longer see her in the distance, heading into the grazing meadow. Talle was right; the only way was to appeal to Raven's lower self. Or...perhaps her higher self. Her sense of justice, forgiveness. What would it take to get to *that* place?

Hawthorne pulled the folder of Raven photos from the drawer. A peace offering might bring them around to "old times" real fast. Maybe she'd even exchange the negatives and photos for the invoice. He opened the folder onto the workbench for an inspiring look at the beautiful and naked Raven tied up in the nest. But the sheath of negatives was gone. That Raven was really something! She'd gotten herself back in here after all, got those negatives! Left the photos, so he might not notice, but got the negatives. On a day like yesterday or tomorrow, he'd be enraged. But now, with bigger things on his mind, the negatives seemed inconsequential. He felt weak and giddy from the pot.

That was it; he'd go to her laughing, he'd pretend it had been just a joke all along, just a sexual tease, all that business about the photos. That now she could have them back. He'd even put a ribbon around the thing. He dug around in the workbench drawer, found an old, stained piece of cord and tied it around the folder. What else? He ~~broke a bit of vine off the practice nest in the~~ corner and wove it around the cord to embellish his gift. Maybe that would help her remember how things had been with them in the nest the first time.

The Ojo de Sombras Saloon. That's where she'd be on a Friday night, right before Fiona Kelly's poetry reading. If he knew Raven at all, he knew that much. He'd have to look the part. He'd stop off at the compound, shower, change into that black silk shirt she always liked. Maybe even wear his black Western hat, his boots. Earring in one ear. Shave, needed a shave.

Hawthorne closed up the studio and headed into the meadow. As he walked and inhaled the twilight air, he had a feeling things had been leading to this moment all along. The break-up with Raven didn't feel real tonight. The shouting match in his *casita* a few nights ago seemed a mistake, a clumsy start. Now they were on the right track. This is where they had been headed all along. Life was gruesome and yet excruciatingly beautiful at the same time. The Green Man knew, Hawthorne felt him watching from the woods, chuckling, raising his fist in glee.

Yes, things were going to be set right tonight. In the universe and in the groin. Hawthorne felt a terrible exuberance he hadn't felt in... years.

Chapter 21: Green Chili Cheeseburgers

It was dusk when Hank pulled out of the forest ranger parking lot on the edge of Ojo de Sombras and pointed his Volvo toward the village center. He'd found the map he'd come for, and had read all the bulletin board announcements about forest fire conditions in the Sierra de Sombras. Earlier he had checked in under an assumed name at the Bear Paw Hunting Lodge – a row of simple motel rooms nestled into the mountainside, made to look rustic with rough-wood siding, a shabby-but-sturdy tin roof, and turquoise bear paw prints painted on each door.

It didn't appear that much had changed in the little mountain community since his investigation into Aisling Devlin's disappearance in 1979. Still no streetlights, neon or convenience stores. His stomach was growling and he recalled the green chili cheeseburgers at the Ojo de Sombras Saloon weren't half bad. And he'd yet to find a bar that could do any damage to a cold bottle of good ale. He drove slowly past the *Extranjeros*. The lights were on, looked like a couple of people were setting up chairs in the back. He had about an hour to do some gastronomic harm. He parked his car and walked back to the saloon.

No one who might remember the Durango private eye would recognize him tonight. In his mind's eye he was debonair (if a little travel-worn from life's events), salt-&-pepper haired, turquoise-wearing Hank Walker. To anyone else he would be Arnie Sawyer, scruffy, bearded, wildlife photographer. He was dressed for an L.L. Bean adventure in a plaid flannel shirt, photographer's vest loaded with film of various speeds, pens, light meter, filters, lens papers, macro lens, batteries, cinefoil, maps and notebooks. Faded jeans and good hiking boots. Over his shoulder was strapped the best camera a Durango pawn shop could supply, and on his head was a dark blue sports cap with the embroidered image of a wolf's head. He thought that last touch was a bit much, but he wanted to hide his hair so the beard would blend in better with his modified sideburns. For this trip, he'd skipped the finer details like coloring his hair and inserting the brown-eyed contact lenses. His concessions to Hank Walker's identity were the vial of Vitamin B12 around his neck and tucked under his shirt, and a 9 mm automatic, safely holstered to a pant clip at the small of his back. And, of course, the pack of cigarettes. He figured Sawyer was either a chain smoker or allergic to cigarette smoke. Either way, the guy would have to suffer.

* * *

Hawthorne was watching the entrance to the Ojo de Sombras Saloon, the folder of photographs next to his elbow on the table. He was ready, the moment Raven came in, to stand up and approach her. Fiona Kelly was already here, in easy view, sitting in a booth near the front, nervously sipping a glass of Ojo de Sombras Blush. She also watched the door.

A surly-looking tourist, decked out in catalogue gear and yuppy camera equipment, passed Hawthorne's booth and sat in the one behind him. Hawthorne shook his head in disgust. Every year more and more tourists, hunters and would-be landowners came through Ojo de Sombras. He drained his beer and signaled for another. Courage. He didn't expect his encounter with Raven to go smoothly, and he was trying to forget as much of this afternoon's conversation with Talle as possible.

He looked good, though, he thought. A little haggard around the edges, but he'd noticed the women noticing him when he came in, wearing his black silk and Western hat. He figured it wouldn't take much talking to go home with any one of them tonight, instead of this mission he was on. He wanted to skip this poetry reading. He wanted to skip a lot of things tonight - skip town, for instance, he chuckled to himself ruefully. But the pressure was on. Talle was really freaked out about the trespasser in the *kiva*. Lately, she seemed to have her own calendar in her mind, and it didn't have anything to do with the reality of daily life. Talle was going over the edge with this Green Man stuff.

The waiter - a local guy in a beat-up T-shirt and jeans; when you were the only bar in town you didn't need cocktail waitresses to sell beer - brought Hawthorne his second beer and moved on to get the order of the catalogue tourist sitting behind him. At that moment, Raven walked through the front door. Before Hawthorne could stand up to approach her, she spied Fiona and slid into the booth with the nervous poet. As if continuing a conversation they'd left off a moment ago, the two leaned across the table, put their heads together and began talking urgently. Hawthorne scowled. Ever since he was a teenager he had dreaded trying to talk to a female when she was clinging to another female.

In the booth behind him, the catalogue tourist ordered a green chili cheeseburger with extra onions and a Bass ale. He grinned to himself at the sight of the woman in black and cleavage who had just sauntered in.

* * *

"Ok," said Raven, as if their conversation had been interrupted only moments before. "I've read some stuff in here..."

She tapped a small paperback she'd picked up at the *Extranjeros* late that afternoon. Fiona glanced at the title: *The Cautious Forager.*

"What if the oil used on Aisling wasn't the same as the oil used on the other poets?"

"How do you mean?"

Fiona felt slightly irritated that Raven hadn't inquired

as to her pre-performance-jitters, but she feigned courage and interest nevertheless, to distract herself.

"What if it was toxic?"

"You mean, what if they – *poisoned* her with the oil they used?"

"Yeah," Raven signaled to the waiter. "Have you had anything yet?"

"I can't eat. Just wine."

Raven ordered herself a tequila and lime and another glass of wine for Fiona.

"It's possible," Fiona mused. "Now I recall when I was in Talle's apothecary, she said she put the toxic stuff up on the high shelf because it was dangerous to even touch the bottles if any of it spilled. Still, that doesn't explain why the gloves with the others."

"Maybe using the gloves is Hawthorne's way of hiding it out in the open that poison was used that one time on Aisling. But who the hell is he hiding that from?" Raven asked. "No one is there but the poet of the month! And Talle, up top."

"The poets told you it's Talle who tells him to use the gloves," Fiona reminded her.

The waiter brought their drinks and the poets solemnly toasted in silence for a moment. Fiona watched in fascination as Raven rubbed lime juice and salt on the back of her hand, licked it off and drank tequila from her shot glass.

"So it's Talle who's hiding something in the open?" Raven finally said.

"Maybe."

"This is making me NUTS! It doesn't make any kind of—Oh! Wait! What if...what if she's hiding it from…"

"Hawthorne."

The poets stared at each other.

"Let me get this straight."

"Talle gives Hawthorne oil that kills Aisling," Raven said slowly. "Hawthorne thinks it's an allergic reaction?"

"A reaction none of the other poets had."

"But they can't be certain, so Talle insists on the gloves."

"Why take the chance?" Fiona wondered.

While they talked, the bar had become so crowded that neither poet noticed a man standing near their booth wasn't just doing so for lack of a place to sit. Suddenly he slid into the booth next to Fiona, set his camera and beer on the table and joined in their speculations.

"Because it wasn't an accident," he said. "Go back to what you were saying...Talle gives Hawthorne oil that kills Aisling. Hawthorne doesn't know the oil is poison. To keep him in the dark, Talle makes sure he uses gloves with all the other poets, even though the oil she gives him to use on their skin is harmless. The big question is why did Talle want Aisling dead?"

Fiona and Raven stared at the up-north-looking tourist guy in the photographer's get-up.

"Excuse me?" Fiona gasped.

Raven suddenly started laughing, slapping her knee.

"No way! I don't believe it! Uh...say cowboy, have we met?"

The man reached out to shake hands with Raven.

"Arnie Sawyer, at your service. Wildlife photographer."

Fiona stared as he turned and shook her hand also, then recognized the handshake. She gave him a big hug, which he wasn't expecting. Even in the dim light of the bar, the women saw him blush.

"So why doesn't Hawthorne turn Talle in?" Fiona asked.

"He thought it was an accident," said Arnie. "Either way, he's an accessory."

"Hell, he looks like the murderer!" Raven added.

"Maybe he looks too much like it," said Arnie, sipping his beer.

"The trip, the gloves, the sex maniac."

Raven pulled the harp string and peg out of her pocket.

"Fiona brought me my proof that it happened there."

"I think it's that old dusty footprint you told us about," agreed Fiona. "I found that caught between the wall and the nest, in the *kiva*."

"It proves that Aisling was in that nest," said Raven. "This peg is broken. Her harp was damaged, they didn't find her poems, something happened to her and it happened in the *kiva*.

Before or after Durango."

"Before? But we went over this with Hank last week," Fiona sighed. "A witness saw her drive out of here, right through Ojo de Sombras, down the highway. The gas station attendant saw her go into the restroom in Durango."

"Well, I don't know...but I do know that I'd better keep my eyes on more than Hawthorne tonight. I'll be checking out Talle's reactions too, when you read Aisling's poem. So, Arnie, what do you have in all those pockets? Anything for us?"

"Matter of fact, I do," said Arnie. He pulled out his steno pad and the list of toxic plants, and proceeded to tell the poets his bad news about Chahil O'Shea and the fact that he'd identified fifteen plants, many of which grew along the river's edge, that a *curandera* could have used to poison a poet.

* * *

Hawthorne was working on his third beer in great irritation. Who the hell was that guy? Obviously some old friend of Fiona's, the way she'd hugged him. Unless she was more of the friendly type than he'd figured her for. He glanced around for a clock but there wasn't one. It was time, though, that was clear. He'd have to brave it. He stood, a little woozy from the fast beers – he really was more of a marijuana man, he smirked – and picked up the folder. As he walked toward the booth, Fiona saw him and made a motion to Raven. Raven turned and frowned. He bolstered his courage and beckoned her to join him at the bar. He watched as she turned and spoke to her companions. Then, to his absolute amazement, she got up and joined him.

"Thanks, Raven. I was hoping we could have a moment," he said, leaning into the bar and beckoning the bartender over. "Can I buy you one?"

Again, to his amazement, she nodded.

"Tequila and lime," she said, and hoisted her sweet ass onto a bar stool. Hawthorne stood closer, putting his arm across her shoulders. Tentatively. She didn't pull away. Wow. This was going much easier than he'd ever dared hope.

"Listen, Raven. I brought you a little peace offering."

He pushed the folder toward her. She gave him a puzzled look and untied the cord.

"What's this?" she asked, holding up the piece of vine from the nest that he'd wrapped around the cord.

"Awww," he grinned, giving her his sexiest look. "Just a little piece of old time's sake?"

She stared at the vine and then realized the source. She opened the folder just long enough to recognize what it held, then closed it quickly and tucked it close inside her jacket. The young man on the stool behind her started to make a comment about what he'd seen in the folder, then saw Hawthorne's evil eye cast his way and thought better of it.

"You got a problem, buddy?" Hawthorne challenged the man.

"Not me, just leavin'," the young man smiled, and carried his beer elsewhere.

"Damn bar, I hate this place," Hawthorne said, sitting down.

"Why'd you come here, then?" asked Raven, pouring salt and lime on the back of her hand.

"To wait for you."

"What changed your mind? About giving me the photos, I mean?"

"I always meant to give them back to you, I just was waiting for the right time. When maybe you weren't so mad at me. I never meant to hurt you, Raven. I don't know what I did or why you got so mad and left but...well, hell...give a guy a break, ok?"

Raven slugged her tequila and stared into her glass, thinking for a long moment. She twirled the piece of vine in her fingers. Hawthorne waited, expecting a verbal dressing down.

But he'd gotten this far; he had to ride the thing out. *In the kiva by midnight*, he remembered Talle's orders. His assignment. Had to keep focused on that, despite the effect of those beers.

"Well...we did have some hot times, I have to admit. You know me, Hawthorne, I can't stay with anyone very long."

Hawthorne blinked and steadied himself against the bar.

"Yeah, we're two of a kind that way, babe," he said.

"You're looking pretty good tonight," Raven smiled, leaning closer. He stared down her shirt. Just like old times.

"Maybe it's the company I'm hoping to keep," he grinned.

"And when and where might you be hoping to keep it?" she asked, touching his thigh.

"Oh...'bout midnight..."

Now came the difficult part. How to get her to the *kiva*? Last time he'd taken her there, he'd had her blind-folded.

"I don't suppose you'd care to take a little stroll through the woods..."

"Like that time we went to the *kiva*?" she asked.

"*Kiva*?" He stared at her.

"Oh, come on Hawthorne, I know about the *kiva*. I found it the other day. I remembered it. That's where you took me that time, right? Where you tied me up?"

Her hand moved up higher on his thigh. It was so warm.

"Look, I'll meet you there. Midnight. I have to get back to my friends now."

And before he could close his mouth, she had her tongue in it. And before he could respond, she was half way across the room, walking back to her table.

She knew about the *kiva*? He turned back to his drink and slugged it down with the taste of her tequila kiss. What the hell? Who cared? Mission accomplished. And a hard on, to boot.

* * *

"Friend of yours?" Arnie Sawyer asked as Raven returned to the booth. He smiled a cool smile in her direction while watching Hawthorne exit out of the corner of his eye.

"Sworn enemy," she responded, pouring salt on a circle of lime juice on her hand.

"Wow. If that's how you treat your enemies, mind if I be your friend?"

"Look, guys. I didn't want you to see that but...he wants me in the *kiva* at midnight."

"Don't they all!" Arnie smirked, pulling out his wallet to pay for their drinks.

"So I made it easy for him. I need to be wherever he is, after the reading. He's going to take me right to her, I just know it."

"It sounds bad, Raven," said Fiona. "Don't go with him."

"You know we can't stop her," said Arnie. "But wither thou goest I goest, and that's the end of that conversation," he turned in the booth to face Raven. "Now listen, young lady. I believe you are, as the saying goes, 'packing'?" He chuckled at her how-did-you-guess look. "I'm trained to notice such things. I want you to give me that gun. Hand it over sweetie," he teased, but he was serious.

"Gun?" squeaked Fiona.

"No way in hell," Raven snapped. "I'm ready for whatever happens tonight." She patted her pockets. "Flashlight, pocketknife, rope, and my trusty .38 derringer."

"You know how to shoot that thing?" asked Arnie.

"Of course. My mom taught me. In fact, she left me this gun in her will."

Raven didn't add that she had her stepfather's switchblade tucked in her right boot.

"God, you western women." Arnie looked at Fiona. "What about you, you packing too?"

"No! My daddy taught me how to shoot, but my gun's back in Oklahoma," Fiona said sarcastically, glaring at Raven.

"Ok, Raven, I'll be right behind you, whatever you do tonight," said Arnie in resignation. "You just be careful with that thing."

"And you be careful with yours, sweetheart," she snapped back. "Geesh, men! Ok, Fiona, it's time. Let's get the show on the road."

"Uh...ladies...wait a minute," Arnie said, taking their hands in his. "There's one more thing you both need to know."

"Yeah?" Fiona and Raven said simultaneously, puzzled at his serious tone.

"Whatever reason Hawthorne has for wanting to get Raven into that *kiva* tonight, I think we've got to watch out for Fiona just as carefully. If not more."

He broke the news to them about the seven-year cycles. And that this was the year of the seventh poet.

Fiona stared at Arnie/Hank in horror. Now she really did feel like the sacrificial lamb, and not at all reassured by all the talk of weaponry. Before Raven or the wildlife photographer could stop her, she gathered her duster, purse and notebook of poems, pushed her way past Arnie, and rushed out the saloon door. Outside she began walking, long strides, fast, pulling on her duster as she went. Raven and Arnie ran out of the saloon to catch up to her.

"So what am I supposed to be doing while you're down in the *kiva* seducing Hawthorne?" Fiona sputtered over her shoulder.

"I'm not going to seduce him, for god's sake!" Raven grabbed Fiona's arm. "That was just to make sure I'm wherever he goes after he hears the poem."

"I'm the damned next sacrificial poet, Raven! They want to *kill* me! I mean, I don't expect everyone to *like* me, but to want to *kill* me? What the hell have I gotten myself into here?"

"You'll be fine," Arnie said, looking around apprehensively to make sure no one had heard Fiona's outburst. "I'll be right there, every minute. If I think things are getting out of hand, I'll take over. We're not going to do anything stupid, you hear? We don't need any heroines here."

"Or heroes, either," Raven admonished him. "I mean, it's nice of you to come and be concerned, but we can take care of ourselves!"

Fiona breathed deeply and tried to pull herself together, thinking she had no problem with the PI playing hero if that's what he wanted to do. She wasn't planning on putting her life in the hands of Ms. Tequila Breath, that was for sure!

"You have to go in there, give a good reading and pretend you don't know any of this, Fiona," said Raven. "You have to go through with this. We're right behind you."

"Why? Don't we know enough now? Let's just go over to the marshal's office and…"

"We need to see how Hawthorne reacts. He needs to lead us to Aisling's body. If we go to Marshal Lopez with this story, he'll just roll his eyes," Raven said. "The Fagans are the most respected citizens around here. They give a big donation to the village every year, if it weren't for them, that new cop station wouldn't have been built last year. Lopez is a lazy old son of a gun, he's out of shape, about to retire, the biggest crime we've ever had around here was speeding tickets. At least, as far as anyone knew. No, Fiona, we have to finish what we've started here. Then we'll call him in. When we have something definite to show him."

Arnie Sawyer listened to the two poets, all the while thinking he hadn't even told them the worst of his suspicions. When he'd stopped for his two o'clock smoke on the highway, he'd had a sudden realization: Aisling Devlin's harp and poems had not been in her car since they had been abducted along with her - or she had never brought them with her to Colorado. He knew now that she wouldn't have intentionally left them behind. Raven was right. Aisling Devlin had never left the Fagans'. She, her harp and her book of poems were all there…somewhere.

Which meant that her abduction in Durango had been

staged. A woman had impersonated the already abducted - or dead - Aisling and had driven her car from Ojo de Sombras to Durango. Stopped at the gas station, made sure the attendant noticed her. Then went into the gas station bathroom and changed from Aisling's clothes to her own, and simply walked away. Leaving behind her a trail of clues leading down the wrong path.

Fooled everyone except Raven and her Green Man.

Hank was sure Chahil O'Shea and his book of poems were also hidden somewhere on the Fagan grounds, but he kept that to himself as well.

Creativity and death. The Green Man was the embodiment of nature's cycles, Hank had read somewhere in his computer research yesterday. The guardian of the life force. Death and birth, winter and spring. To someone, the Fagan prize poets were the embodiment of creativity, of birth. The perfect sacrifice.

Chapter 22: Immortality

Fiona stared out at her audience. She took a moment to ground herself, as she had learned to do when standing before a crowd of strangers and friends, performing that ritual known as "giving a poetry reading". In truth, the ritual felt more like ripping out one's mind, heart and soul and passing them around the room for inspection. With confidence and humor. With pizzazz. With showmanship.

As a young poet, most of the audiences she had met had been of the academic or city coffee house variety - those already inclined toward an appreciation of poetry. This one at the *Extranjeros* in the wild mountains of New Mexico was a new testing ground for her. A truly expectant audience: artisans, electricians, retired hippies, realtors, Spanish, land-owning descendants, young women from the neighboring pueblo. A handful of Los Alamos physicists and their spouses had also appeared, as Talle had promised.

So far it had gone well. So well, in fact, that she almost forgot that there were one or two people here who would like to tie her up and silence her forever. Once again, she hoped this whole murder idea was just Raven's delusion. This was a purely innocent poetry reading, afterward they'd all eat cookies, go home, go to sleep and have nice dreams.

The smell of freshly-brewed, intermission coffee warned her that she was winding toward the end of her first set. It was a good audience, ordinary people who actually wanted to hear poetry. She had become so entrenched in the university and bohemian worlds back in Baltimore; she hadn't known this audience existed. It gave her a feeling of hopefulness, even a lump in her throat. Were it not for her mission on behalf of Aisling Devlin, she could be enjoying this evening, even testing some of her more experimental pieces on them.

"Now I would like to present something special. There is a strong, mythical presence in these mountains and woods. You've probably felt him, perhaps some of you have seen him."

Talle's head shot up and she stared at Fiona as if she was an angel, about to deliver a prophecy.

"He is known as the Green Man. I had read of him before, in my research back east. I'd seen photographs of the historical carvings that depicted him. I had even begun to write about him, in my own poetry."

Talle smiled. The word "beatific" occurred to Fiona, at the expectant radiance of that smile.

"But here, I have actually met him. He is both the spirit of the land and its protector."

Several audience members sat forward, their elbows on their knees.

"I know there are a few scientists here tonight. I beg their indulgence on this one."

A small wave of laughter rustled the room. Fiona took another deep breath. This was the moment. Was Raven crazy or right? She held two poems in her hands, one she had written about the Green Man, and Aisling Devlin's. She looked up at Raven. Raven slowly nodded, her gaze intense. Fiona saw that, in her fingers, the dark poet was slowly winding and unwinding Aisling's harp string and peg. Fiona swallowed hard and looked back to her poems. The time had come to take a stand. For Aisling.

"I was going to read to you from my own Green Man poems," she finally spoke. "But I think I'll hold them until later in the evening. Instead, I would like to read to you someone else's Green Man poem."

Fiona opened Aisling's poem and spread out the creases. The ink was faded. Her hands began to tremble and her guts twisted. A rush of heat moved up her spine. She forced herself to look out at the audience before beginning.

At Liam, sitting in the front next to Talle, dressed in his nicest grey silk shirt and wool slacks, a comfortable sweater across his shoulders, his eyes watching her with all kindness and interest.

At Hawthorne, standing in the back, leaning on the end of a bookcase, politely enduring this event with his eyes on Raven.

At Raven, strategically sitting on the love seat that gave her a full view of everyone in the audience, her fists now clenched in her lap, the harp string wrapped around them, her head held high and her eyes fiercely beaming courage in Fiona's direction.

At Arnie/Hank, who sat next to Raven. He gave Fiona a quick wink and thumbs up, lifted his camera to indicate he'd be documenting the event.

At Silver, in a long purple velvet dress and dangling purple beaded earrings, quietly bustling around the coffee and cookie display, yet watching Fiona's every move out of the corner of her eye, obviously enjoying her role as literary hostess of the evening.

She finally forced her glance back full circle to Talle, who, of all, had a look of impatience on her face. She very much wanted to hear the Green Man poem, apparently no matter who wrote it. Talle smiled at Fiona and nodded encouragingly. Fiona noticed that, in Talle's hand, resting on her lap, she held an envelope. No doubt Fiona's Fagan check, to be presented to her after intermission.

Fiona wasn't sure she could go through with this. Then, she smelled a hint of rosemary and mulch, heard a momentary bristling of leaves behind her, and felt the prodding of a twiggy hand at the small of her back. She began to read.

It was an elegant, enigmatic poem, written in the graceful voice of one who experienced a man as both a fragile human and the personification of the lord of the forest, the purveyor of the seasons, of nature's cyclical immortality. The poet spoke of winter's death as the returning to dust, of the transformation to seed, of the re-flowering in the spring. Of the ambiguous cycle of love. Fiona's voice caught on itself as she read; so aware was she that the poet who had written these words gave testimony to a poignant affection for not only Liam Fagan but for life itself. And that the poet was dead, at the hands of someone in this room. Fiona was also aware, without even looking up from the page, that Talle's body had gone rigid and her smile had frozen in place. That Liam's body had very slightly slumped in his chair, his hands limp across his knees, his eyes downcast and moist. Fiona didn't dare look to the back of the room to see Hawthorne's reaction; she left that task to Raven. She heard Arnie/Hank's camera clicking, saw the flashing of his bulbs.

"This poem reminds me of a line from Edna St. Vincent Millay's poem, '*To a Young Poet*'. '*No thing that ever flew, not the lark, not you, can die as others do.*' I found this poem in one of the volumes of Liam Fagan's own poetry. I assume it was written by a former Fagan winner. It has the initials A.D., 10-4-79 at the bottom."

Fiona put the poem down and forced herself to look at her audience. Some were whispering to each other, others looked stricken. Most of them, smiling softly at the poem, were unaware of the implications of what they had just heard.

"Thank you, this has been a good experience. I believe Silver has treats for us, so we'll take a break for about twenty minutes."

Silver waved, and called out from the back that everyone should stretch their legs and enjoy some coffee and cookies and buy books. She made a circle with her fingers in Fiona's direction and lifted her hands to applaud. Everyone else followed suit, applauding with varying degrees of enthusiasm and vague politeness.

Before Fiona could decide what her next appropriate action should be, she was inundated with a cluster of new fans, babbling questions and comments. She smiled, shook hands and responded as best she could, while trying to observe what was happening with Raven, Arnie/Hank, Hawthorne, Talle and Liam. Talle was still sitting, staring at Fiona. At first her face seemed expressionless, but as their eyes met, Fiona felt a coldness that made her gasp inwardly. Liam was standing, his hand on Talle's shoulder, watching his wife with a confused expression of solicitation. He was talking to her and gesturing toward the coffee concession.

Hawthorne stood near the exit with his hands in his pockets, trying to act as if he wasn't looking for someone.

Fiona felt a panic setting in; Raven and Arnie/Hank were nowhere to be seen. She smiled and nodded and made her way through the crowd. She stepped outside, hit by the cold that seemed intensified in contrast to the wood-stove warmth of the bookstore's interior. Hank Walker's Volvo was parked in front of the store, which was somewhat reassuring. The Fagan van, however, was just rounding the corner, heading back toward the hacienda. As she tried to fight down a wave of anxiety, she felt a hand on her shoulder. She whirled around. It was Liam. His face was lined and sad.

"I don't know whether to thank you or curse you, my dear," he said, taking her hand. "It was very difficult to hear Aisling's poem again."

"Aisling?" Fiona had the presence of mind to pretend. "I didn't realize it was hers."

"Ah. But those of us who knew her realized it. In particular, Talle. She's rather upset, and she's gone home. She begs your forgiveness if she misses the second set."

Fiona doubted Talle had begged anything. Liam was covering for his wife.

"Here, she asked me to give you this. She was going to present it at the end, but - well, I'm not much for making speeches. I hope you'll understand. You've rather thrown us for a loop, you see. It was very tragic, Aisling's disappearance."

Fiona looked at Liam, trying to read him. As usual, it was impossible.

"Well, shall we go in? Your audience awaits you. You've made quite an impression."

Fiona took one last look around as Liam guided her through the door. They had promised to look after her, to stand by her through this whole thing. Where the hell were Raven and Hank?

* * *

As soon as Hawthorne was out of sight, two shadows rose from behind the dumpster next to the *Extranjeros*.

"We've got to follow him," Raven said.

"First we have to tell Fiona what we're going to do."

"She'll figure it out, we don't have time, come *ON!*"

Raven bolted toward the woods.

"Raven!" Hank hissed at her, but she kept moving. He had no choice. Fiona was probably fine, he reasoned as he ran to catch up. It was Hawthorne and Talle they needed to keep their eyes on.

* * *

Hawthorne stood at the edge of the woods, catching his breath after his sprint from the *Extranjeros*. He leaned against a tree and pulled a joint and book of matches from his shirt pocket. *Exposure.* The full impact of Talle's words was hitting him. Her sense of panic now seemed appropriate. No doubt Raven was part of this, he didn't think that frail Fiona could have orchestrated all this by herself.

He finished his joint and crushed out the dregs under his boot, and then stood looking out at his options. If he went left, he'd find the river's edge and hike to the *kiva*.

If he went straight, he'd be back at his *casita* in a quarter of an hour, he could pack and split. Things were not looking good, either option. He continued his sprint, heading toward his *casita*.

Once at the compound, he paused outside the wall, watching. The second-floor lights in the hacienda were on, and those in the greenhouse. He crept around the wall to his *casita*, slipped inside and furtively threw together the bare essentials for a hitchhiking trip. Cash, his stash box; whatever he didn't have time to gather now he could replace on the road. He changed quickly from his seduction clothes into warm layers of shirts and sweater, denim jacket, soft-soled hiking shoes and gloves. He pushed back any cumbersome emotions he felt at leaving his artwork, and slipped out again. The lights were still on at the hacienda. He shuddered and moved quickly down the path through the woods, heading the long way toward the highway.

The thought of never seeing Raven again stood up like a boulder in his path. He heard the chattering of dried leaves, felt a wind kick up and the scratching of tree branches slashed across his chest. Was he headed the right direction to get to Bandelier? He listened but couldn't hear the river. The wind grew fierce; a branch swiped his cheek and stung. He reached to touch the wound and felt blood.

Ok, ok! He thought and turned the other direction, heading for the valley toward Dragon Rock. He'd just go there watch and see what went down. Then he was out of here, for good.

* * *

I am heartily sorry. Oh my Dear, Dear Lord, have I offended Thee? I will right this. You will not regret what You have entrusted to me.

Let's see...plastic bags, Liam's garment bags...We should travel, we're getting older, we should go to Europe. There are Green Men there, on every church. We could see them all, we could go into the verdant, watery forests and find Him there in His other forms...Let's see...

Rope, that's in the greenhouse...scissors, tape...what else will I need to right this situation? Where can we move The Poets to? There's no time to think this through. Somewhere temporary, until there is time...Oh, I can't think, I can't think... Flashlight...matches

...I must change my shoes for the hike, for the Work, this Blessed Work that He requires...It's cold, I must get my scarf...

Oh, Lord, how can I worry for my comfort at this moment? We are coming, do not worry, my Dear, Dear One, we are coming, I will not complain...

The chiffarobe in the apothecary, I can empty it out, put The Poets there for the time being...but only temporary...He wants His dear Poets in the woods, visible and accessible to Him, not in a man-made house, never in a house...Dear One, I am coming, I am coming...

The gun. But He does not like the gun. When I shot the snake that time, He berated me so...my protection must come from nature, from the woods, from the water's edge...Ah, yes, I know...the gloves, I will put them on now, just in case...and this bottle, this one will do...I had made up an extra portion, now I know why. Oh Blessed Be, He guides my every action, even when I am, in my human ignorance, so unaware...Dear One, I am ready, I am coming...

* * *

The audience applauded and waited expectantly. But things were not going well, not like the first set. Silver looked strained, unhappy. Liam, too. The audience had noticed that half the seats were empty - so many people had left at intermission and not returned. Reading the Aisling Devlin piece put a damper on things. Fiona sifted through her folder of poems, searching for something appropriate to the mood, or to counteract the mood, or – and then she simply stopped. She looked out at the audience and shook her head.

"I'm so sorry, all of you. I can't read anymore tonight. I think my friends are in trouble."

Fiona closed her folder, grabbed her duster and ran through the bookstore, leaving her purse and poems behind. Silver stood up, dismayed, her hand over her mouth and stared after Fiona's departure. The reporters from the Albuquerque Journal and the *Ojo de Sombras Monthly* began scribbling rapidly in their notebooks. Liam rose quickly, folded his hands together prayerfully, shrugged at the crowd as if asking their indulgence, and followed Fiona out the door.

"Well, this is most amazing!" he heard Silver speaking to the crowd as he left. "These poets are certainly unpredictable people! All of you please stay, have refreshments. Music! Would someone put on some music?"

"Fiona! Wait!" Liam ran to her side and, breathing heavily, tried to match her stride. "What in god's name are you doing, girl?"

"I'm very, very concerned about Raven. I think she has gone to the *kiva*. She may be in danger. I'm sorry, I'm so sorry, Liam, I've caused such a mess tonight...but there are things you don't know about, I'm afraid, and I must find my friend."

"I'll go with you, then. I am not allowing a beautiful young woman to wander about in the dark on my property!" he kept pace with her and the two moved briskly through the woods behind Raven's cottage, causing a barking tirade from Dingo, joined by all the other dogs in the village. As Liam and Fiona entered the woods, the sounds of the village receded behind them.

"What are these things you say I don't know about?"

Fiona shook her head and kept moving.

"It's not my place to tell you. You need to talk to your wife," she said, and broke into a run.

"You believe my wife killed Aisling Devlin?" Liam

asked, still keeping abreast with Fiona.

Fiona stopped and stared at him, catching her breath. "You know?"

"I must tell you what happened recently to make me wonder about many things." Liam leaned his hands on his knees, trying to catch his breath. In the faint light from the village behind them, Fiona noticed again how frail he seemed. "The other night, after you and I spoke, I went for a walk…"

Suddenly they heard a crashing through the branches up ahead. They stepped back behind a tree and peered out. Someone in silhouette was running toward them.

* * *

Raven and Hank turned on their flashlights and scanned the area behind the Bardic Cabin. All they could see was a stack of logs and firewood where the trap door should be.

"Looks like they've tried to camouflage it," said Raven, disassembling the firewood.

Suddenly they heard a noise, a muffled thumping. Was that a voice?

"Someone's down there!" Raven whispered. Hank helped her move the firewood and then the two of them rolled the two larger logs aside. Hank drew his gun and pointed it toward the trap door while Raven pulled it open.

"Oh thank the lord! Ye've saved my life!" cried out a voice, heavily brogued. Raven knelt and directed her light in the face of…

"Liam? But you were just…"

The man hoisted himself up off the ladder, tossed out a backpack, and sat on the ground, holding his jacket close and breathing heavily.

"It's a wee bit cold down there. I believe ye're known as Raven? I'm Mack Magee, what's left of him. Liam Fagan's brother, if ye will."

Raven stared, her mouth wide open. Fiona was right. Liam had a twin, and here he was.

"And ye would be…?" Mack held out his hand to Hank. "I think ye can put that down. I'm no threat. I've been locked in there longer than I care to say, and even if I were the evil sort, my hands are frozen to the bone. Like ice, they are!"

"Hank". He put his gun away, and shook hands with Mack.

"Listen, I need to warn ye two before ye go down there."

"How do you know who I am?" Raven demanded.

"Oh, I've been watching things a bit. And talking with Liam last week. I think ye are in danger, girl. Whoever locked me in there, they were quite upset because I was digging out the wall. I expect they'll be coming back soon. Meanwhile, I kept busy while I was locked in there. I've dug out a crypt of sorts. There's a couple of poor souls down there. Just bones, is all. There's quite a bit of a stench, hit me like a cloud when I pulled the boards out."

"Yes, we know about the crypt," said Hank. "That's why we're here. Guess you better show us what you've found, but we have to hurry."

Hank and Raven climbed down the ladder and Mack joined them, pulling his bandana back over his nose and mouth. Raven gagged at the smell and held her jacket hem up over her mouth. Hank, a handkerchief to his nostrils. Mack turned on his flashlight and directed the beam at the crypt opening. Hank and Raven followed suit.

Three flashlight beams converged, and Mack watched as the other two absorbed the sight. It was sadly comforting to have the company of other witnesses.

Instinctively, Hank and Raven averted their eyes. Then looked again. Then turned away.

The two skulls held petrified stems in their grins, branches twisted around their temples, reminiscent of the famous crown of thorns. They rested on a gruesome potpourri of branches, jumbled bones, insect casings, and rodent droppings. All wrapped in the webs of spiders. Ankle and wrist bones still bore faded nylon cords of brownish-green. What was left of the poets' notebooks had come to a final rest, melted black from body fluids and rat urine, in the pelvic bones at the center of each pile of human remains. Aisling Devlin's harp was little more than a few clumps of rotted and insect-devoured wood. Only the rusted strings had survived, lying limp, and twisted where the bones of her arms had eventually fallen into them.

"It's a very sad sight, I must say," Mack lamented. "I'll leave ye with this for the moment. I've had all I can stand of the place."

"Ok," said Hank, turning away from the sight, holding his bandana over his nose and mouth. "Are you all right, there, Raven?"

Raven nodded, leaning on a wall, wiping her mouth, staring at the floor. Throwing up like a damned girl after all. After all these months of working her way toward this moment, you'd think there'd be a little dignity in the thing, she thought to herself wryly. She turned to Hank, who was walking around the room, examining the nest, the shelves, the shovels, the pictographs.

"Guess you're used to this sort of thing?" she asked, holding her stomach.

"I don't know if 'used to' describes it. Listen, hon, we don't have much time here."

"I know." She threw her shoulders back and joined him, holding her jacket over her nose. "I was preparing myself to see mummies, with this climate, locked up like that."

"Yeah, I kind of wondered, myself. But it looks like they were buried with their ritual nests as shrouds. Too much moisture, too much protection, too many insects, all because of the nest material. That's why the remains are clean. Did you see all the pupal casings and other bug stuff in there? Looks like the rodents have been gone from their nests quite a while, though. Guess there wasn't much left, old bodies aren't of much interest."

"Yeah." Raven put up her hand to stop him. "So..." the implications of exactly what had been done here over the years began to hit her. "They buried Aisling in '79 and then opened it up again to bury O'Shea with her in '86?"

"Looks like it."

"Is the young lass the missing poet?" Mack asked from the doorway above.

"Yes," Hank called up the ladder. "And we also have an Irish poet, Chahil O'Shea."

"Aye. As if we could spare any of them." Mack shook his head, "tsking" softly.

"Ghouls," Raven's voice trembled with rage. "Absolute ghouls."

"Listen, we have to make sure no one disturbs this," Hank said after a moment. "One of us should go for the marshal now. The other should stay and guard."

"I'll be the one to fetch the marshal, if ye don't mind," called out Mack from up top.

"I need to move my legs around. I'll leave my gear here for the time being."

"I'll stay down here and hide–" said Hank.

"There's another crypt ye can hide in. Behind the cabinetry there–it's never been used, if you get my meaning."

Hank shone the light behind the cabinet and found

the crypt.

"I can just fit there."

"I should wait down here with you," said Raven. She didn't like the feeling that Hank was taking over, just because he was a guy. Or older. Or a private eye.

"No, I need you up top. Cover me from up there."

"Cover you? And who's going to cover me?"

"At least if something happens up top, you can run for help. Down here, I've got to have all my wits about me."

"Mack," Hank called up, "You watch out. We're not sure where everyone is at this point. This guy Hawthorne might be in on all this, too. Watch your back."

"Check the cop shop, or look for Lopez's car parked over near the saloon," Raven added. "Friday nights he watches for drunk drivers mostly."

Mack nodded and took off, heading in the direction along the river toward the village. Raven pulled out her .38 derringer, climbed the ladder, and stashed Mack's backpack out of sight in the juniper. After checking carefully with her flashlight to see if Hawthorne was about, she found a hiding place in some bushes behind a boulder. From there she could see the possible approaches from the river, the Bardic Cabin and Hawthorne's studio.

Down below, Hank took out his 9 mm auto. The handcuffs and extra ammo clips were in his pockets at the ready. He pushed out the cabinet and crawled into the crypt. The smell from the other crypt, which permeated the *kiva*, kept him in mind of his companions. As if he needed reminding.

Above and below, Raven and Hank waited in the dark, alert to the slightest sound.

* * *

"Mack! Over here!"

Liam called out as the man ran past their hiding place, much to Fiona's surprise. The man stopped and looked around.

"Is it ye, Liam?"

Liam stepped out and beckoned Mack over.

"We're on our way to the *kiva*. What's your hurry?"

The man approached Liam. Fiona stared at the two of them conversing so casually. It was her voyeur, only not naked this time; she blushed to herself in the dark. The pale glow of light behind them, from the village beyond, faintly illuminated the two standing there on the path, one gaunt and pale, his hair pulled tightly back, cleanly dressed. The other lean and dark, his hair the same – white and shoulder length - but free and tangled. His clothes worn and dust-covered. The faces were the same, but marked by different experience. Liam's eyes held longing, his lips a desire to laugh. What had he called the man? Mack? That man's eyes were wild and challenging; his was a face full of lines betraying that he was well accustomed to laughing and crying, as he pleased.

"Mack Magee, this is Fiona Kelly," Liam, ever the

gentleman, even in the middle of a crisis. "We finally met," he explained to Fiona, "The morning after you told me he was here."

"I know who ye are," Mack held out his hand to Fiona. But his smile was distracted.

"I don't know if I recommend ye go to the *kiva* now. Raven and Hank are there…"

"Are they ok?" Fiona interrupted.

"They're standing guard."

"Who's Hank?" asked Liam.

"Our friend."

"There's a crypt, there's bodies. Wicked goings-on," Mack interrupted. "Someone locked me in there for the past half-a-day or so."

"My god, are you alright?" Liam touched his twin's shoulder.

"A bit stiff, is all. Afraid I finished off your *poitin*, though. I'm off for the marshal."

"We'll go with you."

"I'm going to the *kiva*," said Fiona.

Liam looked at her and realized there was no way to stop her.

"I'll go with her, then," he amended to his brother. "You'll be fine, Marshal Lopez is…"

"I know, parked near the pub looking for drunkards."

"Right."

Ye be careful. Liam, where is your wife?"

"She went back to the house, she wasn't feeling well."

Mack looked him in the eyes for a long moment.

"Be careful of your wife, Liam," he finally said, "I've watched her doing her chores. That's one strong woman and she's got a wee bit on her mind."

Mack turned and was gone before Liam could respond.

Fiona could think of about twenty questions she wanted to ask Liam, but there was no time. She grabbed his arm and pulled him into a run down the path toward the river.

* * *

Raven held her breath: a flashlight beam was wavering through the red rocks approaching the Bardic Cabin. It was Talle. She had changed from her broom skirt and designer sweater into warm hiking clothes and a backpack. Raven fought her instinct to step out and hold her gun on the woman. Hank was right; they needed to observe her reaction to the bodies first. She would have to let Talle go down the ladder.

Talle saw that the trap door was open, and spun her flashlight beam into the surrounding trees and boulders. Raven was carefully crouched behind a red-rock boulder, out of the light.

"Hawthorne?" Talle whispered. She waited a moment, called out his name louder, then muttered something and flung off the backpack near the *kiva* trap door. She turned off her flashlight, tucked it into her jacket pocket and began her climb down. Her hands looked strange - sleek and shining - on the ladder rungs. From inside the *kiva*, Raven heard her again call out Hawthorne's name.

Raven waited until she heard nothing further, then crept cautiously near the trap door.

Hank held his breath as Talle descended the ladder, calling out for Hawthorne. He couldn't see from behind the cabinet, so had to rely on his hearing and the wandering beam of a flashlight to discern where she was standing.

There was a long moment of silence, then a soft, *"Oh no!"* The sound of something falling, then moaning. Another long silence. Hank breathed as slowly and quietly as he could, his eyes fixed on the floor outside his crypt.

"Oh Lord, tell me what to do..."

Hank leaned closer to the opening, listening intently to her words.

Talle distinctly heard the rustling of leaves, felt a cold breath against her ear. The *kiva* filled with the scent of pine and moss and a potpourri of foreign herbs so complex that even she, the *curandera*, could not distinguish its parts.

Hank heard no leaves rustling. Smelled no herbs. Continued to listen.

"Yes, I had thought so, too. To the house, then? Just until a place in Your natural cathedral can be prepared? Yes, I will do this, My Lord...Who? Oh, it is she, the new poet. She defiled these Offerings I had made to You. She took a poem from the Poet's book..."

Talle's eyes disregarded the truth of what they saw, that

Aisling's poems had not been disturbed by Fiona. That the black, stained binder of poems that had fallen from the skeleton's hands was no longer one from which a poem could have been extracted. No more than could Aisling's wooden harp ever be played again. The poems were lost forever. The harp was silenced.

"...and that other one, Raven, I know she is part of this."

Talle rose, came to the cabinet, rummaged through the shelves. Hank heard and smelled a match being lit, then the warm scent of melting wax momentarily cut into the death smell that filled the room. Talle continued lighting matches until the bit of *kiva* floor that he could see became softly illuminated with the wavering light of several candles. He heard her move away from the cabinet, back in the direction of the crypt.

There was a long silence. Then Talle spoke.

"Yes, I agree. You are so wise, My Lord. And it is time, it is the seventh year."

The sounds of clinking metal and falling plaster.

Then Talle drew a loud, sharp breath. The hair on Hank's arms stood up.

"Oh, My Lord, yes! I had thought this myself, only this afternoon! Yes. *Both of them!* The dual sacrifice will heal the imbalance they have created in Your forest? You will be pleased with my work again, I promise You. I will prepare The Poets for removal now. Then prepare for Raven and

Fiona. See? I brought a bottle of the blessed oil, it will go as You wish."

This was the moment. Hank mustn't let her move the dead poets, or lay one finger on the living ones. Ready with his gun, he silently rolled himself out from behind the cabinet, and stood. He stepped out into the candlelight, saw Talle crouched again, just inside the crypt. He came closer and pointed his weapon at her back.

"Stand slowly with your hands up," he said. "Raven? You there?"

"Right here," Raven's head appeared above, and in her hand, the derringer.

"You heard all that?"

"Every raving word. Are you ok?"

"I'm fine. Hawthorne is probably on his way. Get out of sight."

"Got it," Raven called and pulled her head and gun back out of the opening.

Talle rose slowly. As she turned toward Hank, she slammed her hand against the wall. He heard something shatter. She faced him and, in her left hand, held out one of her blue vials. The glass was splintered and fluid had spilled onto her fingers, which were protected by a translucent glove. Her right arm was still down, slightly behind her. It was hard to tell in the dim candle light, but he figured she was probably holding her gun back there.

"Whoever you are, leave this place now," she hissed.

554

"One drop of this on your skin and you belong to Him forever."

Hank motioned toward the corner with his gun.

"Lady, it's over. Toss that, and your gun too. Then put your hands on your head."

"Who are you?" Talle asked, not moving.

"That's not important. TOSS IT."

"It will be a very slow and terrible death."

Hank couldn't let himself take the woman's threat lightly, even though her brandishing the poison struck him as a caricature of a Wild West stand off, one pointing a gun, the other a bottle of cobalt blue. He had read enough from Dr. Mercer's list of toxic Southwestern plants, and had deduced enough about what kind of death Aisling Devlin and Chahil O'Shea had had at this self-made *curandera's* hands, to know that she wasn't fooling.

"Toss the bottle in the corner and do it now," Hank spoke ominously, gritting his teeth. "I mean it, Lady, or I'll gladly put you out of your god-forsaken misery."

Talle tried to lock eyes with him, but he instinctively kept focused on her shoulders and torso. Suddenly she jerked her arm, as if to toss the oil in his face. Anticipating this, he danced quickly to the side but, as he did, she kicked out with her left foot and caught him in his ankle. He lost his balance and the 9 mm auto went off. The bullet splintered the ladder, and the sound left both Hank and Talle momentarily deaf. In that moment, Talle spun and slammed him in the temple with something heavy and sharp. Hank fell backwards, hitting his head on the ladder and crushing his shoulder against the floor as he fell.

There was no more candlelight.

* * *

Although Raven heard the gun shot down in the *kiva*, there was nothing she could do; her hands and feet bound and tied to a ponderosa. She could see the trap door and Talle's bag of goodies scattered nearby. And her own .38 derringer, lying on the mesa several yards away.

Back in the bushes, watching for Hawthorne, Raven had rummaged through Talle's backpack tossing out garment bags, garbage bags, tarp, tape, rope and knives. She'd left inside the pack an assortment of vials wrapped in plastic that she didn't dare touch.

Just as she finished her quick inventory, she'd felt herself grabbed from behind, thrown to the ground and sat upon. A wad of fabric was stuffed into her mouth and tied behind her head. She grunted and struggled, trying to heave the body off hers, but it all happened too quickly for her karate moves to be of any help. Her captor grabbed the rope Raven had just tossed from Talle's backpack and began to tie her up. The force of the fall threw her .38 several yards across the desert floor, in the direction of the Bardic Cabin. Apparently her captor was not aware of or concerned about the gun. She was lifted and pulled over to a large ponderosa.

"Dmnyhth!" she growled against the gag when she

realized it was Hawthorne.

He wound more rope around her torso and the tree trunk. Raven closed her eyes and groaned, jerking against the cords again, enraged at herself more than Hawthorne.

"Ok, listen to me," he whispered, his hands on her shoulders, trying to hold her still.

"Fkyfkbst!" she hissed.

"Yeah, I know, I know, and next you'll be cursing me in Navajo again. LISTEN. There's no time for this shit right now! Talle is a goddamned dangerous bitch, you hear me? I have to get down there and see what she's done."

Raven struggled but listened intently, her eyes wide and angry, fixed on his face.

"Aisling's death was an accident. It looked bad for me; I sort of have a record, see. And Talle...she sort of black-mailed me, now that I see it clear. But I never meant to hurt Aisling."

Raven kicked again, jerking against his hands.

"STOP IT, for Christ sake! You're wasting your energy. I'm not going to hurt you. I tied you up to protect you from yourself. Talle wants to do the ritual tonight, with you, not with Fiona. When she heard Aisling's poem tonight, she went right over the edge and, frankly, she was already there. I think she went home and got her gun. Are you listening?"

Raven had stopped struggling. She nodded but her eyes were still filled with rage.

"She says there's bodies down there. This is the first

I knew anything about any damn bodies, you hear me? I don't know what she's been up to, but I have a real, real bad feeling. Got it? The only reason I came back was to make sure you're alright."

Raven glared at him. The last thing she wanted to do was believe this man. The wind was kicking up and dust filled her eyes. There was that damned rustling sound again, that sharp, vegetation smell. The tree she was tied to seemed to bend to the contours of her body, wrapping itself gently – but firmly - around her. Something warm breathed in her ear.

That's when she and Hawthorne heard the gun shot.

"What the–?" Hawthorne stared toward the *kiva* trap door. "Who the hell is down there? I thought she was alone down there." He looked at Raven. Her eyes told him sarcastically that she couldn't enlighten him while wearing a gag.

"Ok, look, I'll take it off. But don't you start yelling. You understand? The woman's loco. You GOT IT?"

Raven closed her eyes and nodded, letting her body go passive into the Green Man's embrace. Hawthorne untied the t-shirt from her mouth and quickly put his hand over her lips.

"Now tell me, but whisper. Who the hell is down there?"

"A friend," was all Raven would say. "He has a gun, too."

Hawthorne stared at the trap door.

"So we don't know who shot who."

"Right," Raven said, licking moisture back onto her lips and spitting cotton fibers. "Hawthorne, untie me, for god's sake, this is crazy."

"No. I'm going to go see what's going on. I gotta know."

He tied the gag back over her mouth, crept quickly toward the trap door, and knelt on one knee, listening. Raven banged her head against the tree, growling through the gag.

* * *

Hank was in no position to speak, either. He opened his eyes slowly, trying to remember the weird nightmare he'd just had. He moved to sit up and check his alarm clock but could only fall back and cry out at the pain in his right shoulder. His cries were muffled by something painfully tight and sticky pressing his lips back against his teeth. His head felt like one giant bruise with a hang over, like the ones after his wife died. What was that awful smell? And where were the covers and his pajamas? It was freezing in here. Behind the thing on his mouth, his teeth were banging against themselves in the cold. And who was that over in the corner?

It was a woman, he saw as she turned to look at him. Despite the pain, he tried to move his hands and feet. They were caught, numb, heavy and immovable.

"Be still," the woman hissed from across the room. She was mixing something white in a bucket, pouring water from a jug and stirring with a long stick. She stood and approached the bed. What was all this junk in the sheets? Scratchy stuff, the sheets felt absolutely filthy, caked with dirt and leaves. The woman came closer and peered down at his face.

Then he remembered where he was. What he was smelling. And who she was. He growled protests behind the duct tape covering his mouth. Apparently his false beard had come off in the fall, he could feel the tape pulling at his skin along his cheeks back to his ears. He shifted his head to look down, and realized he was stark naked and strapped with green nylon cords into the Green Man nest. The same kind of cords he had seen on the skeletons in the crypt. A cold dread flushed through his limbs. Just moving his head shot a jolt of agonizing pain along his neck and shoulder. He groaned and laid his head back carefully. Talle Fagan was good at locating all his old wounds, apparently. He had dislocated his shoulder last year, playing football with his nephews. He recognized the re-injury.

"Now you listen. I don't know who you are, or why you came in here wearing a disguise...You do look a bit familiar but...I don't recall. Anyway, the Green Man has chosen you. It is not for me to question. I must trust and do his bidding, as it becomes evident. The one thing he does require is that the mask be made from one who is willing and informed about the ritual. So I am explaining this to you now. Do you understand? Close your eyes if you do."

Hank stared at Talle. Her eyes burned hot and her cheeks were bright red, as if she had a fever. Her hair was damp with sweat, tendrils plastered against her neck and cheeks. He refused to close his eyes, even for a second. She frowned and shook her head and went on.

"Now to inform you. I'm afraid it has to be the condensed version. The Green Man requires a mask every fall. I doubt you are a poet but I see you are a photographer. So perhaps an artist of sorts? You'll have to do. I will make a mask of you as an offering. Usually Hawthorne does this part, with the ladies. I have only once performed this part myself, with Mr. O'Shea, because Hawthorne refused to help - homophobic, you see. Chahil wasn't very willing, either, now that I recall."

Talle chuckled to herself softly, remembering.

"I had to use a bit of chloroform with him. Caught him sneaking in here, he'd seen me getting things prepared for the ritual and was curious. But I won't go into that, there's no time.

I'll take the mask while you are in your most creative form. Then I have other work to do here," she turned and looked back at The Poets in the crypt.

The woman's hand – bare now, she must have removed the poison-soaked glove while he was unconscious - moved down Hank's torso. Despite the cold, he felt a chill of sweat forming across his body. My god, was she really going to-?

She suddenly withdrew her hand and went back to her work across the room. She began ripping strips of gauze. She pulled a small table near the nest and laid out the bucket filled with the white substance - Hank smelled plaster - and the gauze strips. She walked toward the cabinet, picked up Hank's gun from the floor, put it in her jacket pocket. She stood in front of the cabinet, and put on a new pair of surgical gloves.

Hank stared up at the ceiling. He remembered everything now. Where the hell was Raven? Hadn't she heard the gun shot? He yanked his limbs against the restraints. Cried out behind the tape at the pain in his shoulder. He was tied down tight.

Was this woman talking *mask*? Or *death mask*?

* * *

Fiona and Liam slowed their pace as they approached the Bardic Cabin. Neither Liam nor she had had any trouble keeping up the sprint to get here, thanks to the rush of adrenalin and a leaf-scattering wind at their backs the whole way. Liam seemed so different now that they had run into Mack. Even in the dark she could see color in his cheeks, and his hair looked a bit wild from the running and the tree branches catching in it. He looked more like his twin now.

Fiona and Liam crept around the side of the cabin and peered out to the *kiva* area. It took a few moments to understand what they were looking at.

First Fiona saw a small gun on the ground, about eight feet away. She almost didn't see it, but a gust of wind came up, pushing leaves in that direction so dramatically that they caught her attention. When the leaves moved on, the gun remained. Next, about ten yards away, she saw Hawthorne, down on one knee near the trap door, his ear close to the entrance. Nearby, a ransacked backpack, loose tarp and plastic bags scattered in the wind. One of the bags gyrated back into the trees and, another ten yards beyond Hawthorne, slapped into Raven's legs, tied to a ponderosa, gagged and staring lividly at her captor. Fiona carefully lifted her hand behind Hawthorne's back and waved it slowly to catch Raven's attention. She couldn't tell in the dark and distance whether or not her friend saw her.

"Sneak around the other side and see if you can distract him, throw a rock or something," Fiona instructed him. "I'll try for the gun and hold it on him."

Liam raised his eyebrows, but nodded, moving quickly on his mission. Fiona crept back around the side of the cabin and waited. At a sudden crashing off in the trees, Hawthorne leapt to his feet and stared in Liam's direction. Fiona threw herself across the sand, just barely grabbing the gun before Hawthorne turned back. She rose on one knee and held it in both hands, pointed at him. To her surprise, he lifted his finger to his lips, then raised his hands in the air. Liam was already behind Raven, and she was giving him heated instructions before the gag was barely off of her mouth.

"Pssssst!" Raven beckoned to Fiona with her head, while Liam used the knife she had told him was in her boot, to cut the ropes. Hawthorne stood quietly, watching. Fiona moved swiftly to Raven's side, her eyes and gun fixed on Hawthorne the whole time.

"He says he tied me up to keep me away from Talle. She's planning to kill me."

"What?" Liam cried.

"Keep my gun on the bastard," Raven continued. "Hank's down there with Talle."

Fiona nodded, watching Hawthorne with one eye and Raven with the other.

"We heard a gunshot down there," Raven went on. "Hawthorne was checking it out."

Fiona beckoned Hawthorne to move closer, still holding the gun on him.

"What did you hear?" whispered Raven.

"She's talking to someone, I couldn't see what's happening. There's candles lit down there. You said your friend has a gun?"

"Yeah," Raven whispered, rubbing her wrists and stepping out of the loosened ropes. "Good work, you guys, thanks Liam."

Liam smiled at her, patting her shoulder, and handed her back her knife. He was obviously relieved, and confused. He looked at Hawthorne with uncertainty, then turned to Fiona, his eyes filled with pain and fear.

"What does she mean, Fiona? What is Talle doing? You were going to tell me something before we ran into Mack."

"Yes, Lopez is on the way, so don't get any crazy ideas," Fiona said to Hawthorne. She answered Liam without taking her eyes off the sculptor. "It's a long story."

"I'll tell you what's going on, Liam," Hawthorne interrupted impatiently. He turned to Fiona. "The only reason I tied her up was to keep her from doing the crazy thing she's about to do if you don't stop her." He turned back to Liam. "Aisling's death was an accident, but Raven says Talle killed Chahil O'Shea too."

"Oh my god!"

"Your wife has lost her mind. She's fucking dangerous."

"Keep the gun on him, I'll check on Hank," said Raven, moving toward the trap door, kneeling and assuming the same listening pose as Hawthorne had a few moments earlier. She could hear movement below, but she had to get closer to the hole to figure out what was going on.

"Hank? Are you ok?" she called out, staying back from the opening to the *kiva*.

There was no answer. The movement below stopped.

"Talle? Are you hurt?"

Still no answer. Raven looked back toward the others. Fiona kept her gun-holding position, her eyes hot on Hawthorne. Liam joined Raven.

"My dear, I should go down and see if she's been hurt," he said softly.

Raven shook her head.

"Absolutely not. She's dangerous, Liam, we heard her tonight. She has admitted to murder. Aisling Devlin and Chahil O'Shea are down there. In a crypt."

Liam hung his head, closed his eyes and shuddered. He then drew a deep breath.

"All the more reason I should go down. I can talk to her."

"No you can't," called out Hawthorne. "I can though, I've done it before."

Liam knew it was true; Hawthorne was the one to go talk sense to Talle. Her nights at the salon, the huge martinis, the scenes, the broken glass. On more than one occasion – and increasingly over the past couple of years with her menopause, or so he explained it to himself – Hawthorne had been the one to walk her up the stairs to bed, to tuck her in, to calm her. It had been a very long time since Liam had known who Talle was or what she really needed.

"He's right. Let him go down."

"I don't trust him as far as I can spit," Raven hissed.

"I know but...what else can we do? We have a gun up here, we can keep watch."

"But there are two guns down there."

"So are we going to just wait them out?"

Raven frowned at the *kiva* door.

"Hank? Say something, please!" she called down. "Is anyone hurt down there?"

Still no response.

"We'll both go," Raven said. She motioned with her knife for Hawthorne to go through the *kiva* door ahead of her. "You first, Talle won't shoot you."

"But your friend might."

"You'll have to risk him shooting off your legs." Raven whispered through clenched teeth. "But don't forget, Fiona's up here with a gun, and your head would be the most logical target from *her* position."

Hawthorne grinned ruefully, and began to descend the ladder. Raven followed. Liam and Fiona crouched near the entrance, Fiona pointing the gun, ready for whatever.

* * *

Talle stood over Hank, rubbing her gloved hands together to warm the oil she had poured into her palm. He smelled something that reminded him of turnips. A physical panic set in. *Dr. Mercer's list. That root that grows on the banks of rivers and streams.* He couldn't breath, began to hyperventilate. He tried to kick, tried to move his hands, tried to lift his torso despite the excruciating fire of pain in his shoulder, and down his spine. Dr. Mercer's list played across his mental screen. *Seventy percent fatality rate. If not, permanent brain damage and life-long flashbacks. A ten-hour death. Convulsions. Hyper-awake state, hallucinations. Cardiac arrest, muscle breakdown from prolonged seizures. Kidney failure. Drowning in vomit.*

"*Talle, THE GREEN MAN IS SO ANGRY AT YOU!*" a voice cried out from behind her. Talle jumped and turned, horror on her face. The silhouette of a man stepped forward, holding out his hands. "*Stop, Talle. The Green Man says stop.*"

Talle stared at the male form, only a dark shadow against the backdrop of all the candles she had lit for the nest ritual. She would ordinarily have lit the fire, warmed the place up first. The details - which, in Talle's eclectic fashion, she had borrowed from various spiritual practices - were so important. The smudging, the fasting, the incense. But this was all so unexpected, she had not been able to include all the elements that the Green Man required. So she had lit every candle she could find, to create a feeling of warmth, at least. To light up the night in His honor.

If the ritual went wrong, the Green Man's good heart-edness would not survive the cold winter, his hopeful, warm breath would not warm the flowers and saplings, the healing herbs and roots, the nests and wombs of the animals again in the spring. The land would die - drought or fire, government intervention, floods, locusts - there were so many ways. Without the Green Man's presence, without his good will and blessing, chaos was inevitable.

"My Lord, again I have offended Thee?"

Talle fell to her knees, her hands lifted, her plasticized fingers slick with poisoned oil.

"All is ready, My Lord, let me proceed before the others come!"

There was a momentary pause, and then the Green Man spoke again.

"This one is not willing. You know what I require."

Talle's arms dropped to her side and she hung her head. Raven, hidden in the shadows behind Hawthorne, stared at the shiny hands in dread and tensed, clutching her knife. If the theory was correct, those hands must not touch anyone in the room. She didn't dare show herself yet, for fear of breaking the fragile curtain between Talle's hallucination and reality. She tried to peer around Hawthorne to see what had happened to Hank. She fought a cry of horror at the sight of her new friend, naked and bound in the nest – and an instinct to vomit, at the smell and sight of the crypt behind Talle.

"I tried, My Lord. I hoped he would become willing. But at least he is informed."

"Informed that he is to die for me?"

"Informed he is to help create a mask for You, My Lord," Talle pleaded, lifting her hands again. "Please let me put the oil on his skin, it is growing cold. The plaster will set too fast."

"I cannot accept this man. He is not willing and he is not fully informed."

Talle dropped her hands again, staring at the Green Man in despair and shame. His leaves and vines shuddered in the darkness, trailing up the ladder, out into the woods beyond. As her eyes adjusted, she realized He had brought with Him the darker things that crawled in the forest. Snakes and scorpions, centipedes and tarantulas, spiders and beetles, river rats, lizards, bats and toads all quivered and darted in and out of the leaves of His hair, down His shoulders and torso, along His arms and legs. His whole body writhed with subterranean, reptilian, rodent and insect life. Yet His eyes crackled dry red, with fire and rage. She had truly offended Him, as never before. There was only one thing to do. She closed her eyes and smiled.

Raven stared at Talle. There was a look of radiance across her cheeks now, like the faces of the saints on the antique *retablos* and statues in her hacienda gallery. The woman lifted a face of bizarre serenity as if looking to the heavens. The shimmering candlelight created the fleeting appearance of a halo around her head.

"Then I know what I must do, My Lord."

"*You must let me untie him,*" said the Green Man, gently. "*You must do the right thing, my daughter.*"

Talle nodded, tears falling from her closed eyes.

"There is only one who is willing and informed, My Lord. You must forgive her means."

As Hawthorne and Raven watched, horrified, the Priestess of the Green Man, still kneeling, lifted her slick gloved hand and slowly smeared the toxic oil down her forehead, nose, mouth and neck, pausing at her sternum. In a moment of confusion, Raven half expected the woman to move her hand to her shoulder, as if continuing a strange mimicry of the sign-of-the-cross. However, Talle paused in her gesture, opened her eyes and stared into the Green

Man's face, her head lifted in a horrible parody of proud saintliness. In the candlelight, the oil shimmered and glistened on her forehead and lips. Then, before Hawthorne or Raven could react, Talle reached inside her jacket pocket and, quickly, with one clean movement, pulled out Hank's gun and lifted the barrel into her mouth.

Once again, the candles blew out in the *kiva*.

Chapter 23 - Liam's Salon

September 24, 1993

Liam stood in front of his Book of Kells window, watching while the two young poets handed glasses of vintage Macallan around the room. Finally each of them - Fiona, Raven, Hank and Mack - had a glass and all stood, facing Liam solemnly.

"Here's to each of you. We've come through a very strange time together. I think of it as a spell that has been broken. *Slainte.* Thank you for your loyalty and your love."

They lifted their glasses, toasted silently and sipped.

Raven and Hank sat down in a love seat, Hank carefully favoring his shoulder injury. Liam and Mack sat at the chess table and Fiona stared up where the Bamberg Green Man mask had hung. The wall would need painting; time and sunlight had faded the area around the mask, leaving a darker silhouette of his form. Although removed, he was still present.

"I took them all down," Liam said to Fiona in answer to her unasked question. "I have always revered the Green Man, I still do. Hawthorne's were beautiful, but...I can't look at those particular ones anymore and not realize..."

"Of course. So...what did you do with them?"

"All of those things are in storage. Except the two..."

"The two the policemen took into evidence, don'tcha know," Mack filled in, covering for a voice that was about to break. "The one from the young lass and the one from Mr. O'Shea. Along with that big red diary of Talle's."

"I have a toast," said Hank. "Here's to two lovely poets, to their fire, their courage and their caring hearts. Without which we'd not have come to this moment in time."

The men all looked at Raven and Fiona and lifted their glasses, nodding their agreement.

"Well, this is getting maudlin," said Raven, stuffing a brown cigarette between her teeth and patting her jeans pockets for matches. Mack tossed her his lighter. "Tell us about your plans, Mack."

"Well, as soon as my brother can leave this place, I'm taking him on a whirlwind tour of Ireland. Here he is, a full-blooded Irishman, and he's never stood on the Cliffs of Moher or seen a Celtic graveyard or a dolman or drank a pint of Guinness from the tap at the Bogside, if ye can imagine? And yours, Raven?"

"Raven has to be in Baltimore by December to find an apartment and get ready for graduate school," Hank answered for her. "That gives us a few weeks to do a little traveling."

"Traveling?" Fiona looked at her friends. "Why am I always the last to know? Where?"

"Just on the road, wherever we feel like going. Up to Hank's first, he'll need help while his shoulder heals. Then we'll hit the road."

We'll just make it up as we go along," Hank took Raven's hand.

"I want to stop at this little tattoo parlor I know of, over near Mesa Verde. I promised myself a new tattoo before I get too civilized back east," Raven grinned.

Hank rolled his eyes. Fiona didn't dare ask if he'd seen her other tattoo. She gazed at her two friends. Neither of them seemed the settling-down type. Maybe all they'd do is travel together for a while. It was pretty funny the way things had turned out, she chuckled to herself: Mr. Chivalry coming down from Durango to watch their backs, ending up instead on his own back, naked and about to be sacrificed to the Green Man!

No, on second thought, that wasn't funny. But she would always remember that night in the *kiva* as a complete mixture of good, evil, tragedy and comedy. Raven had untied Hank after joking with him that she was tempted to leave him that way, he looked kind of cute and vulnerable. Once she pulled off the duct tape, he growled at her to get him his clothes for god's sake. But everyone was afraid to touch his clothes; afraid Talle might have gotten the poison on them when she undressed him. Raven and Hawthorne had lent him an assortment of their own - two sweaters and a jacket, and extra jeans from Hawthorne's escape back-pack, which could barely zip up and had to be rolled four inches at the bottoms.

About that time, Mack and Marshal Lopez arrived. While they helped bring Hank up out of the *kiva* and radi-oed for helicopter assistance with the the crime-and-suicide scene, Raven and Hawthorne had a long conversation off to the side. Raven explained to Hawthorne about the poisoned oil, that Aisling's death had not been an accident.

"Somehow I knew. I just let myself believe it, because I was afraid," said Hawthorne. "It was obvious that Talle had planned the whole thing, down to making that appoint-ment with Lam's Nursery. It was too easy the way she came up with that idea of leaving Aisling's car at the gas station. I was in shock at the time. But...that's no excuse."

"Why did you keep going to Lam's every year?" Raven asked him.

"She said we had to create a pattern."

"Ah. I thought it was something like that," Raven nodded. "I have hated you, Hawthorne. I have thought the worst of you."

"I know, Raven. And I deserved it. If I had come forward about Aisling's death, at least Chahil might still be alive."

"What are you going to do? You could run now, while Lopez is down below."

"And you wouldn't stop me?"

"I'd try. But you could probably out-run me, after all we've been through tonight."

"I doubt that," Hawthorne smiled ruefully.

"You saved our lives. That was quick thinking, pretending to be the Green Man."

"I can't take the credit for that. I just started talking to her and… it happened so fast… I didn't realize how far gone she was."

Hawthorne stared at the trap door, the flashlight beams gyrating from below as Marshal Lopez pieced together the meaning of the gruesome scene, with Mack's help.

"No, Raven, I think it's time to, as they say, 'face the music'."

Hawthorne had walked away then, toward the *kiva*. He stood and waited for Marshal Lopez to come up top, to turn himself in. Raven figured he was in for a long bout of depression, however things turned out. Technically, he was an accessory. And a few other things that the D.A. would be happy to define for him. Technically, he was no longer someone Raven would take into her bed. Or someone with whom - or on whose behalf - she would even drink another tequila and lime. She figured her Saturday-night binges were finally at an end. She looked down at the brown cigarette in her hand. Maybe hanging out with Hank would help with that.

Hawthorne was an enigma; she thought as she crushed out the cigarette and looked around for Fiona. She would stay grateful to him for what he'd done tonight, but she didn't plan to exchange post cards. She found Fiona near the red rocks, standing over Liam, who was crouched on the ground, his head in his hands. He was shocked and disoriented. Talle had always taken care of his every need. Now he realized just how far she had gone in her twisted efforts. At least Fiona had kept him from going down the ladder into the *kiva* after the gunshot.

The marshal decided Hank should be airlifted by helicopter to an emergency room in Albuquerque. Hawthorne was placed in handcuffs, while Raven and Fiona explained that he wasn't actually the murderer, and had saved Hank's life at the end. Marshal Lopez nodded, made notes and then walked Hawthorne through the woods to his four-by-four.

Watching them go, Raven couldn't help but think there was some kind of odd karmic justice, since Lopez guided Hawthorne along the same river path Hawthorne had led the poets along, every fall for the mask-making ritual. Hawthorne had a lot to sort out about his motivations, and the price he might pay for giving all his power away to his benefactress.

"One thing I never did figure out," mused Fiona, slowly pacing the library. "Who was it broke into Hawthorne's studio that day? Before you got there, I mean," she said to Raven.

"I figure it was Talle."

"What was she looking for? She could have access to the place any time. Why break in and throw things around like that?"

"To make it look like I did it, so Hawthorne and I would have to communicate. She wanted him to seduce me, I think I was truly her next victim. Or else she had it in her head to send you and me off to the Big Graduate School in the sky together."

"And was it she who stole the poem from your cabin?"

"Yup. To make it look like Hawthorne did it, and to find out what I knew. She knew I suspected something, for a long time. By the way, Liam, I need to ask you a question."

"Yes, my dear?" Liam smiled at Raven. It seemed the two of them had come to some resolution of their ambiguous relationship.

"I must do a blessing of the *kiva* before you have it filled in. To balance all this."

"We'll see," Liam smiled faintly, unsure how to react.

Raven frowned. That was not the answer she wanted. Fiona drained her glass and stood.

"More, my dear?" Liam asked, lifting the bottle to change the subject.

Considering it was his wife they were talking about, and whose ashes rested in the urn above the fireplace, he was holding up very well. Fiona shook her head. It was very late and she was extremely tired. Tomorrow Raven would drive her down to Albuquerque to catch a plane back to Baltimore. There, she had a few weeks of course work to catch up on, and would finish out the semester after all, since her New Mexico retreat had been cut in half.

Professor Bregman would return from his sabbatical soon, and would act like he did - and did not - want to hear all about her adventures. Fiona wanted to talk to him about devoting an issue of *The Artisan Review* to Chahil O'Shea and Aisling Devlin, with research articles on the slaughter of the old Irish Bards, the fate of the ancient Bardic Schools. She felt a thesis topic brewing.

By now the news had hit the wires that Aisling Devlin's disappearance and subsequent murder had been solved, and a few of the bizarre facts surrounding her murderess' "ritual suicide" had been leaked. However, while the D.A. did a complete investigation, most of those details were hushed. Fiona and Raven had so far managed to keep the media's attention on their personal lives down to a local whisper, simply by hiding out in Ojo de Sombras and refusing to be interviewed. Hank finally was allowed to play bodyguard for the both of them, following them everywhere they went - which wasn't far. The bookstore, the café, walks in the local ruins - which Raven insisted Fiona see.

Given the way the news was reported, it only took a couple of days' evasion to keep the national and urban-based media at bay, long enough for other stories - international politics, gang wars, a major plane crash, embezzlement at an

Albuquerque bank - to eclipse this one. As for the villagers of Ojo de Sombras, theirs would be a slow and lazy discussion; the details would surface one at a time over beers in the saloon. With false rumors to be dusted off. After all, the story of Aisling Devlin's disappearance had kept them talking for fourteen years. This kind of news should keep them busy into the next millennium.

Fiona put in a call to the Oklahoma farm, the day after the events at the *kiva*. In her exhaustion, it occurred to her that she didn't want her father worrying when he heard the news about the Fagan scandal. She also needed to hear the voice of middle-American sanity.

"Oh, of course, sugar plum, I heard about it on the radio this morning. So...you didn't get hurt or anything?"

"No, Dad. I'm fine. Everyone's fine. I'll write you a long letter all about it."

"I sent you a package last week. Did you get that?"

Fiona smiled and fingered the silver Celtic cross on the chain around her neck.

"It was your mother's, her Aunt Dana sent it to her from Ireland when we got married."

"I know, Dad. I'm wearing it. Thank you for sending it."

"I'll be sending you some more of your mother's things from time to time. She told me before she died, 'Now don't you go giving Fiona these things all at once. You know how she likes surprises, you dole them out now and then when you think she could use a treat.'"

Fiona's eyebrows crinkled up and she felt tears starting. That was just like her mother.

"You take care, sugar plum. You call me in a few days, you hear?"

Fiona promised and hung up. It took her a while to compose herself between the events of last night, the news that Hank was going to be fine, her father's care and her mother's gifts.

She had gone down the ladder to look at Aisling and Chahil, despite Hank and Raven's admonitions that she shouldn't. Before Marshal Lopez arrived, before the area was cordoned off with yellow crime tape. She felt she needed to see them, after coming to this point. Not out of curiosity, but to say a prayer. To whisper to Aisling that one of her poems, at least, was still alive. She would make sure *The Artisan Review* published it. And to tell Chahil that she would research his life in Ireland, and write a eulogy for the magazine. She was sickened by what she saw in the crypt. But she said her prayer, nevertheless.

On her way back up, Fiona saw leaves scattered at the bottom of the ladder, like the ones that night in the hacienda hallway, when she had found herself walking in her sleep.

Fiona would always remember these things she saw by Talle's candlelight that night. She would never forget what could happen to poets' dreams of immortality.

"By the way," Fiona asked, as she passed the chess table on her way out of the library room. "Are you going to finish the game?"

Mack grinned up at her and nudged Liam.

"We've started a new one," he laughed.

"The Green Man really did give me those moves, you know," Fiona smiled back at him.

"Aye, but do you really have need of the Green Man to play a good game of chess? At least one of those moves was from me, lass!"

Liam watched them bantering. What a strange time this was. Losing his life partner only to find she never really was, and gaining his twin whom he had always sensed was just around the corner.

Fiona waved her good-nights to Hank, Raven and Mack, and Liam walked her down the hallway, past the niches, now empty, no candles burning. Their steps on the tiles seemed to echo louder in the absence of the icons, saints and Green Man masks. The emptiness saddened Fiona, despite her relief that the killing was over.

"Fiona, I hope you will not hold against me my awful behavior these past weeks," Liam spoke in low tones, holding her elbow in his hand in gentlemanly fashion. "I am appalled at myself and I have no good explanation."

Fiona nodded, thinking that she had no explanation either for all of the strange eros at the Fagans'. "You said it seemed like we had all been under a spell, and now it was broken."

"I do feel that way."

"So do I. Why do you think all this happened, Liam?"

"Mack says it's a long tradition, the killing of bards. I take some of the responsibility – I should have been more aware that Talle was...in trouble. I had always looked the other way, about her...spiritual fanaticism. And her jealousy."

"Jealousy?"

"Of all the beautiful young poets. There was a history of schizophrenia in her family. She never spoke about her mother but...for many years we sent checks to a sanatorium in New York."

"I see."

"It's...difficult to talk of all that, quite yet."

"Of course."

"Mack thinks I will sort it all out better over in Ireland. He wants to show me the lighter side of my heritage, he says," Liam chuckled. "I guess we'll be doing some pub crawling."

Fiona smiled. Liam would love Ireland: the music and the greenness and the beauty that wraps around your heart like Aisling's harp string around Raven's fist. She had a feeling that a lot of adobe dust would gather here before Liam Fagan returned or opened up these doors again.

"As for the Green Man, I think we all had need of him, in our various ways," Liam mused. "And so he appeared. We conjured him up, so to speak. As he is a fertile presence, perhaps that explains some of our falling into eros while he was around."

Fiona nodded. As good an explanation as she expected to get.

"By the way, that idea of Raven's, her wanting to do a blessing of the *kiva* before I have it filled in. I don't know if such a place *can* be blessed at this point."

"You should let her do the blessing," Fiona said firmly. "A healing is needed. Something good needs to counteract the evil."

Liam winced.

"I know she was your wife, Liam, but we must call it what it was. Raven comes from a long line of medicine men and women. She's the one to take care of this. And she needs to do it, you know, for her own sake. She has been haunted for a long time, by all this."

"You are so right, my dear. Obviously you and Raven have been better mentors to me, in many ways, than I have been to you. My god, you and I haven't had a single session together to go over your own work. I have failed you terribly."

"It's not a problem, believe me."

Fiona didn't elaborate. It was just as well that she hadn't had to sit down with the older poet to look at her work. She hadn't written a single poem since she'd arrived. On the other hand, she had taken a lot of notes this week, sitting at her *casita* table in the evenings, burning as much *pinon* as she could before going back to Baltimore. She would be returning to her city with a wealth of material to work from, given her experiences of the past month in New Mexico.

"You and Raven have become good friends through this ordeal, haven't you?"

"The worst isn't over," Fiona grimaced. "We still have to survive graduate school."

Liam laughed. "Very well, I will let her do what she needs to do in the *kiva*, then. After all that crime tape is taken away."

"Good luck. I mean, you might not be able to make her wait that long."

"Do such things take a long time?" he asked in his innocence of the world's ways.

"I have no idea how long they leave that stuff there. I only meant, if it has to do with waiting on authority, that's not Raven's strong suit. She'll be sneaking in there some midnight, you can be sure."

Liam smiled.

"As for the weird sexual stuff, the Green Man is a trickster. He had his way with us, Liam. Let's just forget all that nonsense. I'm going back to the real world tomorrow morning."

Liam sighed relief at her humor, and hugged Fiona affectionately.

"Rest well, Fiona. Please stop in the morning and say goodbye to me and Mack before you leave for the airport, will you promise?"

Fiona promised, kissed Liam on the cheek and went through the heavy wooden door.

A light snow was falling on the sand and junipers. The scent of it was keen in the air, and the cold intensified the other scents in the courtyard. Fiona inhaled sharply; closing her eyes, then opened them and exhaled. One of Talle's tabby cat orphans crouched at the sight of Fiona, as if terrified, then leapt through the snow and over the courtyard wall.

In her *casita*, she found a familiar sight. Once again, a lamp was lit that had not been left on earlier. Her bags were already packed, tomorrow's travel clothes – the black velour dress, the duster, the green gloves and hat – were hanging to air out the wrinkles. Her books were back in her knapsack. Liam's three black leather volumes were on the table, awaiting her return of them to his shelves in the morning. One lay open. Next to it a flashlight again. And, this time, a smudge stick wrapped in blue thread. Fiona picked it up and smelled: lavender and sage. A note was scribbled and tucked between the open pages, standing up like a little flag:

"Meet me at the hot springs. Then we'll go to the kiva. Midnight. R."

Fiona groaned and then grinned. She was too exhausted for a Raven adventure. She had so been looking forward to that pillow upstairs – under the faded silhouette of the removed Green Man mask that was now down at the D.A's office in an evidence locker.

But there would be no other time for this.

She looked at the page her dark poet friend had left open. It was Liam's Green Man poem. Her eyes fell on the words:

Please the poet to perceive
The undulating dark unknown
And wrest for man a reprieve
From scythes his own seeds have sown.

Fiona kept her duster on, grabbed a towel, the smudge stick and flashlight and headed out the door. It was only nine-thirty. Raven would have to extricate herself from Liam's salon, drive Hank up to the Bear Paw Lodge, drive back to her cottage, and hike the woods to the springs.

That would give Fiona some time to herself in the water first. To think through a poem she was working on. In the dark, without paper or pen.

After all, it was her last night in New Mexico.

Epilogue

He watched from the edge of the woods as the two poets sat together in the water, snow softly falling in their hair, their bodies submerged in the hot steam. He knew it well, that exhilarating sensation of hot and cold, light and dark.

Like those two, the fair one and the dark one, each so necessary to the other. And to order.

He smiled sadly and moved along the path, trailing his skirts of autumn brown leaves, mingled with tumbleweeds and evergreen branches. Crumbs of herbs fell from him, littering the forest floor with a trail of green dust, which his footprints matted down into green paste in the falling snow. He shivered in his branches and shook out his twigs to keep them from going numb with cold. He breathed a sigh of relief and rejoicing - yet tinged with sorrow. True, all was ambiguity in this place of cycles: who could ever tell for certain whether the leaves that curled from the corners of his lips were emerging or being devoured?

Nevertheless, a very long, painful time had come to an end. The dark and the light had come together. Creation and destruction, in equal measure, had balanced the misunderstanding, the loss of self to an illusion of power, which had taken over that one who was now gone. She who - in her fear and jealousy of beauty, voice and youth - had so severely warped what he had intended. His long mourning for the two poets in the crypt could now begin to be healed. He had never wanted the sacrifice. Only to hear their poems, read aloud in the woods.

Like an ancient vine, he coiled himself around an old ponderosa, groaning with pleasure at the sensation. He dangled his leaves from the branches. The aged tree sighed in return, its bark bending to the embrace. A few pinecones fell to the forest floor.

He watched the two poets as they stood to dress and wrap their bodies in towels, blankets and coats. Despite the falling snow, he blew a soft, warm, thyme-scented breeze in their direction as they walked across the meadow, through the woods toward Dragon Rock, shoulder to shoulder, talking softly together. He closed his eyes and fell into a musty sleep, dreaming of the dark, watery forests of Ireland. Free to truly rest and dream, for the first time in many years.

He felt no sadness that the poets were leaving his woods. He would meet them again. Someday. Somewhere.

The Green Man

In days of yore when Druids quested
The forest deeps and faerie lands
The Green Man was often guested
By Elven King and high-born man

All the peoples everywhere
Worshiped the Living god within
Earth and tree and stone and air
And every creature was their kin

The Green Man laughed and gave them breath
And daring heart and dancing feet
And none would dream to fear their death
For merry part and merry meet

Again they came and once again
The Green Man led them through the grave
The laughing, loving, living land
Gave to them as it they gave

Then the days of dream were done
There came a turning of the tide
The Lovers of the Living One
Were hunted through the green hillside

Sacred grove was slashed and burned
Rivers poisoned, the race enslaved
The tender earth was slowly turned
From greenwood path to city paved

Now deep within the darkling gloom
A spirit slips past stem and flower
His passing portends pain and doom
All creatures creep away and cower

Dark and grim this devil broods
His memories - a map of death
Endless grief has him imbued
With blood of bile and bitter breath

The wind will whisper wicked thoughts
That echo through the eerie night
From he whose heavy heart is fraught
With loneliness of Love's lost light

Where he wends and when and why
And who is it for him would weep
He the Lord who cannot die
The wounded watcher in our sleep

Guardian of the Dark School

Please the poet to perceive
The undulating dark unknown
And wrest for man a reprieve
From scythes his own seeds have sown

Grind our flesh and bone to gruel
Feed it to the fiend inside
Set our tortured souls as fuel
Upon the altar of our pride

Liam Fagan, 1992

Lightning Source UK Ltd.
Milton Keynes UK
UKOW05f2250170614

233636UK00010B/133/P